Heroes' Calling

By Edge Celize

authorHOUSE®

AuthorHouse™
1663 Liberty Drive
Bloomington, IN 47403
www.authorhouse.com
Phone: 1-800-839-8640

First published by AuthorHouse 6/29/2011

ISBN: 978-1-4567-6763-1 (sc)
ISBN: 978-1-4567-6762-4 (hc)
ISBN: 978-1-4567-6761-7 (e)

Library of Congress Control Number: 2011907918

Printed in the United States of America

Forewarning:

If you are devoutly religious in any religion that believes in a single god almighty, then this book is not for you. The story at hand WILL offend you outright, however if you still wish to continue reading then please do so at your own discretion. For everyone else who is open minded to accept the following story to be fictional, then I sincerely hope you enjoy it.

Author.

Understanding the format of the story

The story is written in first person, with the action written in square brackets and conversation by and between characters in a script style format. Speeches and thoughts made by other characters while in first person other than Edge, the main character, are in italics. Parenthesis, if applicable, describe the tone in which a thought or speech is conveyed.

The following is a typical conversation between 2 characters:

Character 1: I am so tired today despite sleeping for 20 hours
Character 2: (with disbelief) how could you sleep that long?

When a character other than Edge is in first person, but not talking out loud then it would look like this:

Character name 1: *What Character 2 doesn't know is I had been awake for over 35 hours before I finally got to sleep*

All action that is not described by Edge is written in square brackets which are in bold and italics as such:

[Character 2 stands with disbelief that Character 1 slept for 20 hours, he backs away however not really caring to challenge Character 1's claims]

Glossary

Within the story there are many words in which certain characters will say with an accent. Those words are described below:

Alrighty — Alright
Buncha — Bunch of
Coulda — Could have
Cuz — Because
Dunno — Don't know
Gettin — Getting
Gonna — Going to
Gotta — Got to
Heh — A sound made to signify acknowledgment of something with a sense of weak amusement.
Kinda — Kind of
Lemme — Let me
Lil — Little
Nuttin — Nothing
Outta — Out of
Prob — Problem
Sorta — Sort of
Sumtin — Something
Tryna — Trying to
Wanna — Want to
Whatcha — What are you (Perry/Halo)
What'd — What do
What ya — What are you (Edge)
Woulda — Would have...

Ya _____ You

Yeah _____ Yes

Yo _____ An interjection for 'Hi' and 'Hey' also used to express an exclamation and emphasize sentences when applicable.

-Z _____ Often used in replacement of an "s" in order to give a word a more slang like sound

Prologue:

Long ago before time existed, this world was a wasteland. The two entities of light and darkness fought for what would be the most prized possession in the known universe, life...

Earth would become the center point of all existence, Jehovah and Lucifer fought a never ending battle to create life as they saw fit. The kingdom of heaven where the Angel Sanctuary is held was the home to Jehovah's Army of Light and the empire of hell was the stronghold of the dark army, Lucifer's Grand Force. The fight would be for the creation of known existence as either saw fit, for what is power with no subjects to rule...

But nothing went as planned, rebel angels and deviant demons broke all laws of good and evil and so the first union was created. The joining of holy and darkness, unified and within itself, neutralized. To the demon mother Eve and the angel father Adam, the first true life was born, the first human. A being who was both yet neither genders, no power, no magic or anything special except its purity of innocence. The child matured but never knew anything beyond what it saw with its own eyes. Everyday was like every other, nothing was different, everything was the same and never changed. The child had no perception of time or history, and so it felt its existence was meaningless, its parents seeing their child alone and dissatisfied with life gave up their immortality to create Tempis, an entity of time, without her, life would have no history, no past or possible future. Her existence was the gift of time to human eyes.

And so the child grew up and old, and in time more rebels and deviants followed Adam and Eve's footsteps and had children of their own, the human race was established. Though life had spawned, Earth was still barren, it bore no fauna or flora and existence was harsh. From the help of their parents, the humans were able to understand the most basic of magic and used it to develop science and technology. Life seemed to slowly get better, but to Jehovah and Lucifer this was unacceptable. Life was stolen from them and the creation of a perfect world as either saw fit was gone. Furious at the events that had transpired the two entities stripped the deviants and rebels of their immortality, they are destined to die with the children they created. Lucifer however was still not satisfied, he unleashed his Grand Force and set the planet ablaze. However Jehovah in all his wisdom and patience saw that the cause was not lost, there was still a chance. The gates of the Angel Sanctuary swung opened and the Army of Light was sent downwards to defend the humans and the banished rebels and deviants, and thus The Great War began. Led by the trumpet of Gabriel and the sword of Michael the Army of Light met the blaze of hell led by Testament and Judgment...

The end of the war was long but near in sight, Tempis recorded all the events in the Book of Time. The war's end came with the fall of Testament and Judgment, both whose powers were sealed never again to be released...

Finally, the war was over, Jehovah won, he now had his followers... but Lucifer's voice and power would not be forgotten for he knew that within every human a dark side was present and in time the darkness would grow and he would have his revenge. Earth was ravaged with scars of the war, life just wasn't possible anymore. Select individuals who survived the war pulled what strength they had left and offered themselves as a sacrifice to create me, Saivent. My birth was the final chapter of The Great War, from the meteor which held me, the planet and all its inhabitants were cleansed upon its impact, all traces of the past were gone. Jehovah lent his strength and dimmed the fires that consumed the world, with what strength he had left he took humans and tore them into two halves as best he could, creating the genders of man and women so they can propagate amongst themselves, and creating the heart and soul, so they will forever seek out their other half. In 7 days the world cooled and life slowly started to develop. Tempis protected me, keeping me away from the reach of any mortal and away from Lucifer who was sure to kill me if he had the chance, and finally away from even Jehovah himself who would have used me to influence the existence of mankind. As I grew up so did the planet, life developed everywhere, there was finally peace...

The human race are all descendants of their ancient angel and demon parents, but as long as their blood remained balanced there would be no hint of the past. This is the way it is to remain as agreed by both Jehovah and Lucifer, but Lucifer knew that one day he would have his revenge. And so it came to be *that certain individuals whose blood would become unbalanced would bring forth the truth of the past. These individuals have existed in small amounts as human history progressed, but as time advanced more and more started to show themselves in the world... one individual's story and his group of friends is about to be told. He and his friends will change the face of this world once again, their destiny is more important than they realize...*

Chapter 1

My name is Edge

I never thought my life would take the turn that it did, I never thought I'd meet these people I've come to call friends, and I never believed that I would be considered a hero by some and a villain by all. It started a few years ago when I realized that I would not live my life confined by human laws that allow the strong to govern the weak, I just wouldn't take it. This pyramid of power where everyone is forced to be a follower and if you're rich enough, you get to be a leader for however long your money allows. I once believed the saying "no fate but what we make" well I can say that this is the fate I am making for myself...

[Flashback - Edge is being pushed around by kids all bigger than he is in a school playground]

There were always bullies, its just up to you to take it or fight it, well I took it... I was too scared to fight it. Being the smallest kid in a school playground of Latino's and Black's where you were the only lil Asian boy meant that no one was coming to your aid, if you took their punishment than you wouldn't have to suffer too much. But I kept letting myself get pushed over and over again, and I was already so close to the edge. One day I exploded on a boy who had always found his fun in picking on me relentlessly, I felt the anger, the fire inside grow and become an inferno, the whole school yard was consumed by a flash fire. Everyone was burnt to some degree or another, and me? I was the only kid still standing, they called me the miracle child who survived the freak accident, and the bully? His ashes blew away in the wind. From that day on I knew I had to nurse this fire, I had to control it, and make it my own. This was my lil secret, this is what I would use to define my life...

[Edge is in a confined area of Central Park hard to get to on foot, he is practicing his ability to control fire along with basic punches and kicks]

As I grew up I practice each day to draw out the fire inside. By the time I reached junior high I was able to release it in small fireballs, and by high school I was able to control and wield it as I wish, making it do whatever I want. And by the time of graduation I was even able to fly with it. I started to wonder though, was I the only one? I couldn't be... how would it make sense that I'm the only one? Where would I even start to look? I graduated high school by myself, all my friends left a semester earlier...

I started college only to realize it wasn't for me, and a year later I dropped out. I realized though while taking a course in college that I wanted to be a welder, I loved the feel of the fire and heat, so I made up my mind. That summer off would be the last time I'd be free. I hung out with my friend Perry and went to the beach and such. We all got together, the small handful of my friends, and we spent that summer just having fun. As the summer drew closer to an end I met a new friend from an art website I frequented, he's a friend I've come to know as Cory. When the summer was over I started my new school, it was a trade school that taught HVAC, auto mechanics, engines, and a whole buncha other stuff, I was in the welding department.

Perry never knew about my gift, in fact no one did, it was sumtin I kept to myself... anyway, my friendship with Cory grew and he told me he and his family were coming up to New York for the holidays, I looked forward to meeting him. A few days before his departure he was starting to act strange, he kept asking me if I could change the world, what would I do, what would I want? If there was a war for the human race and freedom from God, would I be willing to fight for it? He told me he would explain in person, so I waited...

Chapter 2

Cory?

I received word from Cory that he had arrived in New York City but due to his mom planning everything out he wouldn't be able to see me until the last day. I had class even though it was the holiday vacation for everyone else, cuz my school is retarded like that. It didn't matter, this whole week the transit authority was on strike so I couldn't get to school anyway. When you think about it, I got my vacation one way or another.

Cory was a tall white dude, he comes from a rich family so he's pretty well off in life. He's pretty typical, the laid back type with short but scruffy brown hair and a goatee, all he knows is work, work, work, and the time he has off he goes and shops like a rich kid. Now Perry on the other hand was quite the opposite, he was a tall brown skinned Puerto Rican kid I met from a mutual friend. Unlike Cory, he's... well for lack of a better term, poor, I may not have known him long but I get along with him great, he's one of my closest friends... granted I been through a few, but you live and learn.

The days passed and the strike ended, I would go out for my nightly lil walks and of course I'd choose the worst neighborhoods to go to just so people can fuck with me. But tonight I decided to go to Battery Park in Manhattan, there was this water fountain that's on at random times and it just so happened to be on this night. It was relaxing and calming, I sat down and reflected on the events of this year. It wasn't long as I stared into the jets of water when I felt a tap on my shoulder...

[Edge is sitting on a bench staring into the water jets, he feels a tap on

his shoulder, slowly turning to see who it is and in shock he falls off the bench]

Edge: (rubbing his tail bone) damn that hurt
Cory: Oh, I'm sorry did I startle you?
Edge: Is that... you?
Cory: In the flesh
Edge: I'm impressed how did you know I was here?
Cory: (winks) I know everything
Edge: Yeah sure, so how are you, how's the city life
Cory: Could be better, then again it could be worse, I'm with my mom, always complaining, anyway, what's up, how are you?
Edge: I'm fine, just thinking about some stuff, that's all. Hey, a few weeks ago you said you wanted to tell me sumtin, all this changing the world and crap. What were you talking about?
Cory: Oh yeah, that... well I'll cut to the point, I need your help
Edge: With...?
Cory: Judgment
Edge: Judgment of what?
Cory: No, his NAME is Judgment
Edge: Come again?
Cory: I know about you Edge, your fire...
Edge: (backs away quickly) what...?
Cory: Don't worry, I'm not here to hurt you
Edge: (with a stern look on his face) assuming you can...
Cory: Technically... yes and no, look all I'm asking is for you to just hear me out?
Edge: Sure... why not
Cory: Hahahaha alright here we go!

[Before Edge can react Cory grabs his hand and pulls him into a bubble like object, and they disappear into a tunnel of light]

Now, I seen some crazy shit before but this can't be happening, was he like me? Was he one of those "special" people out there in the world that I've been looking for? I looked at him while he gazed ahead into the tunnel, I stayed as calm as I could.

Cory: I'm going to show you something that will help you understand
Edge: Where we going?
Cory: Not where, but when, this world you see before you is the outcome of a massive war

[They come to a stop at the end of the tunnel, Cory taps on the bubble gently and they push back into reality, Edge looks through the bubble and he sees a world that is barren with little life, small fires everywhere, but yet buildings that looked as if they were from a sci-fi movie]

Cory: Edge... this is the truth

Chapter 3

Saivent...

[Cory and Edge were in a bubble that kept them from being seen in this strange and yet familiar world]

Edge: What... what is this?

Cory: This is the world as it was before The Great War

Edge: The Great War?

Cory: Yes, it was a war between Lucifer and Jehovah that changed the world into what you know now

Edge: Wait... wait wait wait wait wait... you JUST said Jehovah and Lucifer?

Cory: Um yeah... something wrong?

Edge: (mumbles) oh my fucking god religion is right, I can't believe this...

Cory: Actually no it's not. Religion as it is now is just a facade to cover up the truth

Edge: So then religion is wrong?

Cory: Well... it's been rewritten to conceal the truth if that's what you mean

Edge: WOO HOO! Hhahahaha in your face churches

Cory: Okay... anyway, this was right before The Great War, Lucifer banished the demons who deviated from the darkness and Jehovah banished the angels who rebelled against the holy

Edge: Wait what exactly happened?

Cory: You remember the bible saying that Adam and Eve were the first people that god created?

Edge: Yeah

Cory: Well, it's quite the opposite, they weren't humans at all, Adam was an Angel, and Eve was a demon

Edge: WHOA... that's completely outta this world

Cory: Oh it gets better, they created the first union and had the first child, that child was a human

Edge: Oh... you're shitting me, keep going this is way too interesting...

[As Cory tells Edge about the past they move around the terrain and see the sights of the great towers in the small cities, Edge is in awe of what he sees and is completely taken in by the sights and sounds]

Cory: The world was barren and life was hard, but shit happens right?

Edge: Was it always this way?

Cory: Not even I or my mom knows that, but what I do know is that Lucifer and Jehovah have always hated each other, and everything is because of them, the war, the lies... religion... sadness...

Edge: Wow, this is all too much for me to take in, and who's your mom what does she have to do with this?

Cory: To understand that you need to know about me, my real name is Saivent ("say-vint") I was... created by the survivors of The Great War... and Tempis watched over me when I was young

Edge: The survivors?

Saivent: This world is inhabited by a few races or variations, Elemental Spirits, Elemental Users, Power Users, Chimeras and Avatars to name a few

Edge: (sigh) now I'm gonna have to learn all of this

Saivent: Well, here this will make things easier, you can interpret it as you want

[Saivent puts his index finger to Edge's temple and floods his mind with information about the past and all that he would need to know, Edge blacks out... when he comes around they are back on the bench watching the fountain]

Saivent: This is pretty nice I must admit

Edge: Oh man, I have such a fucking headache

Saivent: Hahahhaaha sorry about that, but hey, I have to go now before my human mom starts to complain, see ya buddy, it was nice to finally meet you

[*Saivent disappears in a gust of wind but thinks to himself...*]

Saivent: *I hope he can help...*

[*Edge is left alone starring at the spot Saivent was just at*]

Edge: Yeah... nice meeting you too...

Wow... I have such a massive amount of information to sort though... but first things first... Judgment...

Chapter 4

The Great War

Saivent filled my head with a lot of stuff from The Great War, half of it I didn't understand, the other half made me feel lied too. Who woulda thought that this was the truth. So where do I begin...

The Great War led to life being the way it is, God ruling all humans and Lucifer being feared by all. Judgment, he was one of the Generals of Lucifer's army, The Grand Force. He was known as The First Dragon of The Dark Flame. Known to all, enemies and allies alike, though short in visible stature his lil body was only a shell for his true dragon form but even though as powerful as he was, he just wasn't strong enough to take on the Army of Light alone, he was soon worn out and defeated. His capture led to the weakening of The Grand Force. The angels and Avatars sealed his powers, separating his dragon form and banishing it to the Black Universe with no hope of return, and his physical form to the Reality Planes. His dragon form was the pinnacle of his true powers. He swore revenge on the human race for taking what was his, and now the present. It seems that Judgment broke free thanks to the help of an unknown power, and Saivent needs my help to destroy him, but Judgment wasn't the only one there was another General, Testament.

After Judgment's capture the second General of Lucifer's army, Testament, began his assault unleashing his power at full force. Testament was in and of himself a god in his own rights, a demon of insane power and strength. Angels upon angels all tried to rush him only to die at the jaws of Leviathan, his personal bodyguard. At the turning point of The Great War Testament unleashed his ultimate attack, The Sky Flood. It wiped out more than half of the world's population putting an end to the fires that consumed the planet and littering the land with drowned bodies. The Sky Flood exhausted his strength allowing the angels and Avatars to come in for the final attack, but he still fought back. Testament was eventually captured and thus, the end of The Great War was at hand. Unlike Judgment who had two forms Testament's power was whole and could not be separated so a young child untainted by darkness was used as a vessel to seal him, the child Kae. And that was the end of The Great War but the beginning of the lie. Everything in the Bible was falsified, though the events were real, how they happened were not, but there's one thing that confused me...

[Flashback - Testament is standing on the highest mountain there was, he holds his right hand towards the sky and a whirlwind of clouds develop, soon the clouds start to spin out of control and water comes crashing down from the sky. Like a broken faucet the sky just fills with water... once the sky was clear and Testament left exhausted, the clouds split open and a ray of light crashes through to the weakened demon. Angels by the hundreds came pouring down towards him with raised weapons, but before they got close, and even though being as tired as he was, Testament raised his hand and from the flood waters Leviathan rose and consumed as many angels as its jaws allowed. Leviathan defended Testament from the Angels... but then a fire bird came, sacrificing itself, it vaporized Leviathan]

That's all that I could see in the memories that Saivent showed me, but who controlled the fire bird is what I wanna know. Anyway, back to Judgment, I'd figure he'd wanna destroy the world for what happened, but the humans, do they know about people like me? I know I'm not alone, but now I need to find them, but at the same time I don't wanna risk being caught. I know what the scientist would do and I know well enough that I'd be a guinea pig for their experiments... and the military, they'd seek me out and try to use me as a weapon. This is so much more complicated than it should be, and where is he? where is Judgment... is he gonna attack outta nowhere, is he gonna destroy the world city by city... what, what is gonna happen, argh! This is so stressful, I dunno why Saivent thinks I can do it, I've never had to use my fire before in this manner, but I gotta admit, the thought of it was exciting, I could feel sumtin inside of me wanting it, I can feel it burn with a desire to fight... wow, I never felt like this before, but it feels good. Lemme go to sleep now, I have school early in the morning, and I don't look forward to waking up tired and sleepy...

Chapter 5

The first strike

I went to school and it was just like any other day, I changed and got right into welding. It was a cold December morning so the heat kept me warm. I was in the MIG class at this point, MIG meaning Metal Inert Gas, basically it's a gun where a solid wire comes out. You aim the nozzle at what you wanna weld and squeeze the trigger, it's boring, but at the same time the light from the electric arc is slightly hypnotic. I was staring into the arc and I started to get entranced or sumtin. As I stared deeper into the arc I heard someone calling to me, it was a voice I never heard before but yet sounded so familiar. Then a face appeared in the arc and I jumped back, I saw... I saw a dragon... could it be Judgment? All of a suddenly I felt sumtin very hot and I saw the leg of my pants on fire, no one was around so I simply just patted it out. Sigh... I need new pants.

School ended early for me cuz there was a fire drill and, well, everyone just sorta left after that. I went home and on the train ride all I could think about was that dragon in the fire... I tried to remember it to see if it jogs anything in my memory but it didn't. When I got home I went to bed and slept till about 7pm and woke up to Perry's annoying "blings" on my cell phone's instant messenger.

[Edge wakes up and has an annoyed look on his face, he crawls to the edge of his bed and stumbles onto a skateboard that sends him crashing to the floor]

Ahhhhhhhhhh fucking shit! Again my ass!

[Edge gets up and goes to look for his cell phone, he begins a texting conversation with Perry]

Perry: YOOOOOOO dude where you is at???
Edge: I WAS sleeping... then you woke me up
Perry: lol tomorrows new years eve whatcha gonna do?
Edge: I dunno I'll probably stay home or sumtin, or go for a walk
Perry: you wanna go to time sq? Mimi said she wants to see the ball drop
Edge: hellz nah I can't stand being around all those people it's mad annoying having them push you and shit
Perry: you sureeeeeeeeeeeeeeeeeeeeeeeeeeeeee
Edge: yes... I'm sure
Perry: ok then dont say I never asked you
Edge: dont worry, it be nice to rest
Perry: what the whole day??? dude you is need to get out more
Edge: lol being brown again
Perry: BROOKLYN! anyway I'll see ya, I got work now
Edge: coolio see ya later dude

I logged off of the messenger, went downstairs to eat dinner and afterwards I got dressed and left the house. I headed towards the highway and felt a need to go into the industrial zone not far from my house. I heard a bit of a ruckus going on but I ignored it, city rats are everywhere and I didn't doubt it was them. I followed my gut instinct to the loading dock, everything was quiet, I sat myself down on the pier and just looked towards Manhattan.

[Edge closes his eyes and sees a world lit up in fire and he opens them quickly]

Whoa.

[Edge stands up and takes a right handed leather weightlifting glove out from his pocket, it's black and the fingers are cut off]

Edge: It's you

[A young man is standing behind Edge, he has long hair that's tied back and a pair of round circular glasses, he has a devious smile that bares his fangs. He's slightly shorter than Edge but has a vicious nerdy appearance, like some sort of psychopath, his voice was sort of high pitched and young]

Judgment: I see I couldn't sneak up on you

Edge: No, you couldn't

Judgment: So you remember me don't you?

Edge: No not really, I just know who you are

Judgment: Really now, you know who I am but you don't remember me?

Edge: You're Judgment, The First Dragon of The Dark Flame

Judgment: My reputation precedes me I see

Edge: Whatever, what'd you want?

Judgment: I just want to talk to an old friend

Edge: Old friend? We're not friends

Judgment: Is that so?

Edge: That's what I know

Judgment: Why did you fail, why did you betray us, all of us

Edge: What are you talking about? What betrayal?

Judgment: I see... so you really don't remember, too bad, I guess you'll die knowing nothing, human

Edge: Sure if that's what you think

Judgment: That's what I know!

[Judgment jumps at Edge hitting him in the chest with his right fist. Edge goes flying back and over the water, but before he lands, he ignites his flames and lands with the tip of his sneakers touching the waters surface. He looks back to Judgment and gives a cocky smirk, his flames rage intensely and he lunges at Judgment]

Edge: STRIKE FIST!

[Edge's right hand ignites into an intense flame, Judgment retaliates and leaps towards Edge. Both of their fist strike, they are equally strong but Edge's flame flickers and intensify. His Strike Fist attack breaks through and sends Judgment flying into the brick wall of a warehouse. The demon picks himself up and out of the ruble]

17

Judgment: I see, the ages trapped in that abysmal plane of existence has robbed me of my strength, don't worry we'll see each other again, and the next time you'll see my true power Fire Lord

[Judgment bursts into a ball of purple flames and disappears]

Did he just disappear? I can't believe that sort of stuff actually happens... so you made the first move then, and you messed up my shirt too.

Chapter 6
A new year with a bang

Well this is it, today is New Years Eve. My friend Isaiah came over to bring me a beer, we played some games and watched TV, then Perry and Mimi decided to stop by before heading out to Times Square, they too brought me a beer, it's only two so far but is everyone tryna get me drunk or sumtin? Anyway, night came and in the end all of us ended up going to Times Square...

You dunno my friend Isaiah or Mimi yet right? Alright, Isaiah is another one of your typical guys, he too is Puerto Rican. He's about my height and is a Christian, that part gets on my nerves now and then but a friend is a friend. He's darker than Perry and tenfold more childish at times. Mimi is Chinese like me but she's way taller though, now that I think about it, everyone is taller than me... anyway, she's tall and skinny with long black hair. She and Perry have been going out for about half a year now? I honestly don't remember, anyway, off to Manhattan!

[Edge, Isaiah, Perry, and Mimi are all heading to the train station to go to the Times Square]

Edge: I can't believe I'm going with you guys to Times Square, you remembered what happened when we went to Whitehall for Independence Day? Shit that last minute decision to watch the damn fire works was horrible
Isaiah: You guys went to see the fire works?
Edge: Yeah, but I wasn't all that happy about it, we bumped into Frank and it was him who wanted to go, I was like whatever

Perry: Oh shut up always whining like an old lady
Edge: (holds up his middle finger) blow me
Isaiah: Yeah man, I agree with Edge it's gonna be so crowded and for what
Mimi: To see the ball drop of course, we are New Yorkers we gotta see the ball drop
Edge: (sarcastically) ahhhh! The ball can blow me too!

[The group laughs... they arrive in Times Square after a 30 minute ride on the train and they get off and head outside, they are met with a crowded of thousands upon thousands]

Edge: OH MY FUCKING GOD! WHAT DID I TELL YOU!?
Perry: Well, still...
Isaiah: (sigh)
Mimi: C'mon, so what, we gonna see the ball drop

It's so not worth, just can't be worth it to be standing out here in a crowded block just to see some stupid ball drop.

[The group waited and waited, then the ball finally began its descent, the count down started, 10,9,8,7,6,5,4,3...2...as everyone gets ready to shout 1 the ball lights up and burst into a giant fire ball...]

What the hell, I knew sumtin bad was gonna happen, but there was sumtin interesting, there was a super shiny purple light before the explosion. Everyone started to run in terror, Perry, Mimi and Isaiah started to run too, but Perry grabbed me so I followed for a short bit. I purposely got lost in the crowd and I just stared at the ball, was it Judgment? was he really exposing the truth out to the world like that. Before I knew it Saivent rushed up to me.

Saivent: This isn't good Edge
Edge: Yeah you're telling me
Saivent: Look I can't stay here long, I can't let him find me I'll explain later
Edge: Sure why not, but what the hell is going on here???
Saivent: He's searching for the fragments of his armor

Edge: His armor???
Saivent: Yeah, in The Great War fragments of his dragon armor were chipped off, they still exist in various forms, and apparently one of them was used in the crystals of the ball
Edge: Damn so that's what's going on
Saivent: Look I have to go now before he sees me
Edge: Go then, I'll take care of things here

He disappeared in that same gust of wind that he comes and goes in, I guess no one would notice in a time like this. I saw a purple comet shooting out from the ball of fire, but it wasn't a comet, it was Judgment!

Chapter 7

Battle in the sky, the first incident

It was without a doubt Judgment, I didn't wanna risk being seen but I really doubt anyone would notice in a time like this. Everyone was running in panic and the cops are swarming everywhere, I think I also see SWAT teams out or sumtin... no, I don't have much of a choice, I'm going after him here and now!

[Flames start to appear on Edge's body, they are small but they pick up in size and intensity quickly, Edge starts to lift off the ground and the moment he does the fire violently flickers. The police all aim their guns at Edge and open fire, he looks back at them with anger and annoyance on his face]

Oh my fucking god, ASSHOLES! Shit I hope my friends are long gone I don't want them to know about me...

[Edge swipes his hand in the general direction of the gun fire, and little molten droplets are seen falling to the floor]

Judgment, I'm coming for you!

[Edge races after Judgment in the sky, but down below the cameras that were documenting the New Year celebration kept on rolling, the camera men aim them at the sky]

Judgment: You're quite the persistent one aren't you!

Edge: Don't need you around destroying my home!

Judgment: YOUR HOME!? HAAHAHHHAA! THIS WOULD HAVE BEEN OUR HOME IF YOU HADN'T BETRAYED US! WE WOULD HAVE LIVED UPON THIS WORLD AS KINGS, INSTEAD YOU BETRAYED US! AND OUR BRETHREN NOW LIVE IN THE UNDERWORLDS OF HELL BECAUSE OF YOU!

Edge: WHAT BETRAYAL ARE YOU FUCKING TALKING ABOUT

Judgment: YOU'LL FIND OUT WHEN I SEND YOU BACK TO HELL

Edge: Oh fuck it...

[Edge speeds up to meet Judgment head on, he knocks Edge back, but he retaliates by using his Strike Fist. It sends Judgment dropping towards the ground but he lands with a concussive force that shakes the pavement, a few people are killed the rest are tossed into the air like rag dolls. Judgment stands up and looks at Edge who is still in the sky]

Judgment: You care about these humans? Then save them as you wish, ERUPTION!

[Judgment strikes the ground hard with his fist creating a fissure, then lights start to shine through the cracks and a split second later, explodes. Even more people are sent flying, Edge tries to save as many as possible, cushioning their landing by catching some of the helpless bystanders. Judgment leaps back into the air leaving Edge to look around at the bodies everywhere. Whatever cameras that were left all point towards Edge who quickly sends streams of fires towards them, destroying them instantly]

Damn what am I supposed to do, I can't save any of these people, and the cameras, they're still rolling? What the fuck, run away, don't stay here... I jetted back up towards Judgment, I wasn't gonna let him get away, this has to end before anymore people are killed, before the media gets even more footage. He started flying faster but I kept up, I shot out streams of flames to stop him but he'd either dodge them or deflect them.

[Judgment comes to a stop and turns around towards Edge]

24

Judgment: You see this? This is a fragment of the past, a fragment of true power

Edge: Yeah, true power, that's why you got your ass sealed, STRIKE FIST!

[Before Edge could land his attack Judgment holds up what looks to be a jewel shard and imbeds it into his right arm. The jewel begins to grow and covers his entire forearm in a crystalline skin with the same purple hue of his flames]

Judgment: ERUPTION!

[Both Edge and Judgment's fist strike each other causing a huge explosion to appear in the sky, Edge is sent flying back while Judgment staggers a bit]

Judgment: Hmm, more power...

[Judgment bursts into a purple flame and disappears]

Shit he's gone again, I better leave too before I expose myself anymore. I jumped off the roof of the building I landed on and started running on the ground. I ran as fast as I could to the closes train station, but they were abandoned, everyone fled in horror so I did what came natural to a Brooklynite, I jumped the turnstiles and ignited my flames, I flew in the tunnels all the way back home. When I got out I calmly walked to my house and I turned on the news, and guess what I saw, me and Judgment were all over the television...

[The TV is on, the news reporter is talking about the events that happened tonight]

News Reporter: Terror arose tonight as the New Year's ball burst into fire, suspected terrorist acts are what people are calling this, but watch as footage shows what appears to be a purple comet and the red asteroid fighting each other, here we also have footage of them being actual people, I repeat these are people...

[Edge shuts the TV off...]

Chapter 8

</H4ck3r>

Oh man what am I gonna do, the whole fucking world probably knows about me. And now Judgment, his attack was a lot stronger, it's that damn shard.

[Edge's cell phone rings...]

I picked up and to my surprise it was Frank, I haven't seen him since like what, August or so, maybe even more. Well here's a new friend of mine for you all to meet, his name is Frank, much like everyone else, he's taller than me. He's an old high school friend, despite his tall and somewhat skinny stature his voice is pretty deep and booming, he too comes from rich parents but they don't share the wealth with him, he often goes to everyone else for money, anyway, he called to say what's up and that we should hang out, reluctantly I said yes. I suppose this was the best way to ignore that bad feeling I have in the back of my head. What if Judgment attacks again, what if he decides to give me grief while I'm out like this, sigh...

[Edge gets dressed and heads out to the train station, he hops on the R train and heads toward Whitehall station]

I headed towards the spot he wanted to meet at, it was that same place where I met Saivent, that fountain in Battery Park. No one was there at the moment so I sat down, tilted my head back to look at the sky and rested. It must've been half an hour before he showed up, now I'm not a patient person at all, but given the circumstances it's nice to get out and relax. He tapped my shoulder and I greeted him with a "hey." We walked to South Street Seaport to get sumtin to eat, we caught up a bit.

Frank: So, Edge, what's up?
Edge: Nuttin much just your typical everyday stresses, school, life, so on and whatever, what about you?
Frank: Just hanging out with people surfing the net and chillaxing
Edge: (laughs and chuckles) "chillaxing"? Haven't heard that term in forever
Frank: Yeah, well, it's just me, hey yo did you hear about that bombing yesterday at Times Square, it was crazy
Edge: (with a sarcastic look on his face) tell me about, I was there
Frank: Yeah I know, Perry told me
Edge: HOLY SHIT I totally forgot about them
Frank: Yeah that to hahahaaa, they said you weren't online last night
Edge: Nah by the time I got home I was like whatever and clonked out
Frank: I see, well they were worried about you, didn't you get their calls?
Edge: No actually my phone was off
Frank: What about a voice mail or anything
Edge: Hmm... Lemme check

[Edge takes out his cell phone and calls his voice mail, he listens to what Perry and Isaiah left then hangs up]

Edge: (laughs) my fault
Frank: Hey so tell me sumtin, how DID you manage to get away? A lot of people were running and screaming, I'd imagine that everyone was pushing and shoving
Edge: Yeah they were... you ever wished that some things never happen
Frank: Sometimes, but it's rare
Edge: Eh, guess we're different
Frank: Oh you have no idea

[Frank rolls up a paper napkin and throws it at Edge and it hits him in the face]

Edge: (chuckles a bit) fuck ass

I picked up that napkin and threw it at him but then what happened
next took me completely by surprised, he held both his hands like you
would when you try to catch a basket ball, then a small portal appeared
and the napkin vanished, then he looked at me and laughed, at this point
I looked like I just saw pigs fly.

Edge: (whispers) WHAT THE FUCK*???*
Frank: (points at Edge) behind you

*[Edge turns around and the portal opens up and the napkin tumbles out
and hits him in the face causing Frank to die of laughter]*

Edge: (still whispering) Yo dude since when could you do that*???*
Frank: I've always been able to do that, but I keep it a secret
Edge: Why?
Frank: Why? Well why did you keep yours a secret?
Edge: So... you know then
Frank: Yeah, thanks to your little show last night, I was there, I saw you,
not to mention you were all over the TV
Edge: Was I?!
Frank: Hahhhaa no, you were too blurry to really make out, that's why
I asked you to come here so I could surprise you
Edge: Sneaky, so what else can you do?
Frank: Not much, I mean these "gates" work both ways or just one
Edge: Wait so all you can do is open up gates?
Frank: Yeah pretty much, it's nothing as cool as you though but it comes
in handy
Edge: Yeah I can imagine
Frank: (with a smirk) oh yeah you know what I mean hahhahhaa
Edge: So, how about you show me what you can do
Frank: What exactly do you mean?
Edge: Let's have a match tonight when everyone is sleeping
Frank: Alright, you got yourself a challenge
Edge: This is cool, Frank, the gate master hahaahaa
Frank: Eww no, shut up, that's so corny dude, call me Hacker
Edge: Oh yeah? How'd you come up with that name?

Frank: I can "hack" the planet

Edge: What ya mean?

Frank: These gates let me go wherever, whenever, take whatever I want, not to mention I'm a computer hacker

Edge: Cool, definitely cool, so Hacker Vs Edge

Frank: Yeah

Chapter 9

Hacker Vs Edge, a new found ally

We chatted a bit and waited for the silent hours of late night, when everyone was gone and everything was still and quite. It was cold, but I didn't mind, Hacker though was a bit chilly. I couldn't wait to see what he can do.

Edge: You ready?
Hacker: As I'll ever be
Edge: Then c'mon!

[Edge leaps into the air and comes down towards Hacker with a kick, but Hacker puts his hands together and creates a gate and Edge falls right through. He then turns around and steps to the side, another gate opens up right beside Hacker who is holding out his arm. Edge gets clotheslined and falls to the ground in confusion. Immediately he gets up and throws a stream of fire at Hacker who just barely dodges it, as Edge is still recovering from the first attack Hacker punches forward in Edge's direction but is nowhere near him, another gate opens up and Hacker's punch goes through connecting with Edge's head at the other end of the gate]

Edge: (grunts) ugh, ok, I see how this works now, alright no probs
Hacker: Thought I was easy didn't you?
Edge: Bah!

[Edge ignites his flames and rises to the air, he swings his arms to the side

and lets out streams of fire that surround the ground area around Hacker. As Hacker is confused by the inferno raging around him Edge Dashes through and catches him off guard with a kick to the face. As Hacker falls back he opens a gate which he falls through, and exits right behind Edge. Without hesitation Edge ignites his fires to a blaze and Hacker's attack is thwarted from the intense heat]

Hacker: Damn!

[Edge continues to throw out streams of fire at Hacker, most of which just barely dodge him]

Hacker: Ok ok ok, I give up, I'm not a fighter
Edge: (laughs) alright good enough, you're not too bad, guess it was a good idea to miss you
Hacker: Miss me?
Edge: Yeah, you didn't think you were able to dodge those fires on your own did you
Hacker: Way to rub salt in the wounds dude
Edge: Don't worry, like you said you're not a fighter
Hacker: I may not be able to fight like you but I'm good with computers
Edge: So you say, c'mon lets rest and get outta here
Hacker: You wanna come over? Get a snack and I can show you what I can REALLY do
Edge: Sure

Hacker opened up a gate and before I knew it we were at his front door. We went in quietly so not to wake up his parents, we both got a lil snack and he showed me his computer. I gotta admit it was pretty tricked out, his room had several monitors which went on with one flip of the power switch. The power consumption must've been outta the world here. He logged into the net and before I knew it he was hacking away at porn sites, secure servers, and even small government sites. Ok, I admit it, this was pretty cool.

[Edge and Hacker stayed on the computer, time passes and Edge falls

asleep on Hackers bed while Hacker himself stays on the net surfing and gathering information regarding the incident in Times Square]

Hacker: *Damn, this isn't good, not good at all. If this keeps up then everyone will find out about us, and then who knows what will happen...*

[Edge hears a familiar voice in his dreams...]

Chapter 10

Saivent's truth, a nostalgic memory...

[Edge is on top of a building that seems to go far above the clouds, he's staring down to the city lights below, this is his dream]

Saivent: Hey

Edge: Oh hey you, what ya doing here?

Saivent: This is your dream it's the safest place for me to talk without anyone finding me

Edge: Oh yeah, so what were you gonna explain to me?

Saivent: Yeah, that, you ever heard that saying "mother Earth"

Edge: Yeah

Saivent: Well there's no such thing, basically I'm the person that gives life to this planet, the animals, the weather, everything

Edge: So your mother Earth

Saivent: Uh, I guess so, that's why I have stay in hiding, if anyone finds me and manages to... well, kill me, then this planet will die and there's no way the humans can manage on their own

Edge: I see, wow so what are you?

Saivent: What am I?

Edge: Elemental Spirit, Elemental user, Power user, Avatar etc etc etc

Saivent: I'm neither, I'm an entity like Jehovah, Lucifer and Tempis, to name a few

Edge: Wow and you trusted me enough to lemme know this?

Saivent: Well you would wonder sooner or later, but I trust you so yeah

Edge: Cool, where is this place? It seems so familiar...

Saivent: This tower? I don't know, maybe it was a second life or something... I'll see ya Edge, have fun in your dreams
Edge: Alright see ya

Hmm, this place seems so familiar but I can't quite place my finger on it, seeing the world from so high up... this hand, this hand of mine...

[Edge raises his right hand and a black cutoff glove appears on it]

This hand of mine, it yearns for sumtin that I dunno of... hmm I can see lightning in the distance, yeah, another life, another world, maybe this is the future, maybe it's the past, who knows...

[Edge gets up and jumps off the building, he closes his eyes and just free falls for a while, he doesn't open his eyes, and he doesn't turn on his flames...]

Chapter 11

Attack at school, the second incident

Hacker opened a gate to my place in the morning so I could go home, shower and get dressed for school. The sun wasn't even out, the train ride was packed as always and getting a seat was next to impossible, I just stood up for the 4 long stops. As I headed to school I looked to the Empire State building like I always do, the sun was out by now but the sky was cloudy, it looks like it was gonna be a pretty nice day, I like grey days... I made it to school and got changed and sat down and rested for a while, I talked to my classmates and such, read the papers, ate some cookies and got ready to weld. The first break came and went and before I knew it, it was lunch, most of the students leave the building to smoke and get food, but I stay behind to sleep. I picked up the Metro newspaper and flipped the pages, I found an article stating that a museum had been destroyed somewhere in Europe, why did I get a feeling that was Judgment.

[A loud explosion is heard in the oxy-acetylene room, Edge puts down the newspaper and runs out of the room and into the hallway to see what it is, the doors of the oxy-acetylene room burst open and Judgment walks through]

Shit, of all the places and times, here and now?

[Edge ignites his flames and dashes towards Judgment, but Judgment leaps back to the hole he blasted in the wall of the building. Edge jumps at him with his Strike Fist but misses and Judgment goes flying out the

gaping hole in the side of the building. Edge reignites his flames and burst out in an explosion of his own, the two are racing against each other. Judgment heads towards the Empire State building and lands on top of the spire]

Judgment: Soon Edge, you will know what it's like to truly burn

Edge: Go back into hiding unless you want me to kick your ass like I did last time

Judgment: This is just to give you grief, the world knows about us, and the humans think it's all terrorist attacks, Lucifer was right, the human race will destroy itself in due time

Edge: I'm so tired of this talk about god and the devil spare me the details, if you think your destroying my home guess again, and as for this grief, go ahead anytime, bring your shit you short midget

Judgment: Big words, don't worry I'll be back for you

Edge: I'll stop you one way or another

Judgment: Go ahead and try, oh by the way here some more grief

[Judgment cuts the spire with a laser like blade that he creates in the palm of his hand and it goes crashing down towards the city below]

Judgment: Ta ta!

[Judgment disappears in a burst of purple fire]

Edge: OH FUCK...

I took out my cell phone and called Hacker.

Edge: HACKER, ME, EMPIRE STATE, GATE TO THE HUDSON NOW!

He didn't get the chance to ask why, I raced to grab a hold of the spire and a gate opened up in the side of the building, Hacker poked his head out and saw my situation, he immediately knew what I meant. He jumped out and he opened up another gate and sent the spire into the Hudson, I grabbed him and flew him up to the top of the building.

38

Edge: Hurry, open up a gate and get us outta here

He did so and just as it started, it ended, we were in Central Park now...

Hacker: Dude, what the fuck just happened?!
Edge: (sigh) Judgment...

I told him about everything that's happening.

Hacker: Ok, this I can help with, we can track him with satellite surveillance
Edge: Damn, you are too nice, let's go then

[Hacker takes Edge back to his home and they access the surveillance satellites and begin tracking Judgment, he's heading towards Egypt]

Chapter 12

Battle in the Egyptian sky

Edge: Look right before he stops, open up a gate far enough from him so he won't notice, I need to stop him from finding anymore shards of his armor, he's getting stronger...

Hacker: Got it, um... it's a bit far... I'll need to ferry you along

Edge: Huh?

Hacker: See, my limit is about 1000 miles give or take, for me to get you to Egypt... I'd have to ferry you along a bit

Edge: ...that's a real inconvenience, alright whatever just do what ya need to do

Hacker opened the gate and ferried me through, we made about 8 or 9 stops that took us from New York, Newfoundland, Greenland, Iceland, London, France, Libya and finally Egypt. I gotta admit that was one hell of a ride...

[Edge and Hacker arrive at Egypt near the great pyramids...]

Edge: Man, you been to all these places?

Hacker: You have no idea

Judgment went to one of the great pyramids and smashed through the side. Me and Hacker followed close by, I wanted to catch him when his guard was down, I'll destroy that shard before he gets it.

Edge: Dude, you might wanna go, it may get bad

Without hesitation Hacker opens another gate and leaps through, gee, thanks for worrying about me.

[Judgment is rummaging through the broken stones that make up the pyramid, a little purple shine is seen and Edge makes a mad dash to knock Judgment down. Edge picks up the Shard and looks at Judgment]

Judgment: NO!

[Edge destroys the shard by heating up his hand with an intense fire that caused the small crystal to crack]

Edge: There's one down
Judgment: You think you've won? I already have two shards, my power continues to grow, even if you destroyed this one there are still more out there
Edge: And each time you find one I'll destroy it!
Judgment: Don't be so arrogant Fire Lord, ERUPTION!

[Judgment leaps into the air and comes down towards Edge with his fist, but Edge grabs his hand just in the nick of time and swings him around using his attack's momentum. Judgment is sent flying back into the rubble, Edge then rushes towards the rubble where Judgment is and hits the ground hard bringing up a tower of flames, immediately Judgment takes to the sky and Edge ignites his own fire to follow, the two continue to battle it out in the night sky of Egypt, they look like two massive fire balls one purple and one red. On several occasion they were able to knock each other into the sand below. The fight continues on the ground as the two rush each other with burning fist. In the distance people start to gather to see what is happening]

Edge: (breathing heavily) look, we have fans
Judgment: (also breathing heavily) then show them what you can do, Fire Lord
Edge: STRIKE FIST!
Judgment: ERUPTION!

[Just like the first time they tried it they both sent each other flying back once again. Judgment staggers to get up...]

Judgment: Next time, you won't be so lucky

[Judgment disappears in a flash of fire]

Edge: Sure why not

[A gate opens up shortly after Judgment disappears and Hacker steps through, Edge is sitting on the ground bloody and exhausted]

Hacker: Damn are you ok?
Edge: (panting) I've had better, come to take me home?
Hacker: (nods)
Edge: (still panting) heh

I think I passed out cuz the next thing I knew I woke up in my room, Hacker was on my computer surfing the net.

Hacker: Hey buddy you awake?

I sat up and looked at my hands and body, I looked like a damn mummy covered in bandages.

Edge: Yeah, you patched me up good
Hacker: It's all basic bandages, you weren't too messed up
Edge: Oh man, what time is it?
Hacker: 12:34pm
Edge: Well I missed school
Hacker: I wouldn't worry about it, it's closed, Judgment destroyed half of it
Edge: Oh yeah that's right
Hacker: Perry and Mimi are coming for a visit they said they haven't heard from you since new years
Edge: Oh shit, damn... I totally forgot about them, shit
Hacker: Hahahhaa you're an awful friend
Edge: (chuckles) yeah, I totally am

Chapter 13

A friendly visit and a white lie

Hacker left before Perry and Mimi came, I rested in bed till they did. The sun was out and bright for the time being, it wasn't long before I heard them calling for me through my window and I began my seemingly long walk downstairs to open the door for them. They greeted me with joy and Perry hugged me, gotta admit it hurt and I wish he didn't do it, but I'm glad he's ok, Mimi too.

[They go back to the room and Edge goes back to laying down on his bed, Perry and Mimi are sitting in chairs by the computer and TV]

Perry: YO! What happened to you that night you disappeared, we were mad worried about you dude

Edge: Well, I'm fine hahahaa

Mimi: What's with the bandages then?

Edge: Oh, you didn't hear? My school had an explosion, I was... in it, fucked me up bad don't you think?

Perry: Damn yo now I feel bad

Edge: Don't, it's not worth it, I'll be fine, these are just lil bruises

Mimi: You should go to the hospital

Edge: Hellz nah, not for sumtin as minor as this, trust me I'll survive. So how are you guys, what happened New Years Eve?

Perry: It was crazy, everyone was running everywhere, it's like everyone went Brooklyn or sumtin

Ok, if by now your wondering what he means by Brooklyn, cuz he

45

says it a lot, it basically means to go crazy and buck wild, almost like a war cry that gets the blood pumping, getting you ready for sumtin extreme to come.

Edge: Hahahahaha!
Mimi: We lost you, Isaiah wanted to go back and look for you but we couldn't cuz the crowd was so thick
Edge: Good, don't ever come back for me, I'll always be alright remember that, I don't want you or anyone else getting hurt cuz you were worried or sumtin
Perry: Why you gotta be so hard, look at you

[Perry reaches over and pokes Edge's chest and he squirms out in pain]

Mimi: Hehehehe
Edge: AHHHHHHHH
Perry: See you're hurt all over
Edge: Bah...
Perry: Did Isaiah call you?
Edge: No, not that I know of, my celly... has been fritzy lately
Perry: He should be ok he got into the train with us
Edge: Wow the trains were still running? speaking of which, did you hear what happened that night?
Mimi: They said it was terrorist or sumtin it's been like that since 9/11
Edge: Oh... I swear they blame everything on terrorist, the government and military are so retarded
Perry: Oh well what can you do
Edge: "Let the world change you and you can change the world"
Perry: Um ok...
Mimi: Hey you wanna get the $5 food tonight?

For those that dunno, there's this lil place on 53rd street in Manhattan that sells this platter of food for $5.00 and the hour long line is WORTH the wait.

Edge: Uh, I don't think I'll be moving for the next day or 2, I'll be lucky to be able to move tonight
Perry: Hahahahahaa

46

Mimi: Yeah, my fault, want a beer?
Edge: What the fuck hahahahaa

They both stayed and we watched some TV for a while, the day quickly darkened and before we knew it night had come upon us. Oh well there's my day for you, a friendly visit, and small lil lies here and there.

Chapter 14

The last shard

[Judgment sits on top of the Empire State building where the spire he broke off was, it's night time]

Judgment: The sword of Michael, Excalibur, managed to shatter a plate from my dragon form. 4 pieces were sent flying around the world, I recovered 2, 1 from the New Years ball, and 1 from the museum, Edge destroyed 1 so that leaves one left... I won't be able to revive my dragon form, but I can regain enough power to rain grief and misery onto this world. And you Fire Lord, you'll get what's coming to you old friend, old ally, old brother in arms. Now, let's not keep destiny waiting...

[A helicopter flies around and spots Judgment on top of the broken spire they shine a spotlight on him but he blast them down with a purple laser from his hand, meanwhile in Edge's house...]

The news have been blaring on about these mysterious "events", they're still investigating the destruction and disappearance of the Empire State spire. Now on the news, a helicopter crashes into the streets killing over 20 people near the Empire State, wanna guess who it is? When is this gonna end...

A few days pass and no word from Judgment, my school was basically destroyed and brought to a halt so I don't gotta worry about missing any days. I haven't heard a word from Hacker on Judgment's whereabouts, things seem to finally be letting up a bit. I took a train all the way to Rockaway Beach so I can stare out at the Atlantic for a while. The train ride there was empty and calm, I mean who the hell really goes to the beach during winter. My fire kept me warm...

[Edge is sitting on the sand and starring at the waves as they wash up against the shore, his fire flickers about violently in the wind. The seagulls seem to effortlessly float above him squawking for food, but he pays no attention to them]

Gotta admit this is pretty nice. I leaned back into the sand, it was moist and cold but at the same time relaxing. My fire quickly heated up the sand drying it out so I was even more comfortable. My eyes closed without me knowing and I started to dream, again I was in that same world that Saivent showed me, this time though I saw my home, New York City going up in flames, the skies were darkened and I heard a roaring. I jerked myself awake though and I saw that the sky really was getting dark, but I didn't move. I stayed laying down and staring up at the sky. The clouds started to swirl in a cyclone formation, but it burst into a purple flame and a fiery dragon came out, I didn't move, I just laid there...

[A gate opens up and Hacker comes through just in time to pull Edge out of the way, the dragon strikes the sand and kicks up a cloud of glass shards]

Hacker: YO! You have to watch out dude
Edge: Huh? Oh shit sorry yo
Hacker: It's him, he's found the last shard, I tried to call you but you didn't pick up
Edge: Damn, I fucked up big time didn't I
Hacker: Dude worry about that later

[Edge looks up to the sky and yells]

Edge: JUDGMENT!

[Judgment appears through the fiery clouds and laughs at Edge]

Judgment: HAHAHHAHAAHAAHAHAHAA! Saved by your friend I see

Hacker: What do you want?

Judgment: I want a lot of things, but in this case I want Edge to pay for his treachery, I have the last shard Edge, do you think you're strong enough?

Edge: Judgment...

[Judgment takes out the last shard and implants it into his forehead. Just as the first two shards had done to both his forearms, the shard in his forehead begins to grow and surround his head with a crystalline helmet like structure]

Judgment: Edge, you will die here, it's a shame you don't remember what you've done, but you'll remember soon enough, when I send you back to hell!

Edge: (sarcastically) ah keep talking!

Judgment: DIE!

Chapter 15

Edge Vs Judgment, flame showdown

[Edge and Hacker are standing on the sand looking up towards the sky at Judgment. The clouds start to grow darker and the wind picks up violently. Edge puts on his right hand glove and ignites his fires to a full burn, Hacker takes a step back from the intense radiant heat. The sand below Edge's sneakers start to melt and crystallize into glass, Edge looks over to Hacker]

Edge: Sorry about that, I'll lower it so you won't feel the burn, but that ass up there, he's gonna feel ever degree of it
Hacker: Go for it Edge, I'll back you up
Edge: No, you're not gonna get involved in this, I don't need you getting yourself hurt or killed, it's gonna end here one way or another, it can't go on like this
Hacker: I'm gonna help one way or another
Edge: Fine, just don't get killed on me

[Edge lunges into the sky towards Judgment]

Edge: STRIKE FIST!

[Judgment grabs a hold of Edge's fist and laughs, he spins Edge around like a centrifuge and sends him flying back into the sand]

Edge: Ok, that didn't work, he got a lot more powerful
Hacker: Teamwork

Edge: Got it, HERE I GO AGAIN! STRIKE...

[Edge again lunges back into the air but this time before hitting Judgment Hacker opens up a gate in front of Judgment and the exit appears right behind him going in the opposite direction]

Edge: FIST!

[Edge strikes Judgment hard in the back of the head and this time he goes flying down towards the sand, but he quickly recovers by putting his hand out and pushing himself parallel against the sand, he's now on course towards Hacker]

Edge: HACKER WATCH OUT!

[Hacker opens a gate behind himself and steps back into it, another one opens up again after Judgment passes but Judgment without hesitation turns around and blasts Hacker with a stream of fire. From out of nowhere Edge comes dashing down in front of Hacker and punches the stream of fire splitting it in down the center. Edge kicks up the sand in front of him and heats them up followed by another stream of fire that send the shards of glass flying towards Judgment, but he dodges them before they reach. Hacker immediately opens up a gate and redirects the glass at Judgment once again. They strike his forearm and he calls out in pain]

Judgment: Enough of this childish game

[Judgment stands tall (as tall as he can) and raises his hand, he snaps his fingers and the sand on the beach suddenly gets pushed aside like some fissure of wind parting the ground. Edge looks on unimpressed at the show of power, instead he takes a stance and ignites his flames to their highest intensity, Hacker backs away from the radiant heat. What's left of the sand on the floor begins to melt and Edge takes off in a dash towards Judgment, they strike fists repeatedly and embers of red and purple flares are sent in all directions as their fists clash, Hacker stands behind and watches the pillars of fires as they fight for the winning blow]

Hacker: *Holy shit, he's really going at it, how can anyone have this much* *power, it's almost like a firestorm fighting itself... those two are at it like no ones business and I can't help out, this isn't a place for me, my powers are useless.*

[Edge and Judgment are pounding at each other and the fight starts to wear them down]

Judgment: Damn you...
Edge: Heh, this is interesting, even with 3 shards we're pretty evenly matched
Judgment: You think were matched?
Edge: Seems so
Judgment: Think again!

[Judgment takes to the sky and focuses his energy into his hands, he puts them together to further concentrate the energy...]

Judgment: DRAGON FLARE!

[The same dragon that came crashing down towards Edge before Hacker saved him is once again coming down on him, this time Edge stands his ground and holds out his hands, he catches the dragons fiery jaws and tries to push it back but he's barely holding his ground, Hacker at this point is being blown away by the intense heat and power. The dragon's jaws start to burn Edge's hands and he calls out in pain, but doesn't back down, he instead envelopes his hands in his own fires and begins to summon all his strength to push the attack away if not to stop it. Edge's own fires start to get drawn to his hand and soon the dragon is being pushed back]

Edge: YOU WON'T WIN!

[A fiery glow appears in Edge's eye and his own fires consume him, pushing the dragon all the way back. Judgment can no longer hold his Dragon Flare attack and instead has to brace himself for Edge's return blast. He easily stops it but following the return blast Edge immediately rushes up towards Judgment and they meet fist to fist]

Hacker: EDGE!

Judgment: You think you can win this?! ERUPTING DRAGON FLARE!

Edge: STRIKE FIST!

[The fiery glare of the Strike Fist collides head on with the Erupting Dragon Flare and the two fires explode in a blaze of energy, Hacker opens a gate and runs through before being caught in the maelstrom of fire. As easily as it starts it's finished... black smoke and fires litter the sky and land. The nearby houses on the beach shore are destroyed, the death of the innocents are uncertain and unknown... moments later a gate reappears and Hacker steps through to see the destruction, he tries to find his friend but both Judgment and Edge can not be found...]

Hacker: *Shit what happened? It's like a war zone, the sky... why is it so clear and blue, where are you Edge?*

Chapter 16

Hacker's grief

Hacker: Edge is missing and I don't have a clue where he is, I don't wanna think he's dead, he just can't be. There're no bodies, nothing, just fires...

[Not too far away on the ground Hacker hears a phone ringing, the light from the screen catches his attention, he opens a gate and reaches for the phone and answers the call]

Hacker: How the hell is his cell phone here?

[Flashback - Edge is laying back on the sand and he takes his cell phone out of his pocket to check the time and sets it back on the sand instead of his pocket...]

Hacker: Hello?
Perry: Hey yo, Edge
Hacker: No, it's not Edge, it's me Frank
Perry: Frank? Where's Edge?
Hacker: He's... I dunno, he's gone
Perry: He's gone? Whatcha mean?
Hacker: If I told you, you wouldn't understand, where are you?
Perry: Huh, whatcha talking about?
Hacker: I'll come get you, just let me know where you are
Perry: I'm home right now
Hacker: Alright can you get to Battery Park and meet me at the ferry?
Perry: Um... ok I'll be there in a while then

Hacker: Good call Edge's cell when your there

Hacker: *I dunno what to do, what am I supposed to tell everyone, that Edge just disappeared or sumtin?*

[Hacker walks around the debris field in search for some hint of Edge. He looks into the sky, clear blue. The sun shines brightly and he has to squint to see clearly, he makes out what seems to be a white silhouette]

Hacker: *Was that Edge? Or am I seeing things.*

[The silhouette turns around and disappears]

Hacker: *He never showed up, He's gone.*

[Hacker sits down on the pier, he hears sirens blaring after what seemed to be hours of idleness, the cops rush in. He stands up and raises his hands, the cops have their guns pointed at him]

Cop 1: HANDS ON YOUR HEAD!
Cop 2: DON'T MOVE OR WE'LL SHOOT
Hacker: (sigh) go ahead officers shoot if you want
Cop 2: WE'RE SERIOUS WE WILL SHOOT
Cop 1: Look we don't want any trouble son, just do as we say!

[Edge's cell phone rings and the cops quickly cock their guns]

Cop 2: WHAT IS THAT!?
Hacker: It's just a cell phone
Cop 2: DROP IT!
Hacker: NO WAY!
Cop 1: Look just do it, we WILL shoot!
Hacker: Fuck you guys

[Just as the cops open fire Hacker opens a gate behind himself and falls back into it]

Cop 1: What the hell just happened?!

Cop 2: Man I got to lay off the drugs
Cop 1: Huh?!

[The gate opens up in the bathroom of the Staten Island ferry, Hacker walks out and searches for Perry just to find him sitting down at a bench eating a piece of pie]

Hacker: *There he is just waiting for me, now I have to break the news to him.*

Chapter 17

Perry's disbelief

Perry: *I met Frank at the ferry, he took me to South Street Seaport and explained everything that happened. I thought it was some stupid joke he and Edge made up. But he proved me wrong, he showed me this thing he could do and I still couldn't believe it. I thought shit like this was only in the movies. I gotz to be loosing my mind...*

[Hacker explains everything that has happened so far]

Perry: *I couldn't believe any of this, he took me to the beach where Edge disappeared. There were still cops all around us so we kept low and outta sight. Frank, I mean Hacker, was really depressed... I was holding myself back. Edge was only in my life for no more than a year or so but he showed me a lot of shit that I wouldn't have seen on my own.*

We waited till night when most of the cops were gone. We jumped over the barricades and looked around, there was no sign of him. The sand was dug up really deep, like a long crater. Hacker went off on his own and I went my own way, I walked the entire crater and I noticed sumtin that was sticking out really weird, it looked like a, baby... wrapped up in a blanket. It was covered in sand and felt like concrete, it was the size of a foot ball so I picked it up and took it with me. Hacker was right, there was nuttin here it's just an empty beach of fire, nuttin more, Edge, he's gone...

Perry: Dude you can go if you want, I'm gonna stay behind a bit
Hacker: Alright, if you need me, just call, here, take Edge's phone

Perry: Thanks, yeah, I'll keep it, see ya…

[Hacker opens a gate and walks through, Perry holds up Edge's phone and looks at it, a tear streams down his left eye. He puts the phone into his pocket and tries not think much about it. The object he found starts to catch his interest]

Perry: What the hell is this thing, it feels mad warm and soft but it's as hard as a rock.

[The object pulses and catches Perry off guard, he ends up tossing it into one of the small fires left from the earlier battle as a result of the shock]

Perry: Holy shit what the hell is that thing? I accidentally tossed it into the fire cuz it scared the shit outta me when it started to shake.

[The object he tossed into the fire started to glow brightly like steel being super heated. It glowed so brightly it melted just like metal would. Perry took a step back in surprise of what he sees. The molten pool starts to form a circle with some rune like characters in its center]

Perry: What the hell is going on… that thing melted and now it's making a circle like it's alive or sumtin. It stopped glowing a bit, then that thing became really bright and all I heard was a baby crying. The light died down enough so I could see again and there was this lil baby in the center of the circle. The closer I walked the louder the baby screamed and then he started to grow. That shit went from a baby to a small crying boy all curled up, he just kept growing. He stopped crying and now he looked like a regular dude, a nude dude. he uncurled himself and stood up, he was a bit shorter than me and I'm pretty tall, 6'1", his skin was a bit more tanned than Hacker's, and his hair was a lot longer, he was also much more toned.

Chapter 18

The calling and the power within

[The nude guy stood up tall and opened his eyes, they glowed white. He raised his hands to look at them. He was completely nude but that didn't seem to bother him, he looked around at his surroundings with a look of unfamiliarity on his face. Perry walked back a bit in caution and the guy stepped out of the circle. His pace was slow but then he quickly picked it up. Perry was scared but didn't run, and the guy stopped right in front of him and spoke]

Mystery Guy: You, you are the one that melted the seal were you not? Only a fire from a powerful demon can break that seal
Perry: Huh, what are you talking about?
Mystery Guy: Does not matter, this world has changed from the days of old, nothing is familiar to me, you, you do not seem to possess any power, how did you free me?
Perry: I dunno I just tossed that thing into the fire and you came out
Mystery Guy: I see, you have my appreciation, this world will soon end, your death will be less painful than everyone else's' human...

[The guy holds out his hand and a jet of water comes streaming out, it hits Perry hard and knocks him down. While Perry is on the ground moaning in pain the guy walks up to him]

Mystery Guy: Tell me, do you fear drowning, knowing nothing you can do will beat the waves that hammer down on you
Perry: (calls out in pain) AHHHHHHHHH, ugh...

63

Mystery Guy: Can you swim?

[The guy picks Perry up with one hand and flings him onto the shoreline and the waves seem to grab him and pull him in, the guy holds out his hand and close his fist like he's crushing an egg, the waves react by grabbing Perry and drowning him]

Mystery Guy: I require clothing...

Perry: I think I musta passed out or sumtin, I remember the waves pulling me in and I couldn't breathe. I dunno if I imagined what happened next but I think I saw a lightning bolt come and hit me, now I'm in this white room, am I in heaven?

Saivent: No not heaven you're in my home
Perry: Who are you?
Saivent: Me? I'm a friend of Edge, my name is Saivent
Perry: Edge?! You know him? Is he alive? Is he ok?
Saivent: No, I'm sorry, he's beyond my reach, I didn't get the chance to save him, but you, I was able to save you
Perry: So it's true, Edge really is gone... why did you save me, didn't I die?
Saivent: You were close to it, I don't know what's going on to tell you the truth, it's like one thing after another, first Judgment and now this... do you know what you did?
Perry: No... I fucked sumtin up didn't I?
Saivent: For lack of a better way of saying it, yeah, you fucked up big time
Perry: Damn...
Saivent: Look I saved you before they got to you, you're the only one that can stop him from destroying the world, I trusted Edge, let me trust you now
Perry: You lost me, I dunno whatcha talking about
Saivent: Remember Hacker, what he told you about the world
Perry: Yeah...
Saivent: I'm giving you the chance to be apart of that world, deep inside of you, you got a potential waiting to be set free, and I'm here to give you a nudge

Perry: So, I get powers?

Saivent: You've always had them, they were just locked up, so I'm gonna unlock them for you, just stop him before he finishes what Judgment started

Perry: Stop who though?

Saivent: Testament, now go, go back to your own world and reach for the skies Perry, find YOUR calling, and you'll find your power...

Perry: No wait!

[Before Perry got his last words out, the white room start to be sucked away and Perry was sent back into the real world, he landed back onto the beach with a thud, it was just barely morning the black sky was being washed away by a tiny bit of sun. The environment was now gray... Perry sat up to look at the horizon before standing up all the way]

Perry: I was on the beach again, I felt... I felt sumtin inside of me, it was surging all over my body, my arms, and legs... wait... wasn't that guy... wasn't that Cory?

Chapter 19

The Angel Sanctuary

All I know is when me and Judgment struck our fist together everything burned and hurt, then it stopped, and for a tiny moment everything was black, but then all the darkness was sucked away and I felt like I was being thrown through space. Everything was spinning so I closed my eyes and curled up into a ball. When I opened them, everything was still and before me stood two giant gates seemingly made of gold. I walked towards it and place my hand on it, it was warm, then suddenly they opened inward and I was greeted by people all dressed in white. But someone walked ahead, I think he was an angel, it was a bit too bright for me to really see but he took my hand and everything dimmed down.

Michael: Do you know who I am?

While truthfully and secretly I did know who it was, it was Michael the archangel of war, he was the one along with Gabriel, Uriel and the others that fought in The Great War, but I pretended to not know...

Edge: No, who are you?
Michael: Come now, do you really not know? I am Michael
Edge: From The Great War...
Michael: Yes, you know of The Great War, do you remember it?
Edge: Remember it? No, Just what Saivent showed me
Michael: Ah Saivent, that... renegade, he defies us and the name of Jehovah
Edge: You don't like him do you

Michael: No we just do not believe what he's doing is right, he goes against all the teachings of Jehovah

Edge: You DO know I'm agnostic right

Michael: Bah, rubbish, Jehovah welcomes all believers and non believers alike, you're here because of the sacrifice, you risked your life to save the world and you stopped a foe of the past, granted Judgment's powers have been diluted but you still pulled off a task even me and Gabriel had trouble with, and that grants you entry into the sanctuary

Edge: So then what, heaven is next?

Michael: Oh no, this is the technical term of heaven, you see when people die their souls depending on their purity are absorbed by Jehovah, in essence they become part of him and they obtain true salvation

Edge: What? you mean they become a part of him to make him stronger?

Michael: Yes, so he can spread the word of true salvation

Edge: Alright so why am I not there then if I sacrificed my life to save the world wouldn't that make me worthy?

Michael: Truth be told your life was not a life of righteousness but you are a warrior no doubt, you fight for truth as you demonstrated when you defeated Judgment

Edge: So warriors come here then

Michael: Yes, everyone here at the Angel Sanctuary is a fighter one way or another, the reason we need this is to defend the humans if Lucifer were to ever attack again

Edge: Like The Great War

Michael: Yes, let us not waste anymore time, there is much to show you, and much to prepare for, you need to ascend in order to gain your full angel status

Edge: (laughs) so I'm gonna be an angel then

Michael: Yes

Edge: Let's get started...

So they want me to be an angel, I guess I have nuttin to object too. I wonder what this new life has to offer...

[Edge gets a change of all white clothes and is then put through training to test his combative abilities, what seemed to be nothing more than an hour or so, actually ends up to be days that extended to weeks and months. Edge

does manage to finish his trials, and he impresses Michael with his skills. It's not long till Edge is finally ready to receive his wings, and so he does, there's just one step left before he's a full angel, and that's to be baptized]

Chapter 20

The truth of the past

I managed to get my wings, it seemed to take forever, but yet time never moved here. I was approached by an angel named Akuma, he hasn't been here very long but way longer than I have. He was killed when tryna save the girl he loved. That sacrifice granted him a seat here in the sanctuary, but he didn't live a righteous life so he didn't make it to true salvation. He dressed like he was a college student, not the cleanest cut but also not to shabby, dress pants and a collared shirt, his hair was shaggy and he had an afternoon shadow, once again, taller than me by an inch or 2. He was one of those light skinned Latinos. I asked him how he came about with the name Akuma, apparently was with a gang, and the word Akuma was Japanese for demon, or some sorta evil spirit. He thought it was cool so that's the name he adopted for himself, he even kept it here in the Angel Sanctuary.

Edge: Is there anything cool here to do?
Akuma: Well besides flying around and having fun with everyone else there's really not much, this is an easy life, I mean you can go and train if you want
Edge: Nah no more training, I'm tired of it, I mean it's great to see your powers improve, but I doubt I'll be using it anytime soon
Akuma: Well have you been to hall of time?
Edge: Hall of time?
Akuma: Yeah it's like a library of history and time
Edge: Let's take a look then

[Akuma spreads his wings and leads Edge to the hall of time, they arrive in a grand hall which seemed to never end]

Edge: Whoa this is wild, how does this place work?
Akuma: You simply call out a memory and your shown what happened and how it happened
Edge: Really? Let's take a look then...

[Edge starts to call out a bunch of stuff from his own life, it entertains him for a pretty long while. Akuma eventually leaves Edge to his own, it's not long till Edge starts to look into deeper matters, he calls up The Great War and sees exactly what Saivent showed him]

I called up The Great War and I saw nuttin different from what Saivent showed me, but I remember those dreams I had, then I remembered what Judgment called me. So I decided to ask more direct questions.

[Edge asked the hall to show him "Traitor, Great War, Edge" and the hall shows him the events of what happened]

I saw... I saw myself. There stood Judgment and Testament, and right behind them in the shadows... I saw myself.

[Somewhere else in the Angel Sanctuary Michael approaches Akuma]

Michael: Have you seen Edge, it's time for his baptism
Akuma: Oh Edge is in the hall of time
Michael: WHAT?! Joke not young one!
Akuma: I'm not, is something wrong?
Michael: You should not have brought him there, he must not know of his past!
Akuma: What?
Michael: Move aside, time is of the essence!

[Back in the hall of time...]

I... I was the third General, that's why he called me a traitor... the events kept playing and I was showed an event not unfamiliar to me. Testament was standing on the mountain guarded by Leviathan, the fire bird that came down, it was Fenix, my spirit calling. I was the one that summoned Fenix... I betrayed Lucifer, but why? I started to call up the reason for my betrayal, but I heard wings flapping and I quickly called out for that childhood event that changed my life...

Michael: Edge what are you doing?

Edge: I'm just looking at my childhood, is there sumtin wrong?

Michael: No... Nothing's wrong, come it's time for your baptism, you wouldn't want to miss that would you?

Edge: No, I guess not, can I finish this last event?

Michael: Very well, I'll wait at the door

I let the event finish but I was thinking of sumtin totally different, why did everyone keep it from me, even Saivent, why was I not told the truth...

Chapter 21

The nature of the fire

I'm the third General, I was a traitor, why did I betray Lucifer...

[Edge walks to the door and meets up with Michael. The angel leads him to a waterfall with a huge pond. The clouds looked like they blended in with the rock face and the water that flowed from the mouth of the fall sparkled brilliantly. Many angels came to watch the ceremony of Edge's baptism, Akuma was front and center for the event. They took off Edge's shirt and he spread his wings fully. Michael stepped into the water and Edge followed, he put his hand behind Edge's head and slowly eased him backwards into the water, soon Edge was completely submerged]

I let Michael ease me into the water, I felt my head break the surface and I was taken by a sudden cold but pure feeling. I kept my eyes closed and before I knew it I was completely submerged, I didn't feel a need to breathe so I didn't hold my breath. I could see the shadows that bounced around the water's surface through my eyelids, the darkness and light kept reverberating, I was soon feeling uneasy, it felt wrong, all of this. There was unrest in me, as if sumtin inside of me was warning me to stop, wanting me to get out and not let this continue, it felt like I was dieing, the real me. The heat I always felt inside of me was perishing, as if it was running outta fuel and couldn't continue burning. The light that pierced through the water and through my eyelids no longer showed, it wasn't a soft warm light anymore, everything was black, it was then that in the darkness I saw myself, I saw myself reaching out to me as if being pulled away by some unseen force. The fire from my hand ignited and

I reached for it, tryna reach myself, but I couldn't, so I reached harder, but the image of myself slipped farther away from me. I began to panic and that's when it happened, that red fire of mine, it raged so violently to reach me that it blew itself out. I didn't see the light anymore, I felt alone and empty, I didn't feel the need to struggle, I felt meaningless, but that only lasted a second cuz my hand was still reached out, I was still calling for the image of myself, calling for that fire to come back, and it did. My fire came back but was no longer red, it glowed blue. The blue flame shined brightly and I saw myself again, huddled in the darkness. I grabbed myself by the hand and pulled hard...

[Michael is holding Edge below the surface and everything seemed calm, but suddenly the water started to bubble, everyone gasped as blue flames started to shoot out from under the waters surface, Michael too steps back in amazement at what is happening, he lets go and jumps back and out of the water, moments later the surface of the water burst and Edge jumps out from the pond, he's soaked and looks like he's gasping for air, floating with his wings wide spread over the pond]

What the hell did they do to me, what are they tryna take from me, my fire!? My essence!? The very being of who I am?!

Edge: WHAT ARE YOU TRYING TO DO!?
Akuma: Edge!
Michael: Son what is wrong???
Edge: You're tryna kill me, tryna take who I am away from me!
Michael: No believe me we're not doing that, your soul must be cleansed of all evil, the fire you posses is from your demon blood
Edge: NO! It's who I am, I'LL NEVER LET THAT BE TAKEN FROM ME!
Akuma: Edge listen to yourself!
Michael: No Akuma, don't get involved
Edge: I was a traitor to Lucifer, WHY?!
Michael: You made a deal with Jehovah Edge, that you were to be reborn as a human and have the chance to live a life without fighting or anguish if you helped him win The Great War
Edge: I... I made a deal with Jehovah? I kept my promise then cuz he

won, now he's tryna take the very being of who I am, I was dieing, YOU WERE TRYING TO KILL ME!

Michael: NO! WE WERE TRYING TO MAKE YOU RIGHTEOUS, TO CLEANSE YOU OF YOUR SINS!

Edge: WHO ARE YOU TO TELL ME WHAT WRONG OR RIGHT?! WE HUMANS LIVE AS WE PLEASE THAT'S WHAT IT MEANS TO BE HUMAN TO LIVE FREE!

Michael: Listen to yourself Edge, you're not human, on Earth you were an Elemental Spirit!

[Edge suddenly realizes Michael is right, he closes his wings and starts to fall, but then his fires ignite to keep him in the air, they are blue instead of red]

Edge: You're right, I was never human to begin with was I? I guess Jehovah made rules for humans to follow, to control them, but he won't control me, and you won't control me either. Humans sin, and you say it's wrong but I'm not human, so what you say that's right or wrong has nuttin to do with me

Akuma: Edge stop this!

Michael: Listen to your friend Edge, Akuma is right, you need to stop this blasphemy, please we're only trying to help you

Edge: No, I don't need your help. I'm taking my own fate into my own hands

Michael: Where do you plan on going, you have nowhere

Edge: I'll think of sumtin

Michael: We can't let you go, I'm sorry Edge

[Michael signals to everyone to capture Edge and restrain him, all the angels immediately rush him and burry him under a pile of bodies, Akuma stands back and only watches in disbelief]

Akuma: Is all this necessary Michael?

Michael: Do not ask a question you know the answer too, you shouldn't have let him in the hall of time, he was not supposed to know of his past for fear of something like this happening

Akuma: What IS happening?

Michael: Knowing the truth must have awaken the deepest part of his demon blood, and now it will not let itself be destroyed. The baptism was meant to cleanse him, and would have done so if his memory was not reawakened

Akuma: It's my fault, I apologize

Michael: It is alright child, the situation is handled

[The pile of angels suddenly start to burst into blue flames, they are all thrown back, and Edge stands up holding out his right hand]

Edge: This hand of mine is what I'll use to make my own destiny!

Akuma: Edge!

Michael: DON'T LET HIM ESCAPE!

Chapter 22

The birth of the storm

Perry: *Saivent put me back in the real world again, everything was wet and destroyed, it had to be Testament. It was a cloudy morning, I had to get home so I went to the train station but no trains were running, I took out my cell phone and it was broken so I couldn't call Hacker. There was just one thing to do, that's to run home.*

[Perry begins to run for what seemed to be hours, but he didn't seem to tire as one would think. There was a path of destruction that followed all the way up from Canarsie to East New York, there were no cops anywhere. Perry keeps running and glances over at Jamaica bay, he sees Testament standing out in the middle of the bay with streams of water jetting out like tentacles. He is now wearing clothes, a pair of jeans, black sneakers a blue vest and a white shirt]

Perry: *There he is, right there standing. What's he doing there looking at the water?*

[Testament raises his hand and collects a sphere of water, he then stares into it deeply and lets it drop. There is still water jets streaming around him, he looks up to the sky and speaks to himself]

Testament: *This world is a strange new world, humans run amok as if they rule all. The loss of The Great War led to this? A society with no order, no respect for those more powerful? Humans, they act as if they rule with an iron fist. I will show them what power is, I will finish what I started, but this*

79

vessel, this body that holds me, it is too weak, it is not meant to contain such power... hmm what is this? A visitor?

[Testament turns around and sees Perry standing at the shoreline, he takes off running in the opposite direction]

Testament: Have I not killed you? A pest such as you still stands though, why... is my power not strong enough? No, you are no longer human are you...

[Testament summons a wave from under his feet and rides it towards the shoreline, as he approaches he reaches his hand out and tries to grab Perry with a wave of water that resembles his own hand, but Perry dodges several times before being caught, he tightens his grip and brings him to eye level]

Testament: You live?
Perry: No you killed me
Testament: (tightens his grip) think stupid human you stand here in my grip before me and you say I killed you?
Perry: I was saved...
Testament: By whom!?
Perry: By a friend of a friend
Testament: So be it, if you will not answer then it matters not, you are clearly alive and breathing, I should just kill you again should I not? Hmm... I was thinking, should I torture you as I did before, or feed you to my Leviathan

[Testament tightens his grip]

Perry: AHH!
Testament: So which shall it be? I will drown you again how is that?

[Testament puts both his hands together and the water consumes Perry in a sphere of crystal blue, but he isn't down yet. Perry pounds his fist against the shell but to no avail. Bubbles start to escape his mouth but Testament just stands with his glowing white eyes, laughing. Perry

pounds even harder but finally succumbs, his limbs stop their desperate flailing]

Testament: That was quick

Chapter 23

The gift of the surge

Perry: I ran outta air but I could still fight, I'm gonna fix this. I felt sumtin in my arm, it felt paralyzing but I grabbed a hold of it anyway.

[The sphere of water suddenly shines brightly and explodes, Perry drops into the shallow water and stands up, his eyes go from a typical brown to a glowing yellow]

Testament: I was right, no longer human, now let us see what challenges you hold elemental user
Perry: This is the power? Oh man, get ready for an ass kicking
Testament: (scoffs) ass kicking? Many who have had such a tongue lived no more than a seconds worth of an existence
Perry: Yeah yeah yeah, pie
Testament: Pie?

[Testament strikes out his arm and a jet of water follows hitting Perry, but he grabs a hold of it and gets pushed back]

Perry: Ugh, more power...
Testament: Yes, more power is what you need

Perry: He pushed me back pretty hard, I suddenly remembered what Saivent said to me, "...look up to the sky..." so I did.

[Perry rises and puts his right arm straight up, the clouds start to thunder

and a bolt of lightning strikes him. The lightning bolt surges through Perry energizing him and dissipating into the ground]

Perry: Yo that feels a lot better
Testament: Does it now?

[Testament again throws a jet of water at Perry but this time he fights back by sending a charged bolt of lightning out from his hand. It hits the water stream head on and splits it down the center, Testament sees the bolt coming at him and he quickly raises a wall of water that stops the bolt dead in its tracks. That same wave now starts to rise and head towards Perry as if trying to crush him, instinctively he shoots a bolt though the top of the wave making an opening big enough for him to jump through. The moment he is out from under the wave another bolt strikes him and he disappears]

Testament: Tricky tricky, are you hiding?

[Testament looks around a bit but then multiple lightning bolts come crashing from the sky and Testament is forced onto the ground, dodging. A few of them hit him and with each one that hits, it's like a flying kick being dealt by Perry. The last kick knocks Testament all the way back and into the ground, Perry tries to follow up with a lightning bolt from the sky but Testament raises his hand creating a shield of water]

Perry: (angrily) I don't get it, doesn't water conduct electricity?
Testament: I am far beyond your skills, my power grows with each moment that passes
Perry: I take that as a no then
Testament: Hmph... We will meet again, that much I guarantee

[Testament starts to give off a mist and suddenly like steam disappears]

Perry: He's gone, the asshole is really gone, I can't believe they really do this sorta stuff in real life.

[Perry stands in the battlefield, triumphant]

Perry: So this is my power, I am... my name is... is Halo, thank god I play games and watch anime...

Chapter 24

Escape from grace

[Edge is holding out his right hand with an army of angels standing around him, his flame glows bright blue]

Michael: You will not leave here Edge!
Edge: Watch me... you know I gotta admit I must seem like the bad guy, but I'll tell you what, I'm not, to me, you're the bad guys, this is just my way of surviving, think of it as a candle flame about to die, you ever seen how it flickers violently? It's cuz it doesn't wanna die
Michael: You've died already Edge, that's why your here
Edge: True enough, we'll see, one way or another I'm getting outta here

[Edge clenches his fist tightly and the flame grows until it starts to swirl like energy, his black glove materializes on his hand and he has a pleased look on his face. He turns and faces the gate of the sanctuary and dashes towards it, a crowd of angels converge to block him but like bowling pins Edge knocks them down with his fist]

I'm not being trapped here, I'll get out one way or another!

[Edge reaches the gate and tries to push it open but it doesn't budge, so he rams it and it still doesn't move, out of frustration he calls out his attack]

Edge: STRIKE FIST!

[The gate moves ever so slightly...]

Michael: Give up Edge, you won't get out, please just stop this, and join us

Edge: Yeah sure, snow balls chance in hell, and quit asking your not changing my mind

Michael: I see, then the hard way it is, capture Edge!

They all started to surround me again, I don't get it why are they so persistent to keep me here, do I have sumtin they want? The angels, they surrounded me from every direction ground and sky, like a dome keeping me from moving anywhere, then Michael walks through, he closes his wings and it looks like he wants to fight me, I guess I have no objections to that at all, if he wants a fight I'll give it to him...

[Michael lunges towards Edge tackling him to the ground and starts to pound on Edge with his fist, but Edge blocks a few before igniting his fire to full burn, the heat forces Michael back and this time Edge lunges ahead. Michael takes the defensive by timing in a punch that was just right sending Edge flying back into the wall of angels who then knock him back towards Michael's direction. Edge appears to be out cold but as he approaches Michael, he calls out for his Strike Fist attack, it catches the angel off guard and this time Michael is sent into the wall of angels who catch him and lands him onto the floor]

Edge: Pretty handicapped fight here ain't it

Michael: You're forcing this on yourself

Edge: Maybe, but now no ones gonna say I never tried to MAKE MY OWN DESTINY! STRIKE FIST!

[Edge jumps up into the air and lands with his fist striking the ground, Michael jumped out of the way in the nick of time, but suddenly Edge turns around and a jet of fire comes streaming out burning Michael's clothing, he's trying to put it out and doesn't realize Edge is coming his way. Edge tackles him and they both fall to the floor where Edge starts to punch him repeatedly over and over again, with each hit the fire becomes more intense. Little embers of blue float away, Edge gets up and jumps straight into the air and then proceeds to throw a rain of fire balls down at

Michael. The angels making up the wall have a look of worry on their face. As the fire balls start coming closer to Michael, he deflects them outward and they hit some of the angels but they shrug it off. Michael regains some of his composure and stands up. Edge once again dashes towards Michael in a head on collision but Michael stands his ground and punches Edge hard and sends him flying towards the wall of angels]

Exactly what I was hoping he'd do, I can't beat him, I'm not strong enough but with the help of his punch and momentum, not to mention a momentous amount of pain, I'll be able to burn my way through that fucking wall and if I can hit it hard enough I can open the gate... as I traveled towards the wall I regained my composure and like superman flying, I put out my right fist and ignited my fire to full burn. I busted through the wall easily, I tumbled onto the ground but recovered in a roll. I immediately dashed towards the gate...

Edge: Now or never, STRIKE MOTHER FUCKING FIST!

[Edge hits the gate dead center and it budges a bit but does not open, he notice the hinges are set so the gate swings inward from the outside]

Oh my fucking god you have got to be kidding me...

[Instead of pushing Edge pulls on the gate and it swings open and he jets through it]

When I realized my stupid mistake I corrected my strategy and finally opened it, once I stepped through though everything became black and the Angel Sanctuary disappeared behind me, I felt like I was in the vacuum of space, everything was chaotic. I was thrown about in all sorts of directions, my limbs felt like they were being pulled apart so I curled up into a ball like the first time, it hurts... it hurts a lot... someone help me...

Chapter 25

The Sky Flood, song of the past

Halo: The sky was still gray and I don't think it's gonna get any better, I beat Testament, I think...

[Halo stands still looking into his palm, a small jolt of electricity is seen running through his fingers. He closes his palm but leaves his index and thumb opened, an electric arc jumps the gap and he looks pleased]

Halo: I need to get home so I can warn my parents and the rest of my family. I started running again as fast as I could, even if my family treats me like shit I still need to warn them and get them outta there. It wasn't long before I reached home, I ran upstairs to warn them but all they could do was yell at me for disappearing the whole night.

Perry: Yo we need to go right now!
Dad: Who the hell do you think you are disappearing for an entire night without telling ANYONE where the hell you were?!
Perry: Can't you yell at me later? This is important, we need to get outta here right now
Mom: Why? What's going on? What did you do this time?
Perry: I didn't do anything, didn't you hear about what happened?
Dad: What the hell did you do?
Perry: You didn't watch the news?

[Halo turns on the TV to see the news on the explosions that occurred in Rockaway Beach]

Mom: Oh shit, what happened?
Perry: THAT'S what happened, we need to get outta here right now!
Dad: Did you do that?!
Perry: What? NO! Where do you come up with all your dumb ideas?
Dad: Boy, watch your mouth!
Perry: NO, fuck it y'all wanna die fine by me, but I warned you
Mom: Perry wait! Come back!

Halo: I got my ass outta there, I'm tired of them not believing a single word I say. When I got outside it started to rain, the clouds were thundering and I felt mad strong. The rain came down even harder and it was cold but I felt warm, each winter has been warmer and warmer, and this winter was just crazy some days it would be hot and some days it'd be cold. The rain got harder and harder, like the sky was throwing rocks down or sumtin. This didn't seem normal though, was it Testament? I ran back upstairs to tell them but they locked me out, they wouldn't listen to me. The streets started to flood and I knew I had to reach higher ground. I think I can actually travel in the storm clouds like I did when I was attacking Testament.

[Halo reaches his hand up towards the sky and a bolt of lightning comes down and strikes him, he disappears... in Manhattan standing on top of the broken spire of the Empire State building Testament stands with his right hand towards the sky summoning all the rain clouds to release their water]

Testament: I am not strong enough yet, my powers will never be realized in this body, they did well to seal me in a vessel which can never see my true strength

[Testament looks downward to the city below with disgust]

Testament: Humanity, a waste of existence... SKY FLOOD.

[Testament calls forth all his power and the clouds thunder violently. The sky opens up and towers of water downpour from the sky. Each drop of rain as big as a gallon of water crashes to earth. They pound on the city streets below, windows are shattered and cars destroyed, people are running for their lives. The maelstrom continues raging as the city streets

drown in Sky Flood's wake. Somewhere in lower Manhattan a lightning bolt strikes the city streets and Halo tumbles out and into the torrent of water, he desperately reaches his hand out to grab something and he grabs a hold of a lamppost. Using the metal surface as a conductor he electrifies his body and travels though the metal post until he reached the top. He jumps up into the air and disappears in a lightning bolt and lands again on top of a building]

Halo: I think I'm gettin the hang of this now. Damn yo, New York is flooded, this has to be Testament...

Chapter 26
Aftermath of the Sky Flood

Halo: The flooding took forever to stop, I stayed where I was and then a portal opened up and Hacker walked through.

Hacker: Perry?
Halo: No it's Halo now
Hacker: Halo then, what's going on?
Halo: I dunno but it's sumtin bad, I think it's Testament
Hacker: Testament? Who's that?
Halo: Remember Judgment? Think of Testament as a water version of that
Hacker: Oh man, you're kidding me...

Halo: I told him what happened and what we had to do. All he could really do was think of how stupid all of this was. We both looked around to see all the destruction.

Halo: Geez what the hell we gonna do
Hacker: Heh, you sound like Edge
Halo: (chuckles)

Halo: We jumped down to the streets to see the mess, it was like a hurricane ran through us. Hacker showed me some people actually looting some of the stores. There were no cops around...

[Somewhere in the mountains of South America a small cloud forms

and rains a bit, the water that fell to the ground starts to take shape, it's Testament]

Testament: That drained me, is that the true extent of this body? No, it will get stronger, I need to focus...

[Testament looks at his right hand, the skin looks like it's peeling off]

Testament: The more power I call up the more this body disintegrates, living in this shell is as good as asking for death itself. I will stay here until this body adapts, until then this world will be at "peace" and when the time is right I will have my revenge

[Testament jumps into a river and blends away with the water, he travels up stream and into a crack on the side of a mountain, he stays there as if resting. His body starts to heal and his muscle tightens...]

Halo: I guess I should go home, me and Hacker parted ways and I headed home in the clouds.

[Halo makes it home just to find it in ruins, half flooded with a worried family inside, they welcome him in]

Halo: I think the next few days will be hard.

[A few days pass and unlike the hurricane of New Orleans a few years back the government immediately sent rescuers to New York City, they supplied people with shelter, food, water and clothes]

Halo: I think a week passed before we got power back and when I turned on the TV it was nuttin but talk about the end is coming or how terrorist are attacking. The churches and government are totally going against each other on this one, saying we need to choose a side or go to hell, or that we need to go into martial law, but me and Hacker knew what was really going on. I wanna tell everyone, but I couldn't, Hacker felt the same way... What would you do? Edge...

Chapter 27

Fall from grace, homecoming

Humanity will never accept us, they'll always fear us cuz they will never see the world from our eyes, from any of our eyes. They proved this time after time. It all began with religion, they fought countless wars based on that one subject alone, and when time passed, they decided to fight about race, and immediately after that government. Even if humans are idiots, I still wish I was alive, I want them to know the truth, that we are all equal in one way or another.

It still hurts, and I didn't wanna open my eyes cuz I was afraid of the pain. I kept tumbling and I just wanted it to stop...

[Edge is tumbling in the darkness then all of a sudden a small pinhole of light appears and the darkness vaporizes like smoke and Edge is hurled into the light, the light soon becomes clear and it's a cloudy but crisp blue sky]

What? Did I get out? Where am I...? The pain stopped is all I cared, there was a windy cold bite on my skin sumtin I haven't felt in a while. I opened my eyes and I saw that I was falling I tried to ignite my flames to fly but they wouldn't go on, I remembered that I had wings, should... should I use them? Oh, what the hell, I opened them and as soon as I did I felt a giant up lift, my decent slowed down a bit, and I flapped a few times to slow down even more. I looked around and the scenery was familiar, it was two walkways that had a tall building at the end of it. The walkways were connected to a very long concrete road...

[Flashback - Edge and Halo walking with their backpacks, they are both wet and laughing at how cool the kayaking was]

Now I remember, that building was the ventilator for the Holland tunnel. There was no one around at all the city seemed almost deserted. As I got closer everything started to look wrecked, sumtin happened while I was away, how long was I gone for? I was a few feet from the ground, a gust of wind ripped underneath me and slowed my decent even further and I gracefully touched down.

[Somewhere far away Saivent suddenly looks up to the sky]

Saivent: Edge?!

[Edge lands and flexes his wings a bit and looks around]

What happened here what did I miss? Hacker... where is he, damn I don't have my phone, not that I'd expect it to work anyway. Why isn't anyone around, it looks like a ghost town. Would it be safe to fly around then? Or should I walk... I guess I should walk.

[Edge closes his wings and they disappear, he begins to walk around]

It looks like a flood ran through here, I don't hear anything, usually the city would be bustling with life. I walked down the street and then I picked up my speed and started running. I made it to Chinatown and that was a whole mess of its own, dead fish from the market littered the streets, and it was then that I heard some noises. I found some people looking around for some food, I didn't bother approaching them and I walked to the Manhattan bridge. I started to walk across and half way through I could see that Brooklyn was no better. It took me a while to make it across but there was finally some more life. Everyone looked like they've been hit hard by some disaster, I didn't wanna interact with them so I did the only thing logical, well not really logical, but the only thing I could think of at the time, I walked into the subways.

The subways were half flooded, the tracks were submerged by 3 feet of water, but there was still space to fly around, I opened my wings and they just barely fit. I was at Lawrence Street and I knew exactly where I needed to go to get home. Living life dependant on the city trains really familiarizes you with the tunnels and subways, it wasn't long before I made it home. When I got out I looked around and I opened my wings to full and flew back the rest of the way, it was only 4 blocks. It of course was empty, no one was there so I landed on the roof and closed my wings all the way.

[Edge is looking down from the roof of his home]

Heh, I gave up being a warrior in heaven for this, but still this is home sweet home.

Chapter 28

Messenger of the heavens

[In the Angel Sanctuary...]

Michael: Young one, you know what you must do
Akuma: I guess I'm supposed to go and get Edge right?
Michael: That is precisely what you must do, his existence on Earth threatens the natural occurrence of events that is to come
Akuma: What if I'm unable to bring him back?
Michael: Then we pray that he doesn't do anything foolish
Akuma: Wouldn't it be easier if you got him back?
Michael: I have my own work to do, and it was not my fault he rebelled in the first place, you were the one that led him to the hall of time, if you can not bring him back then warn him of the danger he places everyone in. If we cannot get him to join us then we must get him to realize it on his own
Akuma: What? Is something going to happen?
Michael: In due time you will know the outcome of your mission
Akuma: I'm going then
Michael: Best of luck to you…

[Akuma opens the gates of the sanctuary and spreads his own wings, a void of wind pulls him into a tunnel of light and he disappears]

Michael: It seems that history will repeat itself once again…

[Edge is standing on the roof of his house, not far in the distance near

the industrial zone a lightning bolt hits the ground. Akuma lands with his right fist against the ground cracking the cobblestone road, blades of wind are storming out from his body. He resembled a meteor of light and thunder smashing into the ground. Akuma stands up moments later after the energy recedes and he stretches his arms and cracks his knuckles, he walks around a bit]

What was that? It looked like sumtin just landed, I went on foot to check it out, and low and behold, look who it is...

[Edge stops and leans back against a building facing perpendicular to Akuma's line of sight]

Edge: Hey there, how you been?

Akuma: Edge, look I really rather not be here or be doing this, can't you come along and make thing easier on both of us?

Edge: Nah you know I can't do anything like that, I don't believe in your world where one can't make their own destiny, I've always thought this way and that will never change

Akuma: Why? Why bother living a life like that...

Edge: Cuz life any other way under subjugation is not worth living, not for me anyway, I gotta be free, it's bad enough living by these laws that humans lay out, and it's bad enough that "we" gotta live in fear of being found out, god knows what they'll do to us. You were once alive, tell me, what did you think, how did you live your life from day to day?

Akuma: I lived as anyone would, I woke up everyday and went to school, I had friends and I fell in love...

Edge: You were always human so you will never understand, you can say you do for all I care but the truth is you have no idea what it feels like to have to live in fear

Akuma: What do YOU know about me? Nothing, how can you even make judgments towards me when you know nothing about me?

Edge: Easy, I stand here, before you, and I judge you just as you judge me, your inability to understand why I need my freedom, why I need to make my own destiny rather than listen to what god has to say all the time, just as you don't understand me for that, I won't understand you, that's how I can make my judgments

Akuma: That's all a matter of beliefs

Edge: No, you're just scared to defy, you're nuttin but a sheep told what to do and where to go, they even feed you don't they?

Akuma: Ok you're starting to piss me off now

Edge: Then do sumtin about it

Akuma: About time...

[Edge turns his head towards Akuma...]

Chapter 29
Duel of spirits (Part 1)

So this is what it's come down to, a fight between two spirits, I've never seen his power before so I dunno what I'm in for, I don't even know what level of strength he's at, then again I took on Judgment without knowing anything either.

[Edge pulls himself off the wall and turns toward Akuma]

I dunno if I can use my flames, it didn't wanna ignite when I was falling, and I tried to ignite just now and they still won't go on.

[Edge lifts up his right hand and clenches his fist but to his dismay his flame won't ignite, there's a disappointed look on his face]

Shit yo, it's not happening, does this mean I gotta fight without it? In the sanctuary I had a sword to use at practice, but I was never good with hand to hand.

[Edge stands tall and spreads his wings wide]

Edge: Let's do this!
Akuma: Fine!

[Edge leaps into the air with one strong flap of his wings and starts a dive bomb straight towards Akuma, but long before he reaches him Akuma cuts his arm across the air in a slashing motion and a blade of wind heads

towards Edge and hits him, knocking him onto the ground. Akuma walks up to Edge and picks him up, tosses him upwards and does his attack again]

Akuma: WIND BLADE!!

[This time multiple blades of wind slash Edge and causes him to fly backwards into a brick wall... Akuma lunges forward and grabs Edge by the shoulders pushing him deeper into the ruble before tossing him into the street, Edge tries to stand up but before he gets the chance to do so Akuma rushes to Edge and starts punching him down, with a kick Akuma sends Edge tumbling around on the ground]

Damn yo, this isn't good, I can't lay a finger on him. Am I actually gonna be beat here like this?

Akuma: What happened, all that big talk and you have nothing to back yourself up, what a let down, where's your destiny now?
Edge: Heh, you're just lucky my flames won't ignite, I guarantee you wouldn't be so cocky then!

[Edge leaps at Akuma locking him in his arms, and flies into the air, he does a 180 and the both of them are sent spiraling down, right before they reach the ground Edge lets go and flies along the ground before landing and tumbling a bit. Akuma is sent head first into the ground]

Did that even hurt him...?

[A gust of wind gushes out from the crater in the street and Akuma rises up and out and then lands onto the ground]

Akuma: That was a good try, but that's the only one you're getting in
Edge: I'll get more in, count on it!

[Edge rushes Akuma but closes his wings, he ends up spearing Akuma into another brick wall, they both stand up and Edge quickly flaps his wings away to get some distance between him and Akuma, but as he flaps *away blades of wind are shooting out from the cloud of debris and they hit Edge. Akuma then walks out from the cloud]*

Akuma: Come on that's not even a challenge, you would've saved yourself a heck of a lot of trouble if you would've just came with me
Edge: (panting) as if that would be happening anytime soon
Akuma: How you like my wind blades?
Edge: (sarcastically) they taste like chocolate
Akuma: Wise guy aren't you, WIND TWISTER!

[A swirl of wind picks up and a small tornado forms, it comes at Edge, but he uses his wings as a shield and wraps them in front of himself. Edge takes the full damage and when it's over he opens up his wings in defiance]

Akuma: (sigh) still wanna keep on going? Edge, don't you ever learn
Edge: Don't you ever shut the hell up?!
Akuma: AIR DRAGON!

[Akuma cups his hand together and a dragon of wind gust forward and bites Edge with its jaws then twirls him around in the air before slamming him into the ground, even after Edge is slammed the dragon continues to drive the rest of its body into the crater where Edge is]

Akuma: *Is he dead? Not much of a fight, what a burn out.*

[A cloud of debris is all that's seen...]

Chapter 30

Duel of spirits (Part 2)

I... I won't die like this, I won't ever give up, not my hopes, and not my dreams... I could barely move, that last attack got me good, what use is fighting back when it's so handicapped. Why won't you ignite damn it...

[Edge hears a sharp calling and he suddenly opens his eyes and clenches his fists tightly, his wings disappear... Akuma walks toward the crater on the floor then suddenly a burst of blue embers are sent into the air followed by streams of blue fire. When the streams subside all that's left is the still hovering cloud of debris with blue fire burning brightly through. Akuma steps back with a worried look on his face]

I'll never give up, I'll always fight no matter what I'll always fight!

[Edge stands up and begins to walk out of the crater]

Akuma: No way...
Edge: I'll never give up and I'll never back down!

[Edge takes a stand and charges up, blue flames burst all over his body, he just stands there, silent]

Akuma: Are you fucking with me?!
Edge: ...

[Akuma rushes Edge grabbing his shoulders and pushing him back, he releases Edge and unleashes his Air Dragon which forces Edge into yet another brick wall, this time Edge doesn't get pummeled through, he instead gently leans back onto the approaching wall. Edge raises his right hand and ignites a blue flame]

Akuma: KEEP FUCKING WITH ME!
Edge: Keep fucking with yourself
Akuma: AIR DRAGON!

[The dragon comes spiraling towards Edge but Edge just smacks it away like a toy]

Edge: Feeling any cockier?
Akuma: Impossible, how'd you get so much stronger?!
Edge: I told you, I'll never give up, I'll never forget my hopes and dreams, and I'm gonna make my own destiny with my own hands!

[Edge shoots out a stream of blue flame]

Akuma: Heh, what can your flames do I can just push it away with my wind

[Akuma attempts to push the stream away but it doesn't work and instead he is engulfed, when the flames subside he falls to the floor in pain]

Akuma: What happened, why didn't it work...?

[Akuma thinks to himself for a second while Edge walks towards him]

Akuma: I get it, that's not regular fire, it's a spirit flame...
Edge: Is it now? Well that would answer a thing or two
Akuma: Damn you Edge
Edge: No, damn YOU

[Edge picks Akuma off the floor and punches him into the air, Edge then proceeds to jump into the air to continue his attack]

110

Our fight continued in the air, we exchanged blows over and over again. I couldn't stay up without my wings, but when I tried to open them I couldn't, I think my flames are keeping my angel powers suppressed. It wasn't long before I landed back on the ground but he stayed in the air, I would send out streams of fire and he'd dodge them. He attempted to fight back with his Wind Blades but what was the use I punched them away like nuttin.

[Akuma dashes in and locks fist with Edge, they look like they are trying to push each other back. A fury of wind from Akuma's side and a blaze of fire from Edge's side fill the battleground as the two continue their fight. Edge finally gains the upper hand and knocks Akuma down into the ground. Edge remains defiant, he charges his right hand and the flames start to spiral like swirls of energy]

Here's my chance to end it!

Edge: STRIKE FIST!

[The swirls pick up their speed and burst brightly in a salvo of light, Edge dives straight down into the crater that Akuma is in. A huge explosion is seen following Edge's strike and a burst of wind pushes out from the crater, a few minutes later the debris dies down and everything begins to calm. Edge stands up, alone, looks around and gives an innocent chuckle, Akuma wakes up in the Angel Sanctuary, Michael looks at him and shakes his head. Back down on Earth...]

Heh... craters and broken walls everywhere...

Chapter 31

First snow

My clothes were messed up after that fight with Akuma... so what else would anyone do? I went home to changed. The majority of all my clothes were wet and moldy. There was one set that seemed to be untouched, it was a pair of black jeans, a white t-shirt and a black button up shirt. I put it on and walked out, there wasn't anyone about and I wanted to take a look around, but guess what? Now my wings wouldn't open, my abilities are just so frustrating lately, I blame it on that stupid baptism. I wanted to go to Central Park but it seemed I'd have to walk there if that's the destination I wanted. It was gonna be a very long walk...

[Edge starts to walk but for no reason starts to jog... then starts to run and he continues running for a long while]

All I know is that it was day when I landed, but the sun started to set now. The city seemed so dead, the lights didn't come on and it was like some horror movie. I remember the lights use to light up even the night sky in an orange tint, now all that lights up the sky is the moon, and it's being partially blocked by clouds. The temperature started to cool down, and rapidly too, for once in a long while I felt cold. I stopped running somewhere at 34th street and started to walk, I was hungry too so I looked around for some food, all I found were bags of chips that didn't seem to be opened...

[Edge sits down on the sidewalk with some junk food and begins to chow down, he finishes in no time and stands up. He looks around in the

darkness to get his bearings, he soon finds north and crosses his arms to keep warm and begins to walk]

I walked for a while, then it started to snow just small flurries but it was enough to put me off, I was near Bryant Park and I knew the perfect place to spend the night...

[Edge heads towards the New York public library and forces down its doors, like many other places it's abandoned. He starts a fire and gets comfortable next to it and starts to sleep... outside a snow storm starts to rage. In New Jersey Halo is with is family staying at his aunts and cousins house...]

Halo: *It's been about two weeks now since Testament flooded the city. The government came in and told everyone to get out, some people even went to hide so they didn't have to go. It looked like a war zone almost. My parents came here to New Jersey, we're staying with my mom's sister and her family. Hacker escaped with his family up to Maine or Vermont and I haven't heard from him since.*

[Halo opens the front door of the house and stands there looking out at the surrounding environment]

Halo: *It's snowing.*

[His aunt comes up from behind him]

Aunt: Perry what are you doing?
Perry: I'm just looking outside, it's snowing
Aunt: Oh is that all?
Perry: Yeah...

[Before he gets to do anything else his aunt smacks him upside the head]

Aunt: WE GOT WINDOWS YOU KNOW, SHUT THE DOOR YOU'RE LETTING ALL THE COLD AIR IN!
Perry: (patting the back of his head) ah ok, damn that hurt

[The night was ending and the sun started to rise, from a window in the New York public library a ray of light breaks through and hits Edge in the face, waking him up]

I guess it's morning already isn't it.

[Edge stretches out and yawns loudly]

The fire stayed alive all night, heh, it's still there for me when I need it. I got up and pushed open the door, the world was covered in a blanket of snow. Unlike the day before I didn't feel as cold this time even though the wind chill was probably down to about 15 degrees or so. I started my walk again, this time it was a lot harder cuz there was about two feet of snow everywhere.

I walked for about an hour and the sky darkened once more to snow. First it was flurries then it became flakes, and from there it was just full snow fall again, but not a blizzard. It wasn't long till I made it to Central Park I was standing under the globe in Columbus Circle and I looked up to it with some form of nostalgia, I remembered all those memories... memories that seemed so long ago, covered in the first snow of the year...

Chapter 32

The Azure Flame

I left the giant globe and started walking into Central Park. The path I always take is completely covered in snow, and the fact that it's still snowing didn't make it any better.

[Flashback - Edge is walking alongside a mysterious friend and the two are laughing and joking, it was autumn so the leaves were brown, yellow and orange. They have their back packs on because they just got out of school...]

There are a lot of memories here and to think they're not so old at all, only a few years ago... things have changed so much.

[Edge walks the snow covered path and without him knowing his blue flame ignites into a tiny fire on his shoulder, the wind is blowing hard and the small flame is pushed backwards trailing along him. The snow continues to fall at a steady pace and the ambient lighting stays gray with a slight blue tint]

I wonder what happened to everyone, was I really gone for a hundred years or so? I use to hang out here a lot after school, me and my high school friends came here when there wasn't anywhere else to go or anything else to do. Now that I think back on it, high school wasn't all that bad, then again that's only cuz I made it "not bad". The first year or two coulda been different, I just wish I was able to show off my fire.

[Flashback - Edge is in high school, it's his fist day and he's being bullied by some seniors, they throw an empty carton of milk at him during lunch and he does nothing but shrugs it off and continues eating. The bell rings signaling the end of lunch and everyone gets up to leave but Edge stays seated for a bit longer, when everyone else had left for class he gets up and looks at the carton of milk with an angry stare, he throws his left hand out towards the carton and ignites it on fire...]

It took me a while to force my way through the snow to reach one of my favorite spots. It was a water fountain, now covered in snow, this fountain lets you know you were close to The Lake, one of many large bodies of water in the park. I stood by the fountain for a tiny bit, I felt sumtin weird pulling on me and I turned around to see what it was.

[Edge stops walking and looks at his left shoulder, there's a small fire being forced back by the wind]

My fire, it's still blue, is this what it's gonna be like from now on?

[Edge raises his right hand and as he does the blue flame on his shoulder slowly goes out but another blue flame ignites consuming his hand, glove and all. He stares at it in awe and wonderment of its existence]

Hmm, for some reason I feel comforted by this flame, this... Azure Flame.

Chapter 33

Fate and destiny

[Edge stands staring at his right hand which is consumed in a swirling flame, he looks completely zoned out as a gust of wind kicks up out of nowhere, a figure materializes and it's Saivent]

Saivent: Edge, is that you?

Edge: Huh? Saivent?

Saivent: I'm so happy to see you!

[Saivent jumps at Edge hugging him like a small child hugging a new toy out of joy, the view is slightly comical due to the fact that Saivent is 6 foot 1 inch while Edge is only a short 5 foot 5 inches]

Edge: Hey, I'm glad to see you too, what happened here it looks like a hurricane ran through here

Saivent: It's... Testament

Edge: Testament?! How the hell?

Saivent: You have no idea do you?

Edge: How the hell do I have any idea what's going on, I don't even know how much time has passed since I was gone

Saivent: It's been almost a month

Edge: That's all? Just a month and all this has happened, what was it, one disaster after another?

Saivent: I'll explain, after you and Judgment fought, you disappeared, then shortly after Testament appeared. He used the Sky Flood, that's what happened, that's why the city looks this way

Edge: Why do I get the feeling I coulda prevented all this

Saivent: Things happen for a reason

Edge: By now you still think I believe in fate?

Saivent: Well fate, rather The Fates are the ones who weaves ones destiny depending on what choices they make

Edge: The hell, I thought God was the one who controlled people's destiny

Saivent: No, Jehovah's existence only influences ones destiny, you see for every choice we make The Fates end up making a new pattern, you heard of them in Greek mythology right?

Edge: No, not really...

Saivent: The Fates were 3 sisters, Birth, Life and Death. Birth, the one who spins the threads of life, Life, the one who weaves the pattern of death, and Death the one who cuts the pattern from the loom and tears it apart for another life

Edge: Wait, Death, is she the one in the hood and scythe?

Saivent: No, that's the agent of Death, he is an entity like myself under the command of both Lucifer and Jehovah, he shows up to escort the deceased straight to Lucifer and Jehovah themselves

Edge: Gees, this just gets more and more complicated...

Saivent: But yeah, The Fates are the ones that determine what pattern to make for you based on your decisions in life, think of it this way, there's a piece of paper, and you take a pen or pencil and draw a circle however small however big, or in fact any shape you want that's your destiny, now take that pen or pencil again and put a single dot inside that circle wherever you want, that's your fate, from the moment you're born, that piece of paper will be made in the loom, then the circle is all that will ever encompass what you will achieve or can achieve, and finally that dot is all the decisions and choices you have made till the very end, all those choices and decisions lead to why that dot is there, it's because you made it go there, you put it there using your ability to chose and decide

Edge: Well, that sure puts a spin on things doesn't it. I guess that saying is true, "No fate but what we make..."

Saivent explained to me what was what, and I got another history lesson from him, he told me that I just need to be strong right now, everything is gonna work itself out, I just need to think and use my brain.

Chapter 34

A week's wait

Saivent left me to my own, after that talk I realize things weren't bad at all, I had a new found confidence in me and I decided to head home, but then again what was the rush, there was no one around so I can technically do anything I want, alright then, for the time being, home was gonna be the fanciest hotel I could find that isn't ruined, and I know exactly where to go. Instead of trekking through the snow like an idiot I just jumped to get around.

[Edge is leaping block long distances at a time from the fountain all the way back down to Columbus Circle]

I forgot what it was like to be alive... usually I'd just fly where I needed to go with my Hell Fire, but I can't do that with the Azure Flame, there is one thing I notice about this flame though, I can move around a lot more easily, my agility, my reflexes, everything feels so... upgraded for lack of a better term. That probably explains the extra distance and boost from my leaps.

I made it down to Columbus Circle and right beside it was Trump International Hotel and Tower.

[Edge has a devious grin on his face]

The lower levels were all flooded through so there wasn't anything useful there. Thank goodness for vending machines and non perishable foods. The lower levels were messed up but the upper levels should be fine, the Sky Flood shouldn't have hit that high up.

[Edge opens the door to the staircase and looks up]

This is gonna take a while but I'll manage. The staircase was one of those types that has a giant column of empty space in the middle while the stair case hugged the walls. I looked up and kneeled down, took a deep breath, ignited my Azure Flame and pushed off.

[Edge goes streaming past the first 20 floors and he grasps the hand rails before leaping again all the way up to the upper floors]

I was on the 48 floor and I must admit what a view it is, the snow though is covering all the damage. I guess it's a bitter sweet view. My next concern was electricity, was there any at all? That's the million dollar question.

[Edge turns on the TV and...]

Yes there is electricity! Great now I can do a few things like watch the news.

[The TV is full of static but Edge turns to the cable channels, they are clearer but still with some interference]

Newscaster: After 3 weeks since the unknown flash flood that consumed New York City, citizens will be overjoyed to hear that within a week everyone will be allowed back in. Most New Yorkers have fled to neighboring cities and left many possessions behind, now they will all be allowed back in so the busy city can continue to thrive and recover from this tragic incident of nature. In other news the Christian and Catholic Church have both agreed that the recent incidents are a warning sign of the end, the military on the other hand have blamed terrorism for the recent onslaught of accidents and unexplained occurrences, stayed tuned for more on...

So I have a week worth to wait eh? I guess I'll relax till then...

Chapter 35

Welcome home

For the whole week all I did was sleep and keep up with the news, on occasions I would head out and just walk around, but at last it was time. Today was the day that everyone would be allowed back into the city.

[Edge gets ready and puts his clothes on, and puts on his signature right hand weight lifting glove. He heads to the window of the room he's staying in, opens it and looks out]

Hmm, here I come...

[Edge leaps out of the window and starts to free fall, after he passes the first 10 floors he ignites his flames and right before he reaches the ground he pushes off against the wall of the building and that breaks his free fall sending him jetting forward parallel with the street. The moment his sneakers touch the floor he begins to run as fast as he can leaping whenever he feels he needs to. The snow has long since melted...]

I need to make my way home, my family is probably worried about me, I dunno where they are though or if they're even alive, and Perry, and Hacker I'll be able to see them as well.

[Edge continues to run as fast as he can downtown, he takes a few breaks along the way and eventually he makes it all the way to South Street Seaport, there he sees people walking across the bridge. Once again he

takes off and head toward the Staten Island ferry and he sees a lot of
people disembarking]

Alright so people are already here I won't be able to use my powers
dashing around anymore, I'll have to be human for the time being. I left
the ferry and headed back to the bridge where I had to fight to make my
way across back into Brooklyn. When I finally made it across everyone
was out and already they started to clean up I managed to hitch a ride
to my home and in all honestly I coulda made it back in about half the
time if I just flew.

[Edge is sitting in the car with the guy who picked him up]

Peterson: My names Peterson, so you're heading home?
Edge: Yeah, thanks for the lift yo
Peterson: No problem
Edge: Hey where are most of the people coming from?
Peterson: Well I'm coming from up in queens right now I'm going to
Bay Ridge to see my sister, but most people fled to Long Island or New
Jersey
Edge: So the Sky Flood mainly effected Manhattan then...
Peterson: The sky what?
Edge: Oh nuttin, I was just thinking out loud
Peterson: I see
Edge: Yeah...

I guess Perry coulda been in either Jersey or upstate since that's
where he has family... anyway, the guy dropped me off on 4th Ave. and
I walked down the block to my home, I opened the door since it wasn't
locked and it didn't seem like anyone was there or ever was there. So I
just went in and waited...

No one showed up and it's night time already, I fear that I might be
a loner from here on out... I turned on the TV on the Third Floor, it was
the only floor that was decent and almost untouched, all I heard on the
news was...

Newscaster: Welcome home New Yorkers

Chapter 36

Reunion of friends

I waited all day and all night, they never showed up, so I put on a black hoody and left. My father had 3 cars in the garage so I took the keys and took the truck, I drove it across the Manhattan Bridge and up towards Central Park, I seem to love that spot don't I?

[Edge is driving the truck on the east side there's no traffic but he's driving at a slow 25mph...]

I heard a lady screaming so I pulled the truck over to see what it was and to my surprised it looked like some sorta monster, almost... like a werewolf, but was that for real do they actually exist? I ran towards her but before I could do anything a bolt of lightning came crashing down from the sky striking the monster, it stopped him dead in his tracks and the lady ran off screaming.

[As Edge watches the lady running away in terror the monster gets up and roars at Edge]

I must've forgotten about that monster cuz the next thing I knew I was that things target but before it got to me another bolt of lightning struck it but this time it managed to dodge. Then the most unexpected thing happened...

[A gate opens up and a fist slams into the monsters face, then from the sky another lightning bolt comes crashing down but right before it hits the

monster Halo materializes and spear kicks the monster, Edge stands back with his hoody on covering his face in the darkness]

That's... that's Perry, when the hell did he get those powers?! I stood back and watched those two take on the monster and defeat it.

[Halo turns towards Edge without knowing who he is]

Halo: Are you ok?
Guy in Hoody: (in a deep voice that sounds obviously fake) uh yeah, how did you two do that?
Halo: It's a secret
Hacker: Yeah, we're super heroes
Guy in Hoody: Really? That's cool yo
Halo: "Yo"? You said yo
Guy in Hoody: Yeah is something wrong with that?
Halo: No, just sounds like sumtin someone I knew would say
Hacker: Don't tell anyone about what you saw ok, it's a secret
Guy in Hoody: A secret? How come?
Halo: Cuz if the world knew about us they would get scared and try to hunt us down, they already know sumtin is wrong
Guy in Hoody: Who does?
Halo: The government AND the churches
Hacker: Especially the churches, they are on the verge of a religious upheaval
Guy in Hoody: Why?
Hacker: Don't worry about it, it has nothing you
Guy in Hoody: I see, I was just curious is all
Halo: Well stay safe we're gonna go now

[Halo and Hacker turn around but before they go Edge stops fooling around and talks in his normal voice]

Edge: I'm glad you guys are doing ok...

[Halo and Hacker stop dead in their tracks and slowly turn around]

Halo: Is that...

Hacker: Edge...

[Edge pulls back his hoody to reveal his face]

Edge: Who were you expecting, the tooth fairy?
Halo: EDGE!

[Halo jumps at Edge the same way Saivent did and hugs him out of joy, Hacker walks up to Edge and gives him a hug as well]

Edge: Heh, I'm glad you guys remember me, I missed you guys too

[Halo is crying and Hacker sheds a tear of happiness]

Edge: Alright, alright, you guys missed me that much?
Hacker: We thought you were dead man
Edge: I was...
Halo: Then how... how did you come back to life?
Edge: Oh man what a story that's gonna be, I'll tell you all once we get home
Halo: To whose house?
Edge: Good point, I don't have much of a home to go to
Halo: Mine isn't too good either
Hacker: Guess mine it is then, the water didn't reach too high up past Central Park
Edge: Alrighty let's go

He opened a gate and we all stepped through, it was nice to be reunited with my friends again...

Chapter 37

A time to recover

Despite what had happened, Hacker's mom managed to cook up a nice dinner for us all. His home was barely touched, turns out The Sky Flood originated at the Empire State. It started as severe downpour of rain at seemingly random areas, severe enough to cause localized flooding. It then turned to massive pillars of water that literally plunged down from the sky, the biggest being the one at the Empire State. The attack seemed sporadic but what the hell, this wasn't the time to think about it, I was with my friends again, that's all that matters.

[Hacker, Halo and Edge along with Hacker's parents are sitting at the table, they eat and enjoy their meal and after they are done they head to Hacker's room leaving his mom to clean up]

Dinner was pretty nice, it's been a while since I had anything to eat that wasn't junk food. When we entered Hacker's room everything was pretty much untouched, he turned on his computer and started hacking away.

Edge: Have you ever been caught doing this stuff?
Hacker: No I like to think I'm pretty good at what I do
Halo: It comes in handy though, his computers mad cool, it's better than yours
Edge: What's left of my computer anyway, my area was hit
Halo: Yeah so was mine
Edge: You live like 30 minutes of walking distance from me

Halo: Yeah hahahhahha

Hacker: You guys live pretty close to each other

Edge: Yeah, he's gotta be the only one that lives so close while everyone else lives like god knows how far away... oh yeah, hey can you check out my home, no one came back so I dunno where I stand at the moment

Hacker: Sure let's check it out

[Hacker clicks away at the keyboard and brings up a satellite video feed of Edge's house]

Edge: (sigh) no one's there... I don't even know what to think right now... hey Perry, won't your parents get mad that you're still out?

Halo: Nope, ever since I yelled at them they sorta stopped caring, oh yeah, my name is Halo from now on

Edge: Halo? Hahhaa nice

Halo: So when you gonna tell us what happened when you disappeared

Hacker: Yeah tell us man

Edge: Alrighty gather around people, for a story of a life time...

[Edge begins to tell them all that has happened, about the Angel Sanctuary, about what happens after death, he tells them everything and they update Edge on the events that have transpired. After the stories were over they all go to sleep]

We all went to sleep soon after, all I wondered was whether I was gonna be alone from now on or not. My eyes closed and I knew I was dreaming cuz everything felt alright. Again I was on a ledge of a building looking down to a world unknown to me, I felt a gust of wind blow past and it was strong enough to almost push me off, but I felt a hand grab my shoulder and hold me back.

Edge: I'm dreaming again ain't I?

Saivent: Hahahaa you're getting good Edge, how have you been?

Edge: It's been rough, hey, why didn't you tell me you gave Halo powers?

Saivent: I didn't really "give" it to him and even if I did would it have made life any more interesting? Wasn't it a good surprise to find out on your own?

Edge: I guess, I dunno...

Saivent: What on your mind? You seemed stressed

Edge: Exactly that, I need a break, just a long vacation

Saivent: Well heads up, I'll try to give you some nice weather alright?

Edge: You can do that?

Saivent: If I try

Edge: That'd be great, we can all use it

Saivent: (smiles) have a good dream Edge

And the same way he came, he left. This city below me looks so familiar, there's just so much nostalgia to it, maybe it's the past, or a possible future, who knows...

Chapter 38

Back to where it all began, ending an old burden

Saivent made true on his word, when we woke up it was all bright and sunny, like nuttin ever happened. It even got warmer too, there wasn't much for us to do though, just stayed home all day. The news said they needed volunteers to help clean up some of downtown Manhattan, I personally felt it was sumtin good to do, it would be a reason to be out and about Hacker though declined and said he had some stuff he wanted to do, so me and Halo went, Hacker just opened up a gate for us.

We ended up doing some volunteer work in one of my favorite spots downtown, Battery Park City, it was a nice lil neighborhood where rich people lived, it was clean and fresh, well not anymore since Testament, but we ended up helping people throw stuff outta their apartments and moving stuff around. I swear at this rate everything would be back together in no time. This went on for a few days and each day Hacker declined, oh well, if not for the crisis of things I wouldn't do volunteer work either so I don't blame him.

On the last day of volunteer work I asked if Hacker and Halo could help me do a few things, Halo agreed, Hacker too amazingly. I had him open a gate to my house, even after so long it still hasn't been touched, I figured the worst had happened. I honestly can't say I am too struck by the thought of what occurred, I've always felt like if such a thing were to happen I'd always be ready. I've always been independent anyway, so it's not like things will change that much.

Anyway I had them help me pack a few things such as clothes and some sentimental objects. My journal which has stayed intact was my most prized possession, it was a gateway into everything about me, but I haven't written in it for so long cuz I only write in it when I'm depressed... there was just one other thing I wanted, my right glove had a left hand companion glove, I never used it but I felt like it would come in handy for some reason, so I took it. I got everything I needed, I left all the pictures behind and anything else that would resemble memories of my family, I didn't need them cuz all those memories exist in my head now, I was on my own from here on out...

[Edge, Halo and Hacker move a few boxes outside then Edge goes back in... moments later the Third Floor burst into flames and then the Second Floor then the First Floor and Edge walks out through the front door with an apathetic look on his face]

And that's that, I had one more thing I asked Hacker to do, I asked him to open a gate to Rockaway beach, and he did. I let them know they didn't have to come with me if they didn't wanna and I don't mind going by myself, but they came anyway. Hacker put my boxes away in his house and then opened a gate to the beach, it seems the people have started fixing everything up and the waves of the ocean fixed up what was destroyed on the beach. The day was still warm so I did what I did last time, I laid back into the sand and closed my eyes, things finally felt ok.

Chapter 39

Things to learn, a time to live

It's been three months since that day, it's June now, New York has returned to its vibrant busy life thanks to the drive of commercialism. Everyone took advantage of the Sky Flood attack three months ago. Insurance companies sky rocketed in new customers, all tryna buy flood insurance. Since then I've reunited with a few friends, Halo met up with his girlfriend again and I met up with Isaiah too. I have no family to go back to, none that knew I was alive anyway, and honestly I preferred it that way, I wasn't ever attached or too close to them so what was the point, it's not like I was gonna allow myself to be taken under their wing anyway. Life isn't bad though, I live on my own, off my own strength and it's done me well, I even managed to get myself a lil studio in Hells Kitchen. How did I come around to that you may ask? Well remember back when I first met up with Halo and Hacker again? And there was this creature? Well lemme fill you in on some details. That monster thing was apparently called a chimera, unlike the Greek legends, a true chimera is a person who has change into some monstrous demon form. I've never seen them until I came back and according to Hacker sightings of them have increased. I took it up with Saivent and he's the one who told me the details. A chimera is a person who changes cuz of their blood imbalance... come to think of it I've never explained it have I? Alright so I guess now is the best time to do so. Elemental Spirit, Elemental users and Power users are the most prime examples of the blood imbalance, cuz humans are descendants of angels and demons their blood is a perfectly balanced mixture of both, meaning they are a complete hybrid, but that's not always the case. On rare occasions the child will be born with

135

an imbalanced blood mixture, meaning they may have more dominant demon or angel genes. The end result is one of the four, Elemental Spirit, Elemental user, Power user and Avatars. Elemental users and Power users exist through natural imbalance. An Elemental Spirit is generally a reincarnation of a person from The Great War. The strength of the spirit forces a shift in balance, however, unlike an Elemental user whose power is tapped through their blood imbalance, an Elemental Spirit taps their powers directly from their spirit. The other way an Elemental Spirit is born is through direct rebirth, if a person dies and is brought back to life immediately then their spirit is released from the body allowing it to gain full potential to their powers, but the person must've been either an Elemental user or a Power user in order to be reborn as an Elemental Spirit. Avatar's are people whose demon and angel blood mix and instead of neutralizing they combine and create new being, I dunno of any in existence but according to Saivent, they are able to control the inner gates also known as chakra gates. This gives them the ability to alter reality almost on par with other entities such as Lucifer and Jehovah. And finally back to the chimera, they are people who have been changed into a demon form against their will. I've met 3 so far, the first was the day I met Halo and Hacker, the second one I met while in the streets one night and same with the third. Which brings us back to how I got that studio, but first, lemme explain how all these beings work.

First off, the Elemental User, this was the minority of the population back in the ancient days before The Great War. These people had the ability to control the elements around them, not only the basic and typical elements but also the lesser known elements such as light, shadow, gravity, etc. As long as they were around their element they could control it, to what degree though was dependant on the skill of the user.

The Power Users made up the majority of the population. Unlike the Elemental users who were able to control the elements, the Power Users had access to one ability. The ability was different and varied greatly from person to person. One may have the ability to fly, while another may have the ability to turn their skin to metal, and still another may have the ability to turn objects into gold. There was literally no limit to the vast amount of variations of abilities this class had.

Now, the time before and during The Great War, Elemental Spirits did not exist, people like me were either directly demons, or directly angels, the pure blood, the ones that had direct access to the vast amount of powers that one could imagine. Demon and angels were at the time the strongest and were often the fighters. However being banished for their crimes of being a rebel or a deviant, they were stripped of their immortality. After The Great War, in fact I think I'm the only one. I dunno of any known Elemental Spirits that existed before me, in any case, "we" have the ability to call upon our element directly through our spirit, even when our element is nowhere around us, we can still use it cuz we draw it directly from ourselves. This however has a draw back, it weaken us when we use our powers unlike the Elemental users. However if need be, we can use what we have in our surrounding environment, doing that gives us almost an unlimited amount of energy to spare.

The Avatars are the ones that made the world what it is today, along with some help. They had the ability to alter reality, allowing them to change the shape and form of their surroundings. They were neither demon nor angel but sumtin unique and new. When The Great War ended, earth was left with the scars of war, life just wasn't possible anymore. So they did two things, create a meteor to smash into earth in order to smooth out an erase the scars, and to create a being that would allow life to flourish in the new world. The Meteor wiped the earth clean, giving it a new slate for life and to be the womb in which the being would be born from. Doing this though required all their strength, the Avatars sacrificed themselves, and that was their last known actions. The meteor cleansed the world in fire, and Saivent was born. Tempis took him into her care and that's his story.

Chimeras to me are new, but according to Saivent they have been around since the time before, during and after The Great War. They are humans who are racked with guilt, turmoil and despair, their suffering and weakened sense of self allowed the demonic blood to take over like an infection, thus causing their mutation. This mutation is currently known to be permanent. Chimeras were mainly used by Lucifer to incite fear and act as a decoy, they were the fodder of the Grand Force.

The Grand Force was Lucifer's army of low class demons and beast of all kinds. Unlike Jehovah's Army of Light who were made up of angel warriors, The Grand Force was just a gathering of monsters, the real warriors were the high class demons that led the mindless beast into war. The Grand Force lacked warriors, but made up for it with the shear amounts of expendable beasts.

Lastly are the entities. They are beings whose existence allows for things to sorta just happen. Saivent for example, his existence allows for life to flourish, without him life on earth would die. I guess they are kinda like gods when you think about it. There are apparently many countless entities out there in the universe, some as powerful as Jehovah and Lucifer, and some almost meaningless in existence, though I have not met or know of an entity whose existence is seemingly so useless.

Now, I return to what I was originally getting at, basically some guy's daughter was being attacked by a Chimera. It attacked and knocked her out, it was some weird rat looking thing, suffice to say I beat it and I took the young lady home, she awoke in my arms right before her father opened the door, and to make the story even shorter he thanks me by giving me the studio free of rent, and that's how I been living since.

Chapter 40

The demon awakens

[It's night and there's a full moon out... Down in South America in the mountain where Testament resides, the land suddenly begins to rumble. The side of the mountain cracks and splits open, Testament gushes out in liquid form and solidifies himself. He's buffed up with muscles rippling all over his body, the white glow in his eye is even more demonic looking. He looks at his hands and sees the transformation that has occurred and is pleased to a degree]

Testament: *This is the outcome? Very well, it will do.*

[Testament changes into his water form again and gushes towards the pacific side of South America, from there he materializes and steps into the ocean like it was solid ground]

Testament: *Where are you, my love.*

[He stomps the water hard with his left leg and a huge wave rises from underneath him and he rides it like a surfer. He starts to head toward the Hawaiian Islands and he reaches it by sunrise. On the island itself the inhabitants look on as they see a huge tidal wave rushing towards them, most run in absolute horror and shock and the others stand there in mesmerized fear. But to their surprise the wave quickly slows and comes to a stop and sinks down. Testament stands before them, a few hundred feet away from the shores with his piercing demonic white eyes, he turns his back towards the crowd of people who have gathered at the beaches to

witness what has happened. As if the water was as hard as the ground we all walk on, he jumps up and stomps down causing the water to rise and fissure, the result is a mega tsunami that rises like a wall of water and head towards the island yet again. On Testaments side a staircase of water forms leading down to the sea bed, the demon walks down and arrives upon a shrine that is sealed with a rock, he puts his hand on the rock and forces a jet of water through cracking it and exposing a small gold pendant. The pendant is an orb shaped mass of veins that wraps around a red gem, all together the size of a golf ball]

Testament: *So this is where your heart and soul lies...*

[Testament steps back onto the staircase and it quickly lifts him up to the surface, the great divide is closed and the water rushes back in, he then begins to make his way to the pacific coast of California... back in New York, Edge is in Central Park by himself basking in the warm summer sun, it's early afternoon]

I guess it was a good idea to take a leave from school, I mean, there's no way I woulda been able to concentrate with all these things going on. Recently there's been a lot of disturbances around, it's almost as if things are destabilizing, like everything is taking a turn for the worst, but yet everything is so nice. I dunno anymore, I'm just gonna live my life the way I wanna.

[Edge is laying back on a rock just basking in the sun with his eyes closed, a shadow looms over and it's Halo making a stupid face, Edge staggers in shock and sits up as quickly as he can]

Edge: Oh crap don't do that again, I thought you were one of those things
Halo: Chimeras? Whatcha saying I'm ugly or sumtin?
Edge: Hahahahaha ugly is an understatement
Halo: That's messed up
Edge: Oh shut up, so sup, what ya doing here?
Halo: What are YOU doing here?
Edge: ...do we really need to do this, again...

Halo: Hahhaahaa I'm just tryna piss you off, I was supposed to meet Mimi later on and I had time to spare so I figure you were here
Edge: Good job, I'm that predictable ain't I
Halo: Yeah

We continued our chat for a while before I felt the urge to wander around. Since we were in the park I knew exactly where I wanted to go for some free food. Me and Halo went to the Time Warner building and went downstairs to the Whole Foods market for some free samples to snack on, afterwards we went upstairs to the Samsung Experience center where we relaxed with some internet surfing.

I surfed the net while Halo talked on the free cell phones with his girlfriend Mimi. I logged in to check my email and before I logged off I notice sumtin that caught my eye. There's was an internet article about a tsunami that killed hundreds in the pacific, I went to read more about it, but before I finished the screen went blank and I just sat there startled wondering what happened. A new window opened up and it was Hacker's face plastered on the screen, he was talking to me telling me that sumtin bad was on its way here. Halo noticed sumtin was wrong and he told his girlfriend bye and came to my side.

[Halo, Edge and Hacker are all conversing via the computer screen]

It's... it's Testament.

Chapter 41

Surging rush

I took Halo to the bathroom and told Hacker to create a gate so we can discuss what's happening in person, in no time we were standing in our "control center" rather, Hacker's room. It seems that Testament caused the tsunami that wrecked the Hawaiian Islands and is now on route to the pacific coast.

[The three are gathered around a mired of screens all displaying relevant information]

Hacker: I can't believe after all this time he's back again
Edge: That's Testament?
Hacker: Yeah, in the flesh
Halo: He looks different though, a lot stronger
Edge: You mean he was weaker back then?
Halo: Yeah when he first came out he was mad skinny, but now...
Hacker: Look, talking about how strong he is right now isn't gonna help the fact he's up and walking
Edge: You think he's gonna destroy wherever he lands?
Hacker: He might, I dunno, either way this isn't good
Edge: Tell me about it
Hacker: No, it's much worse than you think
Halo: Why? What happened?
Hacker: Recently I been keeping up with the media, and it's not good
Edge: When is it ever good...?
Hacker: There's been a media frenzy on the "disasters" that have

occurred, the military are trying to cover it up but more than a few hundred have caught the Sky Flood incident on tape, the battle between you and Judgment at the beach, and even Judgment blowing up the spire on the Empire State, and not to mention that fight in Egypt, they had clear views of you being "people"

Edge: Whoa, I'm on film?

Halo: Nooooo they got me too, watch me get sent to jail cuz I'm brown

Hacker: As racially funny as that is, now isn't the time, the public have posted these videos on the net and I'm doing all I can to keep them off, the government is also trying to keep this on the low

Edge: So what's the problem then? Everything seems to be under control

Hacker: Trust me it's not, I'm able to keep some of them off, but once the information has been circulated it'll be around permanently, and more than 50% of the world probably has a file saved on their computers and a possible hard copy of it as well, I've done all I can to infect peoples computers and delete the files, but for those that have the copies, they are being sent into the wrong hands

Halo: Like who?

Hacker: The churches

Edge: Oh no...

Halo: The churches? What they gotta do with this?

Edge: Everything

Hacker: Exactly, more than 50% of this world, and I'm willing to bet about 80-90% of the whole world believes in some form of religion, some of the strongest ones are Islam, Christianity, Catholicism, and Judaism

Halo: And...

Edge: And that means with all those zealots out there they're more than likely thinking it's either the end of the world or some sorta Armageddon crisis

Hacker: Exactly, there's been rioting in certain places where the churches have demanded an answer to all that has happened, and wanna take actions into their own hands

Halo: So... this is bad?

Edge: Yes you dingus this is bad, this is exactly what I've been talking about, humanity will never accept us

Hacker: It gets worse, if sumtin happens with Testament wherever he lands then the public will know for sure, there's already people ready to risk their lives to expose the truth, just take a look

[Hacker brings up screen of California's coast line, there are people standing on top of their homes with a camera in hand as if waiting for something to happen]

Hacker: They already know he's coming
Edge: Damn this is not good at all, I think it's best to wait and see what happens, is there a way to keep them from filming it?
Hacker: No, I don't think so
Edge: How fast can you get us there?
Hacker: I can't get you there at all it's too far, I can get you up to Texas
Halo: How about somewhere with more clouds? I can get us the rest of the way there
Hacker: Us? More like you and Edge, I can't go, I don't have powers like you guys have, plus I need to monitor the situation
Edge: Chicken...
Hacker: You'd be too if you had to go up against that thing
Edge: I DO have to go up against that thing, look just open a gate as far as you can
Hacker: Alright

[Hacker opens the gate, Edge and Halo steps through, they reappear in a cornfield]

Edge: Hey Toto, I think we're in Kansas
Halo: Oh do the corns give that away, the almighty corns of Halo?
Edge: (with utter incomprehension) the almighty what?! Just get us there
Halo: Yes siree bob

[Halo grabs Edge's shoulder and extends his right arm into the air, a lightning bolt strikes them and they both disappear]

Now it's time to rush, get there as quickly as possible and assess the situation, if all he does is land and leaves everyone alone then maybe no one will overreact, but knowing him that's not gonna happen, we just need to get there ASAP.

Chapter 42

Napalm, hero of the west

[Testament glides across the waters surface splitting it as he draws closer to the Californian coast, people from the shore can see the wave that trails behind. In the sky above Kansas a seemingly regular lightning storm is racing in the clouds, but it's actually Halo and Edge jetting across them at break neck speeds. Testament gets ever closer and before you know it he is clearly visible from a distance by the naked eye, the people on the coast frantically start to take pictures and videos. As Testament approaches the beach, the waves don't stop or weaken, in fact the beach pushes them up into monstrous towering waves that Testament rides right into L.A. killing everyone close to the beach who were trying to take pictures and videos. The waves die down as they move closer inland and Testament comes to a stop on the ground and begins to walk. He gets pretty far before he is confronted by a complete stranger dressed in rugged skater type clothes and long brown hair. He stops right in front of Testament and that apparently enrages the demon to no end]

Testament: You have quite the nerves to do such a thing
Napalm: The names Napalm you dick
Testament: Indeed the nerves you have, you humans have no idea how to respect your superiors in this age
Napalm: I think you can call me human, I'm not sure though
Testament: You think you can stand on the same ground as me? How absurd
Napalm: You think I'm a regular guy, but I'm not and I'll show you what

I mean right now by kicking your ass, but first, what the fuck do you think you're doing destroying my home

Testament: You demand answers from me? I will humor you seeing as you have not long to live, my name is Testament, and I am doing this because it is what should have been done a long time ago if not for that traitor Edge, your home means nothing to me as does humanity, I will be the one to right the wrong, all you abominations deserve nothing less than death, at least in death you have a chance to serve the great lord Lucifer

Napalm: Lucifer? Next thing you'll tell me is Xenu's real as well

Testament: Who is this Xenu?

Napalm: ...come on big shot let's see what you have

Testament: Insolence!

[Testament extends his hand forward and water starts to form and spiral outward like a spear, this is Testament's Water Lance attack, it's approaching Napalm at a rapid speed and he just barely dodges it. Napalm has a look of uncertainty in his face, he realizes Testament is no ordinary opponent...]

Napalm: What? You can use your powers without having it around? What are you...?

Testament: You have no idea of the world around you

Napalm: I have to admit you're like no one else I ever met before

Testament: And you are like everything else I have killed before

[Testament once again unleashes his Water Lance attack but this time Napalm dodges it a bit easier, he starts to run at Testament at full speed like a marathon sprinter, and at a good lengthy distance away he quickly puts on the breaks by skidding against the asphalt. The heels of his sneakers are plated with metal, they create sparks and from these sparks he creates a whirlwind of fire that he sends towards Testament that consumes him in a blaze]

Napalm: Thought that was enough to take him down, I never met anyone like this before, I thought me and my friends were the only ones to have these abilities. He didn't go down, he just walked out of the flames, I can't believe anyone could survive that.

Testament: Fire element, like that traitor

Napalm: Traitor? Don't know what you're talking about, let's have some fun...

Testament: It is no concern of yours, WATER LANCE.

[Before the Water Lance forms Napalm kicks his heel against the pavement causing sparks to fly about, he once again sends them towards Testament as a wall of fire, only a silhouette is seen through the flames. Suddenly the wall of fire breaks open and a spear of water pierces through, Napalm raise his leg and the Water Lance hits the metal plates under his sneakers causing him to perform a summersault, he recovers in mid air and lands flawlessly back down]

Napalm: *Bad, this isn't going to be easy...*

Chapter 43

Battle upon lost angels

[Napalm rushes Testament and starts attacking him with a furious barrage of kicks, but Testament just stands there while tentacles of water rise from out of nowhere blocking all of his attacks]

Napalm: *What's with this guy, the water protects him out of nowhere.*

[A ball of water forms in front of Testament and is shot out towards Napalm who counters by hitting it with a spinning hook kick. Testament's attack is deflected and sent towards a building. The ball of water grinds a hole into its side while watery bullets are expelled from the slowly diminishing ball]

Napalm: *I don't think I should be hit with that sort of attack.*

[Napalm strikes up some sparks with the heel of his sneaker and creates a wall of fire towards Testament, once the demon is completely engulfed Napalm rushes at Testament and leaps into the air right above him. He sticks out his heel with the intention of coming down on Testament's head using those plates under his sneakers. Testament just looks up with apathy, in an instant water starts to swirl around the fires and extinguishes them instantly, they then start to swirl above Testament's head right as Napalm's attack hits, it successfully blocks Napalm's offensive attempt and then forces him upwards in a spin, he lands hard onto the pavement and appears to be badly injured]

Napalm: I... I don't think I can win this. I dropped onto the pavement from like 50 feet up, he really threw me good when he blocked my attack. I'll try, I'll try to beat him!

[In a miraculous show of determination Napalm manages to pick himself off the pavement and as he does so he scratches his heel against the ground and sends a wave of fire at Testament, this time he retains a handful of fire which he uses to set the surrounding cars ablaze]

Napalm: Now I will end you
Testament: You think a few fires will save your useless life?
Napalm: I'll show you my full power!

[The cars soon explode and as they do Napalm uses his powers to direct the flames towards Testament who does nothing but stand there with an arrogant stare, unknown to Testament though, Napalm also controls the stream of fire so it carries along the gasoline from the cars fuel tanks. The gasoline consumes Testament in an envelope of flames, Napalm still stands with a flame in his hands looking onward in the demon's direction. Suddenly the envelope of flame is pierced with a stream of water that gushes outward and spews onto the ground and then begins to move towards Napalm by picking itself up and bouncing along the ground]

Napalm: Impossible! What's going on here!?

[The water then grabs Napalm's wrist and takes the form of Testament]

Testament: That is your power? Pathetic, I know of Chimeras with more power than you

[Napalm calls out in pain as Testament slowly tightens his grip. The lone warrior tries to strike Testament with his other hand but he grabs that too, now both of Napalm's hands are in Testament's grip]

Testament: Simple Elemental User, what hope do you possibly have...?
Napalm: Argh!

[With a few gestures from his fingers Napalm summons the fires from his surroundings and consumes them both in a fiery blaze]

Napalm: *If I raise the heat to my max I might be able to stop him!*

[The fires intensify rapidly and grows in volume, this continues on for a few seconds before they suddenly die]

Testament: I would not want you to die now, I am not done having "fun"
Napalm: Fuck... you

[Napalm passes out and Testament lets go of his left hand. He looks around and then calls forth some water that manifest itself underneath him. It starts to rise lifting Testament up into the air while he stills holds onto Napalm's hand. The column of water takes Testament to the top of a building where he steps off and looks around at the destruction and smiles. Far off in the distance he notices a bunch of people looking at him they are all curious so he calls out to them]

Testament: HUMANS THIS IS YOUR FUTURE!

[Testament holds up the unconscious body of Napalm]

Testament: THE TRUTH THAT HAS BEEN HIDDEN FROM YOU WILL BE REVEALED WITH YOUR DESTRUCTION

[Testament jumps off the building still holding onto Napalm and begins to walk towards the growing crowd of people]

Crowd: WHAT ARE YOU!? ARE YOU THE DEVIL?! ARE YOU GOING TO KILL US?!
Testament: I am the truth of your existence, you are lucky because I will spare you all, go and spread the word, let the world know of terror to come
Crowd: HE'S THE DEVIL! GOD SAVE US ALL! RUN FOR YOUR LIVES!

[In one swipe of his hand he sends a small wave gushing towards the crowd and they disperse immediately running terror]

Chapter 44

Arrival too late the last incident

We raced to LA as fast as we could, I hung on tightly to Halo as he surged through the clouds...

[A lightning storm rages across the skies of Colorado, Utah, Nevada and finally California]

We finally made it, Halo and I fell out from the sky and landed into a crowd of people running in terror, they looked at us and began to scream even louder, I tried to tell them it's alright but what's a short lil Asian dude and a tall brown guy supposed to do? We began to walk in the opposite direction of the crowd of running people, but we didn't have to go far, Testament met up with us instead. Halo stepped forward though and he told me to keep myself hidden for the time being, I dunno why but I nodded my head and stepped back into the crowd, I figure I'd probably be the trump card and step in if Halo needed my help, hell, maybe I should come up with a cool entrance while I'm at it hahhaaahaa, nah I should be serious though, this is the second General of The Great War here.

[Edge steps back and starts to run with the crowd of people and he's soon lost in the hoard. The people soon disappear and Testament comes into full view of Halo, they confront each other for the first time in months]

Testament: You again
Halo: Yup, me again, let him go, he has nuttin to do with this

Testament: This insect? You should be thankful I let him live this long
Halo: Whys that?
Testament: Because your kind are rare in this day and age no?
Halo: My kind?
Testament: Elemental User much like yourself
Halo: What do you know about what I can do...?
Testament: Who do you think I am, I was the General of an entire army of demons, there is a reason for that, and that reason will become apparent to you
Halo: Oh yeah? SHOCKWA...

[Before Halo's attack is released, Testament hurls Napalm towards Halo stopping his attack]

Testament: Lightning element, there is no storm, how do you plan on gathering power to defeat me
Halo: Easy...

[Halo puts Napalm onto the ground and out of danger, he then extends his left hand but holds out his right hand just out of sight of Testament, and in his right hand he gathers a charge and it travels through his body and out his left hand]

Halo: SHOCKWAVE!

[The bolt of lightning shoots outward and a stunned Testament raises a wall of water that disperse the lightning bolt but at the same time burst into vapor]

Testament: I see, you charge up your energy and you direct it forward, but without a storm brewing your power is diminished tenfold
Halo: I got a trump card, but until then...

Halo started to fight Testament and it looked almost like a handicap match cuz everything that Halo does is deflected by that water that constantly guards Testament. From time to time Halo would manage to gather enough energy to perform his Shockwave attack but even that wasn't to much of a success, the few times that it did hit, it sent Testament stumbling back but he quickly recovered and retaliated sending Halo flying back. I remembered hearing that the guy Napalm was one of "us". while Halo and Testament were preoccupied with fighting each other I took it on myself to reach Napalm and try to wake him up.

[Edge heads over to Napalm and starts slapping him trying to wake him up, it works and Napalm blinks his eyes and finally fully opens them. He quickly gets up and looks around and before Edge can say anything he quickly gets up and sees Testament and Halo]

Edge: Hey hey hey, what's the hurry?
Napalm: He's still alive I have to stop him!
Edge: Um, alright you see the brown dude he's a friend of mine, we're the good guys got it?
Napalm: Good guys? We have good guys?
Edge: Look you're tryna stop Testament and so are we so let's work together alright?
Napalm: Whatever you say, but I think you should step back, things are gonna start getting hot in here
Edge: (cocking an eyebrow) is that so?

There he goes, Napalm eh? He was a skinny guy with long brown hair that he left hanging loose I think he was Latino, then again this was LA, so who knows... I guess he's a fire element judging by his name, maybe I don't need to help out after all...

[Napalm dashes forward to join Halo in the fight, when he arrives Testament has an annoyed look on his face]

Testament: Annoying insects, I should have crushed you both
Napalm: You know this guy?
Halo: Long story
Napalm: I see, I guess we both have something in common
Halo: Yeah, team effort?
Napalm: Yeah
Testament: Please, do amuse me, this should be "fun"
Napalm: Oh cheap shot

The two started to fight side by side against Testament and it looked a lil more equal this time, Testament ceased his attacks and started to dodge and parry the attacks of both Halo and Napalm.

[Napalm does a 540 kick and scratches his heels against the floor kicking up a storm of sparks that he ignites into huge clouds of fires that consume Testament, but when they die down it turns out they did nothing, Testament shielded himself with a thin layer of water. Right after Testament lets down his shield Halo strikes Testament with a bolt of lightning that forces Testament to stagger backwards. He retaliates by using his Water Lance attack, it rips through the air almost stabbing Halo but he's saved by Napalm who uses a wall of fire to evaporate the Water Lance]

Napalm: You ok?
Halo: Thanks dude!

[Testament finally goes on the offensive, he raises water from the water pipes underneath the streets and he directs them toward Napalm, like tentacles they strike him now and then as he tries to dodge, from the side though a few bolts of lightning come to Napalm's aid as Halo fends off the waters with his Shockwave attack. Testament notices this and starts to attack Halo as well, a big tentacle of water comes streaming at Halo who does nothing but stands still and holds out his left hand to gather a charge. Small tendrils of electricity start to form and right before the water jet is about to hit him he raises his right hand and all the energy he gathered travels to his extended arm and shoots out splitting the water into two halves, white vapor appears and from the distance Napalm notices something unnoticeable to regular people, Napalm rushes over to Halo's side]

Napalm: I have a plan, strike him with your attack again
Halo: Alright

[Halo charges his attack and unleashes it on Testament who again protects himself with a barrier of water, when Halo's attack hits, it breaks open a small hole and that same white vapor appears]

Napalm: ALRIGHT HERE'S MY CHANCE!

[Napalm runs towards Testament while he's distracted from Halo's attack, he immediately skids against the pavement sending sparks flying out]

Napalm: HELL HOUND!

[Napalm forms the sparks into the shape of a dog that starts to run along the pavement and quickly dashes into Testament causing the white vapors to suddenly ignite and explode, it sends Testament flying backwards and into a building completely destroying its facade. The hell hound continues its attack by running into the debris and exploding in a cloud of flames...]

Halo: Wow, you're pretty good, Edge would be jealous
Napalm: Who's Edge?
Halo: My trump card if that doesn't stop him
Napalm: Trump card?
Halo: Yeah...

[The fire rages and through the flames you can see a pair of white eyes suddenly intensify, the ground quakes a tiny bit and out of the blue a tremendous wave of water expands outward forcing both Halo and Napalm back into the side of a car, they hit it hard and get the wind knocked out of them... the fires are extinguished]

Chapter 45

Powers of the past

[Testament steps out of the water soaked store and walks towards the fallen warriors, he forms two spears made of water that float by his shoulders]

Testament: NOW DIE!

[The lances take on a life of their own as they immediately shoot towards Halo and Napalm... without warning a blue spark appears on the ground a few feet in front of the two warriors and a wall of blue fire forms, it rises high creating a shield. The lances hit the wall of flames drilling into the inferno, but to no avail. The attack comes to a halt in mid air and simply splash onto the ground]

Testament: Failed? What is this...?

[Testament's demonic white eyes sharpen their glare as the wall of blue fire begins to split down the middle. The silhouette of a lone figure is seen standing calmly, with one swipe of the figures right hand the fire simmers down and slowly extinguishes itself. Dressed in a pair of blue jeans with black flames, a plain white t-shirt, and a cut off glove worn on its right hand, the figure walks towards Testament. The demon's eyes suddenly widen in realization to the identity of the lone figure...]

Halo: (breathing heavily with a sigh of relief) see, THAT'S my trump card

161

Napalm: (also out of breath) who... who is that?

Halo: That's my friend Edge

[Without turning around Edge speaks to the two with a cold but reassuring and friendly voice]

Edge: Alright, you guys had enough, I'll take the rest from here

Napalm: YOU!? You're the guy that woke me up!

Edge: Yeah

Napalm: Watch out he's too strong

Halo: You haven't seen anything yet, shit, I haven't even seen sumtin like this before either

Napalm: What's going to happen?

Edge: Sumtin that shouldn't happen

Halo: Go kick his ass dude

[The two slowly get up and back away, Edge's Azure Flame starts to swirl around his body and on the ground, it begins to intensify...]

Testament: YOU.

Edge: Me.

Testament: The traitor

Edge: (shrugs) eh

Testament: Your looks have not changed since I last saw you, even now I remember your face

Edge: (with intrigue) really? I looked like this even all the way back then?

Testament: Why did you do it, why did you betray us...?

Edge: I... don't have a clue, but I'll tell you this much, whoever I was back then, I'm not that person now

Testament: You were supposed to burn the world to ash, your fire was supposed to win the war and give us rule over this miserable planet, but you chose to betray us all, and for what?

Edge: Things happen I guess, sometimes things just don't turn out the way you want them to

Testament: You will always be Fire Lord, the fire that was to end the world

Edge: You flooded it, doesn't that satisfy your ego?

Testament: The humans still live, even flourish, my satisfaction will only come at their total annihilation

Edge: Why you hate them so much?

Testament: Are you absurd, humans are an abomination of our species, the union of Jehovah's children are never to be mixed with the blood of ours

Edge: Oh yeah... good and evil, I forgot

Testament: You stand before me an abomination

Edge: So do you, that's not your body, but I know your eyes... I remember them

Testament: ...

Edge: Even right now your existence is cuz of that kid's body

Testament: That may be so, but my power is absolute

Edge: Really? I dunno about that, I don't think that body of yours is meant to be used in the way you wanna use it, maybe that's why you went into hiding, to adjust your body

Testament: Still believing you know everything, just like the old days

Edge: What can I say, when you open your eyes, you're no longer blind, so when are we doing this

Testament: So anxious to die are we?

Edge: Died once already, I kinda know what to expect

Testament: Then approach

Edge: Here I come...

[Water begins to swirl around Testament ready to defend him at a moments notice, Edge's Azure Flame also ignites as a small spark that quickly burns into an inferno that swirls around him. There is a faint blue tint on the surrounding battlefield...]

Chapter 46

Spirits collide, fire and water

[*A blue streak of flames trails behind Edge as he dashes off, he attacks with a punch that gets blocked by a wall of water. Edge drives his fist into the wall of water while simultaneously increasing the ferocity of the flames that surround his punch. Testament's expression changes as he sees his wall of water failing, without time to react, Edge lands his punch and sends Testament stumbling back. The two begin to fight hand to hand, each one blocking, parrying or countering the other as they attack and defend. Embers of blue fire and drops of water fly off in every direction as fist meets fist. Tremors rip through the ground as the two powers lock hands in a defiant show of power*]

Napalm: That's scary, how can people like those two exist, it doesn't even look real

Halo: I dunno dude, this is the first time I seen him fight like this, he and Testament are different from us

Napalm: How?

Halo: We gotta have our element around to be able to use our powers, that's why you have those plates under your shoes right

Napalm: Yeah, because I need them to start a fire using their sparks, and the chicks dig it

Halo: You show off with them?

Napalm: Well just the sparks, I never show off my fire abilities, only my sensei and classmates knows about that

Halo: Oh...

Halo: Edge and Testament are fucking crazy, I never seen him like this, and Napalm, poor dude doesn't look like he knows what the hell is going on.

[Testament raises his hand and several Water Lances start to form, they fire at Edge like arrows as he runs towards Testament. Edge manages to dodge a few but for those that he can't he just increases the intensity of the fires that surround his fist and simply punches the lances head on. He breaks through them easily and strikes Testament in the chest, but the demon grabs a hold of Edge's hand, spinning him around like a centrifuge before releasing him in a random direction. Edge is sent smashing into the side of a small building which collapses in on him]

Testament: What is this flame of his that breaks through water? His fire has always been red like the halls of hell, but now his fire is different... what about you has changed so much?

[Testament stands proud not even short of breath. The demon stares into the ruble that lies on top of Edge. A slight rumble is felt on the ground followed by a burst of blue rays that shoot out from under the ruble. The debris is sent into the sky as Edge forces his way out. His clothing a bit torn, he raises his right hand and gathers a swirl of energy to it. Testament starts to gather energy of his own which swirls around in the form and shape of water]

Napalm: What the hell is going on, this is like end of the world or something
Halo: My brown sense is telling me we is gotz to get outta here...
Napalm: Come on let's go!

[Edge jumps straight up into the air dragging his right hand as if it weighs a ton and as soon as he reaches his maximum height he hovers a bit and extends his right hand and starts to descend towards Testament like a meteor]

Halo: What the hell is gonna happen when they strike... me and Napalm can't stay here any longer, and I get a feeling this isn't even close to their max.

[Testament holds out the hand that has gathered the energy and braces himself for Edge's attack. The demon swings his arm forward as Edge approaches, the two attacks collide and the combatants cry out...]

Edge: STRIKE FIST!
Testament: COBALT DECEPTION!

[The two attacks meet and suddenly a large explosion consumes the battlefield knocking the combatants back violently...]

Chapter 47

The Aftermath, Xerxes is found

[Edge and Testament pick themselves up from under the ruble and before they get the chance to rush each other again the pendant that Testament obtained from earlier started to pulse]

Testament: *Hmm, you are pulsing... does that mean you have found your body?*

Testament: Sorry to cut this short, but I have business to attend to

[Testament's body begins to turn white and slowly evaporates like steam, in a matter of seconds he is gone...]

Edge: Pfft...

[The battlefield around Edge is like a war zone, destruction littered the wet streets... from out of the rising clouds of smoke and fire two figures approach in an injured manner, they call out to Edge, it's Napalm and Halo]

Edge: Hey you two
Napalm: You're some kind of demon, how could you do all this?!
Edge: If that's what I am then aren't you glad I'm on your side
Napalm: My side!? You totally destroyed my home!
Edge: (innocently smiles) it's not totally destroyed, this is only a small part of... wherever we are

Halo: He's right, it coulda ended up like New York a few months back

Edge: Yup yup

Napalm: How do you even exist...?

Edge: Look, the straight up truth is there's a lot of things in this word that can destroy "us" at any moment, "we" happen to be one of them, I think... my point is, whatever you think you know about your powers, well you haven't seen anything yet. Testament will be back, this fight is far from over

[A gate materializes and Hacker walks through]

Hacker: ...

Edge: Hey buddy

Hacker: Buddy nothing, you guys really did it this time, we better go, and I mean right now, the army is on their way thanks to your little Armageddon scene here, everyone knows now

Edge: This was bound to happen sooner or later

Napalm: What is?

Halo: Are we going back to your place?

Hacker: No we need to go somewhere far and desolate to plan things out, we'll head to my place later

Edge: Where we going?

Hacker: (thinks to himself for less than a second and then rushes out an answer) Australia

Edge: Fine fine, let's go...

[Hacker opens a gate to the farthest location his power will allow, but Napalm is hesitant]

Napalm: What am I supposed to do now?

Halo: Are we gonna just leave him?

Hacker: No, he's coming with us

Napalm: I'm not going anywhere

Hacker: You don't have much of a choice, come with us and be safe, or stay here and take on an army on your own, your choice

Edge: You better come with us, you're nowhere near strong enough to take on an army

Napalm: ...alright

Halo: We is best to go before we get shot up or sumtin
Edge: Yeah, c'mon...

[They all walk through the gate and end up in another state and they do this over and over again till they reach Australia, they pass through Alaska, Russia, China, Singapore, Malaysia, Indonesia, and finally arrive at the out skirts of the land down under]

Halo: You couldn't land us a lil closer to civilization
Hacker: That's what we wanna be as far away from as possible
Edge: Yeah, so what's the situation so far?
Hacker: Massive hysteria, the government is declaring this as an act of war, and the churches have said that judgment day is coming
Edge: (sigh)
Napalm: What? Why would they say that?
Halo: I'll fill him in on that
Edge: Good idea

[Napalm and Halo separate and sit down on some rocks, Halo tells Napalm all about the presumed, now actual, outcomes of their actions]

Me and Hacker discussed the repercussions of our actions, and we both agreed we needed to calm things down as soon as possible, but was that even gonna be possible? When people get scared they gather, individuals who normally are intelligent on their own, start to think with the same thoughts as a collective consciousness and thus become a mere member of what is now a larger being with one single thought, survival, and when survival is the goal, things can get hectic.

Edge: The humans at this point must all think they're gonna be killed in some horrific way
Hacker: No doubt, death by fire, hell on Earth. The religions of the world aren't what I'm worried about, it's the government
Edge: You don't think we can take them on do you
Hacker: I dunno, seeing what you can do, I think you can wipe out a few hundred in a single stroke, but I can't do anything
Edge: That's not true at all you can use your gates as the ultimate defense

Hacker: How?

Edge: How many gates can you open up?

Hacker: About 4, 5 if I really strain myself

Edge: See you can use them to send like 4 soldiers at a time to random places, and god forbid you close the gate on them half way through, fucking cut them in half

Hacker: I... never killed anyone before...

Edge: I...

Hacker: Anyway, we need to be ready for whatever happens

Edge: Do you think they know what we look like?

Hacker: Very likely, in fact I bet on it

Edge: What about you? Do you think they have anything on you?

Hacker: Now that I doubt, I hope anyway

Edge: I see... we need a base, a place where we can meet up

Hacker: What like the Justice League?

Edge: Sorta, but not with such a corny name

Hacker: (scoffs)

[Somewhere back in America, Testament holds out the pendant which glows like a homing beacon, a soft white light outlines the red gem and shoots out directing the demon in its desired direction, it leads him into the museum's Egyptian exhibit. Testament walks around until he comes across a pillar of stone, he places his hand on it...]

Testament: There you are, my love... my Xerxes.

Chapter 48

The voice of the people

[Testament places his hand on the pillar of stone and begins to feel its surface as if trying to discover something. His hands come to a stop and he punches that spot casing the pillar to crumble. A mummified corpse falls forward as the pillar collapses, Testament picks the corpse up and heads outside. When he reaches the front door he is met with a squadron of cops all aiming their guns at him. Without hesitation the demon swipes his left hand in front of him causing a torrent of water to coalesce washing the law enforcement away. Testament looks at the corpse in his right hand and slowly disappears in a fine mist. Back in Australia Edge, Hacker, Halo, and Napalm are discussing what to expect when they get back to New York City]

Napalm: I won't be going back to New York with you guys
Edge: It's ok, will you be safe in L.A.?
Napalm: Yeah, I know I will be
Edge: Alright so we'll just drop him off
Halo: You think anything is gonna happen when we get back?
Hacker: I dunno, there's nothing I can tell you right now
Edge: We'll just have to hope for the best, let's get going
Hacker: Off we go then

[The group takes off following the same route back, they drop off Napalm, and they start heading towards New York, when they reached home they land on the tip of Manhattan in Battery Park right in front of the East Coast Memorial eagle sculpture]

Edge: Seems pretty quiet and normal
Hacker: A bit too quiet don't you think?
Edge: Times Square, we need to be in Times Square
Halo: Why?
Edge: Well, any park or any mass gathering area is good enough
Halo: But why?
Edge: Cuz anything they would announce they would do it in a big open area. Hmm, hey Hacker can you take use to Union Square?
Hacker: Sure
Halo: But WHYYYYYYYYY?
Edge: (with an annoyed look) ...

[They all head into the gate and appear inside the train station at Union Square, they head upstairs into the park itself and see a huge crowd, they move in to see what's going on]

It seems worse than it really is, there was a crowd gathered around a few speakers. They preached about the coming end and that we all need to convert to be saved. Everyone was too entranced by the speakers words to notice us, there was this one guy who spoke out against all of this, I listened to him try to speak some sense into the crowd, but they wouldn't listen. It's apparent that things were gonna be taken too far, I decided to speak on my own, Halo tried to stop me cuz he knew where I stood with all this, he knew my words would cause a riot, but I refuse to stay quite, I refuse to stay censored under fear of the possible outcome of my ideas and beliefs...

Edge: (talking loudly over the crowd) HOLD ON A SECOND! DO WE ALL NEED TO HEAR THIS? IS THIS WHAT YOU ALL REALLY BELIEVE? THAT IF YOU CONVERT NOW, IF YOU CHANGE YOUR IDEAS AND BELIEFS THAT YOU WILL BE SAVED? DO YOU ALL BELIEVE THAT THIS IS THE END OF THE WORLD, IS THAT WHAT HE KNOWS FOR A FACT?! USE YOUR OWN JUDGMENT, I KNOW I AM NOT ALONE WHEN I SAY THAT IT IS NOT THE END OF THE WORLD, BUT IT'S A START OF A NEW BEGINNING!

Suffice to say I failed speech 101 in my short stay in college...

Head Speaker: DON'T LISTEN TO HIM HE'S ONE OF THOSE DEMONS! THOSE THINGS THAT HAVE DESTROYED OUR CITIES, OUR HOMES, OUR WAY OF LIFE!

Edge: AND WHAT PROOF DO YOU HAVE?

Head Speaker: EVERYONE LOOK TO THE SCREEN HE'S THE ONE IN BLUE FLAMES, THE FLAMES OF SATAN, THE FLAMES OF A DEMON!

[They all turn their heads to the screen and then turn to Edge and his friends, they all back away from him in horror]

Edge: WHAT YOU SEE IS NOT A LIE, IT'S THE TRUTH, BUT THERE'S MORE TO IT, IF NOT FOR ME MORE PEOPLE WOULD'VE DIED, I'M NOT THE BAD GUY HERE, but I know it's hard to understand right now...

Head Speaker: DON'T LISTEN TO HIM HE'S TRYING TO TRICK YOU HE'LL LEAD YOU INTO THE DEPTHS OF HELL AND YOUR SOUL WILL BE LOST

Edge: Gees, CAN YOU SHUT THE FUCK UP? IS THAT ALL YOU CAN DO? IS PREACH ABOUT THIS SO CALLED END OF THE WORLD? YOU WANT THE FUCKING TRUTH, HERE'S THE FUCKING TRUTH, ALL OF YOU HUMANS OUT THERE ARE NO DIFFERENT FROM US, WE ALL HAVE THE SAME BLOOD, HUMANS ARE THE OFFSPRING OF DEMONS AND ANGELS AND THAT'S THE TRUTH! I WAS FIGHTING TO SAVE YOU GUYS FROM A DEMON, IF ALL OF YOU SHEEP CAN'T DETERMINE THE TRUTH ON YOUR OWN THEN YOU ALREADY BEEN BRAIN WASHED, BUT FOR THOSE OF YOU WHO CAN SEE THE TRUTH ON YOUR OWN THEN THINK FOR YOURSELVES AND DON'T LET THIS PREACHER OF IGNORANCE LEAD YOU TO YOUR... WHATEVER...

Fail.

Head Speaker: (the crowd dies down) you see folks, profanity, blasphemy, lies, spoken from the mouth of a demon

Edge: People, I'm a New Yorker like all of you, I know for a fact you can all think for yourselves, don't let this one person dictate to you what you should and should not believe, but whatever, who am I to say right? do your own shit, fight amongst yourselves, I said my part...

[*Edge turns around and starts to walk away, Halo and Hacker follow close by, Edge's face turns apathetic. He knows what he's done and he's just trying to understand what is about to happen, before he gets any farther though cops, FBI, and even SWAT teams all appear at once, they all surround the 3*]

I see this is how it's gonna be eh?

Edge: (sigh)
Halo: Great, I'm brown, they gonna shoot me up first
Edge: Ha, funny at the worst times
Hacker: Guys, this is bad

[*The enforcers lock their crosshairs on the 3 and demand they put their hands up and surrender*]

Enforcers: PUT YOUR HANDS UP AND GET ON THE FLOOR YOU ARE ALL UNDER ARREST!
Edge: (baffled) is he serious? Are they fucking serious?
Halo: We can beat them any time we want right...?
Edge: (appalled) ARE YOU FUCKING KIDDING ME?!
Hacker: Hey Edge calm down, let's just see what they want
Edge: (still in disbelief) fucking dick shit assholes, please tell me they're kidding right?!
Halo: Uh, I don't think so dude
Hacker: Let's just do as they say we can't make ourselves look like the bad guys here

[*The 3 let themselves be taken into custody. Somewhere around the world Testament takes the mummy of Xerxes and lays it into a huge fountain and places the pulsing pendant around her neck. The veins that wrapped around the gem extend their grip and sink themselves into the mummy's chest. The dry corpse immediately begins to absorb the water in the*] *fountain... the dried flesh slowly begins to rehydrate. The gem pulses and glows as if it were a beating heart...]*

Testament: *The Fountain of Youth will restore life to you, and soon we will be reunited and the human race will be exterminated.*

[The lush green forest that surrounded the Fountain of Youth begins to wither and die. The beating glow of the gem begins to pulse faster. Vines suddenly burst out from the ground in an attempt to wrap and bind Xerxes, but prove to be futile. The vines slowly begin to dry and turn to dust, in a seemingly last ditch effort, the surviving vines pull Xerxes into the ground]

Testament: *It is too late Mei there is nothing you can do now to stop the rebirthing. Xerxes, soon your body will be full of life again, and we will be reunited my Xerxes.*

Chapter 49

The white room

[Hacker, Edge, and Halo are taken to an unnamed military base, they are put into a room of all white with a large rectangular mirror at the far end. Hacker seems bored and contempt, Edge is annoyed and Halo is paranoid, he starts to play around with his powers by arcing a small jolt of electricity back and forth between his thumb and forefinger]

Edge: Quit that or else we'll be in more heat
Halo: I can't take this, what the hell they plan on doing with us?!
Edge: Probably run test, or dissect us
Halo: Shut up!
Hacker: You guys thirsty?
Edge: Water would be nice
Halo: Pepsi...

[Hacker opens a small gate and pops his head through, after a small survey of the unknown destination, he pulls his head out and reaches in with his right arm, pulling out a bottle of water and two cans of soda. From a distance behind a two way mirror two military leaders talk]

Leader 1: Do you see that? He just made some sort of portal
Leader 2: The other one was impressive too, he seems to have electric control
Leader 1: And the third one, he's the one that's been all over the news
Leader 2: Do you think he was the one that caused the Empire State incident?

Leader 1: I don't doubt he might have had something to do with it
Leader 2: Let's begin
Leader 1: Yes

[The two open the only door into the room and head towards the group, before they get more than two thirds of the way Edge loudly says...]

Edge: Come any closer without telling us why we're here and I will burn you alive...

While in fact my Azure Flame is completely useless at burning anything seeing as how it can't set anything on fire.

[The two stop their approach and reply with a reassuring tone that they won't be hurt and that they only want to talk]

Leader 1: We only want to talk, that's all, I'm General Westing, and this is Colonel McDraff
Edge: You coulda talked to us outside where we were
General Westing: Because of national security, we can't allow that, these are... delicate situations
Colonel McDraff: Yes, we have no idea what you are exactly, you could be aliens, or super soldiers from other nations
Hacker: We're neither
Halo: I'm a citizen yo, I got my birth certificate and social security!
Colonel McDraff: We know that, we ran a background check, you're all American citizens, look, we just want information, know what's going on... assess the current situation is all
Edge: The current situation is not for you to know, let those two go and maybe I might be willing to reveal what I know to you
General Westing: We can't allow that, we do guarantee your safety, you won't be harmed, any of you
Hacker: You, the government, all you do is lie, you say you're trying to protect the civilians and citizens, but all you do is hide stuff from them, you keep them in the dark, I know what your gonna do, your gonna get Edge to talk somehow, then once you have all you need to know you'll try to get us to join you, if not, then you'll threaten us or try to control us somehow

Halo: ...we're gonna die aren't we

General Westing: No, please don't say such things, this is nothing more than an investigation. As you already know the recent events in California have exposed the world to whatever you three are

Edge: You sure it's us?

Colonel McDraff: Positive, there's video footage. As you can understand, your... abilities are very destructive and we need to know what your purpose is

Edge: Look there's more going on than you can understand, even if I told you, you wouldn't be able to believe me even if you wanted to

General Westing: Why is that?

Edge: Cuz humans simply aren't ready to accept the truth about the world

Halo: The truth?

Edge: Yeah the truth

Hacker: What is it?

Edge: Like I said humanity isn't ready, I need to know sumtin first...

General Westing: Make some accommodations for them, they need some rest

Hacker: I'm not staying here, I'm going home

General Westing: I'm sorry, we can't allow that, if you leave we will be forced to take actions

Hacker: What do you think you can do...?

Colonel McDraff: Please, we don't want any trouble

Edge: Just chill out, we'll be fine

Halo: This is gonna turn out bad I know it

Chapter 50

Answers I don't have

Saivent was the only person I can turn to for advice, he's the oldest and most experienced person I know... that night I slept in a typical military bed, hard as rocks, but oddly comfortable enough...

[Edge falls asleep easily, in the dream world he appears to be standing on that same building's edge he seems to like. He looks around and calls out to Saivent]

Edge: Hey yo, Saivent you there?

[A gust of wind blows against Edge and he feels a hand rest on his shoulder]

Saivent: That was a pretty awesome fight you had
Edge: Yeah? I try hahahahahaa
Saivent: So what's up?
Edge: I need your advice, you know the situation I'm in right?
Saivent: Yeah... you want to know if you should fight your way free or let them know the truth right?
Edge: Yeah, basically, I just dunno what the outcome of either one will be
Saivent: Well, technically I'm not supposed to meddle with human affairs...
Edge: Human? Ha! What a word to use...
Saivent: Your still human, just, special is all, but anyway, it's all up to

you, I'm not your father, I can't control you, but I can advise you, and I advise you do what feels right, ultimately it is you whose affected more than I am, my job is simple, keep the life of this world in motion
Edge: (sigh)
Saivent: I know you'll make the right decision
Edge: Thanks...

[Saivent walks away and before Edge turns around he disappears, Edge keeps on looking out toward that mysterious city, he stays on that ledge thinking to himself...]

If I tell them the truth, are they gonna spill it to the world or lie about it. If I tell the world, is everybody ready for the truth? Or if we fight our way out what repercussions will there be... gees, why are these types of decisions so hard to make.

[Edge stays a bit longer thinking, he soon stands up turns around and free falls with his back facing the street below, he closes his eyes and prepares for the impact that wakes him up in the real world]

I got your answer...

Chapter 51

Incidents confirmed, the world is torn

I woke up and was soon greeted by General what's his name. I told him my answer and that I'd let them know what "we" are, but only under one condition, I tell the entire world at once, and at the United Nations. It took a while to convince him, he had to talk it out with his superiors, and finally with the approval of the President they agreed. I ask them to release Halo and Hacker, they didn't wanna do that, so instead I asked them if they could join me in the spot light, but they said no. So what ended up happening was me alone with a dramatically large amount of cameras pointed at me, standing behind a podium, about to address the whole world, exposing the truth.

[Edge stands behind a white podium, he seems nervous and scared, he closes his eyes and takes a deep breath, remembering memories, trying to find some sort of drive, some sort of justification for doing what he's about to do]

Edge: Um, alrighty, I guess I'm gonna tell you sumtin you all wanted to know, sumtin you all been dieing to know, so where do I begin... "We" are not unlike you, in fact we are all alike, you guys can be like us as much as we can be like you. The events that have happened lately, are... events that are catching up from the past. If I told you the straight up truth you would all be angry, afraid, pleased, and scared, all sorts of stuff... I guess it's best I lay it out for you, for all of you right here... so I'll start off like this then, no lies, no sugar coating anything. Agnostics, rethink yourselves, atheists... your so wrong... and to every other religion out there, your wrong too, half wrong anyway... the devil and god are real, but that's not how it all happens as it's said in the Bible. We... are all children of them, them both. But some of us... like me... like some of my friends... like the people who try to destroy the world... "we" are special... cuz we... are different... what I'm tryna say is basically, people like me, are not aliens, not demons nor angels, not an experiment, not terrorist, not "mutants" not anything but regular people with special gifts. I'm not here to hurt you, what has happened was all outta defense, there are people out there who wanna destroy the world, I'm not calling myself a defender, but just a person who wants to survive, so I fight...

[The speech goes on a bit longer, by the time it's all over, people around the world are in shock, riots have broken out, protestors cover the streets in anger and hatred. Some people are scared of the possible future, others are angry at Edge for outing them, some are shunned by family members for coming out after seeing Edge's speech, others with powers have started using them to fight back against people who have turned on them. Others finally accept their powers and use them to attack people who have belittled them, who made fun of them. The world has been torn apart... Edge, returns to the military base... Colonel McDraff addresses Edge telling him how his speech was one of the biggest mistakes ever to have happened]

Colonel McDraff: That was the biggest mistake to have ever happened, I don't know what the hell the President was thinking letting you do that

Edge: Well now the world knows, isn't that what ya wanted?

Colonel McDraff: Not at the cause of war!

Edge: You think this is war? You have no idea what real war is, you and your guns and bombs, you have no idea

Colonel McDraff: Look boy I was in Nam fighting before your mom was even born, don't you tell me about war

Edge: Pfft, apparently I was fighting wars before your kind even existed asshole so why don't you shut up before you really get me mad

Colonel McDraff: (takes out a pistol) I should kill you where you are

Hacker: That's not a good idea

Halo: Oh shit...

Edge: Really? You think your fast enough to pull the trigger?

Colonel McDraff: Don't tempt me

Halo: Stop it, does everything have to be a fight

Edge: Get that gun outta my face or you die

[Hacker quickly opens a gate and grabs the gun out of McDraff's hand]

Hacker: This is not gonna solve anything people, can we go? Or do I have to get us outta here?

Halo: Calm down dude, you don't wanna start a war do you?

Edge: If everyone is like him, then a war is already starting...

Chapter 52

An escape into fire

Edge: So are we going, or do we have to force our way out?

Colonel McDraff: You really think I'm going to let you leave so easily?

Edge: You think you can stop us? Let alone just me?

Hacker: Oh fuck it

[Hacker creates a gate and pulls everyone through in a blink of an eye they return to Battery Park in New York City, they see fires and burnt cars, people are fighting and rioting...]

Hacker: What did you do man...

Halo: It's almost like judgment day...

Edge: I did what I had to do, do you really wanna hide what you can do from this world? Do you really wanna live under a rock, hiding everyday? I dunno, I'd rather fight for our freedom, fight for a place to belong, it's happened throughout history, this fight to belong in the world has always happened

Hacker: Listen to yourself, you sound like a self proclaimed genius trying to free the world!

Edge: WHO ELSE WOULD DO IT THEN?! I'M FUCKING TIRED OF HAVING TO HIDE MY POWERS FROM THE WORLD, EVER SINCE DAY ONE WHEN I FOUND OUT ABOUT THEM I HAD TO HIDE THEM... what'd you know, your powers don't cause destruction, doesn't cause death

Hacker: No, but you can't save the world with fire

Edge: No, I can't, but I can sure as hell blow my enemies the fuck up with it

Halo: What about me...

Edge: Your new to this Halo, you were human once, we are all still human

Hacker: What are we gonna do then...

Edge: I dunno, I have no clue at all... I wonder if there's anyone like us here, it be good to gather them all, see what they think

Halo: You guys are crazy, what do you think you can do

Edge: Can you just shut up and stop worrying?! You always worry about stuff that you don't be worrying about, I mean what the fuck, you have powers don't you? What, you dunno how to use them to defend yourself, to make your life easier, or do you like being told what to do and not think for yourself, gees

Halo: Don't gotta be so mean about it...

Edge: (sigh)

Hacker: Well... I might be able to help, I can probably give you access to local TV's

Edge: What ya mean?

Hacker: Send out a message

Halo: If you're like us then join us right?

Edge: You can do that?

Hacker: Sure, it's not hard, just takes some setup is all

[Testament notices something in the life flow of the world]

Testament: The world is in chaos. What has transpired? Have the humans finally accepted their doomed fate?

[The demon gets up from his meditative state, turns into mist and disappears... back in New York City...]

Heh, everything is in ruins... it's like nuttin I do leads to any good, so why continue right? I'm just so compelled to make my life worth sumtin, it's my life right, who else does it belong to...?

Halo went home and I went to Hacker's, there we set up a small telecast. We planned to get everyone together, and maybe we can all work sumtin out.

[A day goes by and the telecast goes off without problem, Testament stands on top of the Empire State which has been rebuilt by now, he looks at the chaos below]

Testament: Fool, what did you expect these humans to do, such meaningless creatures, they die so easily they might as well not live at all

[People are rioting still, in Times Square where the huge LCD billboards are Edge's face suddenly appears, and before long Edge's face is seen throughout the nation he sends out his message to all that are like him, he calls to them telling them to gather with everyone else at a safe place and that place would be at Central Park of New York City, with that said he was off the air, Hacker created a gate and they both proceed to Central Park. Testament also caught sight of the telecast]

Testament: Central Park, is that where I will destroy you in front of the world? Let us see, Fire Lord...

Chapter 53

Gathering of friends and foes, the fated hour

We were in Central Park at the Great Lawn, smack dab in the middle. At first it was just me and Hacker, but soon some more people showed up. On one side there were people just looking at us, and on the other side we had people screaming at us, telling us we're all going to hell, guess who they were. I stayed in the middle with Hacker, the sky started to get darker and lightning struck here and there, it wasn't long till I saw some familiar faces, Isaiah, and Kareem, then came Halo and his girlfriend Mimi. Then other faces I've seen here and there and some old forgotten friends. All I did was just look on as they gathered by the tens and... Tens. There wasn't many of us... On the other side of the field were the angry mob of hatred and righteousness, they got bigger and bigger. They would march on and try and force us apart, but there was no way in hell I'd let them do that. I opened my palm and lit a small blue flame in it as the mob pushed closer, I shook my head telling them no. The people behind me and Hacker looked at the fire and seemed to feel a bit comforted.

[A few people come up to Edge, it's Isaiah and Kareem, two more approach but soon stop seeing as how Isaiah and Kareem got to Edge first]

Kareem: You crazy Asian
Edge: No way, you to?

Kareem: Didn't I tell you I wanted to make a super hero club? You thought I was kidding didn't you

Edge: Yeah hahahaahahaa

Isaiah: Hey you're that guy Frank right?

Hacker: Yeah, do I know you?

Isaiah: Nah but I seen you in Graphics though

Hacker: Really?

Edge: Oh yeah, that's pretty cool, we all went to school together, I forgot about that

Isaiah: Yeah so you do your fire thing right?

Hacker: What do you do?

Isaiah: You ever saw that show Full Metal Alchemist?

Edge: I did... so what, you do things like transmutations or sumtin?

Isaiah: Yeah, sumtin like it

Hacker: What about you?

Kareem: Force fields, shields whatever you wanna call it

Edge: That's all? Gees where we're you when we needed you?

Kareem: You never told me about you

Edge: And you never told me about you either

Isaiah: What do you think is gonna happen man?

Hacker: Got me

Kareem: Whatever it is I don't think it's good, this mob wants to kill us, they really want us dead

Edge: Well, we won't let that happen will we?

[A giant wave of water rushed towards Edge but stops in front of him, Testament gets off and faces Edge]

Edge: Ok this is where everyone has to leave right now, no questions asked

Isaiah: I trust you man...

Hacker: Good luck Edge

Kareem: You crazy Asian

[Halo tells Mimi that she needs to leave but she doesn't listen, she walks off but stays around, Halo screams back at her to leave this place right now so she turns around and runs off, Halo runs up to Edge]

Edge: Go away Halo, this is not a fight for you

Halo: I got powers don't I? Besides I'm at my strongest right now, it's storming

Edge: (nods) alrighty, fight your best

Halo: BROOKLYN!

Testament: What have we here boy

Edge: You just called me boy?

Halo: Bring it on

Testament: What is the Hurry? Show these humans their worth

[Testament forms two lances and launches them at the angry mob and at the crowd of supporters, Hacker immediately opens two gates and redirects them towards Testament himself who simply waves his hands causing the water to drop back down]

Testament: You are quite the annoyance

Edge: EVERYONE LEAVE THIS PLACE AT ONCE!

[People from the crowd of supporters yell back at Edge telling him that they can help, but Edge yells back telling them they are better to him alive then dead, they all slowly start to scatter but stay close by to watch. Edge then turns to the crowd of haters telling them that if they want to live, they'd better leave right now, they go nowhere so he threatens them with a blue stream of fire aimed above their heads, they all duck in fear but still don't move]

Edge: Suit yourself, your own deaths

Angry crowd: DIE YOU FREAKS!! YOU DEMONS!

Halo: Let's do this already

Testament: (to the crowd of supporters) you humans have no idea of your worth, it is nothing, you simply exist as an abomination of reality, Jehovah does not favor you because he created you, he favors you as a last choice, I am your truth, Edge is your lie, this future belongs to the darkness, and I will right what was wronged all those years ago, all those eons...

[He points to the crowd of supporters]

Testament: In all sadness of truth, they are the closes to the forgotten reality, but this day and age has made you weak, you are all weak

Edge: You never get sick of hearing yourself speak do you? Let's finish this already, isn't that what you wanna do so badly

Testament: So eager to die, very well Fire Lord, let this be the final match

Edge: Yeah about time

Chapter 54

Battle of the ancient powers (Part 1)

[The crowd of supporters all looked on from a distance knowing something bad is about to happen. Not knowing what to expect the angry mob pushes forward towards Edge. He takes out his right hand glove and ignites a blue flame in his hand while putting it on, the flame slowly starts to swirl from his hand to his body... Small droplets of water begin to form around Testament as he starts to summon his power, floating weightlessly in mid air. Some of the droplets merge to form a lance which Testament aims at the crowd and releases it. The lance dashes off and begins to branch into smaller lances as it reaches the crowd, but suddenly the atmosphere around the crowd abruptly distorts and the lances are repelled by a force field]

The feeling was eerie, as if this has happened before. There was a primal feeling inside me yearning to break free, I can hear its calling, I can feel its presence. It's small and barely noticeable, as if being overpowered by another force. I ignored it and focused on the task at hand, the last fight I had with Testament was one of my most forceful battles, not even the one with Judgment was comparable. Testament was the real deal, the only other Elemental Spirit that could be a match for me, if not more. His raw strength was insane, I did all I could to keep him from breaking my bones with his melee attacks...

[The clouds roared with lightning and thunder, flashes of light illuminated

the dark grey sky. The two warriors looked at each other with piercing eyes, neither one making the first move. A single drop of water around Testament begins to grow larger than the rest and begins to drop towards the ground. Both Testament and Edge begin to tense up... the moment the droplet hits the ground the two dash off towards each other. A lance forms in Testament's right hand and he hurls it at Edge who counters by smashing it with his right fist, breaking it apart into a shower of water. The two Elemental Spirits draw closer to each other and right before they meet they pull their right fist back and release. The energy released when the two fists met forced everyone flying back including Halo, but Edge and Testament remain standing with their fist pressed tightly against one another. Edge throws a kick to the side of Testament's head and sends him to the ground, but the demon hurls a lance that barely misses Edge. The two distance themselves from each other and begin to gather their element in their right hands. Testament unleashes a blast of water and Edge releases a stream of intense azure fire, the two attacks collide in an earthquake of power and force. The ground below the collision point is pummeled into a crater, dirt and grass along with everything else in the ground is thrown into the air. The angry mob has disbanded in terror and disbelief but the crowd of supporters all look on in an awe of amazement protected by the force field that Kareem has erected]

Hacker: This is like the first fight all over again

Kareem: He fights like this all the time?

Halo: The last time was in LA, me and Napalm barely made it, then came Edge... he and Testament destroyed almost everything

Isaiah: Dang, I can't believe it, this is crazy that anyone has this sort of power

Halo: You have no idea do you

Hacker: The first time I saw him was with Judgment, he saved my life

Kareem: He's really that good? He's an asshole to me, a complete asshole

Halo: We'll... he is pretty fucked up, but he's there when you need him, he's there for me is all I can say

Isaiah: For me too actually

Halo: You guys should get outta here it's not safe

Kareem: We can take care of ourselves

Isaiah: Yeah, we can do it

Halo: That's whatcha think, it's gonna get bad this time, real bad

Hacker: I'm going, Edge can definitely take care of himself here, we'd only be getting in his way

Kareem: I'll crush him up with my Force Smasher

Isaiah: I'll blast him with my Ion Cannon then

Halo: Sure...

Hacker: See ya guys...

[Hacker disappears through a gate]

Kareem: So what's your power?

Halo: It's Halo, my power is lightning

Kareem: I'm Apollo

Isaiah: Yeah, I'm Raven, and I have one of the most awesome powers, matter manipulation

Halo: You're full of yourself, just hope for the best with Edge, I'm gonna go in

Raven: Hey what you think you can do?

Halo: Plenty

My fight with Testament here in New York was the same as the one in LA, he's stronger now, but I can do it, I know I can, I have to... our attacks kept clashing, neither of us giving way. Halo jumped out from behind and lent a hand, he released his Shockwave attack, spiraling it around my stream of fire. It began to force Testament's attack back but he just put more power into his water blast tryna force me and Halo back... but we forced back harder.

[Halo and Edge are putting all their power into their attacks, it slowly but surely starts to overcome Testament. When it seems like it's about to overtake him, Testament dodges to the right and throws a Water Lance at Halo, Edge sees this and quickly redirects the stream of flame at the lance, Halo sees what happened a split second later, both Halo and Edge's attacks have subsided, they now stare at a smiling Testament]

Halo: Damn yo he's fast

Edge: Just keep your eyes peeled

Testament: That flame of yours Edge, it is different from your other
Edge: Still mine...
Testament: Apparently, interesting enough, it stops water and is unaffected by it, intriguing... it is a spiritual flame
Edge: What? Grandpa wants a cookie or sumtin for figuring that out?
Testament: MWAHAHHAHHAAA only one place would be able to subdue your flames enough for it to change itself
Edge: Yeah yeah yeah...

[Testament raises both hands to eye level causing two waves of water to form from the ground up, he then crosses them and the waves of water immediately rush forward like a tsunami. Halo reaches to the sky and disappears within a bolt of lightning. Edge raises his gloved fist above his head and ignites his Azure Flame to a full burn and slams it down into the ground as the wave hits, splitting it into two halves that passes by. From out of nowhere Testament lunges out from the oncoming water and punches Edge, sending him back and into the ground. From the sky a bolt of lightning comes ripping through the air striking Testament, but he quickly recovers and reaches out and grabs Halo's leg which was the lightning bolt and swings him around violently before letting go, sending him hurling into a tree. Edge gets up from the ground seeing an opening for attack, lunges at Testament and starts pummeling him with a furry of punches and kicks, Testament fights back. The two look like a blur of power, punches met by the others fist, kicks met by the others shin. The fight continues relentlessly...]

Testament was strong alright, Halo is knocked out slumped over a tree so once again this fight is mine and mine alone...

Chapter 55

Battle of the ancient powers
(Part 2)

[Flashback... atop a mountain that nearly reached the skies Testament stands weakened but resilient. The clouds open up and an army of angels pierced through the dark sky with swords raised and armor shinning in the bright sunlight. Testament raises one hand and the ocean below erupts as multiple towers of water whips into the incoming army. The towers then begin to wrap themselves together to form an eyeless water serpent, Testament's spirit calling, Leviathan. The beast opens its maw and releases a blast of water that finishes off the rest of the angel army. As the heavenly soldiers fell to their watery grave the sunlight that pierced the dark sky suddenly began to glow with a burning rage. The clouds all disperse as the sky ignites, a fire bird of immense size, comparable to that of Leviathan, comes crashing down like a meteor smashing into the watery serpent. Leviathan is evaporated in a shower of water and steam. The fire bird, barley smoldering, opens its beak and releases a fireball at Testament consuming him and knocking him off the top of the mountain. The fireball clears up and turns out to be a humanoid figure, both it and Testament plummet to the ground creating a small crater. The two lay side by side, one facing down and one facing up... Testament rolls his head to see his foe... it's Edge, who simply looks back with a small grin...]

Testament: Traitor... what have you done...
Edge: Fate, maybe destiny, I dunno...
Testament: You have destroyed us all...

201

Edge: I only did what I thought was right

Testament: You are one of them, one of those deviants

Edge: Yeah... I guess I am

Testament: You have no idea what you have done Fire Lord...

Edge: I made a new life for myself, with the end of this war... comes a chance for peace

Testament: You are a fool, you are a demon one way or another. You will always be consumed with that fire of yours...

Edge: Maybe not, just maybe...

[The clouds open up again and this time, Michael and Gabriel step forward and slowly descend, their wings only flapping slightly... Gabriel confirms Testaments further weakened state. Michael goes to Edge and picks him up]

Edge: Maybe I made a mistake...

Michael: No Edge you did the right thing, rest now...

[Edge closes his eyes and is taken up by Michael. Gabriel calls for a team of angels who comes down to deal with Testament... Present day New York City]

The two of us stood our ground never letting go of our resolve, but I dunno how much longer I can keep it up, I'm getting tired, this blue flame of mine feels like it takes more energy to use than it outputs.

[Testament calls forth a tidal wave that begins to form as small materializing bubbles, and then into a wall of water, and then finally an ocean sized wave... he sends it surging towards Edge...]

Fuck, that's gonna be painful if it hits... I summoned what strength I had left and I literally cut the wave in half down its center. Even though they went in separate directions I didn't have the strength I needed to keep it up, I was soon completely taken by the wave.

[Edge is knocked back and tossed around in the wave... he's finally thrown out and lands back down on the muddy ground]

Testament: What is wrong Edge, you seem weaker, much weaker than you use to be

Edge: (panting) ugh... your one to speak, your hiding it but I know damn well you don't got much power left...

Testament: No, I will not be the one to destroy you, someone else will do that, it has waited eons to see you again

Edge: What...

Testament: BEHOLD!

[Testament raises his hand towards the clouds, they begin to swirl around chaotically, a single bolt of lightning comes crashing down striking the muddy ground. A massive explosion of mud is thrown into the air along with an outpour of water, the bolt of lightning struck and ruptured a water pipe... the crowd of spectators have all fled in horror long ago, only a select few remain...]

Testament: Say hello Fire Lord!

[From the stream of water a silent yet familiar moan is heard, it slowly becomes a thunderous roar... the stream of chaotic upward spraying water starts to take form... the form of a leviathan...]

Edge: Ah... crap.

Testament: AHAHAHAHAHAAAAAHAHA!

Chapter 56

Battle of the ancient powers (Part 3)

[The leviathan rose up and darts toward Edge...]

Crap!? How the hell am I supposed to fight against sumtin like that...? I barely got enough energy to stand up and now I have to dodge that thing...

[As the leviathan approached with its jaws wide open, Edge could do nothing but ready himself for its attack. Suddenly from out of nowhere a bolt of lightning strikes Edge causing him to disappear. The leviathan ends up smashing into the ground, bursting into a thick spray of water but quickly reforming itself]

Testament: He is gone...

[From not so far away another bolt of lightning strikes the pavement and out comes Edge and Halo, they tumble to the ground...]

Edge: (panting) so your back in action I see
Halo: (also panting) yeah, a splash of water woke me up
Edge: Thanks for the quick rescue, but you should go, there's nuttin more you can do here
Halo: I can't...
Edge: What? Why?

Halo: Cuz I can't leave you here, you were about to be eaten up by that thing

Edge: Dude I can take care of myself, remember? I'm the one he wants

Halo: Yeah yeah, say whatever you want you can't get rid of me

Edge: (sigh)

[The leviathan comes around and Testament hops onto its head, it brings them in the direction of Edge and Halo]

Halo: Look, I may have a plan

Edge: What is it?

Halo: Back in LA, with Napalm...

Edge: Yeah?

Halo: My lightning caused this white vapor to appear, and Napalm was able to set it on fire

Edge: ...oxygen and hydrogen...

Halo: I guess

Edge: That might be a prob

Halo: Why?

Edge: My Azure Flame doesn't set anything on fire

Halo: God you're useless

Edge: ...

[Edge hits Halo over the head]

Edge: Give it a try, I'll see what I can do

Me and Halo stood our ground, Testament approached with the leviathan and Halo took to the sky through his lightning bolts. From outta nowhere catching Testament by surprise from the shear speed, multiple lightning bolts all strike down on him hard. They continue to keep striking and eventually Testament raises a water shield. And I noticed that white smoke that Halo was talking about...

[Edge ignites his right fist and lunges towards Testament]

Testament: Are you mental...

Edge: STRIKE FIST!

[*As Edge's strike fist is about to land, Testament enlarges the shield, the azure flames strike the white vapor but nothing happens*]

Shit... I knew it, it won't ignite.

[*Edge hears a whisper in his head...*]

There was a voice in my head, it whispered sumtin to me, Azur... Azurath... what the hell is an Azurath? I tried to ignore it but the voice got louder, like it was yelling at me to listen... for a split second I closed my eyes to concentrate on shutting the voice up, and that's when Testament made his move. He forcefully expanded his water shield outward, it knocked me back and causes Halo to tumble outta the sky and onto the ground, the voice just kept getting louder...

[*Edge calls out loud in anguish*]

Edge: FINE YOU WANT IT THEN YOU GOT IT, AZURATH!

[*Almost instinctively Edge forms his hands into a sphere and pulls it back, everything that is alive around him starts to give off a blue tint, a blue sparkle of light that begins to head towards the sphere shape formed by Edge's hands*]

Testament: What is this...?
Halo: Ugh, Edge?

[*Edge gathers more and more energy, the look in his eyes are that of a blazing blue inferno*]

Testament: No. I will not let you finish! LEVIATHAN GO!
Halo: Oh shit...

[*The leviathan lunges towards Edge with its jaws wide open, but Edge doesn't react almost as if he was in a trance...*]

Not enough, I don't have enough yet...

[*The leviathan closes in on Edge and out of nowhere Halo jumps in *front and fires his Shockwave attack in full force, it's enough to keep the leviathan at bay for the time]*

Edge: HALO GET OUTTA THE WAY!
Halo: YOU KNOW WHAT WILL HAPPEN IF I DO?! HERE'S YOUR CHANCE FIRE YOUR DAMN ATTACK!
Testament: I DON'T THINK SO! WATER LANCE!

[Testament pulls his fist back and draws out a water lance bigger than the usual ones and hurls it at Halo, piercing his chest]

Edge: NO!

[Testament stands on top of Leviathan's head and laughs maniacally as the lance migrates through Halos chest and towards Edge]

It's now or never...

Edge: IT'S NOW OR NEVER!

[Edge draws the collected energy forward and releases it in a blast that smashes through the lance, and rips through Halo, the leviathan and finally reaches Testament, but the demon raises a water shield that manages to repel the attack for the moment but is quickly being overtaken]

Testament: INCONCEIVABLE!
Edge: DIE!
Testament: NO! NOT THIS TIME! YOU WILL NOT WIN THIS TIME!
Edge: AHHHHHHHHH!

[Edge puts all his effort into pushing his blast forward and it shatters Testament's shield, the blast engulfs the demon and as it does a demonic aura is seen being vanquished from the body...]

The blast hit him head on and sent him back, he flew off the leviathan and was air born for a good amount of time. The moment he left the leviathan though, it turned into a giant puddle of water that came crashing down onto the ground... is it over...? I'm so tired... oh no, Halo.

Chapter 57

Death.

I rushed to Halo, he was lifeless on the floor. My attack went right through him but left no physical injuries, but still my friend remained lifeless.

[Edge kneels over Halo's lifeless body in sorrow... the rain stops, the whole scene is filled with destruction, mud and dirt thrown around... soon the clouds start to clear up slowly... out of nowhere Saivent appears in front of Edge]

Saivent appeared in front of me, he tried to console me but to no avail.

Saivent: Edge...
Edge: Saivent, can you save him?
Saivent: I'm sorry, I don't have that sort of power
Edge: He's gone then isn't he...?
Saivent: Edge, I'm sorry...
Edge: Damn it!

[Edge picks Halo's head up in his arms and a blue flame, small but clear and bright ignites in Edge's right hand]

Saivent: Huh?
Edge: What? wait a minute, can you tell me where he is?
Saivent: What do you mean? He's right there...

Edge: No I mean where his soul is

Saivent: No... You don't mean too...

Edge: Yes, I do, now can you or can't you tell me where his fucking soul is?!

Saivent: It's... It's closing in on the gates to the Angel Sanctuary...

Edge: I get it...

[The blue flame flickers out and a bright white light appears from Edge... out of nowhere Edge's shirt rips from the back and a pair of white wings emerge and open defiantly]

Saivent: Edge...

Edge: I'll be back, and so will Halo, I won't let him die, not like this...

[With one strong downward stroke, Edge takes off into the sky then slowly disappears in a scattering of shinning white spheres]

If I can get to Halo's soul before it enters the Angel Sanctuary, then I might be able bring it back to Earth and back to the body. He'll live again damn it, so help me I won't let my friend die this way!

[Edge flies through the darkness before meeting up with Halo's soul...]

There he is, I see him, he's just about to exit, if I can get to him before he does I might be able to avoid a fight with Michael. I flapped my wings harder to catch up but it was no use, he was soon tossed out and I followed. We were both in front the golden gates, but they hadn't opened yet. I picked Halo up and tried to open the portal to bring us back home but it wasn't opening, instead the gates opened up and guess who walks on through, Michael and Akuma.

[Edge ignites his right hand into a blazing blue fist]

Michael: Don't worry Edge, I'm not here to fight you

Edge: Then what'd you want

Michael: You really wish to help your friend don't you?

Edge: Yeah, he didn't deserve this... it was my fault

Michael: (nods) things will reveal and work themselves out in the future, so go Edge, do what you must

Edge: (stands there silently) I... can't open the portal back

Michael: I know, in order to do that you must sacrifice your angel status

Edge: Give up my wings you mean

Michael: Yes...

Edge: I see, it's either fall down to my death knowing full well I can't fly with my blue flames... or join you

Michael: It's not a hard choice Edge, use your better judgment

Edge: Sorry, but I'm Asian... ciao!

[Edge opens his wings wide and they start to shine brightly, they suddenly explode in a ray of energy and feathers... a portal opens up]

Michael: I hope you know what you've done

Edge: I never know, I'm just taking things as they come

[Edge jumps through with Halo]

Ugh here we go again, the darkness, the chaos... I closed my eyes and just rode it out the whole time never letting go of Halo. It wasn't long before we broke through into reality and now we were tumbling down like we just jumped out a plane or sumtin, Saivent... where are you... I need your help.

[Edge and Halo are plunging towards the ground at break neck speeds]

I can't do it, I can't ignite it, Saivent... I need your help!

Saivent: Edge, no, you can do it Edge... I know you can, reach deep down inside and ignite the spark of your flame.

Heh, when you need people the most... you realize all you can really depend on is yourself. No one can ever help you the way you can help yourself. I opened my eyes to see our descent, c'mon, ignite... I know you're in there, I can feel you... stop being such an asshole and ignite... IGNITE MOTHER FUCKER!

211

[Edge and Halo are falling through the sky rapidly. A bright light is seen shining in Edge's right hand he extends his hand forward and clenches his fist tightly]

Last chance, I'm telling you... IGNITE!

[His right hand burst into the red flames of hell and they instantly surrounding him. He rights himself from a head first falling position to an upright position, and lets the fire burn brightly and fiercely, from down below Saivent snickers]

Saivent: *Told you so.*

[Edge and Halo look like a giant meteor crashing to Earth, but as they reach the surface Edge opens the throttle and releases his fire to their maximum burn and they start to slow down. They hit the ground with a loud crash, the fires incinerates everything within the small crash zone]

Halo! I quickly took back into the sky and flew over to Halo's body, the moment I got close though, Halo's soul disappears from my arms and seemingly darts ahead back into the body.

[Halo's soul enters the body and the wound is instantly closed leaving behind a slight but noticeable scar...]

Edge: Did it work? Is he alive?
Saivent: (smiles) see for yourself...

[Halo coughs a bit, rolls over to his side and sits up]

Halo: I had this weird dream, what's this scar in my chest?
Edge: (smiles and hugs Halo) ass... I told you to get outta the way
Saivent: I should leave you guys, take care kids

[Saivent disappears into the wind]

Halo: Dude what happened?

212

Edge: Long story, I'll tell ya about it some other time, but for now let's get outta here

Halo: Where to?

Edge: Anywhere, I need a long...

[Edge suddenly passes out]

Halo: Oh shit Edge, EDGE! Damn, he's out cold...

[Halo looks at the sky, it's bright and clear, then he looks at his hand, and a small surge of electricity jumps across his palms...]

Halo: *That's weird, that's never happened before.*

[Halo takes Edge to his apartment...]

Chapter 58

Witch's birth

[Cops, SWAT, FBI and all sorts of other government agents are standing at the fight scene, between Edge and Testament. By now Halo and Edge are long gone...]

Agent 1: Seems like we have a casualty
Agent 2: What is it?
Agent 1: It's a guy
Agent 2: A guy? Wadda ya mean?
Agent 1: Here take a look for yourself

[The first agent takes the second to see a guy on the floor, it's the body of Testament]

Agent 2: Is he dead?
Agent 1: He's unresponsive, out cold that's for sure
Agent 2: So is there any danger?
Agent 1: Maybe, the scientist will figure that part out, it's not our job

[The body is taken onto a stretcher and then into an ambulance that drives off]

Agent 2: What a mess...

[The ground above Xerxes starts to stir and an arm breaches the

surface, a female figure climbs out, nude and covered in dirt she laughs maniacally]

Xerxes: Hahahhahahahah AHAHAHHAHAAHAHAHAAA!

[The dirt below her suddenly shoots out vines that try to grab her but she cuts them with a whip of energy similar in color to fire... the whip gives off a slight electric discharge when it hits the vines, but it cuts them and Xerxes jumps into the air, a pair of butterfly wings with sharpen tips sprout and she head towards New York]

Xerxes: Testament! TESTAMENT!

[Back in New York, Mimi, Halo's girlfriend is dead on the edge of the battlefield crushed under some trees and rocks. The same vines that tried to over take Xerxes are now wrapping themselves around Mimi and they pull her underground]

I dreamt a dream... I don't remember how I got home, but all I know is that I'm in my bed, I'm tired and sore, and when I got up no one was around. There was a note on the table beside my bed so I turned over to pick it up, it read:

"yo its me, sorry I couldn't stay, but I had to go find Mimi, I wanted to make sure she's safe, see you later dude, Halo"

And with that I got up and outta bed, my now... dirty bed, cuz someone threw me in with my dirty clothes on, Halo. Then again, when I think about it, I'm glad he didn't take them off, talk about awkward.

Once I changed I took a long hot shower and immediately went to the fridge for some food, I ate whatever was there, eggs, cheese, some chicken and a can of corn. When I was done I sat in front of the TV and turned it on, guess what I saw? The ruins that were once Central Park, some news reporter lady started talking and said how a young man, by the looks of it not more than 23 to 25 was found unconscious at the scene.

[The TV shows a close up of the young man...Its Testament]

Damn, if he's not dead... then it means he can wake up at any time now and start this mess all over again. I called Hacker to tell him what I just saw. He suggested we pay him a visit once things have calmed down, but even then there would be plenty of security guards posted around.

Later that day I went out for a walk, the streets were calm and not as busy as they usually were. I went to South Street Seaport, one of my favorite spots. They had a balcony area with plenty of seats so I sat down and laid back, the hot summer sun didn't bother me much, just yesterday, I think... there was that huge fight, and it was cold and gloomy.

[From behind Edge, Hacker walks up and sits down]

Edge: Fancy meeting you here

Hacker: Yeah, so... what are we gonna do about Testament?

Edge: I dunno, your plan is the best one, I can't think of anything else at the moment

Hacker: I don't even know where they're keeping him

Edge: You for real? Damn...

Hacker: What about Saivent?

Edge: What about him? In fact when did you meet him?

Hacker: Long story, but can't you ask him for help?

Edge: I guess, but I don't like asking him for favors. It's like I'm just using him at my leisure

Hacker: Well we can do it ourselves I guess, I just dunno how that's gonna turn out, or how long it will take

Edge: Can't you hack the info out somehow

Hacker: There's nothing, don't you think I already tried...

Edge: Damn it

[A few days passed and the body of Testament remains motionless, then out of nowhere an explosion followed by screams and gun shots break out... a figure of a young female burst through the cell that was holding Testament, she smiles... The face of the female figure never shows itself, it is masked by solid black hair that hangs in front. She picks Testament up, grins and blasts another hole into the adjacent wall, she flies out with incredible speed]

Chapter 59

Mother earth incarnated

The news of Testament's disappearance was no surprise to me, but my hands were tied at the moment to care... there were no signs of any trouble brewing, and there was nuttin in the papers, so I decided to relax my guard a bit. Halo on the other hand was in a fit, his girlfriend Mimi has been missing and she's nowhere to be found. Halo suspects that she might have been killed, he's been looking for her, I feel bad for him...

[In the early afternoon of late summer in the middle of Central Park, still in ruins... a hand reaches up and out followed by vines. The vines dig upward lifting the body of Mimi up and out, her hair is now a shimmering deep forest green as well as her eyes and a small diamond shape jewel on her forehead. Her skin, wherever it could be seen, seemed to have roots that latched themselves in a twisted and knotted fashion, they dug into the skin and looked almost like veins and arteries, the color of her skin was that of a light brown, almost like dry dirt. She seemingly examines her new body and then looks around at the decimated park, her face grows sad. She kneels down to touch the ground, when she does the same color that envelope her hair and eyes now spread out onto the floor. Suddenly all the fallen trees and the upturned grass are beginning to fix themselves. In a few minutes all of Central Park is back to the way it was before the battle and even more intense in life than it had been. The enchanted body of Mimi seems pleased and she starts to walk about]

I called Halo and told him if sumtin bad did happen then there wasn't anything he can do at this point he reluctantly agreed. We went for

219

a walk in downtown Manhattan along Hudson River Park. We talked and caught up a bit. It's been a while since me and him have hung out, even before the whole fight with Testament my friendship with him had been growing apart, but it's to be expected, we were growing up, our lives were headed in different directions, I wasn't gonna hold it against him, even I've been changing as a person. Anyway, we walked up to about 40 sumtin street or was it 50 sumtin, it was a few blocks away from the Intrepid, a naval battleship turned museum. There was this small park and we sat down and looked over to New Jersey.

[Halo plucks a flower from the bed of grass besides him and whispers the name Mimi into it, then drops it on the grass again. Back in Central Park the enchanted Mimi seems to hear it and immediately sinks beneath the soil and begins to traverse towards Edge and Halo]

Edge: Yo dude, you feel that?
Halo: Yeah, what is that?
Edge: I dunno, but it's coming towards us
Halo: Damn it, already some shits gonna be up?

[The grass below the flower that Halo dropped splits to reveal a hand that grabs the flower, followed by the rise of Mimi. Halo stands there in absolute shock and Edge just looks on with a dumbfounded look on his face]

Halo: MIMI!
Edge: Wait dude, I don't think that's her
Halo: Whatcha mean? That IS her, just look!
Edge: Exactly, look AT her
Halo: Mimi what happened?
Mimi: Mimi, that is the name of this girl?

[She spoke with a dual tone voice, one young and feminine, the other a bit more masculine, but the younger voice shines through a lot more clearly]

Halo: Mimi don't you remember me?
Mimi: Mimi, yes, this was the name of the original owner, but she has long since gone

Halo: Gone?! What do you mean gone?!

Mimi: She died upon my arrival, the resurrection of Xerxes required my immediate action, I could do nothing without a body

Halo: Wait no, none of this makes sense, you said that Mimi was dead when you found her?

Mimi: Yes

Halo: So who are you?

Mimi: I am a protector

Halo: Of what?

Mimi: Of nature

Edge: Oh... Saivent

Mimi: My brother, is he well?

Halo: The hell...

Edge: (with confusion and annoyance) let's find out... SAIVENT!

[Edge calls out loudly and in a subtle gust of wind Saivent appears and turns to Edge]

Saivent: Mei... What brings you out into the open?

Mei: Xerxes

Saivent: (sigh) her again...

Mei: She's been revived, I tried to stop her but was unable to bind her

Edge: Ok what? NOW what he hell is going on here?

Halo: ...

Saivent: If Xerxes is out... then this means that Testament's disappearance is because of her

Halo: ...

Mei: Testament was the one that brought her to me, he revived her body with water from the Fountain of Youth, that is where I tried to bind her but it only hastened her revival

Saivent: Hmm, Testament was defeated by Edge

Mei: But life still remains in his body

Halo: (with impatient anger) WHAT THE HELL IS GOING ON HERE!? MIMI IS YOUR SISTER?!

Saivent: So to say, but that's not Mimi. My existence allows ambient life to exist, Mei is the person who regulates the life that comes into existence

Halo: Meaning?

Mei: Extinction, evolution

Halo: ...

Edge: (pinches the bridge of his nose) I beat him with my blue flame, it works differently than my red

Saivent: Yeah, I remember now. Your blue flame attacks spirit energy

Mei: He possesses the Azure Flame?

Edge: Yeah, it was a side effect of my baptism in the Angel Sanctuary

Saivent: This is becoming quite the predicament

Mei: Indeed...

[Xerxes lays Testament down in a patch of withered grass within the forest in which the Fountain of Youth resides]

Xerxes: Testament... my love... what's wrong, why won't you wake... HAHAHAHAAHAAHA, Testament...

Chapter 60

The innocent vessel

[Xerxes stands right beside the body of Testament that has laid motionless except for the rise and fall of his chest due to his breathing. She stands there playing with a butterfly that glows with a fiery hue. Suddenly Testament twitches a bit before giving out a subtle moan and rolling over, Xerxes stops paying attention to the butterfly and diverts her attention to Testament]

Xerxes: My love my Testament you are alive, you are well yes?

Testament: Huh? Testament? What testament are you talking about, where am I...

Xerxes: Love... my love... it's me...

Testament: Who... who are you?

Xerxes: I am Xerxes, you are my love as I am yours... you are my Testament...

Testament: Your testament to what? I do not know who you are

Xerxes: This... this can not be... you are Testament... my only love, my love who revived me... that is you...

Testament: My name is Testament? No, my name is Kae

Xerxes: ...no...

Kae: Where am I? what's happening?

Xerxes: No... NOOOOOOOOOOOOOOOOOOOOOOO!

[Xerxes throws her head back and a violent screeching is heard, she grabs Kae by the head and clasp her hands around his ears bringing his eyes to

meet hers. She stares deeply into the brown eyes of Kae as if searching for something... after a few seconds she releases him]

Kae: What's wrong with you woman, release me!
Xerxes: He is gone... this can not be... he is gone and this... this frame remains... his soul is gone... but this frame's original soul is alive...
Kae: Why are you talking to yourself?

[Xerxes turns to Kae and gives a shriek so loud the land shakes]

Xerxes: AHHHHHHHHHHHHHHHHHHHHHHHHHHHH!
BEGONE WITH YOU... INSECT, INFECTION... MURDERER...
yes... murder... death... you will die!
Kae: What?! There must be some sort of misunderstanding
Xerxes: ...
Kae: Maybe not...

[Kae quickly gets up and runs as fast as he can in the opposite direction of Xerxes, she just stands there with a cynical smile, she puts her hands together and opens them and gently blows, a cloud of dust flies out, the same color as that butterfly she was playing with earlier. They begin to flow forward and each dust particle starts to grow in size and soon each one becomes a butterfly. They fly towards Kae and they try to attach themselves onto him but he dodges them. Two of them touch each other and violently explode]

Xerxes: You who has taken the soul of my love will never escape me!

[Xerxes opens her wings and dashes into the sky with incredible speed and zips to him in an instant. Grabbing him by the collar of his torn punisher shirt she takes him into the sky and heads out to sea. She tosses him into the water below and heads off in the direction of New York City]

Xerxes: The traitor, the betrayer, I will avenge my love with anger and pain, joy wrapped in agony! AHAHAHAHAHAHAAHAHAAA!

Chapter 61

Choices and decisions

[In the White House...]

General Westing: Sir, the situation has become increasingly urgent

President: Is it Edge?

General Westing: No, with the multitude of attacks that have recently occurred, the incident in LA and the destruction of Central Park in New York, not to mention the disappearance of the spire atop the Empire State ALSO in New York

President: Are you trying to say...

General Westing: Yes sir, we must take action, and soon before there's another attack, or before there's nothing left to defend

President: What do you suggest we do? March into New York and demand Edge to surrender, you seen what he can do, you seen what his friends can do, are you really willing to aggravate him?

General Westing: There's one possible solution

President: And that is?

General Westing: We have nuclear weapons, all we need if your consent

President: My god... do you know what you're asking? You're asking me to allow the destruction of New York

General Westing: These people must be stopped, you of all people should understand the urgency, there are also other concerns...

President: More?

General Westing: Yes sir, the civilian sectors are being over run with religious zealots proclaiming the end of the world is near. If we don't take action then all of this can blow out of hand

President: Do you have any idea what the death rate of innocent people will be if you ask me to do such a thing

General Westing: I don't believe that will be to much of an issue, we've received reports from Cherry Point, a Marine Corps air station in North Carolina of a mysterious object on route towards New York

President: Dear god, are you saying there's gonna be another battle?

General Westing: We don't know yet, but in the worst case scenario of a battle all the civilians will be instructed to leave the city and take refuge as far away as possible, the bombers will then proceeded to target the area for complete annihilation

President: God help us all

General Westing: Sir, according to the churches it's already too late...

[Back in New York City...]

I left Halo to Mei and went on my own way, Saivent had left long ago. I can't really imagine what Halo's feeling. The only thing that's running through my mind is what the possible future holds for us. As I walked through the streets people stared at me with fear and anger, as if it was all my fault, maybe it is, I dunno... but what I do know is that I feel what I am doing is right, for myself that is, hell, if you wanna make an omelet you gotta break some eggs right?

I went back to my old home, the ashes were left untouched, all that remained was the brick skeleton that made up the house. I flew all the way to the top of the third floor and just stood on the ledge for a while. Slowly but surely my old neighbors started to come out and stare at me, but I didn't pay much attention to them, I stayed to myself. The whole world knows about me, knows my face, knows who I am and what I can do. Suddenly someone picks up a rock and throws it at me, it was someone from the church that was 2 blocks away from my house. Then I saw more and more people come from the church's direction and they all had stones in their hands. Now this is an absurd sight, like we were in the medieval times again. They surrounded me and all started to throw stones at me.

[Edge just stands on the ledge of the roof while people throw rocks at him,

they're all stopped by swirls of fire that surround him in a blaze. He stands there with a look of dumb shock, the crowd formed by the church's people start to yell at him but they sound like nothing more than incoherent mumbles]

This is just stupid, alright, I'll amuse them, let them toss all their stones and when there's no more stones I'll see what else they can throw my way.

Edge: Go ahead, throw it all, throw all your damn rocks, and when you fucking run out lets see what else you can pull out your ass to throw at me!

[An hour or so passes and there's a big pile of molten rocks under Edge, and Edge just looks on with absurd amazement at the determination of his attackers]

This is beyond stupid, they actually think they are gonna hurt me this way? Some guy actually took out a gun an unloaded an entire clip at me earlier. I think he went to go buy more bullets or sumtin...

[A giant explosion causes the ground to shake violently, Edge stumbles around a bit and loses his concentration for a second allowing a single rock to hit him in the head, he calls out in pain like a little girl before another ground shaking explosion is heard]

Whoa, where the hell is that from? I looked around for the origin of the sound before witnessing a third explosion of light. It was from Manhattan... man, there's always trouble when I don't need or want it.

Chapter 62

The fury of Xerxes

Halo: Damn, I was talking to Mei tryna understand what the hell happened and then this banshee comes outta nowhere, starts to throw these damn butterflies that explode and then Mei starts to get all weird.

[Xerxes hovers in the air looking at Mei]

Xerxes: You of the Earth, who tried to bind my power...
Mei: I will not allow you to destroy this world as you once sought to do
Xerxes: Destroy... HAHAHAHAHAHAHAHAAHAHHHAA destruction broods creation... my love... destroyed... but so much destruction will be born...
Mei: You are unstable, you are not as you once were
Xerxes: Stability means nothing to me!

[Xerxes shoots out a whip that glows like fire, it wraps around Mei binding her arms and discharging small jolts of electricity that run through her body. Mei's eyes glow bright green but Xerxes takes her and hurls her into a building breaking the whip into particles of light. From underneath Xerxes the ground suddenly breaks open and roots shoot up grabbing the banshee by the ankle, she tries to fly away but the roots grip strengthens. From the rubble Mei walks out with her hair messed up]

Mei: I will not let you befoul this world, so much life has come into existence, too much for you to destroy
Xerxes: Like the way you destroyed my love, my TESTAMENT!

[Xerxes breaks the roots that hold her down with her whip and materializes a butterfly in her hand and sends it towards Mei with a gentle wind blown from her lips]

Mei: Interesting

[The butterfly speeds towards Mei who does nothing but stands there. She holds up her right hand and catches the butterfly which instantly changes color from a fiery hue to a subtle green glow like the emerald on Mei's forehead]

Xerxes: IMPOSSIBLE!
Mei: Hmm I see, you take the creatures of this world and turn them into your slaves, how disgusting
Xerxes: ARGH!

[Xerxes cups her hands together and blows hard, a cloud of dust flies out and each particle takes the form of a butterfly and they are sent speeding towards a pissed off Mei. Mei just holds up her hand which still has the captured butterfly and that cuts the stream of fiery glowing butterflies down the middle. But the two streams now touch everything else blowing it all up. Xerxes sees an opening and quickly dashes in and slams a butterfly into the gut of Mei causing her to fly back from the violent explosion. Halo catches her just in time before she lands]

Halo: Mimi... I mean Mei
Mei: You still care for this girl, because I look like her?
Halo: I... I dunno
Mei: Her death will not be in vain, there are still remnants of her being inside me, left over when this girl passed
Halo: What?
Mei: Fragments of thoughts, memories
Halo: Mimi, I'm so sorry I couldn't protect you...
Mei: She cannot hear you, I'm sorry...
Halo: ...

[Halo gets up and unleashes a bolt of lightning that jets through the air and strikes Xerxes causing a big explosion]

Halo: This fight is mine

Mei: No, let me deal with her first, your powers will not be effective on her

[Xerxes gets up and gives a cynical laugh, she spread her arms open and from her hands multiple whips jet out all over and try to bind Mei and Halo. The two dodge but are eventually caught. Xerxes materializes a butterfly and sends it towards Mei, her eyes glow green and the butterfly she obtained from Xerxes flies straight into the path of Xerxes butterfly in a head on collision. The fiery butterfly is destroyed but the green one is left floating around. It then severs the whips that bind Mei and Halo]

Xerxes: Traitor... enemy...

Mei: This one belongs to me, and shall serve only me

[The ground suddenly cracks open and multiple roots shoot out trying to bind Xerxes but she counters by unleashing her whips. The whips and roots tangle themselves instantly. Xerxes takes to the air but Mei throws a green ball of energy at her and it strikes her in the back. The ball breaks open and reveals itself to be acid, it burns Xerxes badly causing her to land. The moment she touches the ground Mei dashes forward running on the roots then leaping into the air before landing a punch on Xerxes face which sends her down into the ground. Mei picks the banshee up by the throat but she strikes Mei in the gut which causes her to keel over, Xerxes grabs her by the throat this time and tosses her into the air]

Xerxes: FLAME SNIPER!

[Xerxes motions her hands as if she's pulling an arrow back, as she pulls back two whips appear and fold into the shape of a bow, in her arrow hand another whip thins itself out and becomes an arrow with a flaming head. She releases the arrow and sends it speeding towards Mei, but before it connects a bolt of lightning intercepts the arrow. Xerxes grins and with blinding speed takes flight and appears behind Halo]

Halo: *Damn she's fucking fast, but not fast enough!*

[Halo instantly vanishes, to the amazement of Xerxes he's now behind her.

She gives a cynical laugh before dashing off again, now Halo and Xerxes are locked in a battle of speed. Halo clearly is faster but lacks the tactics and experience that Xerxes has. She quickly knocks him to the ground]

Xerxes: Mayflies... motes of dust... this will end as did the life of my love... with agony and destruction yet unheard!

[Xerxes spreads her arms above her head and spins around rapidly, releasing a huge cloud of dust which quickly takes the shape of a cluster of butterflies...]

Chapter 63
FINALLY EDGE!

Mei: This isn't good...

[Mei raises her hands, suddenly tree trunks burst forth from the ground consuming the entire battleground in a forest. The Butterflies come into contact with the timbers and violently explode in a shower of splinter. The explosion produces a concussive force that forces the remaining trees onto their side]

Halo: Damn, what else she has up her sleeves
Mei: I don't know the extent of her power as it is
Halo: Where the hell is Edge when you need him
Mei: Will you assist me?
Halo: I thought you didn't want my help...
Mei: It is apparent now that her power is exceeding my own strength
Halo: No prob, all you gotta do is ask

[Halo discharges a bolt of lightning out of his hand straight at Xerxes, but the banshee lashes out her whip into the path of Halo's Shockwave attack. The whip wraps around the bolt of lightning and they vaporize each other]

Mei: A direct attack with your lightning arcs will not work, she must be attacked physically
Halo: Aright, let's try this then!

[Halo suddenly becomes a blur while standing still, he then instantly vanishes and multiple Halos appear running in different directions encircling Xerxes. She laughs and flaps her wings of energy just enough to lift her feet off the ground by an inch or 2. Mei raises both her hands and surrounds the battlefield with a new forest, this time the trees are twice as tall and thick, and the radius is three times as wide as the original...]

Damn it, I hope what ever is happening isn't gonna get too serious I don't have my cell phone with me so I can't call Hacker. Damn it I wish he could just teleport me.

[The multiple Halos start to attack Xerxes from different directions one at a time, but she elegantly dodges them all. Mei sends the emerald butterfly towards Xerxes and it latches onto her back with its barbed limbs weighing her down enough for Halo to strike her multiple times sending her into the ground. She calls out a shrilling cry and reaches onto her back to rip off the shimmering green insect. Before the butterfly is sent spiraling away, Mei runs in and quickly rams a sphere of acid into the gut of Xerxes. It breaks open spilling its corrosive contents onto the banshee, but unknown to Mei one of Xerxes's butterflies appears from behind and touches the enchanted girl. The explosion sends Mei soaring back while Xerxes doubles over in pain from the acid. Halo stops his attack and sends a bolt of lightning into the ground in front of Xerxes kicking up a small cloud of debris]

Xerxes: Trickery can only be your last hope... to learn is to be weak!

[Xerxes clasps her hands together and the cloud of dust is drawn into her hands, she spins around like a drill and the dust flies out forming butterflies that automatically seek a target. Halo quickly runs to Mei and catches her before she lands...]

Damn it, where's Hacker? He should be seeing all this happening, why isn't he opening a gate? Maybe... does he feel used? I hope that's not it. Damn it I'll fix all of this... I flew as fast as I could and as I drew closer I saw a small forest, this took me by complete surprise, what the hell is going on?

[Edge turns up the intensity of his fires and he jets there as fast as he can... Halo and Mei are standing there in front of Xerxes, pretty beat up but not down or out yet]

Mei: Stand back Halo...

[Mei stands straight up and opens her arms wide, the emerald jewel in her forehead starts to glow. It intensifies before firing a laser like beam of energy out at Xerxes, but banshee dodges it with grace and elegance. Mei takes her arms and closes them and puts her hands together in a two finger praying position]

Mei: Emerald Cascade!

[The space around Mei suddenly distorts slightly, the gem on her forehead abruptly sprays out an abundance of laser like energy that all lock onto Xerxes but she snickers and holds out her hands and from each finger a whip shoots out and she whirls them around forming a barrier that protects her in all directions from the Emerald cascade]

Mei: She is too strong, my power is not what it once was... this world has been polluted by humans... I cannot defeat her
Halo: Damn it Edge, where are you...
Xerxes: I WILL RIP YOU TO SHREDS!

[Xerxes extends her arm and sends a whip lashing out towards Mei, suddenly the canopy of the forest burst into embers and then fire]

Edge: DRAGON FIRE FLAMETHROWER!

[A stream of white hot fire jets down and consumes Xerxes, she screams as her body feels the scorching flame]

Edge: Damn I leave you guys for a while and I come back to this?
Halo: FINALLY you show up, be careful yo, she's strong
Edge: So was Judgment, so was Testament
Halo: This one is different
Edge: Oh yeah? Have you ever known me to back down?

Halo: Just be careful yo, lightning doesn't work on her and her butterflies explode on contact

Edge: Butterflies?

Halo: Yeah, butterflies...

Edge: What else she got?

Halo: A whip, an arrow attack called Flame Sniper and she's fast, almost as fast as I am

Edge: Joy, alrighty my turn then, STEP BACK

[Edge pulls his right handed cutoff glove from his pocket and puts it on snugly]

Halo: Crap...

Chapter 64

Edge's new attack...

[Edge stands his ground firmly and ignites his Hell Fire, Xerxes looks on with her head cocked to the side and a big grin on her face. The hellish fires swirl around Edge, lashing violently as they stirred through the air]

Xerxes: Mine... ALL MINE!

[Without warning, Xerxes snaps her hand out unleashing a whip at Edge, but he simply catches it with his right hand. Small jolts of electricity sizzle outward where the whip meets glove]

Edge: Now that's new
Xerxes: Hmm...

[Xerxes breaks the whip and pulls her arm back and calls forth her Flame Sniper]

When I saw the arrow of fire forming I dashed forward to try and stop her before it finished shaping itself. My speed while in my Hell Fire form was nuttin compared to my Azure Flame, I was just too slow. Xerxes appeared behind me in a blink of an eye with the tip of the arrow pointed to the back of my head. This can't be good, I can't dodge at this distance and I dunno what damage that attack can do, we were at a stand still.

[Xerxes doesn't move and neither does Edge. The two just stay there motionless while Mei and Halo stand back contemplating what to do]

Edge: ...
Xerxes: ...

[Suddenly as Edge tries to dash side ways Xerxes quickly lets go of the arrow before Edge even gets an inch away. The explosion is violent and extreme, all the trees are felled. Edge is sent skidding on the pavement before he manages to stop himself by digging his gloved hand into the ground ripping it up. Xerxes quickly sends out a whip that wraps itself around Edges left ankle and she swings him around like a toy hurling him into the side of a tree trunk. The whip breaks off and before Edge can recover she opens her palm and blows into it sending out a cloud of butterflies. Mei sees the attack and quickly plunges her right foot into the ground causing a wall of rock to rise in front Edge protecting him from the butterflies' kamikaze attack]

Damn, I can't even touch her as I am, she's not as fast as Halo but she's a hell of a lot more vicious and intense. Mei's rock wall protected me from that attack, but I can't fight this way, maybe now it's a good chance to try out that new technique.

[Flashback - Hacker and Edge are sitting in the balcony area at South Street Seaport, it's night and the balcony is bathed in the warm colors of the incandescent street lights]

Edge: Hey check this out, I been messing around and I think I came up with a new attack
Hacker: A new attack?
Edge: Yeah remember when we sparred and I couldn't attack you head on and instead I just raised the heat around me so you couldn't touch me?
Hacker: ...don't remind me...
Edge: Hahhahaaha yeah, exactly, anyway, I figure maybe I can do sumtin like that with my flamethrower
Hacker: What like... explode your flamethrower outward?

Edge: Well when I was fighting Testament I heard this weird voice in my head saying the name "Azurath"

Hacker: Azure wrath... blue rage?

Edge: I guess if you cut it into two words... but yeah, anyway, with the Azurath I was able draw energy in from the surrounding, like I could actually feel the life energy from plants and animals drawing into me

Hacker: Oh so that's what you were doing

Edge: ...you really like sitting back and watching the action don't you...

Hacker: (sips his soda) I can't help it if I'm not a fighter

Edge: (sigh) anyway, so I tried to do the same with my Hell Fire, but low and behold the fire charges itself

Hacker: And...

Edge: And I can compress it

Hacker: Compress it? Like concentrate it?

Edge: Exactly yeah

Hacker: Then what happens?

Edge: (in a Japanese accent) biga boom...

Hacker: How powerful is it?

Edge: I dunno, I never really unleashed it... cuz I dunno how strong it will be or what it will do

[Edge holds both his hands up and in the space between it he ignites a fire that slowly starts to expand but suddenly it's forced inward on itself as if something was sucking it in. Then Edge strains a bit and increases the intensity of the fire in the center of his hands, it expands doubling in size and once again it collapses in on itself, this continues another five times, and by the fifth the sphere resembles an orb of dense plasma. Hacker leans back away from the intensity of the heat the orb radiates]

Hacker: Oh shit, that's intense...

Edge: Yeah I know

Hacker: And that doesn't burn?

Edge: Nope, I don't even feel it... BUT I do feel the pressure it exerts, like it's tryna... pop or sumtin

Hacker: Well pop it away from here, I don't feel like being fried, and as it is I'm already feeling the burn

Edge: Hhahahaah yeah, the burn...

[Present day - Xerxes slices the rock wall down with her whip, Edge quickly jumps into the air, up and over Xerxes landing beside Mei and Halo]

Edge: I want you guys to listen to me carefully, I'm gonna try sumtin, I don't even know how this is gonna turn out, but I want you guys as far away as possible, this can definitely hurt you if you get caught up in it...
Halo: Edge, whatcha up to...
Mei: He means what he says, I sense he is already gathering up a large amount of energy... your attack will level this area
Edge: Maybe, maybe not... we'll have to see, but you two have to get as far away from here as you can
Halo: Alright, c'mon Mei

[Mei nods her head and back flips right into the ground, she effortlessly disappears into the depths below]

Edge: (with a disturbed look on his face) ok, yeah... that's freaky
Halo: Yeah...

[Halo disappears in a bolt of lightning]

Edge: Time to play
Xerxes: HAHAHAHAHAHAHHAHAAHAAAHHAHAA

Chapter 65

The Firestorm unleashed

I rushed at her to try and lure her in, my goal was to get her to willingly get close enough to me so I can unleash the new attack...

[Edge holds up his right hand and it ignites into a rage of fire. He runs towards Xerxes who jumps back and sends her whip out at him. Edge manages to catch it with his left hand and he pulls her towards him and as she nears he sends out his Dragon Fire Flamethrower attack, Xerxes breaks the whip and folds her wings of energy around herself and it just manages to keep her safe as the jet of fire is cut down the middle by her wings. Before the attack ends Edge jumps into the air and with his right hand still ablaze, hits her with his Strike Fist attack, Xerxes is sent back...]

Good if I can weaken her then I can land my attack with more accuracy.

[Edge charges up by increasing the intensity of his fire and puts his hands together, in the empty space between his palms he starts to compress a small flame over and over again each time doubling it. Edge is just barely able to keep the sphere of plasma like energy from releasing itself, the pressure it exerts is clearly too much for Edge to keep holding onto. Xerxes gets up and in less then a second appears in front of Edge grabbing his hands]

Xerxes: What have we here... a shiny ball...

Edge: To late...
Xerxes: Never to late...
Edge: FIRESTORM!

[The sphere of plasma like energy that Edge was collecting suddenly burst. The force expands outward at a geometric rate, the entire forest is instantly leveled and incinerated. Edge holds onto Xerxes arms as she is thrown back by the force to keep her in the epicenter of destruction...]

God damn, what the hell did I do? When I released the energy it violently expanded outward and as if time slowed down. I could see everything incinerate and burn up from stable matter to cinders of ash. Reality rippled from the intensity of the heat, everything glowed brilliantly with the color of molten steel and sunk downward from the pull of gravity. Xerxes was forced back and I could see her wings of light and energy burn off and disintegrate into embers of sparks. She screamed violently and fiercely as the heat burned and scorched her flesh. Unlike most attacks this was not over in seconds, this attack drew on for what seemed like forever. As far as I could see at the time, everything was consumed by fire nuttin was left unburnt, nothing was spared... there was no mushroom cloud like Hiroshima, there was no radiation, all there was, was fire, heat, and incinerated mater. Ashes floated in the air...

[Edge stands straight up but stumbles a bit, everything within a five block radius is destroyed and consumed by flames, Xerxes lays on the floor catatonic. Moments later the ground burst forth to reveal Mei and from the sky comes Halo]

Edge: Hey guys
Halo: What the fuck did you do...?
Edge: Stopped Xerxes?
Halo: Yeah and almost destroyed Manhattan
Mei: Your power is returning to you
Edge: Returning to me?
Mei: During The Great War your power was...
Xerxes: (moans) flies... motes of dust...
Edge: Guess she still has some fight left in her
Mei: She has been weakened by your attack, she can be defeated now

Halo: What are we waiting for then
Mei: Agreed
Edge: Let's do this...
Xerxes: You won't...

[Halo holds out his hand and sends out a bolt of lightning that hits Xerxes and pins her to the side of a crooked structural beam. Mei sinks her right foot into the ground and vines burst from below and bind her to the beam]

Edge: I guess it's my turn...
Xerxes: AHHHHHHHHHHHHHHHHHHHHHHHHHHHHHHH

[Edge walks up to Xerxes and as she screams a shrill cry Edge holds up his hand and extinguishes his Hell Fire, the Azure Flame slowly ignites into a blaze and he places his hand on her chest]

Edge: It ends now
Xerxes: IT WILL NEVER END!

[The flames suddenly ignite into a full blaze that consumes Xerxes from head to toe, the vines that bind her slowly begin to die and turn to dust right before everyone's eyes, and slowly following the vines death is Xerxes demise, her skin turns black like decaying flesh and her eyeballs collapse. It's as if all the life is being drained from her body but in fact her life force is consumed by the Azure Flame, burning off like sheets of paper. Xerxes body was now a dried up mummified corpse, as it was when Testament found her]

Halo: What about that necklace?
Mei: It is useless now, its purpose was to contain her soul, separate from her body, but now that her soul is destroyed...
Halo: And what about you? Where you gonna go?
Mei: ...I will leave this body, and return to the earth where I belong
Halo: And Mimi?
Mei: She is where she should be
Edge: I'll leave you two...

[Five jets fly overhead and release a cloud of smoke that covers the battlefield]

Halo: What's going on?
Mei: (with a confused look) I have no idea...

[Another jet flies towards the group from the down town area and releases a single missile]

Edge: Oh shit...

Chapter 66

Countdown to destruction

[In the White House an hour before the fight with Xerxes...]

President: No we're not launching a nuke into New York City
General Westing: But sir...
President: This is not up for discussion there has to be another way

[The door to the room burst open and with no resistance from the secret service a man steps through. He is dressed in all black with military insignias sown throughout his uniform, his hair pitch black and heavily gelled back, he bares a firearm on a holster that's strapped across his chest]

Man in Black: President, General, I am War Commandant Stavrite, I am assuming immediate control over all military branches beginning... now, General please leave.
General Westing: Under whose order?
War Commandant: By the command of the DIE
President: DIE?
General Westing: ...

[The General walks out with little hesitation]

War Commandant: DIE is a military branch unknown to all personnel within congress and all ruling houses. We are to immediately assume control once the situation is beyond the hands of... the lower branches.

Beginning now and until the situation is resolved you are relived of all duty and will be transported to a safe location
President: This is insanity, I've never heard of such an organization

[Armed soldiers walk through the door]

War Commandant: Please Mr. President if you'll follow them you and your family will be kept safe
President: This is outrageous!

[The president gets out of his seat and is escorted out by the armed soldiers, the War Commandant picks up the phone...]

War Commandant: This is War Commandant Stavrite, connect me directly to DIE...
Operator: Yes sir
War Commandant: Captain Treis, begin the decimation of Manhattan, leave, nothing and no one alive
Captain Treis: Yes sir, we will begin immediately
War Commandant: Operator connect me to all the highest commanding officers within the United States military, one way audio only
Operator: Yes sir... your connected sir
War Commandant: Attention all commanding officers of your respected branches, by now you should have received an encrypted transmission of the highest authorization requirement, access the file and follow the instructions, any insubordination will be dealt with accordingly, you are to relay your orders to your subordinates and immediately mobilize, we are now under a state of martial law.

[The War Commandant leaves the office and gets into a helicopter that takes him to an unidentified location. He exits and heads into a facility and gets on an elevator which brings him a few stops down. It exits into a room with a person strapped to a table with his arms and legs spread apart]

War Commandant: Are we comfortable? You know you and your friends have caused a lot of trouble, the entire nation is in a state panic, in fact the entire world has been turned upside down. Don't bother struggling, your powers won't work here, we know how they work, we might not be able to "fix" it but we can suppress it for the time being.

[The War Commandant points to a small pillar with a figure attached via cables that stands behind him. The figure is humanoid in shape but its skin is white as milk and shines like polished plastic, its face has no nose or mouth, just eyes that do not blink, eyes as black as midnight, its limbs were absent and in their place were stumps that had an assortment of wires coming out, only the head and torso were kept...]

War Commandant: See that? Know what it is? It's a genetically engineered human with the power to suppress other powers. It was quite a lucky find for us, unfortunately the original subject did not survive testing, but instead we managed to clone him and modify him... there are so many more out there with unique abilities like you, and we can't just let you run rampant like Edge and Halo are doing. You... you possess a very desirable gift, if you help us you'll find yourself in a much more favorable position

[The War Commandant pushes a button that tilts the table upright]

War Commandant: What do you say? Help us stop Edge and you can save yourself and your entire race from extinction

[A monitor blinks on and shows 6 jets in mid flight]

War Commandant: Know what that is? A nuke powerful enough to level half of Manhattan, they're going to destroy New York City, you can stop it, kill Edge

[The person on the table drops his head down to look away from the monitor]

Hacker: You better pray that nuke kills Edge because if it doesn't he's gonna find you and send you to hell personally...

Chapter 67

The massacre begins

The jets flew over head and released this cloud of... sumtin, it looked like smoke. Then from way farther down I could see another jet coming, it released a missile, but it wasn't a regular missile, it was way too big... it could only be one thing.

Edge: Damn it Halo get us the FUCK OUTTA HERE!

[Halo nods and grabs a hold of Edge who grabs onto Mei and he tries to bolt them out but noting happens]

Halo: The hell, I can't...
Edge: What ya mean you can't?!
Halo: I can't get a connection!
Mei: It must have been the cloud of smoke they released, it is blocking the ionic charge required
Halo: Can't you fly us outta here?
Edge: I can but not fast enough, that a fucking nuke!
Halo: Oh shit...
Mei: There is nothing I can do

Crap, there has to be sumtin I can do... I can't push it away... I can blow it up though... damn it to hell, where the fuck is Hacker when you need him the most? There's only one thing I can do...

Edge: Mei, erect a wall with the strongest material you can get and protect Halo, I'm gonna try and destroy it before it reaches us...
Halo: What's gonna happen to you?
Edge: I dunno, I'll be fine... now get outta here...

[Mei raises her hands and a dome like structure erects around her and Halo]

I stood my ground and ignited my flames, I called forth all the strength I had and released it in a wave of rippling heat, it expanded outward and filled the area with a haze of fire...

[Edge's pupils start to fade away and his eyes are consumed by a white blaze...]

I felt my spirit blaze with a force I've never felt before. I had complete determination in me to keep my friends safe and to destroy that nuke. I heard a calling deep inside of me, a familiar calling... I was never able to understand it, it never spoke to me, but this time it beckoned at me, pulled on me, begged me to listen to it and this time I could not ignore it. It felt like a force tryna break free, it felt like a rage of anger looking for freedom, so I did the only thing I could do, I let it out.

[Edge throws his head back and calls out]

Edge: COME OUT!

[The fires that surrounded Edge suddenly increase in volume and swirls around at increasing speeds, the sharp calling Edge hears in his head suddenly becomes audible...]

Halo: What the hell is he doing outside? I wanna see so I told Mei to open a small hole in the dome, and I saw some shit I shouldn't have saw.

[The fires swirl upwards and suddenly out burst a pair of fiery wings from the inferno... followed by a head of a bird, its beak was sharp and hooked like an eagles and its eye glowed like Edges, it was a Phoenix...]

I heard it, it called out to me and I listened... it wanted out and I let it out. It was my spirit calling, and it told me its name... its name was Fenix.

[The fire bird was about a quarter of the Empire State in size. It takes flight and in doing so finishes demolishing any building that wasn't already destroyed by Edge's Firestorm attack. It instinctively flies towards the incoming missile and with a single wing stroke knocks it off course, sending it tumbling upward into the sky before flying back to Edge, Halo and Mei, Fenix lands and wraps its wings around the three. The missile was no longer on a direct route to the group but still in danger of exploding... and as programmed the missile detonated... The warhead's explosion sends out a shockwave that should have wiped out everything in sight but Fenix forcefully opens its wings redirecting the majority of the shockwave in the opposite direction towards Staten Island. Reality ripples from the intensity of the heat and all evidence of the missile and its explosion is sent southbound. The fire bird looks up to the sky breaking apart into particles of embers that blow away and dim down. All of downtown Manhattan is destroyed, midtown and upwards suffered heavily from the force of the shockwave and surrounding boroughs suffered as well, anything left standing were just structural support beams from sky scrapers and buildings...]

Halo: *Edge just stood there with his fires going crazy around him, the danger seemed over for now. When the missile exploded a bright light filled the area and Mei closed the small hole, then everything went silent, and when she dropped the dome that's all I saw... just Edge. The phoenix was gone, the fires around Edge cooled enough for me to get near him.*

[Halo begins to slowly walk towards Edge]

Fenix had left already, but I know its presence now, I know what the force of its power is like. I slowly let the fires dim down and disperse, the only remnants that remained is the dieing glow of molten metal...

Halo: Edge...
Edge: (panting) yeah?
Halo: What are you...?

Edge: Hahahaahhaha, I'm a monster...

Halo: We gotta get outta here

Edge: I dunno where Hacker is, try calling him

Halo: How? Any sorta cell phone network is long gone

Edge: Damn, Mei, can you stick around? We could use your help

Mei: My help is needed right now regardless, the nuclear material left behind has tainted this area, I must rid it before I do anything else

Edge: Alright then, we need to go to Hacker's, we'll meet up later is that alright?

Mei: That is the best course of action

Chapter 68

Rescue Hacker!

Me and Halo arrived at Hacker's place on foot to find it damaged by the shockwave, but everything inside was gone, there was no one around at all, the streets had been empty the entire way up to his place. The computers were all gone, everything... was he mad at us? Did he feel like we were using him? What the hell is going on damn it... sumtin was definitely wrong.

Edge: Ok look I need to go get my cell phone, make a few calls, you... go do... whatever...
Halo: ...that's the worst command you ever given
Edge: (leaps into the air) it's not a command, it's a suggestion!

[Edge takes flight on route back to his studio apartment]

It wasn't until I took flight that I realized the devastation that nuke attack caused. New Jersey, Queens, Brooklyn... parts of those boroughs were destroyed. My home was destroyed too... I don't like what's going on, were they really willing to sacrifice the city? And more importantly was it aimed for me or Xerxes? or maybe all of us... Hacker, where are you...

[Edge lands in a pile of ruble that use to be his home...]

Damn I can't stay long, I think the radiation is getting to me already,

I didn't even get the chance to rest after that battle damn it, why does everything happen so fast...

[*Before Edge leaps back into the air he notices a little blinking light on the ground*]

Wow... of all improbabilities...

[*Edge picks up his cell phone and removes the sim card*]

This is the only thing I should take since everything else is radioactive.

[*With that, Edge heads back to Hacker's place to find that Halo is napping on the couch. Edge sits down besides him and turns on the TV not expecting anything to show up, after channel surfing for a while he manages to come across a news report*]

News reporter: THE ENTIRE NATION IS IN A STATE OF MARTIAL LAW THIS IS A WARNING TO ALL CITIZENS, GO HOME AND STAY IN...

[*The news reporter is shot dead by soldiers. Edge's face becomes apathetic and his eyes slowly pull themselves shut, he too has fallen asleep...*]

I was jerked awake by sumtin, I guess it was my dream, I saw Hacker being killed in a massive explosion. I must've fallen asleep at some point, I guess I was more tired than I expected. It's already beginning, they plan on wiping us out, but how? How are they gonna be able to tell... that's it I need to talk to Saivent.

[*And as he thinks that, Saivent appears in the other room but is looking out of the window, Edge gets off the couch and heads over. He comes up besides Saivent and looks out the window with him*]

Edge: The hell is going on... how the fuck did things end up like this...
Saivent: I dunno, it all started off with Judgment's escape and then it led to one event after another

Edge: Yeah, that's about it... I need to know sumtin, they have Hacker don't they...?

Saivent: ...

Edge: (angrily grabs Saivent) WHERE IS HE!?

Saivent: He's in a holding cell, not too far...

Edge: Can you get me there?

Saivent: ...no...

Edge: Can't or won't...

Saivent: Can't...

Edge: Why not?

Saivent: I'm not even supposed to be talking to you. I wasn't even supposed to ask you that favor. I'm supposed to stand back and let history write itself out, but I can't... I've already changed everything when I asked you that favor... I changed the future

Edge: So what the hell was supposed to happen then?

Saivent: It doesn't matter now, that future will never come into existence...

Edge: ...where is Hacker...

Saivent: Go south, to Washington DC and head into the Pentagon, I'm not sure where but there's a branch called DIE, it's a secret branch so no one knows about it you'll have to find it on your own, there will be a hidden elevator that leads below ground a few stories, from there it will lead you into some corridors, but knowing you, you'll just blast a hole straight through. You'll find Hacker at the end of one of those corridors...

I went outside and broke into the neighbor's house, no surprise, it was empty. I looked around for a cell phone and found one on a desk, the battery was full so I slipped out the old sim card and put mine in.

[Edge quickly dashes outside and calls to Halo, in mere moments he wakes up and rushes outside]

Edge: Look, you don't have to come with me but I need some help, I need to rescue Hacker... he's being held captive...

Halo: How you know?

Edge: Saivent told me, and to make matters worse the entire nation is in a state of martial law, they have orders to hunt people like us down and kill us on sight

Halo: I'm in dude...

Edge: You sure? We need to go to the pentagon

Halo: Yeah I'm sure, he's my friend too you know

[The ground rumbles a bit and Mei burst out from the pavement in the streets]

Mei: It is done...

Edge: Alright Mei, I need you to do me a favor, I can't let any more people die, especially innocent ones cuz they are who they are. I have a few friends, they are in the boroughs... I think... I hope... can you gather them and with your powers create a stronghold or a shelter of some sort? We need a place of safety

Mei: I can do as you wish

[Saivent appears behind Mei]

Saivent: The city is empty, all humans are gone, except the homeless and stragglers

Edge: ...alright, Mei, do you have the power to do what I asked?

Mei: I may, and if I do not...

[She looks towards Saivent]

Mei: I will simply call in some favors

Saivent: How bothersome

I told them who they needed to get and without hesitation Mei was on her way, Halo bolted us into the sky and in about 15 or so minutes got us to the White House, from there we go on foot to remain as inconspicuous as possible...

[Halo and Edge land a few blocks away from the White House. The entire city is in a state of panic, people are running around screaming and soldiers are patrolling shooting anyone that gets in their way]

Damn, there are people everywhere running around as if it was the end of the world. To my left there are bodies on the floor not moving and bleeding... to their right is the soldier that shot them. Me and Halo made our way as fast as we could to the pentagon, but that place was heavily guarded with military personnel at each entrance and all throughout the perimeter... the only way we could really get in is by complete brute force, unless we were able to create a distraction, that way we can get in without being seen, and even then how are we supposed to find the way that leads to Hacker...

[Edge's cell phone rings...]

Edge: Hello?
Raven: Hello? It's me Raven
Edge: Yeah, sups?
Raven: I just called to see what you're doing
Edge: Yeah, right now is not the best time to be calling
Raven: I know, I know, I got this green lady in front of me and she said that you told her to come get me?
Edge: Yeah, that's Mei, in case you haven't noticed the nation has been put into martial law, your not safe any more and neither is your family, get them outta the city, and you have to stay away from them, they are after people like us, if you stay with them you'll only get them hurt...
Raven: I see, I'll go then... where are you right now?
Edge: I'm in Washington DC just outside the pentagon
Raven: What the heck are you doing over there?
Edge: They kidnapped Hacker and I gotta rescue him
Raven: Wait hold up...
Edge: What?

[Raven tells Mei to continue what she was doing and she does not argue, he runs upstairs to his room and turns his computer on. When it is fully booted he touches the computer and is instantly drawn in]

Halo: What happened?
Edge: I dunno, he just hung up
Halo: ...

Moments later I hear Raven calling to me, I turn around in complete amazement and am wondering how much more of a curve ball life can throw at me...

Raven: Yo what's up?
Edge: (angrily) WHAT THE FUCK!?
Halo: Yo how the hell did you get here so fast?

[Raven holds up both his hands and an arc of electricity jumps the gap like a tesla coil. A jolt of electricity quickly jumps from Halo's hands into the ground]

Edge: (hits Raven over the head) idiot! You coulda told us that sooner and saved us a shit load of trouble!
Raven: Sorry man, so what's going on?
Edge: Hacker, he's in there somewhere and we dunno where he is, so we're tryna figure out how to get him out as quickly as possible
Raven: That's all? Alright hold on

[Raven gets up and goes to the nearest payphone and zaps into the circuits by simply touching the phone. Not more then two minutes pass and he reappears]

Raven: Ok, I found him
Edge: ...

Chapter 69

Out of Character...

Edge: You know, anything else you can do you should just tell us right now to save us the trouble

Raven: Hold up man, there's sumtin strange going on, I can't get close to him without feeling like I'm losing my power, like I can't control it anymore

Edge: What ya mean?

Raven: Like I can't use or feel my powers

Halo: That's probably why he hasn't gotten himself out...

Edge: That's true, you and Hacker are both power and elemental users, but me and Halo...

Raven: What you mean?

Halo: That we won't be affected, right?

Halo and Raven started to bicker for a while over who had cooler powers, I just sat back and watched the childish stupidity unfold. For a good three minutes this kept up, then I had to step in and remind them of the situation we were in. When they finally stopped Raven explained to me where he was and the best way to get there, in the end we agreed that a full on assault with blunt force would take them by surprise and that would allow us the time we needed.

Edge: Alright let's do this shit, Halo, go create the diversion

Halo: (nods) k

[Halo walks up to the first line of guards who immediately open fire on

him without warning. He instantly uses his speed and multiple clones appear out of thin air, the soldiers all rush to him and open fire with everything they have but Halo dodges them all without ever being hit]

While Halo lured the guards away I took flight into the sky and put my glove on. The fire ignited and swirled around me and I focused all the strength I had into my right hand. I plunged downward towards the ground at break neck speeds with my fist extended and the fire violently ripping past me. As I drew closer Halo and Raven both took cover. My fist sunk deep into the roof of the pentagon instantly leveling the entire impact zone as the shockwave from the impact expanded outward. Raven quickly comes up besides the rubble before the dust even settles down and he puts his hand onto the ground. Arcs of purple electricity shot outward and the rubble quickly starts to reshape itself into a wall that surrounds the perimeter, Halo bolts in through the top and joins me and Raven. Without hesitation Raven once again puts his hands onto the ground and quickly creates a staircase by reshaping the material around him. The staircase descends to the corridor that leads to Hacker. Halo took the lead while Raven traveled through the electric conduits, I ended up igniting my Azure Flame and running as fast as I could down what seemed like a mile long path. Finally we reached Hacker...

[Halo makes it to the end of the tunnel first and is met with a giant door, Edge comes in second and stands with Halo as Raven burst through the electric conduit and tumbles to the floor]

Edge: Yo what's wrong?
Raven: My powers don't wanna work anymore, I dunno why
Halo: Well mine still do
Edge: Mine too...
Halo: SHOCKWAVE!
Edge: STRIKE FIST!

[Both Edge and Halo strike the door and smash it down revealing a laboratory of scared scientist that surround a person strapped to a table in the center of the room, it's Hacker]

Edge: HACKER!

War Commandant: Edge, I see you come for your friend, but if I were you I'd stay where you are unless you want to see your friend dead
Edge: Who are you and what'd you want with him
War Commandant: I am War Commandant Celsius Stavrite, I want his powers of course, the power to stop you and everyone like you
Edge: The hell...
War Commandant: Your kind is dangerous, look at what you've done to the world already
Edge: ...so what did you do, how did you manage to keep him here
War Commandant: I was hoping you could answer that for me, how is it YOU still have your powers when you're THIS close
Edge: Sometimes things are beyond your understanding
War Commandant: Is that...

[Without warning Halo blasts the War Commandant with a bolt of lightning before dashing off in a flash to Hacker, the scientist all scream in horror and flee for their lives. One of them presses a button that sets off an alarm]

Edge: Dude, that was so outta character...
Halo: Um, Brooklyn?

Someone pressed the alarm button and then all hell broke loose, the War Commandant was down, but I didn't go to see if he was dead or not, after a shot like that he should be more then dead.

Halo was unable to break Hacker free so I grabbed the shackles that held him down and I told him to hold still. I heated them up and broke them off once they were soft enough to be pulled apart. Hacker was now free...

Hacker: (in a weak voice) about time
Edge: Can you get us outta here?
Hacker: No, my powers don't work with that thing suppressing them
Edge: What thing?
Halo: I think he means this thing...

Halo pointed out this white figure that was connected to a series of wires and cords. It was held in a tomb like structure of some kind, exposing only its upper body and stumps where limbs use to be.

Raven: What is that thing?

Hacker: It's a human clone

Edge: You sure?

Hacker: It use to be one of us, with a power, but these people found him and used him to create these, these things...

Raven: But what does it do?

Hacker: You don't pay attention do you? This thing has the power to suppress our powers

Raven: Then how come Edge and Halo aren't affected by it?

Edge: Cuz me and Halo are not really what you are, your powers are directly related to your blood imbalance. That's why you can tap into certain abilities

Hacker: But Edge is different, aren't you Edge...

Edge: Yeah, my powers come directly from my spirit, and so does yours, Halo...

Halo: Mine to?

Edge: When I brought you back I changed you, you're like me now

Halo: That... that's cool

Hacker: Look this little science lesson is fun and all but we need to get the hell outta here before this place self destructs or sumtin

Edge: Alright

[Edge holds his hand out and blasts the white object with a stream of fire that disintegrates it into ashes]

Hacker: Let's get the hell outta here...

[Hacker opens a gate back to New York City]

We landed in what was left of Battery Park, a place we were all familiar with, a place we can... could call home, but when I turned around to see the flattened city I saw sumtin that clearly did not belong there... an enormous tower, Mei...

[Back in the lab, Stavrite gets up and smiles...]

Chapter 70

The Stronghold and the light of hope

The stronghold seemed like it was made of several towering pillars of semi iridescent pearl colored crystals that leaned against a main pillar, towards the top was a section where multiple smaller crystals clumped together in a mass, and on the very top was a spire. Mei came out from the main entrance along with Apollo, they and Raven took Hacker inside. I stayed out front with Halo to just look at the shear size of the structure, there was nuttin that big in the city, not anymore anyway. As tall as the Empire State if not more so, in fact I'm pretty sure it was much taller. The stronghold was located either on top of or near the Wall Street area, frankly I wasn't too sure since I never go to those areas, but it was within walking distance of Battery Park, what's left of it anyway. Halo enjoyed himself by bolting to the top and looked around the city. I followed him by flying up, but the view was less than comforting, New York was pretty torn up. It was night by now, the fight with Xerxes and the whole nuke shit took the whole afternoon and went into the night. Then the whole situation with Hacker took most of the day immediately after. I managed to rescue Hacker with ungodly speed though when you think about it.

I hope the temperature cools down soon, the heat is really starting to get to me... Halo and I headed inside shortly after. The inside of the stronghold was made up of corridors and chambers, rooms and more rooms, it was as if it was meant to house an army and then some. Mei took me to the highest point and it was a room that had a 360 degree field of view of the city. This was supposed to be the command center, it was stationed within the spire...

Edge: So you know...

Mei: The extermination has already begun, I can feel the lives of this world being terminated

Edge: We gotta do sumtin...

Mei: What is there to do...?

Edge: Here, we can bring as many of them as we can here. The walls of this place...

Mei: Made of minerals stronger than diamonds

Edge: ...wow, that's... a lot more than I expected, but you see, this place can withstand attacks right?

Mei: That is its purpose

Edge: Will it... will it be destroyed if you're gone?

Mei: No, my time here is not too short, but I won't be able to exist for that much more, when I am gone, this fortress will remain as a defense for everyone's sake

Edge: And how much time do you have left?

Mei: That I do not know

Edge: We need to get everyone here, but I dunno how...

[Hacker walks in, he is rested up but not entirely at 100%...]

Hacker: A signal, we need to signal them here, let them know

Edge: How do we do it?

Hacker: A beacon of some sort, but first we need some stuff, we need to let everyone know and for that I need to get my equipment, but those assholes destroyed everything...

Edge: Could you do it with new stuff?

Hacker: Yes, but give me a bit to rest, I don't have the power right now

Mei: Take this...

[Mei touches her chest and a blue light shines from beneath her skin, it slowly pushes its way out and drops into her hands]

Edge: What is that?

Mei: This will be your beacon, your light of hope, to bring forth all who are being hunted

Edge: Where do I put it?

Mei: The top, it will shine brightly and all will know its meaning

Edge: And what about the bad guys?

Mei: We are here, we can defend this place if need be, also, only the ones who seek refuge will be able to see its light, anyone who wishes us harm will be blind to it

Edge: (nods) alright...

I flew to the top and sure enough there was a small space to house the lil blue gem. When I placed it down a forceful light erupted from the gem and pushed me back a bit, the light was so intense I had to close my eyes and move away to a safe distance to see what was going on. Like a sword piercing the heavens at night, the ray of light shined brightly as it reached into the sky. From the distance I could see the faint glow of the sun, morning was on its way, and it's been one hell of a long night. Even though I'm tired, I haven't felt a great need to rest yet, usually by now after a battle like that with Xerxes I'd be passed the fuck out, but no... I'm not alone anymore in this, I feel myself drawing from the strength of Fenix... ah fuck this I'm gonna go to sleep.

[Edge heads into one of the rooms]

Even though everything is made from a crystal like substance it was really comfortable, someone had taken the time to furnish it with blankets at least. The bed was a flat elevated stone, the base was polished smooth like marble and it had a slight warmth to it while still cool enough for the summer heat.

I probably was asleep for a handful of hours at best before I heard a knocking, it was Raven.

Raven: YO MAN COME OUTSIDE!

Edge: Wha... why? What's going on?

Raven: Just come out and you'll see!

When I stepped to the window I saw about twenty or so people all gathered by the front entrance, Halo and Mei were there already treating the injured. I rushed down to ground level to see what was happening. A guy named Dak stepped forward to greet me.

Dak: Howdy, um... my name is Dak. I didn't know what else to do or where else to go. I saw your broadcast on the internet a while back and so I came here to find you

Edge: Where did you come from?

Dak: I came from North Carolina, everyone I know is gone or turned their backs on me, so I didn't know where else to turn

Edge: What happened to you guys?

Dak: We were attacked, my family is gone, even some of my friends. But let me ask something. What is this place and what's going on here?

Edge: This is a stronghold, it's the last safe haven for people like us

[Hacker walks out from the back]

Hacker: The people who attacked you were soldiers following government orders, people like us are being exterminated

Dak: The government? Why would the government do something so horrible...?

Edge: Cuz people like us are "dangerous" humans don't understand us, and they fear what they don't understand

Hacker: Well that's not too surprising, look what happens every time you get into a fight, half the city is blown to bits...

Edge: That's beyond the point, I really don't have a choice

Dak: Isn't there another way though? Without harming other people? More like, why can't we just live in peace, if they left us alone then everything would be fine

Edge: And what about those people behind you? I take it they're in the same situation

Dak: We found each other along the way. Figured it'd be easier if we were together than apart. Some of them I've known for a while and others I only just met not so long ago

Edge: I see, alright, the last most important question, what can you "do"

[Dak holds up his hand and tiny sparks of light start to gather and collect into a hand ball sized orb that spirals around with electricity that reaches out]

Chapter 71

Nostalgia is an old friend

I let Halo deal with Dak, I took everyone else into the stronghold and found them all rooms. Each room was able to hold about 4 people and with plenty of free space to move around too so I don't think anyone will feel cramped. Mei tended to the injured with incredible ease, with just a touch their wounds were healed almost instantly, but I could tell that she was wearing herself out.

Edge: You alright?
Mei: I am fine
Edge: You look really out of it
Mei: My energy is growing weaker
Edge: Is there anything I can do? Like, get you some... water or sumtin
Mei: No, I'm not meant to exist in this corporeal form, this was meant to be a temporary existence, but with the events that have transpired I will try to remain as long as I can to be of as much use as I can
Edge: Your color...

When I first met her she had a vibrant green glow around her, green hair green eyes, just green everything, but now her skin was much darker in color and the green glow is slowly but surely becoming a yellow glow...

Mei: "Nature's first green is gold, her hardest hue to hold. Her early leaf's a flower, but only so an hour. Then leaf subsides to leaf. So Eden sank to grief, so dawn goes down to day. Nothing gold can stay."

269

Edge: Robert Frost, I remember hearing that when I watched that movie, The Outsiders, it was a good movie, and book
Mei: (smiles)
Edge: If I recall, I've never seen you gold
Mei: That poem is only part way true
Edge: Oh?
Mei: When green subsides to cold, thus returned to gold, but only so an hour
Edge: (nods) thanks for helping us out
Mei: My task is far from done, as is yours
Edge: I know, I know...

I left Mei to let her rest. I took some time off for myself and just walked around, I made my way to Battery Park City and I just looked out to New Jersey. The weather was definitely starting to get cold and at this time of year that was abnormal, usually it would still be as hot as 90F if not hotter. Mei doesn't have much time left, I didn't know where things could possibly end up going from here on out. It all felt like there was so much more to all this, that this is nuttin more than just a prequel to sumtin so much more, this adventure is far from over...

[*A stranger appears behind Edge. He is as tall as Halo but much more muscular, he had a Caucasian complexion but there was something off, just enough to make one question his racial origin*]

Stranger: Usually nostalgia is caused by a once familiar memory... how's your fire?

[*Edge turns around slowly and it takes him a second to recognize the person that stands before him, but when he does he is totally shocked*]

Edge: Oh shit I know you, yeah... talk about familiar memories
Stranger: So you finally made sumtin outta yourself you bum
Edge: Yeah, I did... and you?
Stranger: Nuttin much, just training
Edge: Training for what?
Stranger: To control the power within
Edge: Power within?

Stranger: Yes, just like you

[Edge holds out his right hand and a small fire envelopes it]

Edge: Like me?

[The stranger brings his right hand to his mouth and blows into it, enveloping it in fire as well]

Stranger: Like you...

[They shake hands and the fire swirls around violently before extinguishing themselves]

Edge: When I said different time and different place, I didn't think it was gonna be so literal
Stranger: Me neither, but I saw you on TV a long while back and I saw the things you could do, and I have to admit I was jealous. You can do shit I can't even think of
Edge: That's cuz I lucked out
Stranger: Oh yeah? How so?
Edge: Long, long story
Stranger: I've got time
Edge: Let's just put it simply as, I've been through some tough shit to get where I am now
Stranger: I can agree with that, so how you been all these years
Edge: Well the most recent you seen but after I graduated I took some time off then I went to college and dropped out to pursue a different school, how about you?
Stranger: More or less the same, I graduated and started working right after school
Edge: Oh yeah? Was it a good job?
Stranger: Eh, maybe, maybe not... Anyway, I'm interested in what else you can do, I wanna see what you got
Edge: Still the same, always looking for fights and challenges
Stranger: Yeah, just keeping it real, you know me
Edge: Alrighty

[*Edge jumps back about a hundred or so feet and ignites his right hand again, then puts on his black glove*]

Stranger: Alright, let's do this!

[*The stranger blows a stream of fire into both his fist and the two dash towards each other. Edge leaps into the air and as he is right above the stranger he lets a stream of fire descend upon him, but the stranger literally grabs the stream, turns it around and hurls it back at Edge who simply puts out his right hand and extinguishes the fire. The stranger takes in a deep breath and breaths out a stream similar to Edge's flamethrower but he cuts it short effectively turning it into a projectile*]

Shit, where is he getting his fire from? Is he an elemental spirit like me? No, he couldn't be, that's the funny thing about elemental users, they find the trickiest ways to get around their handicap. Halo, before I saved him and brought him back to life, would charge up his lightning strikes by collecting the bioelectricity from his body and condensing it, Raven does the same, and then Napalm used pieces of metal under his sneakers to make sparks. whew, I'm telling you, there's a way around everything.

[*Edge clasps his hands together and bats away the fiery projectile. He doesn't notice that as he does so the stranger races up and manages to lay in an uppercut that sends Edge flying back into the ground. He breaks his fall by rolling back, his Hell Fire suddenly disperses and extinguish. A smirk is seen on Edge's face as he stands up and a blue ember passes by in front. Without warning or hesitation Edge jets forward with a sidekick to the gut with such speed that catches the stranger by surprise. As the stranger is sent backwards he manages to send out multiple fireball like projectiles. Edge literally holds out his right hand and catches one of them and squeezes it until it snuffs itself out with a pop. The moment the strangers feet touch the ground he breathes out a continuous stream of fire that Edge counters with his Strike Fist, it cuts the stream in half like a hot knife through butter. The stranger manages to rush in and grab Edge's attacking fist and with a flip, tosses Edge into the air like a doll*]

Heh, not bad at all, adaptive, and can make his own fire without special tools.

[The stranger holds up his right hand and ignites it into a blaze and then clenches his fist... Edge holds up his right hand as well and subsides his Azure Flame, only to replace it with his Hell Fire. Instinctively the two run towards each other and as they near, their fires burn as bright as the sun and as intensely as a firestorm. They meet fist...]

Edge: STRIKE FIST!
Stranger: DRAGON FIST!

[Their fists collide and the energy that is sent outwards incinerates everything in the surrounding area, the two are sent back violently. When everything subsides the two fighters stand up and see that everything is on fire. Without hesitation they quickly use their powers to silence the fires that were left over from the explosion...]

When we killed off the renegade fires that were burning everything up we sat down on the sidewalk and just talked for a bit... it's been like what, 3 or 4 years since I've last seen him, there wasn't much to catch up on though.

Edge: I gotta know, where the hell do you get your fires from, there's no way you can be like me
Stranger: I was gonna ask the same thing
Edge: Heh, I asked first
Stranger: Fair enough, I took martial arts a long while back and they taught me the importance of breathing exercises. Before I could only take the fire from surrounding areas and control it that way but the more I practiced my breathing, I just, suddenly one day burped fire
Edge: (with a dumbfounded look on his face) ...
Stranger: Yup, what about you?
Edge: I get my fires from myself, it's hard to explain, I mean, I just feel it, I know it, it's who I am
Stranger: Oh yeah, yo what's with that blue fire of yours?
Edge: That's a different story, it's sumtin way beyond you
Stranger: Oh yeah? Try me
Edge: Trust me, it's not sumtin you obtain so easily, he'll I'm not even sure how I obtained it
Stranger: Well what happened when you got it?

[Edge stands up and starts walking back to the stronghold]

Edge: I was baptized!
Stranger: Get the fuck outta here

[Edge turns around as he is walking away]

Edge: Yo Josh! You just gonna sit there? Let's go get sumtin to eat!!
Josh: Yeah!

[Josh gets up and heads towards Edge]

Josh: Yo the name's Phenix...

Josh was a friend from high school, in some form or another a friendship developed, he always had a smile on his face but he also had that look that let you know that at any moment he could snap and break you. We had a few classes together, we didn't hang out much, but when we did I always felt like there was a connection, like he understood me without me having to say a word. We didn't see each other at graduation, mainly cuz we didn't graduate with everyone else, hell I just got my diploma and left. The last time we ever saw each other I remember we both said that maybe in a different time and place perhaps a proper friendship could come to surface, maybe that time is now. Phenix... damn that's the same name as my calling.

Chapter 72

The testament of water

The telecast that Hacker had set up a while back was finally shut down, but even for the time it was on the air hundreds came forth. Once they reached the outer edges of the surrounding states Hacker took it upon himself to bring them straight to the stronghold with his gates, no soldiers dared to follow. Most were refuges looking for safe haven, others were fighters wanting to wage a war and fight back. The majority of them were power users with a handful of elemental users scattered throughout the bunch. They all sought me out seeking advice, advice I didn't have. I knew we couldn't stay like this forever, we would eventually have to fight, but would I be able to make such a decision? Would I be able to put so many lives at risk?

[Edge is at the command center of the stronghold, he looks out towards Brooklyn and notices something weird]

It feels like a force that pushes against me, sumtin familiar. Halo came into the room and told me he felt the same thing. We decided to go check it out, I didn't ask Hacker to open a gate, he's been doing enough already. Halo teleported the both of us to Brooklyn within a bolt of lightning. Whenever he does that it feels like I am being pulled apart, as if my legs are pinned down and someone is pulling on my head and tryna tear me in half, all this while being consumed in a tunnel of blinding light. Halo describes it as a blink of an eye, I begged to differ. We reached Brooklyn and we just walked around, going wherever the force felt the strongest. We walked all the way to Coney Island and that's where we found him... Testament. He was face down on the sand, and not moving. It was Halo who was brave enough to walk up to him and poke him. But he didn't move, then I followed and rolled him over. He was completely out but he was still alive cuz I saw his chest rise and fall as he breathed.

Edge: Geez, what a predicament...
Halo: What the hell does that mean?
Edge: It means what the fuck are we gonna do
Halo: Why couldn't you just say that?!
Edge: ...
Halo: Why don't we just kill him...
Edge: That seems wrong, I mean look at him, he's almost innocent looking

[Just then Testament coughs violently as if he was drowning, he rights himself and spits out large amounts of water]

Halo: Crap KILL HIM!
Edge: NO! Wait...

Testament came back to life suddenly and all I could think of doing is waiting to see what his next move is...

[Testament turns back over onto his back and opens his eyes slowly, the sun causes him to put his arm over his eyes to shield them from the intense light. He gets up slowly and looks at Edge and Halo, who are both in a ready to fight or flight stance]

Testament: Where am I?
Halo: That's the oldest trick in the book
Edge: What'd you mean?
Testament: Where is this place? That crazy lady, where is she!?

[Testament looks around a bit as if something had startled him]

Edge: What crazy lady?
Testament: The one with the butterflies and wings!

Halo: Xerxes...

Edge: What about her? She's not here

Testament: She tossed me into the ocean that is the last thing I remembered... she was trying to kill me, accusing me of killing her testament

Halo: Uh stupid, that's your name

Testament: What? My name is Kae, not Testament

Halo: Yeah ok, and I'm lil Miss Muffet

Kae: Miss who?

Edge: Whoa you said your name is Kae?

Kae: Yeah

Edge: You don't remember anything?

Kae: All I remember was waking up then being accused then tossed into the ocean

Edge: Do you remember anything before that?

Kae: Not really, but I do remember a voice, I wasn't able to move but I heard a voice, like it was thinking to itself

Edge: Hmm...

Sumtin seems wrong here, it IS Testament, but he has no idea of anything... no wait, when my Azruath hit him, I saw some sorta aura fading off of him. I never really paid attention to it since Halo was my first concern at the time.

Edge: No, he's telling the truth Halo

Halo: What? How do you know?

Edge: Cuz I know, when I beat Testament, I beat Testament, the soul who was inhabiting the body at the time

Halo: And?

Edge: This is the original soul of the body

Kae: How come I don't remember any of it?

Edge: I dunno

Halo: So what do we do?

Edge: We take him back, there's nuttin else to do... Actually can you still use your powers?

Kae: Powers?

Edge: Can you control water

Kae: I... don't know...

Edge: Give it a try

Halo: This isn't a good idea

Kae: How though?

Edge: See the water as part of you then just like you would move your hand or legs without thought, try to move the water

Kae: Ok...

[Kae struggles a bit to levitate an orb of water from the shore, but nothing happens. He concentrates even harder and suddenly his eyes widen and shift from human looking into a clear blue watery wave and an orb rises with ease]

Edge: I take it as a yes

Halo: Look at his eyes

Edge: No, Testament's eyes were white, his eyes look like the surface of water

Halo: That means?

Kae: It means I remember...

[Edge and Halo suddenly jump back and ready themselves for a fight]

Kae: No, I remember everything now, though the entity known as Testament is gone, his powers and memories remain, they have tainted me

Edge: Is that sumtin we should worry about?

Halo: I told you this was a bad idea

Kae: Kae, that is the innocence in me that is now gone. The demon's actions, memories...

Halo: So who are you?

Edge: Testament

Testament: That will forever be my name, the name of this power, the name of the actions and memories

Edge: And whose side are you on...

Testament: I have... no allegiance, just as I have no use

Edge: Join us then

Halo: Are you crazy?

Testament: Join you? And fight for what, what purpose would there be in my allegiance towards you?

Edge: Not allegiance, friendship

Testament: Friendship...

Edge: Yeah, I'll explain later though I think we should get back

Testament: ...I accept your friendship then

[Testaments eyes, suddenly shift back to regular human eyes and the orb of water drops back down]

Wow, that was wild...

Chapter 73

A fighting plan

It took a while for Testament to ease himself into the crowd. He was totally outta place and had no idea what to do. He spent the majority of his time just walking around in the hall like he was unsure of everything. When he was still Kae he seemed innocent and oblivious to everything, but when he awakened his powers the innocence looked like it shattered to the realization of who he was and what he's done, rather what the entity that was in him had done.

The Light of Hope remains active, like a beacon to all the heroes out there, never once did the light dim. Mei was in a room sitting cross legged on a bed of soil, I could actually see roots that have extended outwards from her thighs and into the soil. Like a plant keeping itself alive, I didn't disturb her, I just let her be.

More and more would arrive each day, usually just handfuls, but it adds up quickly. It wasn't before long that they all came to me and asked me what we were gonna do. Truthfully I didn't know what we could do if there was anything to be done. The military hasn't made their move yet, but they were gathering their numbers, as if they planned to attack all at once. Hacker has been tracking their whereabouts and it seems like they are tryna surround us. Everyone kept coming to me asking me the same questions, but I had no answers for them. Finally I decided to call a meeting, all the heroes gathered in the largest edifice of the stronghold.

[Edge stands in the center of a giant crowd with Halo, Hacker, Mei and Testament by his side]

Dak: What are we gonna do? We know what they are planning

Raven: Are you gonna do nothing? C'mon man, we gotta do sumtin

Apollo: I don't like violence but I agree, we got these gifts, we should use them

Edge: (sigh) look, I don't have any answers to your questions cuz personally I dunno what the right course of action is, nuttin we do would help us, it would only make us look like the bad guys, I dunno what to tell you guys yo

Raven: Right, but that's not the Edge I know

Edge: No offence the Edge you know was whoever I was in high school, I'm not that person anymore, and neither are you the same

Apollo: You were an asshole in high school

Edge: (flabbergasted) is that really the point here!?

Hacker: Edge is right, anything we do would only look like an attack on our behalf

Dak: We have the right to be here, why do we have to be the ones to be pushed to the edge

Mei: That is the eventual fate of your species it seems. I have seen this tragedy unfold long ago

Halo: You know I agree with them, you can't just stand around and do nuttin

Edge: Halo, what can I do, what'd you WANT me to do, I'm not gonna put everyone's lives at risk just for a stupid idea

Hacker: You have a plan?

Edge: I've always had a plan, it's just whether it's the right course of action that bugs me about it

Hacker: What do you plan to do?

Edge: Sumtin bad, sumtin very bad...

Dak: Tell us your plan

Edge: It's completely absurd and absolutely wrong, but it's the only choice we really have

Halo: Say it already

Edge: (sigh) who's really in control here? Who has the say on what happens to us?

Hacker: The military and churches

Edge: Exactly, more or less, and what are they tryna do?

Dak: Apparently wipe us out

Edge: Right, what does a rat do when it's cornered? it fights back

Raven: So that's what we should do man fight back!

Edge: Fighting back is only temporary, I had sumtin more permanent in mind...

Hacker: ...your not...

Edge: It's a thought, now you can see the morality issues of it?

Dak: What is it?

Testament: He plans to destroy every single military establishment there is, every soldier, every force that would stand against us

Edge: Way to ease it on them

Testament: When you gain power, you learn to destroy everyone who opposes you, that way you keep the peace without enemies at your door

Hacker: ...

Edge: This plan is for me, Halo, Mei and Testament only, no one else is strong enough

Dak: Why you 4?

Hacker: Because they are the only ones with the power to do this, we would only get ourselves killed. Edge, this is insane, this is too much even for you

Edge: Everyone, this is your choice, if you have any better ideas, let us know, you're all in this too, you're part of this family, this alliance of power. Your voices count

[The crowd starts to all cry out at once and in an uproar...]

No one could possibly like this plan, it's nuttin but murder, then again we are the ones at the end of the muzzle. We have the strength to fight back yet we don't, is that the way it's supposed to be? No, Raven is right, this isn't like me, never back down and never give up, that's who I am. This entire war started as a result of stopping the destruction of humanity and now in order to save ourselves we need to destroy humanity a lil more, is this just? This course of action, we have the right to exist, no one should ever have power over someone else...

Phenix: Edge, think, is sitting around doing nothing really what you want? We both have a fire inside of us, we both yearn to burn free and fierce. I know you thought of this plan cuz in your heart it's what you truly want, it's what I'd do, EVERYONE LISTEN UP!

283

[The crowd goes silent...]

Phenix: You all agree that we need to do sumtin, we can't just sit back and do nothing, Edge's plan involves fighting back, think people, how many of us have lost loved ones, friends and family, should their death be in vain?! We want our freedom right!? SO LET'S TAKE WHAT'S OURS! OUR FREEDOM TO EXIST AND BE WHO WE ARE! ENOUGH OF THIS OPPRESSION!

[The crowd stays silent...]

Edge: Spoken true, like the fire that burns in both of us
Hacker: I... agree, so many of us have died. We need to fight back, protect what's ours
Halo: Let's kick their asses
Testament: Follow no ones ambitions but your own, like a hurricane, let your intentions roar loudly
Raven: Right, we gotta fight man
Apollo: I will fight, I won't be afraid
Mei: Such desire
Dak: I lost my family and those closes to me, whatever it takes I won't let their deaths be in vain!
Edge: This is what everyone wants? To fight? Heh, I was stupid to think that everyone would think it was wrong. You all know that they are aiming to kill us right? When we leave the stronghold it's up to you guys to defend your home. I have faith in you, I know you guys can do it, I know you're strong enough, hell I can see the desire in all of you, such potential. The strongest men and women stand before me, I'm honored, Halo, Testament, Mei... you know this will be dangerous right?
Testament: I will fight
Mei: Natures first green is gold...
Halo: I'm in, gonna kick some ass!

[The whole crowd goes crazy in an uproar]

Halo: So... when do we do this?
Edge: No idea...

Chapter 74

The last snow

The weather has been acting crazy, the summer was hot as hell but everything is cooling down really fast, is sumtin wrong with Saivent? I haven't seen him around lately, I wonder what he's been up to.

I woke up in a nice warm bed and looked out the window to see lil white flutters of dust falling from the sky, it was the second snow of the year. Snowing in September, heh... I got outta bed quietly so I wouldn't wake anyone. It's been a long time since I been in the snow so I was anxious to get out and be taken in by the whiteness.

[Edge puts on his regular clothes and heads outside, the moment he ignites his flames the snow on the floor around him instantly melts into a puddle of water, he smiles a bit and takes into the air]

The sky was totally blanketed by snow, I didn't feel cold at all, my fire kept me really warm this time. I flew all the way up the mostly destroyed Empire State building to get a better view of the city, the snow covered a lot of the destruction. There I stayed for a bit just thinking to myself and it was nuttin but bliss...

[Edge sits down and crosses his legs with his fire surrounding him, suddenly a bolt of lightning streaks across the sky and strikes the empty space in front of him. Halo appears upside down with a smile and throws a snowball at Edge and then is suddenly struck by another lightning bolt and disappears. Edge stands up with a look of confusion on his face then suddenly a gate opens behind Edge and Hacker appears just long enough

285

for Edge to see him before he throws another snowball at Edge, then falling off the building's side into another gate and disappearing]

What the hell was going on?! Catch me off guard then disappear, damn it I should had my fires on a hot blaze. I jumped off the building and landed on the streets below, melting every inch of snow that came into contact with my fires, I even managed to dry up the puddles of water closes to me. I walked around a bit but soon found nuttin of interest so I decided to head back home.

[Edge starts to head home]

When I reached the front entrance low and behold there was Hacker and Halo pointing and laughing, I just looked at them with a face like an adult would have if they were dealing with two annoying children.

Hacker: So, what's up?
Edge: (sarcastically) ha ha, funny with that whole snowball thing
Halo: We should have a snowball fight
Edge: I'm so not in the mood for sumtin like that
Halo: Why? It'll be fun!
Edge: Go play with Apollo or Raven
Halo: I don't like Raven... and Apollo is too busy playing some handheld game
Hacker: Your thinking aren't you
Edge: Yeah...
Hacker: About the plan right?
Edge: What else? This is gonna be sumtin massive, and it's gonna take a lot of energy
Hacker: We really have no other choice do we?

[Dak opens the front door and steps out, by now the sun has broken through the grey clouds and slowly warming the city up, the snow is beginning to melt]

Dak: Hey Edge, I've been thinking... this whole plan...
Edge: Second thoughts?
Dak: I mean it's a lot of innocent lives

Edge: Yeah, we're innocent too aren't we, most us anyway

Dak: Isn't there another way? There's just this pit of gloom I feel, something about this all feels so wrong

Hacker: What would you have us do? Right now it's peaceful, but it won't last like this, I say we make our move first at least then we have a fighting chance

Halo: Whatever yo but it's not right that they do this to us

Hacker: Agreed

Dak: I'm just saying if this plan goes through... I dunno...

Edge: I know people are gonna have their objections, but in this case the majority rules, we all agreed sumtin has to be done

Hacker: Question is, when we do this?

Edge: Hacker, is there anyway to get us the locations of the biggest bases?

Hacker: Sure, that's easy enough to do

Edge: This what we'll do, the 4 of us will attack the largest bases, that should cripple them, then we head onto the smaller bases, I know they'll retaliate with their nukes...

Hacker: This is only for America?

Edge: I dunno what's happening around the world, so we should keep this as close to home as possible, let's avoid unnecessary deaths. Since everything is at peace right now, lets keep it that way, we're gonna have to organize everyone so everyone knows what needs to be done

Hacker: Got it

Dak: This just isn't good...

Chapter 75

Talk within powers

[In a room of white, Saivent stands in front of a maiden dressed in a snowy garment which seems to be lifted up and flowing with an unseen and unfelt wind. Her hair stretched as far as her garment did and was platinum white, her eyes never opened and in front of her lies a book that floated in place seemingly with the same wind that blows against her apparel, this is Tempis, the maiden of time]

Saivent: Where do you think this is all going to end up?

Tempis: Time will tell my child

Saivent: Do you know what will happen? Have you seen the future?

Tempis: The past, the present and the future all exist as one

Saivent: What does that mean?

Tempis: It means the events unfolding will play themselves out as they are destined to

Saivent: So now your Destiny as well?

Tempis: Hmm, child, still your soul, the humans will decide their own fate as they have the ability to do so

Saivent: Damn it I hate doing this, sitting back and doing nothing, not being able to do anything, and when I can there's nothing for me to do, damn these rules, and whose to stop me anyway, whose going to be there for the follow through if just walk out and fix everything myself

Tempis: That is beyond your powers to do so in the first place, and if you could do so you would destroy the balance of existence

Saivent: This whole existence crap belongs to Jehovah and Lucifer, I don't need followers

Tempis: But the followers need you, if you were to be destroyed this world would no longer be able to support life, the lands would dry and the skies would darken

Saivent: And Mei? Can't she just evolve some new species to handle it? Isn't that her job, isn't that what her existence is for?

Tempis: Your sister's existence coincides along yours, when you were created, the Avatars who gave their life not only created you but they also created your sister as well, the two of you are harmoniously one

Saivent: (sigh)

Tempis: Time will tell

[In a military establishment somewhere War Commandant Stavrite speaks to a figure hidden in the shadows]

War Commandant: So Edge plans to wipe out all the major bases...?

Dark Figure: That's the plan so far

War Commandant: And you don't know when this is to take place?

Dark Figure: No

War Commandant: Then your job is to find out when this is to happen and report back, once he and the strongest leave the stronghold that's when you destroy everyone inside

Dark Figure: I got it

War Commandant: And what of the chimeras

Dark Figure: What about them?

War Commandant: Their numbers should be growing

Dark Figure: And?

War Commandant: Just like Edge, you have no respect for your elders

Dark Figure: ...

War Commandant: The chimera's role is pivotal, you alone won't be able to kill everyone in the stronghold

Dark Figure: I'll turn that place into an oven and roast them alive

War Commandant: ...the chimeras will take care of the stragglers left behind in the rest of the country, you make sure you do your job

Dark Figure: The chimeras are all over New York, they keep themselves hidden, Edge won't find them

War Commandant: And so the plan plays out...

[In the angel sanctuary Michael stands in front of a giant crystal sphere,

he looks at Edge but is distracted by the approach of Akuma who also starts to view the sphere with him]

Michael: Akuma, what brings you here?

Akuma: Edge, is there any new news on him?

Michael: Plenty...

Akuma: Such as?

Michael: At this rate Lucifer will make his move first, many have already died, and many more in anguish. Chimeras are running rampant on earth, so many souls have turned, so many lost...

Akuma: Hasn't he already made his move when he released Judgment?

Michael: My boy, Lucifer was not the one who released Judgment, Saivent was

Akuma: Saivent!? Why did he do that? Isn't he on our side?

Michael: Why he did that is beyond me, it would have been beneficial to all of us if Judgment had remained sealed, and no he's not on our side, much like everyone else not under Jehovah's might

Akuma: So then he's an enemy?

Michael: Young one, everyone is our enemy

Akuma: (sighs displeasingly)

Michael: What is wrong?

Akuma: I dunno, everyone is against us, why?

Michael: They do not wish for the peace that Jehovah's power would bring everyone, they do not accept that he is King

Akuma: But why is he King?

Michael: He is almighty, just and true, his might is absolute

Akuma: That really doesn't help

Michael: (chuckles) are we losing our faith young one? You've seen his power, the wonders he created, and this beautiful sanctuary we live in

Akuma: I guess it's easier for you to accept, since you were always an angel

Michael: Don't worry young one, your purpose is as important as mine or any of ours, Jehovah cares for us all equally

Akuma: I guess...

[Akuma turns around with a worried look on his face, unnoticed by Michael who gently smiles an innocent smile... back in the stronghold...]

How long has it been since all this started? I remember not so long ago I was going to school... oh shit, I totally forgot about school didn't I? Not that it matters now though. From Judgment to Testament, then death and life again... I need some fresh air.

[Edge heads to the top of the stronghold where the command center is]

It was empty, the command center... the night sky was darker than usual without the city lights. The only thing that shined brightly was the Light of Hope. Its bright blue hue lit up the surrounding area, almost like a light house, it was September now, a few more days and it'll be my birthday, I'll be 24.

[A strong wind gust through one of the windows, Edge goes to look outside to make sure nothing foul was astir]

That was an unnatural wind, came so quickly and went...

[A voice speaks from the back startling Edge causing him to ignite his right hand ablaze]

Saivent: Whoa Edge, calm down, it's just me
Edge: Saivent, it's been a while
Saivent: It has hasn't it
Edge: Sumtins wrong, by now I can tell
Saivent: Edge, you know too don't you? That something bad is coming
Edge: Yup, some mad fucked up shit is on its way...
Saivent: You wouldn't by any chance have a clue would you?
Edge: (shocked) how the hell would I know!? Aren't you the super natural entity here?
Saivent: Truthfully I don't even know
Edge: (sarcastically) oh, great, just great, I guess were all fucked?
Saivent: Hey life screws us all sooner or later, you know I wish I could help
Edge: Yeah yeah, I'm not holding anything against you but hell if you dunno anything, then there's no way I know anything
Saivent: How's Halo?
Edge: He's doing fine

Saivent: And Hacker?

Edge: Just as well

Saivent: I see you made plenty of new friends

Edge: Yeah, your sister's helping hand made that possible

Saivent: Well I'm glad you're doing fine, I just wanted to stop by to see how you were and wish you a happy early birthday, I don't got much to give you but I'll see what I can do

Edge: Gee thanks, I feel so special now hahahahahaa

Saivent: (nods) goodnight Edge

Edge: Yeah you too...

And just like that he was gone with the wind. He's right though, sumtin is gonna happen, and it's gonna happen faster than I expect it to. The Angel Sanctuary has stayed quite for too long, chimera attacks are gone, the military is silent for the time being, and the churches are silent too, this is the calm before the storm isn't it...

Chapter 76

HAPPY BIRTHDAY EDGE!

That morning everyone was up way before me, did I over sleep? Back and forth people came and went as if busy doing sumtin. Halfway down the hall Halo approached me and dragged me outside and without even asking me teleports me away in a bolt of lightning. I hate when he does that cuz it's not sumtin I can get use to at all. Personally I just don't understand how teleportation works, Judgment, Testament, Halo, Saivent, they all do it, hell even Hacker up to a certain extent, I just don't get it. Halo took me to a place that wasn't unfamiliar, in fact I'm pretty sure I remember it from somewhere.

Edge: Where are we? Why does this place look so familiar?
Halo: Dude your kidding right?
Edge: I'm not, seriously where are we?
Halo: We're at Knick's house fool
Edge: OH shit... I can't believe I've totally forgotten about him
Halo: Well don't worry no ones here, no one is anywhere actually, it looks like it's been abandoned a long while back
Edge: Why'd you bring me here?
Halo: I dunno I guess cuz we haven't been here in years
Edge: Hell I don't even remember the last time we were here

[Edge and Halo open the door and head to their friends room]

Everything was abandoned, all his games, his toys and models. Everything was left alone. Me and Halo sat down and reminisced on some memories we had. This was all before Halo knew about my powers, even before I had fully mastered them in fact. I've come a long way I must admit, but that was so long ago. By Knick's bed was his weapons, he had a combat steel Chinese styled broadsword which was in perfect condition, all it needed was to be sharpened and it's ready for use. There was also a kendo stick and a small dagger, useless to me and Halo.

Halo: You think he'd mind if I used his sword?
Edge: Hell if I knew, I'm wondering where he is...

[Halo unsheathes the sword and holds it up laterally and sends a charge through it, small jolts of electricity can be seen jumping around on the surface of the blade]

Halo: Guess I got myself a blade
Edge: ...you're so Brooklyn...

We stayed for a short time or so it seemed, by the time we decided to leave it was dusk. The sun wasn't down yet, but it glowed brightly and vibrantly with the colors of a dieing day. The same way we got there was the same way we got back to the stronghold, things were eerily quite... Halo opened the door first but just enough to let himself in first and then closed it on me...

[Edge stands there silent and dumbfounded...]

What the hell, this is a terrible joke... I pulled on the door some more but it wouldn't budge so I just stood there. First a few seconds then a few minutes, in fact I even sat down on the floor after a while of standing. I'm not a patient guy, but I can only imagine what they are up too, is it betrayal? Are they gonna hand me over to the government, or maybe an angry mob of religious zealots who wanna crucify me or sumtin? No... None of those I know for sure... so then what... I know...

[Edge takes to the sky and heads toward the command center, there he slips in through the windows while uttering incoherent profanities]

When I made it in everything was silent and on the floor were individual pieces of skittles, my favorite candy of all time. It then hit me like a ton of bricks, they are leading me somewhere to surprise me, maybe a surprise attack or betrayal? No... Lemme shut up I am becoming paranoid. I followed the trail only picking up a few pieces to eat on the way and it led me to the dining hall, one of the biggest edifices of the entire structure. I opened the door and I expected a whole crowd but there was no one... now I am confused beyond all logic, where the hell was everyone? None of this makes sense, why lead me somewhere and have that place be empty, unless they are tryna throw me off. Halo closed the door and locked it cuz he didn't want me to enter from the front, but up in the command center there was a trail, that means they knew I would head up there... so if they are guessing my movements, where would I go next...

[Edge sits down on the floor and thinks a bit, he suddenly gets up and runs to the front entrance of the stronghold only to find a note on it that says "other side fool!"]

"Fool"? That must be Halo. What the hell are they planning? why would they possibly need to distract me this long.

[Edge speed walks to the back entrance and when he opens the door everyone who lived at the stronghold at the time all yelled HAPPY BIRTHDAY! Edge has a nervous and embarrassed look on his face, he turns bright cherry red]

Edge: You guys...
Halo: Surprise fool, yeah it's your birth, it's your party
Hacker: You like it? Took us basically all day to set it up
Raven: Yeah man, for all the things you did you deserve sumtin nice
Edge: Heh... well wow... I dunno what to say
Halo: Who cares lets have some fun
Raven: Yeah c'mon it's your party lets celebrate
Edge: Well then what's everyone waiting for lets enjoy ourselves!

People turned on boom boxes and blasted the music loud and defiantly, I enjoyed myself at the snack bar chowing down on food of all sorts. The "backyard" was decorated like some sorta Hawaiian beach party, there were lights and those party ribbon things. To the side were lawn chairs set up, now personally since I'm not much of a party animal I decided to enjoy myself by sitting down and relaxing. A drink by my side the starry night above, my friends and music, we were all just enjoying ourselves and having an overall good time. The party lasted a pretty long while, people danced and sang, ate and passed out. When the party had ended everyone went back inside and went to bed or sumtin, but I stayed out, I was pretty tipsy at this point, but still in control of my movements and all that other stuff. Halo and Hacker came and sat down besides me and asked me how I liked the party.

Hacker: Did you enjoy yourself?
Edge: Yeah, it was sumtin everyone needed, I think this relaxed them a lot
Halo: To bad there wasn't any pie, I love pie
Edge: You and your stupid pie...
Halo: They didn't have cheese cake either, god I love cheese cake...
Edge: ...
Hacker: As long as you had fun, that's what's important
Halo: Yeah, well I'm tired I'm heading in, see ya guys
Edge: Ciao
Hacker: See ya dude

[Halo gets up to leave. Hacker gets up to yawn]

Hacker: You know what, I think I'm gonna head in too, I'm tired as hell myself
Edge: Sure...

[Hacker turns around and starts to head in, before he goes all the way in Edge calls out to him]

Edge: HEY YO!
Hacker: Yeah?
Edge: My birthday isn't for another 3 days!
Hacker: What the hell...

[Somewhere far away...]

Saivent: Ahh fuck I got it wrong...

Chapter 77

Difficult arrival

The party, even though it was on the wrong day was fun. We all needed it to relax and get our minds off of stuff. But we all knew that the war wasn't far and soon this stillness would be lost in mayhem, death and fighting.

There was never anything to do in the stronghold so I would always go out and walk around, sometimes one of my friends would come and accompany me, but that was rare. Hacker provided everyone with entertainment by connecting to the television networks, everyone else would play video game consoles. The stronghold had become a giant hangout center. The kids played while the adults did whatever it is they do.

I walked around everywhere by myself, at this point there's nuttin in Manhattan that I haven't seen yet, what's left of it anyway. Hell I even walked around in the subways. Either way my walks would all lead me back to the stronghold. Sometimes me and Phenix would spar for a bit in the "front yard", that was always a spectacle cuz we'd go at it rough, fires flaring up everywhere. Everyone would come and watch, the lil kids would ogle and stare then have lil sparring matches of their own. It was Apollo who came up with the idea of using our days to train everyone in the stronghold to use their powers and how to fight.

Apollo: We should train everyone to use their powers, to use them for the better
Edge: Hahahah what like a school or sumtin?
Apollo: Yeah, wouldn't that be a better way to spend our days?

Edge: It would be, but sadly I have the patience of a 5 year old in an all you can eat candy store, I hate being a teacher

Apollo: I'll be the one to do it then

Edge: You? Hahahaha your qualified?

Apollo: Sure why not? I'm special too, I have powers just like everyone else

Edge: Yeah but you're a power user, you can only do your shield thing

Apollo: So what, that doesn't mean anything

Edge: Look, you know this is gonna be a tough job right, it's not sumtin that you just pull together and then drop when it doesn't go your way

Apollo: I know that

Edge: Then knock yourself out

Apollo: Where should we train though?

Edge: Wherever you want, free country, actually no it's not, free city if anything

Apollo: We'll use the backyard

Edge: Be my guest

Apollo: Cool, I'm gonna get everything organized

[Apollo leaves Edge by himself in the front of the stronghold]

The Light of Hope is still up and still just as bright as ever, but no one is coming anymore... we haven't had a new comer in a few weeks, the end of the year is drawing ever closer and the temperature has finally cooled to a chilly 45F or so, just the way I like it. I was gonna head inside but my attention was thrown when some guy in a soldier's uniform came up from behind and collapsed in front of me. It was Napalm...

[Edge calls to Hacker and he immediately creates a gate to bring him to the medical bay]

Damn he looks really beat up, it must've been hell to get here all the way from California.

[Halo comes into the medical bay...]

Edge: Halo?

Halo: Yeah, I came when I heard, how is he?

Edge: Pretty bad, hey Hacker do we have anyone who can heal?

Hacker: I already sent for her, she should be on her way

Edge: Good...

Halo: Damn he looks like shit

[Napalm is laying on a bed, he's covered in dry blood, dirt, and soot]

Edge: Yeah I know, imagine what he's been through...

Hacker: That would be a lot, haven't you kept up with the news?

Halo: No, not when I have Halo to play

Edge: ...

Hacker: ...

Edge: Loser...

Halo: What? What would you do all day if you had nuttin to do?

Edge: ANYTHING!

Hacker: Things are bad, almost every channel you turn to within the states are all talking about us, outside the USA especially in Europe it's nothing but hell, ever since the Vatican authorized the murder of our kind...

Edge: ...WHAT THE FUCK!?

Halo: They did that?!

Hacker: Yeah they did, basically like our martial law, riots immediately broke out, desperate parents trying to save their kids, while other parents saw them as demon children and killed them, and it gets worse... the Europeans are predominantly Christians while heavily Muslim in certain areas. And everyone who didn't believe in anything suddenly believed in Heaven and that they were gonna be condemned to Hell if they didn't change their ways, and they believed that the best way to show their faith is to kill our kind, because we're demons...

Edge: I can't believe this, see what I mean, this is a perfect example of how religion fucks us all over

Halo: What else happened?

Hacker: They claim they have almost gotten rid of our kind over there...

Edge: You mean they claim they almost succeeded in genocide... is there anything we can do?

Hacker: We're too late, there's nothing else we can do

Edge: Fuck it all to hell...

[A little girl walks into the room, and Hacker takes her to Napalm and she does what she is asked to do]

Halo: What do you wanna do?
Edge: I dunno, we can't let that shit happen over here, I dunno how many of us are out there, if this is it then we're in trouble, everyone in here is part of an endangered species
Halo: Damn...

[The little girl leaves with a smile on her face. Edge and Halo turn to Napalm]

Halo: Hey budddddddddddddy long time no see
Napalm: Ugh, Edge... Halo...

[Napalm slowly starts to get up, but falls back down in pain]

Edge: Slowly...
Hacker: How you feeling?
Napalm: Ugh like shit, this is the stronghold right?
Edge: Yeah, you made it alive, but just barely
Hacker: How was the trip?
Napalm: Shit, you wouldn't believe all that had happened
Edge: At this point nuttin would surprise me

Chapter 78

To the east, Napalm's journey

Napalm: My story begins in a land far away...
Edge: ...
Hacker: ...
Halo: ...
Napalm: Ok I guess the theatrics suck, it all happened really fast, soldiers came into the streets and anyone in their way were shot at, anyone who resisted were shot on the spot. Then it was announced all over that the country had been put into martial law, and that all non humans would be arrested and any resistance would be met with immediate termination. The small band of us rallied and fought back, we held our own for a bit... but we were overcome really quickly when they set up these white human figured statues. Our powers suddenly stopped working, my sensei protected me and told me to head towards you, he died trying to save me...

[Flashback - Napalm, a chubby middle aged guy and a handful of other young guys are all standing in one line as an army of soldiers approaches]

Moe: Hey you better know what you're doing Napalm
Napalm: We got powers they got nothing, we'll kick their asses for sure
Sensei: Hmm... Do not be so decisive, this battle will test everyone's skills
Napalm: Well get ready because here they come

303

Luke: I dunno how you talked me into this...
Napalm: You always wanted to be a hero so here's your chance
Sensei: HERE THEY COME! NAPALM!
Napalm: GOT IT!

[Napalm jumps ahead of the line and scratches his sneakers against the pavement just as the soldiers begin to open fire. The wall of flames that rises acts as a distraction while Moe gets out of the way to higher ground and prepares his attack. Luke stops the molten bullets after they passed through the wall of fire with his mind and redirects them back at the soldiers. Sensei stomps his foot onto the ground in a show of defiance and hits his belly with his fist, a blast of wind is released from his mouth and rips through the air concussively knocking the other soldiers back. Moe, now on top of a car, raises his hands and the ground underneath the tanks and vehicles the soldiers brought with them suddenly cracks open and swallows them into a small fissure. More soldiers arrive this time with heavier fire power. One of them launches an RPG at Napalm, Sensei pushes Napalm to the side and smacks his belly sending out a wind blast that pushes the RPG out of the way. Luke then grabs the RPG with his mind and redirects it to the soldiers. Moe once again cracks the ground underneath the backup soldiers and swallows them in a fissure]

Sensei: Good, keep the offense up, do not falter!
Napalm: Got it sensei
Luke: Will do
Moe: No problem
Sensei: Hmm... They will not succeed if I have anything to say about it.

[The battle continues in favor of the small band, other friends of Napalm do whatever they can to help out along the side but the primary fighters are clearly distinguishable. Sensei leads the attacks, Napalm acts as backup, Moe and Luke are the follow through. Everyone else fights just as tough and as resiliently. Not too long into the fight the soldiers bring out pillars that they drive into the ground, the pillars have white human like bodies attached to them]

Sensei: Hmm... Be on the look out they've brought out new weapons

Napalm: No matter what they bring I will end them
Sensei: Hmm...

[*Napalm scratches the pavement with his sneakers to bring up the sparks but they won't ignite into a blaze*]

Napalm: What the fuck!? What's happening!?
Sensei: Hmm...

[*Before they realized what happened the soldiers immediately open fire killing Luke and Moe. Napalm and his Sensei get behind cars to dodge the bullets*]

Napalm: MOE! LUKE!
Sensei: No!
Napalm: Sensei what's going on why won't our powers work!?
Sensei: It's those white statues, they are blocking our powers

[*The soldiers continue to fire, the bullets rip through the gas tank of the car the two are hiding behind, the others create sparks that ignite the gasoline... the car explodes throwing Napalm and his Sensei into the air, they land violently*]

Sensei: Hmm... Napalm, go, there's not much more you can do now, I will cover your escape
Napalm: But Sensei!
Sensei: Go, go and seek out the one called Edge, if he is as powerful as you say he is, then he can surely help us
Napalm: There is no US if you stay behind!
Sensei: This is something I must do... to protect you and the future, now GO!
Napalm: Sensei!
Sensei: Go now my student!

[*Napalm gets up and runs for it, the soldiers start to open fire but Sensei gets up and with one last stand he forces what power he can muster up into a blast that completely blows the soldiers, the pillars and vehicles away,*]

Napalm doesn't look back, he focus on the journey ahead, he can only shed a tear as he runs from the battle... Present day]

Napalm: That was the last time I saw Sensei
Edge: Damn, I'm sorry...
Hacker: How did you make it here?
Napalm: I had to walk, my metal plates are all worn out now. I traveled at night when I could and I stayed hidden in the morning, I caught a break when I found a lighter, that alone saved me from a lot of the soldiers that did find me. My big break came when I finally got a hold of a working car and with that I burned rubber as fast as I could, and when it was out of gas I had to dump the car and continue on again by foot, anyone who spotted me either gave me away or helped me in secret with food. When I made it into Washington DC there were soldiers everywhere, I couldn't get through at all so I had to pretend to be a soldier
Edge: What ya did with the actual soldier?
Halo: You killed him didn't you?
Napalm: I ended him, he wasn't going to just lend me a uniform just because I asked
Edge: What happened after you got through?
Napalm: From there on it was easier, I followed that blue light and the closer I got the more deserted it was, and I finally made it here
Hacker: That explains the uniform you're wearing
Napalm: If you have anything else to change into, it would be great, I can't stand to be in this
Hacker: I'll find you sumtin...

Damn everything is in ruins, this really is like the apocalypse or sumtin, and we're here doing nuttin about it. I can't stand this, sumtin has to be done, and soon...

Chapter 79

Nature's first green is gold, the countdown...

Napalm settled himself in and started training the others along side Apollo, there's only 3 months left in the year, and hopefully that will be 3 months of ease.

[Edge sits on top of a rock in Central Park taking in the warmth from the sun on a cool afternoon, a gate appears and Hacker sticks his head out]

Hacker: Uh, Edge? We may have a problem...
Edge: Hmm?
Hacker: Check this out...

[Hacker takes Edge to the communications room. It's filled with computer equipment and wires running everywhere]

Edge: What's going on?
Hacker: Me and a few elites around the world hacked the super computers of DIE, we discovered they planned to attack us on the night of the lunar eclipse
Edge: Lunar eclipse? There's one coming?
Hacker: Apparently, it's gonna be an all out heavy attack, what should we do?
Edge: Call Apollo...

[Apollo is summoned and is brought to the room via a gate]

Edge: Hey Apollo how strong are your force fields?
Apollo: Stronger than you can imagine
Edge: I'll take that as "very strong" then, and how long can you keep them up?
Apollo: As long as I can keep my concentration on it I guess
Hacker: You don't plan on evacuating the stronghold?
Edge: And go where? Besides we all have powers, we can all defend ourselves if need be, you'll be here too, you can just gate them all to a safe location if it comes down to that right?
Hacker: If they aren't waiting for me already at the exit point and if I have such a place to go
Apollo: What going on?
Edge: Hacker just discovered the plans of DIE
Apollo: DIE?
Edge: Defense Initiative of Extermination, it's a military branch specifically developed to fight and eliminate people like us
Apollo: See I told you we should have made a group back in high school just for such occasions
Edge: How was I supposed to know you were being serious?!
Hacker: ANYWAY, they plan on attacking on the night of the lunar eclipse
Apollo: When is that?
Hacker: ...
Edge: Yeah when IS that?
Hacker: ...in 3 days
Edge: What the fuck, that doesn't give us a lot of time at all
Apollo: Shit, do we have a back up plan? Anything at all?
Edge: Hmm, We'll stay, were gonna fight, everyone should have good control over their powers by now, and the ones that won't fight... take them somewhere then, I dunno where
Hacker: So this plan of yours, you're really going through with it?
Edge: Yeah
Hacker: Best of luck then...
Edge: Won't need it

Deep inside me I had no second thoughts, I knew that this was sumtin I had to do, that it was the right course of action on our behalf. To be safe, and to be free, if we are the monsters they say we are, then so be it, these monsters will hide no more, we're done being bullied around.

[In a dark control room in a military establishment a shadowy figure appears from the darkness]

Dark Figure: It worked, we forced Edge's hand, he'll attack when we want him too

War Commandant: Good, then Hacker was fooled, get things ready, 5 minutes after Edge's first attack you begin yours, and ready the Chimeras for their attack

Dark Figure: And what about you guys? You're going to just sit around?

War Commandant: The human military means nothing to me, for all I care Edge will be doing me a favor

Dark Figure: And what about the Angel Sanctuary?

War Commandant: They will not get involved, not yet, they will make their move but only when they see fit

Dark Figure: Finally, I'll get my revenge...

The first day passed and we all prepared ourselves. We trained and rested, tensions were high. The seniors all met up in the command center to make sure we all knew what would be happening. Me, Halo, Hacker, Napalm, Apollo, Raven, Phenix, Mei and Testament, we all discussed and went over each of our roles, to make sure there are no mistakes, we finalized the plan and went our own ways.

The second day, we, the seniors all took a day off to do whatever we had to do just incase we didn't come back. I went to Mei's room to see how she was, to my surprise she was doing better than ever. She was tending to a plant when I walked in, her skin had started to change from a pale tone to a glistening gold...

Edge: Your skin...

Mei: Natures first green is gold... it is odd that they should choose such a time to strike, be weary Edge, something is wrong

Edge: Everything is wrong

Mei: This is probably the last time we will see each other, I wish you the best of luck in your mission
Edge: You too, and thanks for everything
Mei: (nods)

I left Mei to herself, there was nuttin left to do now. I had nuttin left to do now... so I waited, the second day passed...

Chapter 80

The plan unfolds

Night fell and with it came the full moon. Its brightness was only seconded by that of the Light of Hope. The city hasn't had power for as long as I remembered now, but that didn't matter cuz ever since Mei cleaned up the nuclear fall out the air became cleaner, the stars shined and "nature" started to take over the city, where there once were buildings and streets, now had patches of dirty, and overgrown vegetation. Some green still, others brown and dried from the coming cold...

The moon was still round with light, no hint of the eclipse came. The seniors all gathered up in the command center and we waited patiently, none of us had much to say. We all knew what was coming and we knew that we had to be strong for what's to come. They wanted us dead and we wanted to survive...

A few hours passed and we went right through midnight and then suddenly a small shadow crept over the moon. Slowly it inched its way over a quarter of its face then half. The atmosphere was tense, all eyes were gazed upon the moon. We knew that the moment it was blacked out they would attack. Apollo got himself ready, he sat down Indian style and relaxed himself.

[Apollo is sitting cross legged on a huge pillow and he gathers energy around him, his body starts to radiate with a yellowish energy that resembles calm water moving about]

Edge: Are you ready?
Apollo: Yes, whenever I hear the first shot

Edge: Yeah... your half deaf lets just say when you're given the order
Apollo: Why do you have to be such an asshole to me all the time?!
Edge: HAhahahaa, remember make the shield big enough so they can't use those power suppressors

That was laugh well needed, everyone chuckled a bit, and in that time the moon totally covered itself, we all froze in our spots...

[Outside the stronghold military vehicles are starting to gather, they all aimed their weapons at the stronghold, soldiers, vehicles, and even helicopters]

The first shot was fired from an artillery shell, that familiar whistling sound before its destructive impact was enough to signal Apollo.

[The yellowish energy around Apollo suddenly expands outward in a rapid pace, the artillery shell approaches even faster, and the two meet. The explosion caused a rippling effect over the force field which immediately corrected it self by shimmering then stiffening into a smooth sphere]

The rest of the armed forces began firing, all that was heard was just a maelstrom of explosions, the stronghold just barely shook.

Edge: Ok Hacker now it's your turn, open a gate and send us on our way
Hacker: Got it

Hacker opened a gate for each of us. Each person was assigned to 5 major military establishments and whatever else there was in their paths. From the farthest from home and working our way back here as fast as we can to defend the stronghold.

[Hacker opens a gate for Testament, Halo, and Mei to walk through one by one, Edge is last to leave]

Edge: Now it's up to you guys to keep everyone safe, I'm depending on you two the most
Napalm: I got it, I won't let this place be taken over like my home was

Phenix: No problem man, you can count on me
Hacker: I'll monitor everything and make sure nothing gets through
Edge: Good

I went through my own gate and then I took to the air, this was it, this was the battle that would show them that we won't back down. This would end the war in the states, with no military to attack us, we would be safe, then afterwards maybe we can help out our kind in the other nations...

[Edge is flying through the night sky with his fires blazing, out in the distance lights are seen on the floor, it's the first base...]

Chapter 81

Halo strikes!

[Halo exits his gate and quickly bolts into the sky and heads to his destination]

Halo: I can't believe this is it, this is supposed to keep us safe... I hope Edge knows what he's doing.

[Halo reaches his destination and lands right in the middle of the base, everyone freezes and stares at him, he stands alone and defiant... The first shots are soon fired and Halo quickly dashes off with horrifying speed. He dashes around the soldiers causing them to shoot each other out of fear. A commanding officer orders the soldiers to use gas to subdue Halo, they all put on their gas masks and release canisters that empty out a toxic white cloud. Halo gets caught in the smoke and stumbles to the ground in pain. Before the soldiers open fire again he manages to dash off to the safety of a bunker rooftop. Bullets whiz by and with continued ease Halo dodges them all]

Halo: Screw this...

[Halo bolts to an open area and reaches his hand towards the sky...]

Halo: SKY THUNDER!

[A massive bolt of lightning strikes Halo who instantly redirects the energy outward. Dozens of electric arcs rip through the air striking all the nearby soldiers instantly killing them. From afar tanks are deployed, they release a volley of artillery shells that cover the eclipsed moon. He releases his Shockwave attack and instantly takes out half of the incoming shells. From behind the tanks the soldiers set up the power suppressing pillars but they have no effect on Halo... He continues to combat all resistance till no one opposed him anymore]

Halo: Damn that shit was harder than I thought, why can't Edge ever plan anything easy.

[Halo closes his eyes and takes a deep breath, he opens them and arcs of lightning twist outward, he once again reaches his hand upwards towards the sky and multiple bolts of lightning strike him this time they arc out into a dome and strike everything in the surrounding area, the buildings are immediately set ablaze and the weapon silos explode violently. The attack ends and Halo keels over in fatigue]

Halo: Damn that took a lot of energy, and I'm supposed to do this 4 more times?!

[Halo bolts into the sky and heads for his next location]

Halo: I wonder how everyone is doing...

[Back in the stronghold the soldiers continue their attack, Apollo is calm and steady never once losing hold of his concentration. Hacker is deep within the communications room monitoring all outside activities. The rest of the senior members are at their post making sure nothing gets in...]

Halo: I hope this one is a bit easier than the first.

[In the skies above a military base a raging thunderstorm stirs. Bolts of lightning strike down on the buildings and structures, the soldiers run for cover as the base is hammered by arcs of electricity. Halo drops out of the sky and lands on an open field. He dashes off in blinding speed]

Halo: Damn, it would make things easier if I can find the bombs and crap, I can just blow it all up and this one will be done for, but where are they...?

[*Halo continues to search around and he finds a nuke...*]

Halo: Damn, if I set this off then the area will be fucked up big time, maybe I can teleport it outta here.

[*Halo takes out his cell phone and calls Hacker but there's no connection*]

Halo: Fuck, I gotta get rid of this some how...

[*He grabs onto the missile and tries to bolt it out but instead he triggers the war head, he realizes his mistake and quickly dashes out of the silo and moves away as fast as he can*]

Halo: When I tried to get that shit outta there I fucking set it off instead, so I got my ass outta there as fast as I could, when I stopped I looked back and all I could see was the mushroom cloud, everyone is dead... I know that. All of them. Damn man...

[*Halo continues his route and by the last one he's completely worn out... his speed has dramatically decreased. He stands in front of his final base clutching his left arm to stop the pain and bleeding. The bases have all contacted each other by now and they have word of what is happening, this last base is prepared for Halo. Before he is able to make a move the soldiers quickly fire off gas grenades that consume Halo in a fog of poison. He tries to escape but is too tired and too slow to get anywhere fast enough, he tumbles to the ground as he trips out of a hastened pace...he closes his eyes and blacks out...*]

Chapter 82

Testament's assault

Testament: *My task is simple and yet it feels as if a mountain of work is on my shoulder. Somewhere inside me I feel a hatred for these things, these humans, and yet I am one of them, but yet I am not... instead I am sent forth to destroy their armies and end this war, this war of survival...*

[Testament simply walks up to the entrance of his first base, the soldiers immediately recognize him and open fire without question]

Testament: *Stupid humans, lives so worthless you might as well not live at all... I remember those words... from the demon, and now they are spoken from my lips.*

[The bullets hit Testament but inflict no wounds, they rip right through him... the bullet wounds ripple like the surface of water and simply reform, instantly healing themselves. In one motion Testament raises an arm and multiple streams of water rush out from the ground and make their way through the soldiers lungs drowning them slowly...]

Testament: *So fragile, such a simple task.*

[He walks around with no fear on his face, his eyes shine like the surface of a pond, no longer are they antiseptic white as they were in his full demon form, they now glow a faint blue with subtle ripples of water. He continues his assault relentlessly leaving no one alive. He finds the weapon storage and doesn't really know what to do with it]

319

Testament: Such frail creatures with such immense power, like a fly trying to hold up the world.

[He creates a giant sphere of water around the storage house and crushes it. The weapons which consisted of everything from bullets to grenades explode forcing the sphere to break and showering the entire base with water. A radio washes up beside Testament and on the other side a soldier cries out...]

Radio: A THUNDER GUY IS ATTACKING US WE NEED BACKUP ON THE...!

Testament: So the lightning one has begun his attack as well. Edge is brave for deciding on such a plan, his demon blood runs true.

[Testament finishes up the base and dematerializes into vapor and disappears in the wind. A few minutes later in another base, the ground shakes violently, the soldiers all stop and prepare themselves for an attack. The ground burst and streams of water shoot up from below. Testament begins his attack immediately by taking the streams of water and bending them downward so they blast everything they touch. Like lasers they rip through building walls and soldiers alike. The initial attack is fast and instant, the soldiers were not prepared]

Testament: If this is their defense then they have no hope of winning.

[Testament slowly raises his hand and the ground begins to shake violently. Water starts to seep through the ground and cracks the concrete, liquefaction occurs and in moments the entire base is more then half way sunk into quicksand. Testament looks annoyed and vaporizes away]

Testament: They offer no resistance, they are helpless against me, I have yet to come to a base worthy of taking on my power.

[Testament rides atop of a giant surf wave on land as he rushes towards the next base. This base is surrounded by an electrical fence and experimental energy based weapons. Testament lifts one of his eyebrows in curiosity as he jumps off the wave and over the fence]

Testament: For such weak and defenseless creatures they make up for it in their magic of science.

[*The soldiers all come out with high-tech looking riffles and begin firing at Testament, he lets them hit him but this time they rip through him violently and cause him and immense amount of pain, before any more of them hit he quickly liquefies his entire body and dives through the ground. Within seconds the ground right below the soldiers crack and streams of water rush out from under and into their mouths and noses. They are all drowned in a matter of seconds as Testament forces the water out of them, exploding them like balloons. More soldiers begin to fire electrified nets onto the ground and they shock Testament back into solid form. He pants a bit and stands up, he smirks and crosses his arms*]

Testament: So they forced me to fight in my solid form.

[*Water starts to form around him and he jets it out controlling them like they were part of him. The soldiers fire more rounds and electric nets at him but he swats them away like toys. He starts to walk to the center of the base with the water swirling around him protecting him. He once again sinks the base into the ground, but this time he wasn't aware of the immense power grid underneath... the moment his waters reach the power generators the electricity travels upward and catches him. Testament quickly drops to the ground and liquefies. The atmosphere is enclosed by the sound of live electricity... it soon stops and the entire base explodes violently...*]

Chapter 83
Mei's gold, her hardest hue to hold

[In another base far away from Halo and Testament vines of varying thickness spring up and entangle themselves in everything from cars to antennas. As quickly as they sprouted upwards they begin to pull down and into the ground, effectively destroying the entire base from the ground up. The soldiers are left untouched and any that could have escaped were allowed to escape. The base which was surrounded by a gate with watch towers and assorted vehicles all around was now nothing more then a giant sinkhole of fire and metal debris... The war Commandant is contacted...]

Dark Figure: He's gone
War Commandant: Then let's begin

[Mei continues her mission with ease, she is not encountered by any resistance... she approaches her final target visibly exhausted. She stops far enough away so she remains undetected, a wind blows passed her and she speaks knowing all too well who it is]

Mei: Brother, have you come to see this body go?
Saivent: I guess
Mei: This is the last act on my behalf, this body will not last any longer
Saivent: I know... tell me, do you wish you could do something to change something
Mei: It's crossed my mind now and then, is that why you released Judgment?

Saivent: So you know...

Mei: Yes

Saivent: I released him cause... I just had this idea that by releasing him the world might unite together, BUT, low and behold look where we are

Mei: It did not go as you hoped did it

Saivent: Not even close, Edge beat him alright but that led to his disappearance which was not supposed to happen, then Testament was released, and by trying to fix that I just made the problem worse, then Edge shows up again and I'm thinking he might be able to correct things but his nature is so temperamental that he made all the wrong choices for the right reasons, or was it the other way around, and mother won't help me out on this

Mei: Things will play themselves out

Saivent: Exactly what she said

Mei: But they will

Saivent: Worse still is Edge doesn't even know this, I meant to tell him, but I might as well just kill myself and save him the trouble

Mei: (chuckles) I have to go now

Saivent: I'll see you later

Mei: Things will work themselves out

[*Mei starts to walk towards her final base, the soldiers immediately target her and open fire. Each bullet that hits her tears away her skin like bark from a tree. Beneath is a golden light that shines through brightly and brilliantly. She walks into the center of the base and unleashes the golden light. In a blinding flash everything is vaporized and consumed in a sphere of light. When the corona starts to fade what's left behind is a baron surface of cracked mud and soldiers standing about, confused at what had just happened. In the center stood a sapling, it instantly starts to grow at a rapid rate all soldiers run for cover. Soon it reaches well into the skies and its branches begin to stretch outward, heavy with leaves, they swayed ever so gently as the wind blew passed them. At the base of the trunk, its roots where as thick as buildings and its bark as tough as rocks... all that remains of Mei was a small locket that was on the ground, the wind blew, and it was soon covered by loose sand and dirt... Back at the stronghold Hacker monitors the surveillance cameras from the communications* room, computer monitors flicker around everywhere. Apollo is still in the command center sitting cross legged concentrating as hard as he can. Outside the soldiers continue their assault. Unknown to everyone, soldiers and defenders alike a gathering of figures is forming right outside the radius of the military. The figures start to move in closer and in the light of gun fire their forms can be seen... they are the chimeras...]

Chapter 84

Wrath and warmth of fire

When I exited my gate I immediately flew to my base and landed dead center unleashing my Firestorm attack. It destroyed everything in the blast zone, buildings soldiers, vehicles, everything. The base was not destroyed though, only everything within a five block radius. I went around and looked for a weapon storage facility, that was the easiest way to create a big enough explosion to destroy the base.

[Edge walks around till he finds the storage facility, he then blast a stream of fire into the housing and takes flight, within moments a huge explosion is seen from the distance and Edge is off to his next base]

With each base gone I am just one step closer to home. And when they are all gone there will be no weapons to hurt us, to hunt us, to destroy us. This is the right thing to do, it's them or us, and I'll be damned if I let them walk all over us anymore, one way or another, this ends now.

[Edge arrives at the front gate of his second base. He intensifies the fires around him and walks right through the front gate melting the steel instantly. A hail of gun fire is set upon Edge but each bullet comes to a grinding halt as they near him. Literally the copper casing and the lead slug it surrounds melts and simply fall to the ground creating a pool of molten metal around Edge. In one violent release of energy, waves of fire are sent outward, incinerating everything in the surrounding area.

The rest of the soldiers all abandon station and in no time the base is left empty]

This is a first, usually they fight till the very end, hopeless as it may be, but they all just surrendered, what's going on? Did they realize there's no point in fighting back and just leave? No, this isn't like them...

[Edge walks around for a while, the soldiers have long gone and the base is silent. Edge looks for the main weapon storage , but the moment he opens the door he finds a bomb, before he realizes what sort of bomb it is, it goes off. In a rattling violence the entire base is instantly wiped out... once the mushroom cloud settles a bit and the dust is blown away by the wind, a sudden release of power expands outward and forces away the remaining bits of debris. In the center of that fiery energy is Edge kneeling on the floor. The moment he stands up the energy opens up to reveal a pair of huge fiery wings, it's Fenix. From afar the soldiers were watching, when they realized their plan had failed they send in a barrage of artillery shells, Edge simply takes to the air along with Fenix]

They're willing to go as far as sacrificing their base to try and stop me? They seem just as desperate as I am... to bad, cuz they just pissed me the fuck off, and it just so happens they are in my way.

[Edge heads towards the group of soldiers in his way and lands, Fenix comes up from behind and unleashes its energy incinerating everything in the area. When the attack is over Fenix is nowhere to be found]

Go back to sleep, I'll ask for your help again in due time. I can feel the final battle coming, through all this the moon has remained eclipsed... that's a bad sign. Sumtin is gonna happen, and I need to get home as soon as possible. I only have a few bases to go, I gotta make them quick as I can. Damn, was that a nuke that they just set off?

[Edge takes to the sky and continues his assault. He's met with resistance and he dispatches them with relative ease...]

It's kinda funny, I remember what Hacker said to me a long time ago...

[Flashback - Edge, Halo and Hacker are in an argument, and one sentence from Hacker stuck in Edge's mind till now...]

Hacker: ...you can't save the world with fire...

[Edge finishes off the last base with a bang, it's the biggest base so he used the Firestorm at full power, it severely weakens him and he has trouble standing up afterwards]

I'm so fucking tired, all these bases, all this trouble. I need to make it home, I need to make sure everyone's alright...

[Edge takes to the air but tumbles around like a fumbling bee, he tries his best to gain his composure and begins to climb into the sky. He finds the blue glow of the Light of Hope and follows it on his way home, slowly but surely picking up speed...]

Chapter 85

A traitor within trust

[10 minutes after the departure of the team, a shadowy figure appears from behind Apollo and in one quick strike knocks him out. The shield instantly falls and the soldiers quickly attack the stronghold with everything they have. The artillery shells that hit the side of the stronghold explode violently but barely does any damage. Hacker quickly opens up a gate to Apollo to see what has happened, the moment he steps through the gate he sees the person who has knocked out Apollo]

Hacker: YOU!? You're betraying us!? WHY!?

[The betrayer fires a stream of flames at Hacker but he creates a gate and reflects it back to him. As if expecting that, right after he launches the jet of flames, he quickly picks up Apollo with one hand demonstrating his strength, leaps out the window of the command center and takes to the sky just like Edge. Hacker follows him to the window and opens a gate to grab Apollo back but the moment he opens it an oven of flames pass right through keeping him from entering]

Hacker: *Damn, he's just like Edge he knows how to keep me away. I can't do anything... what the fuck are those....?*

[Hacker looks out to the streets below and there are red eyes that litter the streets]

Hacker: Oh no...

[*The soldiers quickly launch the power suppressing pillars in a circle around the base. The chimeras instantly attack and all Hacker can do is warn everyone of the coming danger. Raven, Dak, Napalm and anyone else who can fight are all alerted but the moment they head outside and try to stand their ground they all realize their powers don't work and they quickly head back inside and towards Hacker*]

Raven: Dang it's those things again!

Dak: Why aren't my powers working?!

Napalm: It's those white bodies they stick into the ground, they prevent our powers from working, damn it I will end them or this!

Dak: What are those things?

Hacker: They're clones of person, he was a power user with the ability to stop others from using their powers, the government took him and experimented with him to try and find a way to fight people like us, he died and they cloned him discovering that his clones, while brain dead and soulless, still possessed the ability to keep other users from using their powers

Dak: They would go that far to play with people like they were gods?

Hacker: They go even further, they experimented with him and genetically modified him, that's why they look that way. He's no longer human, he's completely artificial... they found out they could alter him to remove his human qualities and boast his powers, they were design to be more "durable" in battle

Raven: Dang where's Edge and the others?

Dak: What good would he do?

Hacker: The pillars don't work on him

Dak: Why him?

Hacker: We assume it's because he's an elemental spirit

Napalm: What the hell is an elemental spirit?

Hacker: Unlike Napalm who gets his fires from sumtin that produces his element, Edge is able to create it from his own spiritual energy

Napalm: How does that keep him immune?

Hacker: He was once a full demon

Napalm: ...

Dak: ...

Raven: Dang...

Hacker: Look we don't have time to discus this anymore we have to go, there's a passage way that leads far enough for us to use our powers
Napalm: Wait where Phenix and Apollo?
Dak: Yeah they're not here
Hacker: Phenix is a traitor, he kidnapped Apollo...

Chapter 86

Dynamo.

[The soldiers surround Halo ready to fire the last shot, they all edge closer to him, all with fear...]

Halo: *Where am I? Am I in the sky?*

[Halo wakes up to find himself suspended in mid air high above the clouds, he rights himself and looks around curiously at what has transpired]

Halo: *Crap did I die again? Edge is gonna be mad pissed if I did. This don't look like hell or heaven though, so where am I?*

[Off in the distance a roar is heard, so thunderous and loud that Halo felt his body shake from the bass. From out of the clouds a massive tiger the size of a school bus seemingly made of electricity steps out and slowly and looks at Halo]

Halo: *What is this? How come it feels like I know him, like he's a part of me, I'm not afraid. This is so weird, I approached him and he stepped forward to greet me. He lowered his head and I pet his nose.*

[When Halo places his hand on the tiger's nose he is suddenly consumed by light, in the real world the soldiers quickly back up and cover their eyes from the immense light. Halo awakens on the floor and stands up to see that time has seemingly stopped. The soldiers are frozen in place and the area is consumed by an ambient light]

Halo: *What's going on? Why is everything still, did I stop time or sumtin? I walked around to see if everything else was like this, and it was. Far away I could see that tiger, I walked towards him and it looked like he was* tryna *take me somewhere so I followed. He took me to the weapons storage and I knew what to do.*

[The moment Halo touches the door, time unfreezes and everyone is active again. Halo quickly unleashes his Shockwave at full force and instantly as the silo explodes time immediately freezes itself once again and the tiger reappears, Halo instinctively jumps onto its back and it starts to run. As it heads towards the exit of the base time slowly begins to reestablish momentum, soon they are in normal time again. Halo looks back and in the distance he sees a mushroom cloud that quickly becomes a tiny spot of light]

Halo: Let's go home Dynamo!

Chapter 87

Devastated home

[*Halo rides on the back of Dynamo and in no time he is home, but when he arrives he arrives to a devastated battlefield. He gets off of Dynamo's back and the tiger roars loudly before dematerializing in a flash of lightning. Halo walks around to find a field of dead bodies everywhere, soldiers and users alike*]

Halo: *What happened here, did I miss sumtin?*

[*In the distance past the stronghold red eyes start to glow first in a few pairs then in larger and larger numbers. The only light there was, was from the Light of Hope, anything beyond that was shrouded in darkness. The glow of the red eyes slowly made their way towards the stronghold, the ambient illumination from the Light of Hope revealed to Halo the owners of the crimson eyes... chimeras*]

Halo: *Shit, that's a lot of chimeras... what are they holding...?*

[*Halo takes a closer look and realizes they are holding dismembered parts of human bodies, he shudders in horror...*]

Halo: *UGH! What the fuck?! That's fucking nasty! They were never like this, they're like savage animals in human form now... shit and they're after me!*

[*The chimeras drop their body parts and start to head towards Halo, slowly at first and then a faster pace until they are running. Halo stands his ground and as a bunch of them got near him, he unleashes his Shockwave attack. It pierces them and they drop to the floor dead. More and more start to rush at Halo, he takes one step to the side and all time seemingly stops. He runs up to as many of them as he can and uses his Shock Fist attack to impale them, when time resumes its normal pace the impaled chimeras fall to the ground dead on the spot. Seeing their comrades fall in battle does not faze the legions of others out there]*

Halo: *Damn there so many...*

[The chimeras all continue their attack on Halo relentlessly but Halo uses his new found speed to literally slow time down to a crawl and attack the chimeras with his Shock Fist, this takes its toll on Halo very quickly...]

Halo: *Damn it, where's everyone else?*

[Halo bolts himself to the entrance of the stronghold and bangs on the door]

Halo: *Fuck, what if no ones inside... wait the top.*

[Halo bolts off to the top of the stronghold where he enters through the window]

Halo: *What exactly happened here? There're flame marks, it looks like someone had a fight here, but who did this? I wonder if anyone is left.*

[Halo begins to descend the tiers in search for survivors... within the stronghold he sees many dead bodies, most are chimeras but some are also users]

Halo: *Oh man how did sumtin like this happen. The chimeras that were dead didn't have any marks, it looked like they just dropped dead on the spot. The users looked like they were ripped to shreds. I yelled out to see if there were any survivors, but there wasn't any. I walked around a bit and there he was in the dining hall... Hacker.*

Chapter 88

Edge's arrival

[Halo runs to Hacker...]

Halo: HACKER!
Hacker: (coughing) ugh...
Halo: Are you alright!? What happened here?!
Hacker: I'm alright, I think...
Halo: What happened here?
Hacker: We were betrayed
Halo: What? Who the hell would betray us?
Hacker: Phenix, he betrayed us and kidnapped Apollo, he's gone now
Halo: What why? Where's everyone else?
Hacker: I sent them away, Napalm, Raven, Dak and a few others are with them
Halo: Damn I didn't make it back in time to stop all this
Hacker: We should be safe now, I managed to seal off the door and stop the ones that got in
Halo: How did you do it?
Hacker: Do what?
Halo: Stop the chimeras?
Hacker: I just took out their heart
Halo: Damn

[Halo takes Hacker to a near by table and sits him upright but Hacker just falls back into the chair...]

Hacker: You're the only one that made it back?
Halo: So far...
Hacker: Shit...
Halo: I haven't heard from anyone
Hacker: You were outside?
Halo: Yeah
Hacker: How is it out there?
Halo: Soldiers are all dead, but the chimeras are all over the place, the white pillar people things...
Hacker: Power suppression pillars
Halo: Yeah, those things are down
Hacker: Good we should be safe for now

[Halo and Hacker are resting within the stronghold, moments later there are explosions heard outside, continuous blast that causes the entire stronghold to shake, faintly between explosions you can hear vulgar profanities being shouted out]

Hacker: Heh, Edge is back
Halo: Yeah
Hacker: Let's go greet him...

Chapter 89

Arrival to devastation

I finished my mission and started to head home. Suffice to say it wasn't easy, then again, staying alive isn't easy either. All I had to do was look to the sky and I could see the Light of Hope pierce the darkness, all I had to do was follow it and I knew I would be home. It wasn't a long flight, below me I could see the other bases that had already been destroyed. What did catch my eye though was a huge tree located in... Well somewhere, it seemed to reach into the sky and I had to stop to look in wonder. I knew this was Mei's doing, I guess she's gone now, but she left this giant tree to us, why though? She never mentioned doing sumtin like this... whatever its use was we'll just have to wait to find out. I can't just ogle at the sight of the tree when my target was home.

I flew as high as I could above the clouds so I could cover more ground. The sky though was black, the moon still hasn't revealed itself after it had eclipsed. That can only mean sumtin bad is gonna happen, all the more reason to get home faster.

[Edge turns up the fire and dashes off even quicker]

As I soared in the clouds I felt small drops of cold water condense on my face, I just burned my fire hotter and all the clouds around me just sorta wafted away from me. As I edged closer to home I saw the sky of the city covered in a dark shroud, I flew over New Jersey and started my descent. A descent that should've been a relief cuz I knew home was right there, a descent that should have made me feel justice in my actions, but I descended into a silent war. Soldiers dead everywhere, silence, the

341

white pillars of humanoid looking figures have all been toppled over and eviscerated. Their organs were spewed all over the ground. The stronghold which I expected to be teaming with life was silent, the shield that should have been up was down. All I could wonder was if sumtin had happened. Did the soldiers get in? Was everyone alright? I walked up to one of the bodies, and to my surprise it wasn't a soldier's body, in fact most of them were... they were chimeras. Each one had a hole blasted through its chest, each one laid dead with no apparent struggle. Who did this? Was it Hacker? No, his attacks don't cauterize or even leave such a wound. Was this Napalm or Phenix? I have to get into the stronghold, I have to find out what happened.

[Edge walks toward the stronghold but as he nears the front entrance a swarm of chimeras run out from the shadows and attack Edge. Edge simply turns around and unleashes a wave of fire that incinerates the chimeras in the front. Several break through and manage to grab Edge and choke him to the floor, he simply uses his Strike Fist attack and sends the chimeras back explosively]

Mother fuckers are really starting to piss me off!

[Edge cups his hands together and unleashes a weak Firestorm that destroys all the chimeras in sight]

What the fuck is going on, where is everyone? Why is the shield down?

[Right then and there the entrance to the stronghold opens and out comes Halo and Hacker]

Edge: (with a worried but angry voice) guys! What happened here?
Halo: We've been betrayed
Edge: ...
Hacker: (with slight signs of pain) it was Phenix, he betrayed us

[Edge's face loses all emotion, all the fires in the ambient area suddenly cease and die. With no signs of emotion Edge just walks past them and into the stronghold looking around]

Halo: Oh man, he lost it
Hacker: Good thing or bad thing?
Halo: I have no idea
Edge: ...
Halo: Dude?
Hacker: Dude?

[Edge's shoulder drops and his fist unclench...]

Edge: I... I can't do this anymore
Halo: You ok?
Edge: I just can't, everything is against me, against us...
Halo: Against you?
Edge: (chuckles) everything I do, everything that seems right, it just leads to one epic fail after another, I just can't do it anymore
Halo: I'm sorry, but we gotta do sumtin
Edge: Do what? What else is there to do? I'm on the edge of just quitting
Halo: Dude, shut the fuck up, after all this shit you choose now to be a lil bitch about stuff?
Edge: ...
Hacker: (with a shocked look) wow...
Halo: I mean c'mon what happened to never give up never back down
Hacker: You really think it's a...
Halo: I mean you didn't just make us go through all that shit to just sit there and whine and complain like an old lady
Hacker: Dude...
Edge: ...
Halo: GET A HOLD OF YOURSELF!
Hacker: Uh dude...

[Edge in one swift motion turns around and plunges his Strike Fist into Halo's chest and sends him flying back. Edge's eyes are consumed in a fiery blaze, the surrounding area immediately ignites into an inferno that blazes out of control]

Hacker: I TOLD YOU NOT TO PUSH HIM!
Halo: This is for his OWN GOOD!

[Halo sends a Shockwave at Edge, but Edge simply holds up his hand and catches the lightning bolt taking its full force. Edge's hand is forced back but he resists the entire way as if catching a fast heavy ball]

Halo: IF THIS IS WHAT IT TAKES!
Hacker: This is so not a good idea...

[Edge's eyes are still consumed in fire and he looks like he is devoured in apathy. Edge and Halo continue to battle relentlessly, Hacker tries to stop them but is completely overcome]

Hacker: C'MON GUYS THIS IS STUPID!

[Suddenly the sky opens up and a downpour kills all the fires in the area and snaps Edge out of his rampage. Suddenly a figure takes form and a pillar of water hammers both Halo and Edge back pinning them against a wall. Testament fully materializes from the figure]

Testament: (with a hint of pain in his voice) enough, at a time like this allies should not be at war
Hacker: Finally someone sane...

[Edge's rage cools down and he seems to snap back into reality, when he does he seems a bit lost]

Sumtin in me clicked and I sorta blanked out, when I did though I felt like I had nuttin to worry about, like I was at ease, I was tired, so fucking tired, but I got pulled back here, to this existence. Before me stared three pairs of eyes, Halo, Testament, and Hacker...

Chapter 90

Coming end

Hacker filled me in, I just couldn't believe that Phenix would do that. But why? He's not a bad guy, we were friends in high school, and he was the only other fire user that I could relate to. On some if not many levels he was the only one that understood me, better than even Halo. Why did he betray us...?

A lot of people died, those fucking chimeras... It's bad enough we have all these groups pressing down on us but now we gotta deal with a traitor and these mutated idiots. First things first, we need to get Apollo back, I dunno what they plan to do with him, but we have to save him. I asked Hacker if he knew where they were going but he had no idea. Before I even knew it, it was day break, the moon stayed in the shadows the entire night, this breaks all laws of physics and I KNOW sumtins up, I just dunno what.

Edge: Where is everyone?
Hacker: They're in a safe place up by the Catskills
Edge: Hmm, leave them there, they'll be fine, we have to get Apollo back, and then... I dunno what will happen then
Hacker: Maybe I can locate him
Edge: Go and try, anything is better the nuttin at this point
Halo: And me?
Edge: Uh, I... dunno
Testament: I will go rest, I am fatigued
Halo: I think I'll do the same

[Halo and Testament both head in, Hacker opens a gate and steps through, only Edge is left standing there]

Apollo is gone, the moon is eclipsed, Mei is gone, there's a giant tree, what the hell does all this have to do with each other? I flew up to the sky to see if anything looks weird, and indeed there was sumtin wrong. All around where there should be green, there wasn't, all there is, is dead brown, dieing plants everywhere. As if the entire world was drained of life.

[Edge quickly flies back down and calls the others back outside]

Edge: Guys sumtin is wrong, it's like the entire world is dead or sumtin
Hacker: It's everywhere, the plants are dieing
Halo: What the hell is going on?
Edge: Did you find anything on Apollo?
Hacker: No not yet, there's... there's no power
Edge: No power?
Hacker: Yeah, there's no electricity or anything, like everything just died

[Halo holds up his hand and releases a bolt of lightning]

Halo: I still seem to work
Edge: ...
Hacker: ...
Halo: What?
Edge: ...damn it, what's going on...

[Testament steps out of the stronghold with an annoyed look on his face]

Testament: Can I not get some rest here, what is the problem?
Edge: The world is dead
Testament: Explain
Edge: There's no power, the plants are dieing
Testament: Hmm... The moon was completely eclipsed last night was it not? I have never once seen it reappear after it was covered in darkness
Hacker: You know... I noticed it too

Halo: Too busy being beat to the ground to notice...

Edge: I noticed it

Testament: As for the rest of the world I cannot answer that mystery, but...

Edge: But...

Testament: If the moon is gone, that can only mean one thing

Hacker: What is it?

Testament: Lucifer

Halo: The devil?

Edge: What about him?

Testament: He is breaking free, he must have gained...

Edge: Gained what?

Testament: He must have gained enough tortured souls to feed off of, enough to give him the energy to break through, but he can only do that on an eclipse

Hacker: That doesn't explain why the moon didn't reappear though

Testament: He is a demonic entity, he has vast powers, far beyond ours

Halo: Great, how we supposed to fight sumtin like that?

Edge: (hits Halo on the shoulder) never give up and never back down, we fight fire with fire

Halo: You're the only fire dude here

Edge: (with an annoyed tone) it's a figure of speech!

Hacker: Hey Testament, you have any idea where Apollo could be?

Testament: Apollo?

Hacker: He was kidnapped by Phenix

Testament: Phenix must be working under Lucifer

Hacker: So you know where he is?

Testament: No, if this is the case then it is too late, we must stop him at the moment he comes out, until then we can do nothing

Halo: Hacker, what about everyone else?

Edge: Leave them outta this, when this battle starts it's only gonna be the 3 of us

Hacker: (with an assertive tone) hey what about me?!

Edge: Don't you get it, haven't you seen what we can do?

Hacker: So? What does that have to do with anything?

Testament: It is obvious he cares, otherwise he would not bother to warn you of the upcoming danger

Halo: Yeah, besides, don't you remember tryna stop me and Edge? You couldn't even get near us

Edge: (sigh)

Hacker: Good point I guess

Edge: Go to the rest of the group, tell everyone to find safety far away from here, take them to a place where it's not too hot and not too cold and wait there

Hacker: Wait for what?

Edge: I dunno...

Hacker: This is it isn't it

Edge: Yeah, how much time do we have?

Testament: In two more days. First day to seal the moon, second day to drown it in blood, and third for the gateway to open

Hacker: Why does he need Apollo though?

Testament: To keep the gateway from being closed or destroyed

Edge: I hope Apollo doesn't turn on us

Halo: Wow, this REALLY is it isn't it?

Testament: It appears to be so

Edge: Yeah, it seems that way doesn't it

Hacker: I guess I'll be on my way

[The group holds out their hands and they grab each others forearms forming a circle]

Halo: Alright guys...

Testament: To the coming fight...

Edge: Yeah, an adventure...

Hacker: To friendship...

Hacker parted ways with us after that, from here on out I'm just winging it.

Chapter 91

Always waiting...

Why does it seem like we're always waiting for the worse to come? Then again everything has a purpose doesn't it? Nah, fuck that, after all that's happened, after all I found out, I don't believe in that anymore. We cleared up the stronghold of all the bodies, users and chimeras alike, and outside, the soldiers. Testament dug out the ground in a small area of dried grass in Battery Park City and we laid the bodies there. I incinerated the pile and we spread the ashes into the sea, uh, rather the river that is, from there, we rested and relaxed, gathered up our energy and did what we had to do. How many times have we've done that already? Each time we'd think that was the end, the last time we would have to be in that position, but here we are again. This should all be me, I started all this, I should be the one to finish it, but look at the reality of it all. I'm not actually alone...

[Edge sits on a chair staring out into the Hudson River, Testament walks up to him from the side]

Testament: Fire Lord
Edge: Why do you always call me that?
Testament: That was your title
Edge: Sometimes I wonder what goes on in that head of yours
Testament: What do you mean?
Edge: Who are you really, Kae? Or Testament?
Testament: Testament is the name I take on. The name of this power, Kae is the name given to this body, but my soul, who I am, I am neither

Edge: Then who are you?

Testament: I am just memories and fragments that exist of the old demon, given life by the soul

Edge: So, you're like a fusion

Testament: Fusion?

Edge: Never mind, how much do you remember about that old war?

Testament: Not very much, I can only feel the memories in certain instances, and in certain times I can recall facts and details

Edge: It's funny, you act just like him

Testament: Perhaps

We stopped talking after a while and we headed back to the stronghold to meet up with Halo. That night we looked into the night sky and just as Testament said, the moon was red like blood. It would be one more day to go before we would find out where the gateway would be.

The sun broke the night as it always did and when it rose we awoke to a barren world, the buildings almost seem to be slowly deteriorating, the pavement was cracked and jagged and I think... I think I even saw a tumble weed role by. Anyway the 3 of us went to the command center and looked out the window that day. We didn't have much to say to each other, we just waited. The day seemed to pass by so fast as if almost in a blink of an eye it was over.

The sun started to set and the blue sky became orange then red, and finally the dark blue of night. The moon started right off as a red giant in the sky, it was almost directly above us.

[The ground below suddenly lit up with red dots, the eyes of the chimeras. They surrounded the stronghold and began to climb their way up]

Testament: They are trying to reach us

Edge: Lets keep them as far back as we can

[With no warning Testament surrounds the command center in a ring of water and releases it. All the chimeras are washed back to the ground]

Halo: Now it's my turn

[Halo reaches his hand to the sky and a bolt of lightning strikes the ground electrocuting all of them]

Edge: That's not gonna stop them, look, in the distance

[More red eyes open themselves up and they begin to re swarm the stronghold, this time in greater numbers]

Halo: Dude we need to get outta here, we're basically pinned, and we need to save our energy
Testament: Then let us go
Edge: Let's go to Central Park, we can each get there on our own
Halo: Right
Testament: Agreed

[Edge takes to the air and starts flying north, Halo grabs his broadsword and just disappears within a lightning bolt into the sky, Testament leaps out the window of the command center dematerializing into a stream of water and dives right into the steam pipes below the city streets]

I feel bad for Central Park, that place is always being fucked up somehow. I thought that within the darkness I wouldn't be able to see the wave of death that seemed to have suddenly consumed the planet but I was wrong. The grass had dried up and the floor was dusty. When all 3 of us got there we waited, just waited to see what would happen next. And so it came in the form of more chimeras...

Edge: Damn it they don't give up
Halo: How many you think there are?
Testament: Too many, I will take care of them, it takes too much energy for you two to deal with them
Edge: Just don't wear yourself out

[Testament lifts his hands up to shoulder level and slowly closes his fist. Streams of water come rushing up from the cracked ground, and with a twist of his wrist, he extends his fingers causing the water to jet forward. They all rush ahead and dive right into the nostrils of the chimeras. The stream would fork in two and then four in order to reach the others that

escaped the first wave, in moments all the chimeras were on their knees drowning. The streams of water quickly left those that were dead in search for a new victim to asphyxiate]

Edge: Wow, that's useful
Halo: That's just creepy...

The more that fell the more that came, it was almost never ending...

Halo: Where the hell are they all coming from?!
Edge: Fuck this shit...

[Edge holds up his right hand and fires start to swirl around his gloved fist. The fires start to shine brightly and more intensely, he suddenly drives his fist into the ground and within moments they are surrounded by a ring of fire that erupted in a 5 block radius]

Edge: That should keep the rest of them out while you take care of the rest of the ones inside
Testament: They will be dead in no time

The firewall should keep the rest of them out, we need to keep our focus on the blood moon.

Edge: How do we know when to strike?
Testament: A red light will shine upon the gateway
Edge: Damn what if it's all the way on the other side of the states
Halo: I can get us there
Edge: How?
Halo: Dynamo...
Testament: You did not...
Edge: Dynamo?
Testament: His spirit calling...
Edge: Oh shit...
Halo: Cool right?
Edge: No not that, oh shit to that!

[The moon starts to shine brilliantly for a second and then a ray of crimson light breaks the sky and pierces the darkness]

The time is here, now we have to figure out where the light is going...

Halo: Alright get on!

Halo released a stupid large amount of lightning from his body, enough to cause us to dart back from it. The lightning quickly struck the sky and disappeared, not even a second later another larger bolt of lightning struck the ground and a giant tiger like figure ran out from it. This was his calling?

[Halo quickly dashes off in a blur of lightning grabbing both Edge and Testament pulling them onto the back of Dynamo]

Damn this is insane, in a split second I was watching a giant tiger run past me to being on the tiger itself, damn I hate when he does this. This is like that pain I get when I'm traveling through the bolt of lightning that Halo travels in, just 100 times worse.

[Dynamo starts running and time around them slows down to a crawl]

Literally in not more than a minute from what it seemed I was outta that world of speed and back in reality. Before me stood 3 figures, and around them was a yellowish dome of energy, below them was the mark of the gateway, a pentagram the size of a city block, how cliché...

[Edge, Halo and Testament get off and Dynamo disappears in a flash, they stand before 3 figures, one is knelt on the ground. The moon above shines a giant pillar of red light upon the 3 and below them glows a bright red pentagram]

Phenix: So you made it after all

Chapter 92

Pairing up before the end

Edge: Why'd you do it yo

Phenix: (laughs with disbelief) you really are slow aren't you?

Edge: ...

Phenix: Didn't you notice from before? I'm just like you

Edge: What ya mean...

Phenix: Please as if any real elemental user could create fire from his breath, not even a master elemental user can do that, but it was the only lie I could come up with at the time

Edge: So why, what's all this for

Phenix: You really have no idea do you?

Edge: If I did I wouldn't be fucking asking now would I

Phenix: Years ago, so many years ago, when you first discovered your power... do you remember what happened

Edge: ...

Phenix: That's right! You got it! It's me

Edge: It was all a lie, high school...

Phenix: Bingo! I just thought I'd fuck around with your head a bit. But I guess now it's time to bring it to an end

[From the back of the person kneeling on the floor, a figure steps out]

War Commandant: Edge, nice to see you again

Edge: You...

Halo: I killed you

War Commandant: So it seems you did, let me change into something your more familiar with seeing shall we?

[*The War Commandant steps up and tears open his blazer, from his bare chest we can see the hole that Halo blasted out. The hole though was now filled with a purplish blaze*]

Edge: It can't be...

[*The purple blaze begins to incinerate the flesh and in no time all that's left is a shell of char. The shell immediately cracks and a small fiery figure steps out, the flames subside and a familiar face is seen*]

Testament: Judgment
Phenix: Ah the failure recognizes you
Judgment: So it would seem
Edge: No, no no... What the fuck is going on here, I killed you, and you killed me
Phenix: Like I said you're the slow one, what happened when you died? Took a visit to the sanctuary didn't you?
Edge: That means you went back to hell
Judgment: Yes, that's right, Lucifer gave me one more chance to redeem myself, sadly I can't say the same for that abomination, you completely killed him and now all that's left is that imitation
Testament: ...
Phenix: You're too late Edge, Apollo is under our control, and while his shield is up, you can't get through, not that it matters even if you did, you'd have to destroy the moon somehow in order to stop the gateway from opening
Edge: ...
Phenix: I'm itching to take my revenge
Edge: Fucking asshole

[*Edge's right fist ignites into an inferno. Phenix steps through the shield and raises his right hand and ignites it into a crimson fiery blaze. The two stare at each other with intense hatred*]

Judgment: You're mine...

Testament: Quarrel?

[Judgment steps out of the shield and ignites his entire body, the flames start to extend and grow into the form of a serpentine dragon]

Testament: If that is the way it is to be...

[Water drops start to form around Testament and coalesce into streams of water. His eyes glow with the hue of crystal blue water and with a slight tilt of his head the ground shakes violently, from the earth burst forth Leviathan...]

Halo: Great, what the hell am I supposed to do...?

Chapter 93

The two flames

[Edge and Phenix take to the sky and vanish within the clouds, both their fires ignite the dark heavens into a cindering hell]

Phenix: You know how long I waited for this day? How long my blood boiled with this inferno? Just the sight of you makes me sick, the fact that you're in front of me is enough to make me wanna destroy the world!
Edge: You lied all this time, just to get to me, at the cost of so many, you really are a piece of shit!

[The two beings of fire jet towards each other and exchange blows, flares and sparks break the darkness of the night sky]

Phenix: I spent an eternity in hell, tormented by your face, ravaged by the demons, only my hatred for you and my anger kept me intact and sane, the thought of seeing you again one day and TEARING YOUR FACE OFF!!

[Phenix unleashes a wave of fire at Edge who manages to stop most of it with his Strike Fist]

Edge: You can't even begin to imagine how much I hated you back then, add on the fact you betrayed us all makes you nuttin but dead shit to me!

[Edge dashes forward and grabs Phenix by the ankle and throws him

*towards the earth and immediately follows. The two plummet and Edge
fires off a few streams of flames at Phenix, but Phenix dodges them all]*

Phenix: You're gonna have to do a lot better than that Edge, you thought
Judgment was bad? Wait till you see what I do to your friends, the look
on your face when I gut them all with my bare hands...

*[Edge dashes forward even faster and grabs a hold of Phenix and thrust
forward as fast as he can driving the both of them into the ground. A large
explosion kicks up a cloud of debris. The two quickly right themselves and
stand in defiance towards one another with their flames lit brightly]*

Edge: The only thing I regretted when I turned you to dust was that I
didn't get to see the look on your face as you burned!

*[Phenix unleashes a flamethrower at Edge who counters wit his own
flamethrower. The two streams collide and repel each other in a fury of
sparks]*

Phenix: You're not gonna win this one!
Edge: I'm not fighting to win, I'm fighting to kill you!

*[Edge suddenly stops his stream of fire and Phenix's flamethrower quickly
consumes him]*

Phenix: YOU LOSE EDGE!
Edge: Think again...

*[Within Phenix's crimson flames that now consume him, Edge braces his
right arm with this left hand and unleashes his Azure Flame. It quickly
over takes Phenix's flames causing him to jump back and out of the way]*

Phenix: You know you can't beat me so you resort to that grotesque
flame, that imitation
Edge: The only imitation is you, you dumb fuck!

*[Edge ignites his Azure Flame to a full burn and collects it in his right
fist]*

Phenix: When this is all over there's just gonna be one
Edge: You don't have shit to fight for...

[Edge strikes the ground with his flame lit fist and a fissure of energy erupts towards Phenix, but Phenix takes to the air and extends both his arms outward releasing rays of energy that pierce through the air and into the ground like lasers. Edge's speed in his Azure Flame state allows him to quickly dodge them all]

Phenix: Run all you want Edge, that's all you could ever do!
Edge: AZURATH!

[Edge stops dodging and forms his hand into the shape of a sphere as he summoned his attack. The rays that Phenix shoots out are pulled into the revolution of energy and immediately expelled outward toward Phenix. Realizing what attack this was he now quickly starts to dodge to the best of his efforts only narrowly missing the curving beam. Edge's attack quickly subsides and it visibly leaves him drained, the Azure Flame extinguishes itself]

Phenix: You don't have the energy to sustain that flame at the level your using it at, HA! How pathetic
Edge: What's pathetic is you, not even a true demon, just given their powers, you don't got a clue about anything
Phenix: Who cares?! I sure as hell don't, as long as I get my revenge on you that's all that fucking matters!

[Edge falls to his knees as Phenix slowly approaches him]

Edge: (breathing hard) it's kinda funny, you're pissed off at me cuz I killed you and you were sent to hell, but in reality, I don't even know who you are, all I remember is the feelings I had when I set you on fire...
Phenix: Oh shut up, look at you, you can't even stand up, don't talk to me about irony or any of that shit, you know what's really ironic? It's this whole situation, you, the Fire Lord, reduced to this pathetic shell, while I stand strong, that's real irony
Edge: Heh, it doesn't really matter, no matter what you say, what you do, you'll just never win, you didn't before, and you won't now

361

Phenix: HA! Do you even hear yourself, god, you really are full of it aren't you

Edge: Yeah, but it's cuz you have nuttin to lose, and therefore nuttin to fight for, I on the other hand can't afford to lose. You really dunno anything about me do you... I thought you'd be able to understand me since we're so alike sometimes but I guess I was wrong. It's people like you who made me who I am, and it's cuz of people like you that give me the reason to fight and to keep on fighting...

[Edge slowly starts to get up, Phenix stops approaching...]

Edge: It's cuz of people like you that piss me off...

[Edge reignites his Hell Fire and it begins to swirl around him]

Edge: BRING IT OUT
Phenix: What are you babbling about...?
Edge: Bring out that crimson fire of yours, and I will show you why I was called Fire Lord by smashing it!
Phenix: (scoffs)

[They both ignite their fires intensely. Within each of their eyes an inferno rages...]

Chapter 94

The dark flame and the Torrent

Judgment: Not only are you just a shell of power and an abomination but you ally yourself with that traitor
Testament: I exist as I exist, who I am is who I choose to be

[Judgment, fully surrounded by his flames which have taken the form of a serpentine dragon, takes to the sky. Testament steps onto Leviathan's head and a jet of water blast out from its maw, it cuts into the air like a laser but Judgment dodges]

Judgment: Let's see the ultimate battle between the oldest of powers!

[Judgment heads towards Leviathan and releases a violet laser from his hand. Testament erects a shield of water that absorbs the attack just long enough for Leviathan to release another jet of water that pierces through the shield and takes the laser head on. The two assaults collide and dissipate each other]

Judgment: HAHAHAHAHA! It's a pity your true power is no more, you might have actually been able to beat me
Testament: I intend to crush you and drown your flames!

[Leviathan and Judgment spiral towards each other and intertwine their bodies locking themselves in a helix of mayhem. Testament quickly runs down the back of Leviathan and summons a coil of water that he aims at Judgment. The water puts out the violet flames causing Judgment to fall

out of his fiery dragon. The moment Judgment touches down the dragon dissipates]

Judgment: What a pity that I don't hold with me the Azure Flame like Edge does, that's what he used to defeat you wasn't it
Testament: You talk as if I am moved by your words, I am not

[Testament raises his hand and releases a jet of water that cuts through the ground like a laser, it heads towards Judgment and right before it hits, Judgment opens his mouth and a blast of black flames erupts out. The black flames hit the water jet head on overwhelming Testament's attack causing him to jump out of the way. Judgment shifts his head to follow the movements of Testament but Leviathan comes to his aid by coiling its body around its master. The flames hit Leviathan and evaporates a portion of its body into steam]

Judgment: Yes, you see the power of fire now don't you... I was the first... the first General, the first dragon, the first flame... THIS WORLD RIGHTLY BELONGS TO THE DARKNESS!
Testament: We will see...

[Testament draws out more water from the ground and increases Leviathans size, Judgment opens his mouth and releases an inferno that takes the shape of the same serpentine dragon, but this time Judgment stays outside the dragons fiery body]

Judgment: Leviathan, meet Malico

[Malico, Judgment's spirit calling appears as a dragon with black scales that shimmer violet and glow with black flames. Visually resembling a snake with limbs, Malico stands behind Judgment with pride and ferocity]

Testament: Malico...

[Without warning Malico lunges forward and attacks with a vicious bite sinking its fiery fangs into Leviathan. In one quick twist Leviathan turns and disperses into giant bodies of water that hit the ground. The water

quickly leaps upward like a web and encapsulates Malico entrapping the dragon in a sphere]

Testament: CRUSH!

[The sphere of water collapses in on itself mixing with the fire to create a gust of steam that expands to cover the entire area]

Judgment: You really think it's that easy?
Testament: Hmm...

[The steam starts to recollect and reforms Leviathan's body]

Testament: Seems like Malico is no more
Judgment: From the darkest of all shadows my fire will burn

[From the shadows cast by the surrounding objects a pair of black fiery eyes forms. Black flames burst from the scattered shadows and Malico pulls himself together from the darkness]

Testament: Hmph

[Testament rushes forward and transmutes into a torrent of water. Malico steps in front but Testament pierces through the dragon and reaches for Judgment, the demon release a stream of fire that keeps Testament at bay]

Testament: *I will never defeat him if this keeps up. I need to make multiple direct attacks, towards him and his dragon.*

Chapter 95

Halo's decisive task

Halo: Yeah, what the hell am I supposed to do, Edge is fighting Phenix, Testament and Judgment are going at it... there's Apollo still, hmm...

[Halo looks at Apollo...]

Halo: Hmm that shield he has up is gonna be a pain, I should probably take it down. I guess that's what I'll do... or should I help Edge...

[Halo thinks to himself if he should help Edge, but in his mind he only sees Edge yelling at him to stay out of his fight]

Halo: Or should I help Testament...

[Halo once again only sees himself being yelled at for butting into someone else's fight]

Halo: Fuck that, down goes the shield.

[Halo reaches for his sword and draws it forward, he sends jolts of current down its blade causing it to glow slightly with arcs of electricity]

Halo: Alright, let's go!

[Bringing the blade over his head, Halo swings downward and slices the wall of the shield causing it to ripple slightly, nothing else happens...]

Halo: Damn, not even a scratch, maybe...

[*Halo leaps back a far distance and raises his sword high into the air, multiple bolts of lightning all strike down on it consuming both Halo and the sword in a flash of sparks. He pulls his sword back and calls out his spirit summon as he draws his blade forward*]

Halo: DYNAMO!

[*The stored energy in the sword suddenly jumps forward as a bolt of lightning that increases in size and into Dynamo's form. The spirit beast dashes forward in a blink of an eye as the rest of the world seems to slow down. It makes contact with the outer wall of the shield ripping at it and tearing it with its claws and fangs but nothing happens. The shield does not decrease in size or strength*]

Halo: Damn it! I can't believe how strong that shield is.

[*Flashback - Halo and Apollo are in the stronghold*]

Apollo: Yup, that's my nickname, ultimate shield

Halo: Go figure, damn it there has to be a way in, maybe Hacker, but damn I don't got my phone on me...

[*Halo looks back at Judgment and Testament fighting, he then tries to look for Edge but only sees flashes of light off in the distance...*]

Halo: I don't gotta choice, I need to go get Hacker, he's the only one that can get me passed the shield.

[*With that said Halo bolts into the air surrounded by arcs of lightning. From the arcs Dynamo reveals himself and pulls Halo onto his back*]

Chapter 96

The final battle of the flames...

[Edge and Phenix stand facing each other defiantly, their eyes consumed with the wrath of the Hell Fire]

Edge: LET'S DO THIS!

[Edge dashes forward instantly with his flames lit strong and bright. He raises his right hand, bathed in fire and calls out his attack...]

Phenix: DIE!

[Phenix grabs his right forearm as he rushes towards Edge, it glows and pulses releasing waves of flames]

It was like the whole world had slowed down for this one instance. Seconds that passed by in a blink of an eye seemed to be as long as the minutes they created. In front of me I see someone who I had thought to be an old friend, turns out to be the person who ignited the fire in me and brought back the memories of hatred and anger. Was our friendship in high school a lie? Stupid question, it was, and nuttin more, but even so... I coulda believed that there was someone who I could relate to without my fire.

[The two rivals rush each other with their attacks charged and ready. Their surroundings, charred from the fires of their battle, glow red with the anger of their flames]

369

I saw him coming, his fist glowing, mine ignited in flames, two fires born from the same parents, against each other...

Edge: STRIKE FIST!
Phenix: DRAGON FIST!

Just like that time we sparred, what seemed like only yesterday, I thought this person before me was a friend, stop kidding yourself Edge, you know who your friends are. I thought this crimson flame in front of me could understand me, he's the one that kindled the flame within me. Just like the last time our attacks hit, this time, all I felt was anger, resentment, hatred... pure utter hatred flowing from his fist, his flames. I understood, recalling the torment I suffered at his hands when I was a kid, I understood, cuz I felt the same.

[The two attacks clash head on, the battlefield suddenly lit up in a blinding empyrean of light]

Edge: I won't lose...

[Somewhere in the universe a pair of eyes open slowly as if awoken from a long and deep sleep]

Mysterious Being: ...

[The light from the attack shines more bright than the sun itself and for a moment that seems to be frozen in time, night becomes day. The two attacks, shrouded in the corona of the false sun play themselves out, all that can be heard are the thunderous concussive blows of two rivals...]

Phenix: I'll have my revenge...

[The mysterious being who seemed to have been awoken closes its eyes and releases a wave of energy. Its prison's surface, a neutron star, quakes and tremors with the ripples of energy released. Continuous waves of energy are discharged outward, the surface of the star seems to crack and bleed light as an envelope of illumination is shot outward and starts to orbit the star. The being quickly opens its eyes and sharpens its focus, from its embryonic position it flexes its wings and opens them... the star explodes in a super nova with no equal in the universe...]

Chapter 97

Frozen shadows

[Leviathan and Malico are in a maelstrom of fury as they battle each other, a serpent of fire and a hydra of water]

Judgment: How long do you think you can last eh?!

[Judgment releases a stream of black flames at Testament who blocks by creating a shield of water with his hand. He counters the fire stream with a wave of water he pulls from the ground below. Judgment releases a sphere of black flames which shield against the water wave]

Judgment: Is that all you got?!

[Judgment leaps onto Malico's head and the two release a violet laser type attack, Judgment from his hands and Malico from its maw. Testament leaps back next to Leviathan]

Testament: I will have to merge...

[Leviathan coils itself around Testament and begins to glow brightly]

Judgment: Hmm?

[Leviathan uncoils itself from its cobra stance and falls to the ground, Testament is inside Leviathan, he begins to transmute his body into water and in no time the two become one. Leviathan struggles in pain a bit and

then a pair of arms and legs burst from both of its sides, Leviathan speaks with Testaments voice]

Testament: We shall end this

[Leviathan lifts its body up from the ground with its new limbs. It opens its jaws and releases a call that pierces the night. It starts to develop scales of ice that slowly takes over its body]

Judgment: Hmm this will be interesting
Testament: Now this ends

[Leviathan springs forward and releases a breath of ice shards that it sends towards Judgment, Malico intercepts with a black flamethrower that vaporize the ice shards. Judgment jumps through the flamethrower but is met with a tail swipe by Leviathan that sends him into ground. Malico lunges at Leviathan and the two lock jaws. Judgment gets up from the ground and rushes towards Leviathan, but before he gets close Leviathan releases a stream of water from its side, right above its left shoulder that jets out at Judgment. Judgment takes the water stream head on but the stream of water starts to form a jaw and then suddenly a head]

Judgment: I see, so you can attack from multiple directions...

[Judgment engulfs himself in a whirlwind of black fire which causes the second head to pull back, Malico pulls back to Judgments side]

Judgment: You're starting to be a real pain...

[Leviathan forms another head that juts out from above the right shoulder, with 3 heads Leviathan lunges forward, each head acting on its own, one of them throwing itself at Judgment and the other two pinning Malico to the ground, but Malico manages to break free from Leviathan's jaws and take to the sky. Judgment cuts Leviathans left head off with his laser attack and takes to the sky along with Malico. The two fire off their lasers down at Leviathan, engulfing the beast in an explosion of black flames. The ground shakes and moans are heard. Judgment and Malico keep up

their attack increasing the power output... they cease their attack after a while but the dust doesn't settle down... moments later from the debris 3 pillars of water rush upward and slowly taper into a mist. The mist shrouds Malico and Judgment]

Judgment: Mist? You'll have to do a lot...

[Judgment begins to choke and Malico struggles to stay afloat, the two drop to the ground like rocks]

Judgment: (choking) what the fuck is this...

[Judgment tries to get up but falls back down again chocking. His face turns pale white and then blue, he opens his mouth and a gust of cold air comes out, he starts to freeze over in solid ice and Malico begins to disintegrate... moments later Testament materializes from the mist floating around Judgment...]

Testament: (with signs of fatigue) Shattered Diamond Dust...

Chapter 98

Breaking the shield

[Halo appears at a camp site near the entrance of a cave, users, and senior members are gathered around upon the arrival of Halo]

Halo: Yo Hacker, I need your help right now dude, Edge and Testament are fighting Phenix and Judgment
Hacker: Whoa what? Judgment?
Halo: Yeah, it's a long story, they have Apollo, he's protecting the gateway
Hacker: You need me to break in...
Halo: Yeah, can you do that?
Hacker: Lead the way

[Halo and Hacker quickly head back to the gateway... in no time, the two are standing before the shield]

Halo: Alright do your...

[Hacker quickly opens a gate inside and Halo quickly steps through. He shakes Apollo but nothing happens, then he's smacking him around like a rag doll]

Halo: Damn it WAKE UP!
Hacker: Uh... I don't think that will help
Halo: Wait, maybe...

[Halo grabs Apollo's shoulder...]

Halo: Can you make the gate bigger and above us?
Hacker: Sure

[The two bolt right out and the shield is gone]

Hacker: Uh... what next? Anyone?

[Halo reappears a few seconds later]

Hacker: Where's Apollo?
Halo: I dumped him on a beach
Hacker: That's all you could come up with?
Halo: We gotta do sumtin about this gateway now

[As Halo says that, the ground begins to shake violently causing the two to fall down]

Halo: Ah fuck...

[The pentagram on the ground which was the size of a city block, lit itself up...]

Halo: Shit this ain't good
Testament: He is coming...

[Testament comes up from behind Halo, he appears to be worn out and tired]

Halo: Damn your pretty beat up
Testament: My status means nothing compared to what will happen when the gate opens
Hacker: How do we stop it?
Testament: We cannot, neither of us are strong enough
Halo: Fuck yo, this is just impossible

[The pentagram ignites into a blaze...]

Hacker: FUCK!
Halo: SHIT!

[Testament creates a barrier of water around the group and pulls them a far distance back]

Halo: What the hell?! Those flames are way hotter than Edge's
Testament: That is the heat of the Hell Fire, Hacker, you must go now, it is no longer safe for you
Hacker: I wish there was more I could do
Halo: Actually, find Apollo, try and wake him up from his trance his shield might be able to keep everyone safe
Hacker: (nods) see ya later guys

[Hacker opens a gate and steps through...]

Halo: Now what?
Edge: Now we tear him down...

[Edge steps up from behind Testament and Halo]

Edge: This is finally it

Chapter 99

Rise of the king himself

The earth shook in front of me, there was nuttin I could do except watch the gate incinerate the ground. The fires were hotter than even my own, for the first time in a long time, I could feel the burn...

[The gate suddenly cracks and the ground caves in on itself leaving a giant sink hole consumed in flames, out poured hundreds of winged demons, staggering numbers...]

Edge: Wow...
Testament: This is the last fight
Halo: Damn it don't say that, you're just gonna jinx it, watch there be like ten other fights now...
Edge: Shit, here they come...

[The winged demons all started to head towards the three lone fighters. Weapons in hand, ready to be dulled on their victims]

The sky was filled with fire as the demons rained down on us. They got closer and we saw nuttin but suffering waiting for us, without warning Testament called forth Leviathan. He stepped up onto its head and headed off into the cloud of demons, then Halo summoned Dynamo and leaped onto its back and disappeared in a flash, demons fell from the sky like chunks of rotting flesh at the mercy of their attacks.

Edge: RISE FENIX!

[Edge ignites his fires and throws them into the sky, they burn rapidly into an inferno and out from the fires comes Fenix]

Fenix flew off on its own and in one stroke of its wings felled a group of demons. I took to the sky, getting as close as I could to the Hell Gate, and unleashed my Firestorm attack. I saw the plasma like energy expand and incinerate the winged creatures. They all fell with lil effort on our behalf... suddenly the ground which was still for a time abruptly and violently shook. I looked to the Hell Gate and saw a massive hand reach out, the blaze was so intense that I had to shield myself and back off. The hand extended and became an arm followed by another arm. It pulled the rest of its body out from the hole, a pair of solid black horns, polished like onyx emerges from the ground followed by the rest of the evil king's body. Fully standing, he was comparable to a ten floor apartment complex, his voice was thick and echoed deep into the night, there was a dual voice effect one very creature like and the other very human. He had hooves for feet, polished black like his backward curved horns. His skin was crimson red with veins that bulged, muscles that seem close to bursting...

Lucifer: Reap the land of its life and burn the world to its core, no human shall be left alive...

[The demons stop in place and all cheered as Lucifer spoke]

Lucifer: But the traitor is mine

[Lucifer points to Edge...]

Edge: Then c'mon!

[Edge charges his Firestorm, but instead of releasing it like an explosion he thrust it forward like the Azurath]

Edge: FIREBLAST!

[The flow of plasmatic energy races towards Lucifer, he does nothing but stare at the beam disintegrating it before it ever reached him]

Edge: Ah fuck...

Chapter 100
Against the king (Part 1)

[Fenix and Edge take to the sky above Lucifer and begin attacking him with everything they have. The two dash in and dash out in sequence but none of their attacks even faze The King]

Lucifer: What hope do you have of winning traitor?

[Lucifer swats at Fenix like an annoying fly buzzing around]

Lucifer: You, born of my power and fires, dare to think you have what it takes to defeat me? How absurd...

[Fenix dashes forward like a meteor crashing into Lucifer with unbelievable speed, but to no avail as Lucifer grabs a hold of Fenix and tosses the fiery bird aside...]

Edge: If you created me then you know me better than ANYONE ELSE!

[Edge Rushes forward along the ground and ignites his Azure Flame for an extra boost in speed. He succeeds in getting near Lucifer's left leg and attempts to unleash an Azurath but The King's giant body betrays its full speed. Before Edge has time to gather enough energy for his attack Lucifer has turned around and unleashed a flamethrower at Edge, but Edge just manages to unleash what he has gathered and it rips through The King's

flamethrower striking him in the eye. The King's roars of pain echoed loudly through the chaotic night... from a distance away...]

Testament: It has begun
Halo: Damn it, these fucking bats just keep coming
Testament: We must defeat them so we can help Edge, he alone will not be able to end this
Halo: You know he will just yell at you right
Testament: ...yes...
Halo: Let's do it then!

[Halo and Testament unleash their most powerful attacks wiping out a wave of demons, only to have more fill their places]

Halo: Oh my god this is never ending!
Testament: We must endure!

[A gate opens up and grows larger, suddenly a small but sizeable army of fighters step out]

Napalm: Don't care what you say, we're here to help.
Halo: The hell...
Dak: This is like, the end of the world or sumtin, literally, we need to work together if we're gonna stop this
Testament: You are all putting your lives at risk
Hacker: Tell me about it
Testament: Then unleash your strength!

[Together the band of fighters all unleash their most powerful attacks clearing out a wide radius of demons enough for Halo to bolt himself and Testament out of there]

Dak: Now what?
Napalm: Now we END THEM
Hacker: Which is pretty literal

[The King rubs his injured left eye before opening it to reveal the Eye of Fire]

I recognize that, but where... where have I seen it before? A pupil with three black irises surrounding an equally sized central iris, this looks familiar, as if...

[The King looks at Edge with the Eye of Fire]

I felt the air around me begin to quickly heat up, as if I was thrown into an oven and the heat was already on high. I looked at The King as Fenix came to me, I knew exactly what was happening, but I couldn't do anything about it cuz before I knew it, the air around me ignited and I was trapped in a whirlwind of fire.

[Testament and Halo burst out from a bolt of lightning and see The King, they immediately look at The King's line of vision to see a small body of flames]

Halo: EDGE!

[Halo sends a lightning bolt at The King, distracting him long enough for Testament to put out the flames. As the steam vapor is blown away, a cocoon of blue flames is seen before it dissipates. Edge falls out and drops to his knees, Fenix just arrives and lands behind Edge]

Edge: Damn it, if not for the Azure Flame I don't think I woulda survived that
Halo: Don't you control fire
Testament: These flames are from hell itself and controlled by Lucifer, even Edge can not withstand them
Edge: Yeah, shit is insane hahahhaa

[Edge chuckles a bit before getting up]

Edge: I told you guys to not come
Testament: No, you did not actually
Edge: Oh, then... I guess here we are then

Chapter 101

Against the king (Part 2)

[The trio summon forth their spirit callings. Three elemental spirits stand before The King himself and Armageddon]

Edge: You know, who woulda thought that it would all lead up to this
Halo: (towards Edge) I blame this on you
Testament: (towards Halo) I blame this on YOU
Halo: (in shock) the hell did I do!?
Edge: Pfft, I blame this on Saivent, but either way, we're here...

[The King looks at the 3 defiant warriors...]

Lucifer: A traitor, a half breed, and an abomination, against the core of all that is dark, how laughable
Edge: No, what's laughable is the truth, that deep down inside of you, your core is light
Lucifer: ARGGHHHHHHH!

[Without warning, Leviathan, Fenix, and Dynamo lunge forward and attack. Dynamo sinks its fangs into Lucifer's arm and electrifies him. At the same time Fenix swoops down diggings its fiery talons into Lucifer's back while Leviathan binds his legs from below causing him to stumble forward]

Lucifer: PESTS, ALL PESTS!

[Halo grabs his sword and electrifies it before jumping into the air... Testament transmutes his body into water and lunges forward... Edge calls out his Azure Flames to full burn and initiates the Azurath]

One straight blast right through his heart, that's all I need, and this can all be done and over with.

[Halo comes down on The King with his sword but doesn't even make a scratch, it just send stray bolts of lightning out in every direction. Testament engulfs The King's head in an attempt to drown him, all this happens while Edge gathers the energy needed to unleash his Azurath]

Just a lil more, c'mon guys, I know you can do it...

[Tiny spheres of blue tinted energy fill the battlefield and are being drawn to Edge as the Azurath slowly takes form, but Lucifer decides to make his move. The King opens his mouth and releases a cauldron of flames that quickly evaporate the water surrounding his head, he then aims his fiery breath down at Halo who just manages to bolt away from it]

Edge: DAMN IT! NOW OR NEVER!

[Edge unleashes his Azurath, it bursts forward like a stream of plasma aimed at The Kings heart]

Lucifer: Insignificant nuisances

[The Azurath approaches The King at break neck speeds, but he simply looks at the stream with his Eye of Fire causing it to burst in a plume of glittering sapphire energy]

Edge: SHIT!

If that energy touches any of us in a large enough amount then we're dead...

Edge: HALO GET THE FUCK OUTTA THERE!

Testament is nowhere to be seen, the best I can do is pull the energy towards me and throw it off to a safe direction.

[Edge extends his right arm forward and his left to a perpendicular direction, the shining energy is instinctively drawn towards Edge who then streams as much of it off to the side as possible, but not all of the energy was drawn away, and the amounts that were left behind cling to the surfaces of any object it touches like a magnet]

Fuck, that shit messed up big time.

[The King holds his ground and unleashes a wave of fire outward from his body causing Fenix, Dynamo and Leviathan to release their grip...]

I managed to pull the remnants of the Azurath to the side, but there's a good amount still left.

Halo: Shit, what just happened?
Edge: He popped the Azurath like a water balloon, water... shit where's Testament?
Halo: I dunno, I thought he was with you
Edge: Satan blasted him away, we can't win...

[The ground starts to get wet as if water were seeping through the cracks. It forms itself into Testament]

Testament: (panting) giving up already? I did not know the Fire Lord was capable of such
Edge: Testament, are you alright?
Testament: I will be fine, however, we need a plan on taking Lucifer down, at this rate we will greatly fail
Halo: Great, we're gonna die
Edge: ...guys... you guys should probably go, I can't fight if I have to worry about you guys all the time, just now the Azurath coulda killed you both
Testament: I will not back down
Halo: Same here

[Lucifer stomps his foot on the ground causing the earth to violently shake]

Edge: ...

I looked to Lucifer and I wondered what our chances were, and all I saw was just an empty future...

Chapter 102

The third General

Edge: LET'S DO IT!

[Edge, Fenix, his friends and their spirit callings all dash forward as a wall of power, each one firing off their own attack. The King takes them all head on, deflecting some, dodging others, and taking the blunt force of the ones that make it through. The team works together with all their might and power to bring Lucifer down, but The King counters with his own attacks. As easy and annoying as swatting flies away, the group is slowly being beaten one by one...]

Edge: (panting) this just isn't working, we're not strong enough
Halo: (panting) damn it
Testament: (also panting) we cannot give up
Lucifer: Did you really think you could defeat the origin of darkness? I am the first evil within the universe, and you, a handful of nuisances

[The three spirit callings come to rest at the trios side... one by one they start to fade away... Leviathan breaks into a mass of water that hits the ground in a loud splash, Dynamo collapses and vanishes in a furry of stray lightning bolts, finally Fenix fades away in waves of fire and embers...]

Testament: Our callings...
Halo: Dynamo...
Edge: Heh, is that how it is...?

[Edge starts to laugh to himself and walk towards Lucifer]

Halo: Dude, did you lose it
Testament: Edge, what are you doing...?
Edge: Hahhhahahaha heh...
Halo: COME BACK HERE!

[Halo rushes to Edge, but Edge stops him from approaching]

Edge: Don't worry dude, I know what I'm doing
Testament: It seems quite the opposite
Edge: Guys, you should probably back away for this, it can get a bit messy

I had a feeling, just a gut feeling, there was sumtin that I needed to happen. I dunno, it's just a voice in my head, no, not even a voice, just a desire, a push if you will. I just hope I know what I am doing, cuz if not... then wow, this woulda been the biggest mistake I have ever made. I ignited my Hell Fire and it swirled around me in the familiar warmth.

Lucifer: Have you finally come to your sense? Are you finally realizing how useless the fight is?

[Edge continues to walk ever closer to Lucifer until he's just far enough from Lucifer to look down on. Edge looks up towards Lucifer, with bruises and scratches from the battle, he smiles...]

Edge: I'm right here
Lucifer: PRETENTIOUS FOOL!

[In one quick step, Lucifer comes down on Edge crushing him like an insect. Fires burst from beneath Lucifer's foot as he twists and pushes deeper into the ground, Testament and Halo look on in shock...]

Halo: EDGE!
Testament: It cannot be!
Lucifer: MWAHAHAHAHAAAAA the traitor is dead, now it's your turn

[*Lucifer looks at Testament and Halo, their surroundings quickly heat up and distort. Halo realizes what's happening and quickly grabs a hold of Testament and bolts him to a safe location, but due to his weakened condition the two land not far away*]

Halo: SHIT... shit shit shit, he's gone... he's really gone...
Testament: ...he may be gone... but there is still a battle to fight, still a war to be won

[*Lucifer lifts his foot off of the crater he created when he crushed Edge, all that remains are fragments of bone and ashes*]

Lucifer: How pitiful, just a pile of ashes, I expected more

[*Testament calls forth Leviathan, but only a pillar of shapeless water comes forth*]

Testament: I see
Halo: We're too weak...
Testament: I believe it is time to retreat, we can no longer effectively fight here

[*Lucifer calls out in victory...*]

Lucifer: NOW REAP THE LAND, THE NIGHT IS OURS!

[*From the Hell Gate hordes of demons rush outward into the night, flying, crawling, running, all types of demons are unleashed onto the world*]

Halo: ...no, we need to stay and fight, Edge wouldn't give up, and I won't either
Testament: We do not have the strength to summon our callings, much less take on an entity
Halo: No matter what I have to try, it's the only way I can honor my friend

[*Halo reaches his hand to the sky and a lightning bolt takes him to Lucifer*]

Halo: Edge may be gone, but I'm still here!

[Halo charges his sword and rushes The King. With lightning fast reflexes he dashes in and attacks with his sword only to instantly dash out as The King counters... a short distance away...]

Testament: Honor? I know of no such word, only victory, but defeat... I will not settle for!

[Testament calls forth a torrent of water and rides it to The King]

Lucifer: With no leader to follow you still fight? How foolish, you might have lived to see a few more hours of life had you escaped, but now you will feel the fires of hell!

[Lucifer unleashes a shockwave that sends the two lone fighters back, immediately following the shockwave the battlefield distorts with the rippling waves of heat and then instantly ignites. Testament grabs a hold of Halo and surrounds the both of them in the densest water he can create]

Testament: Hold your breath...

[The fires approach and engulf the two fighters, what seemed like an eternity is over in just a few seconds, the water shield breaks open and the two fall out covered in steam]

Halo: (coughing) what the fuck are we, steam buns or sumtin?
Testament: (falls to the ground) that is it. It took what was left of my energy to create and sustain that shield, I am afraid I have nothing left to give
Halo: (looks at his blade and shakes his head) I don't have anything left either, this sword is absolutely useless

[Halo tosses the sword to the side...]

Lucifer: Now, you die

[Lucifer lifts up his foot and is about to come down on the two like he had done to Edge earlier, but a sharp piercing cry breaks the night]

Lucifer: What!? Impossible!

[From the ashes and bones within the crater that Lucifer created when he stepped on Edge, a spark of fire ignites. It burns outward ferociously and forms a pentagram of fire within the crater. From the bones and ashes a hand emerges covered in blood. Another hand emerges and pulls itself out from the ground. The naked body of a human is seen standing in the pit of fire, covered in blood, the figure smirks and reveals his fangs. Testament wearily looks up and in shock manages to stand himself up right]

Testament: It cannot be
Halo: ...

[The blood soaked figure raises his left hand and the blood burst into flames, the flames then die down revealing a spiked glove with the finger tips cut off, the figure then raises his right hand and the same happens... the blood on his body begins to ignite and burn away leaving behind a black short sleeved shirt and black pants. The pupils of the figures eye's burns with fire...]

Halo: EDGE!
Testament: No, that is not Edge
Halo: Whatcha mean it's not him?
Testament: That is the third General, Torment.

Chapter 103

Torment, the traitor

[Torment looks at himself and then smirks to The King...]

Lucifer: How...

Torment: Edge is an idiot, what did you think would happen if you killed him? All he needed was a little push, once he realized where he would end up after you kill him, the rest was just getting you to actually do it. When you killed me, rather Edge, you left behind a bit of yourself, your flames that is, and Fenix did the rest, from the ashes I rise anew

Lucifer: Impossible, such a thing can't happen

Torment: But thank goodness it did, because then I wouldn't be here would I? Boy, what a major mistake that would've been right?

[Torment yawns obnoxiously loud and stretches out a bit, clearly demonstrating how cocky his nature truly is]

Torment: (winks at Lucifer) well now, where were we?

[Without warning Torment dashes into the air and stops right in front of Lucifer's face]

Torment: Boo!

[As quickly as he is able to raise his hands, a jet of white hot flames comes rushing out of Torments open palm and right into Lucifer's face. The King stumbles back in visible pain]

Lucifer: You...

[Before Lucifer could finish, Torment rushes forward and lands right on Lucifer's shoulder besides his right ear]

Torment: You know, it's been a while since we had such a one on one like this pops
Lucifer: You wretched plague!

[Lucifer releases a wave of energy from his body that ignites into flames, it forces Torment to stumble off of Lucifer's shoulder and take to the air for safety]

Lucifer: To think you're capable of such a feat, to rid yourself of your humanity and revive in full demon form
Torment: (smirks)... who said I'm rid of my humanity? Though true, in this "full demon" form I'm the only one able to match you and possibly defeat you, it doesn't mean my humanity's gone, just... resting for a bit. It's apparent that everyone is useless and can't handle a simple task... hey by the way, that was a nice attack, let me show you the upgrade!

[Torment holds both his hands slightly above his waist and flames quickly surround it and compresses into a small sphere in each hand...]

Torment: PLASMA STORM!

[Torment brings both hands together in one quick motion and a burst of light is released. Almost instantly everything in the surrounding area is incinerated leaving nothing but ashes behind]

Torment: (stumbles back a bit) whew, that was a dozy wasn't it?

[Lucifer gets up from the ground with smoke coming off his body]

Lucifer: You...
Torment: Me?
Lucifer: Smart ass fool, you really think you have the upper hand?

Torment: For the time being I KNOW I have the upper hand, but the game is really up to you isn't it?

Lucifer: Hahahahaha!

[A short distance away Testament and Halo find a safe place to rest up]

Halo: Whatcha mean that's not Edge? It looks just like him

Testament: That is in fact Torment, the third of us

Halo: Us? I don't get it

Testament: In the days of The Great War there were three primary commanders on each side, Michael, Gabriel, and Uriel on Jehovah's side and Judgment, myself and Torment on Lucifer's side

Halo: You mean Edge?

Testament: Edge was his preferred name, unlike me and Judgment who showed absolute loyalty to Lucifer, Torment would question his authority amongst other disloyal matters

Halo: So Torment is...

Testament: Torment is Edge's birth name, he was the one in charge of torturing all the souls that entered hell, he alone made sure of each souls eternal suffering

Halo: Wow, that's... that sounds like the way he is in real life now that I think about it

Testament: It was not a name he wore around proudly, and so he named himself Edge, why though, I do not know

Halo: How powerful is he?

Testament: Very, he was Lucifer's trump card, should Judgment and I fail in our task, he alone was to strike the final blow in Jehovah's army and win the war, however...

Halo: He betrayed Lucifer, that's why everyone calls him the traitor isn't it

Testament: Correct

[Torment looks towards the sky with a cocky smirk while Lucifer stumbles back to his feet]

Lucifer: You really are something unique, when I created you I made sure to make you from the deepest fires of hell, to ensure absolute loyalty I even took a piece of myself to include in your creation

Torment: ...

Lucifer: But who would have thought you would deviate, my own soul, your defiance, your arrogance... your disloyalty proved to be the greatest blunder of all time, perhaps I should have created you from dirt, to instill fear within you. To think you alone have caused the future to be what it is

Torment: I don't know pops, what does dirt really fear? Nothing is lower than dirt is there? Maybe scum? What was that saying... "fear nothing but fear itself"? You're afraid of me because you made me, you're afraid of your mirrors reflection aren't you

Lucifer: Come now, you want to test yourself, then test yourself upon my true form! Witness fear in its true nature!

[Lucifer's body begins to glow red hot and suddenly his horns start to melt like molten steel. An incredible amount of heat is released and even Torment has to retreat to safety before igniting a wall of fire to protect himself... when the heat subsides, all that is left is a figure standing about seven feet or so in height, very reminiscent of Lucifer's previous form. This new form is toned down and hornless, however it had a tail that bore a sharp ivory black stinger at the end. His feet were still hooves and his skin a crimson hue that shinned like polished metal. He wore an asymmetrical armor that shined like the spike at the end of his tail...]

Torment: Now that's more like it, and I thought this was going to be boring

Lucifer: Are you sure you wish to allow your mouth to run so disrespectfully? You have never faced my true form

Torment: Oh I'm sure, I need you in this form if I wish to kill you, you know

Lucifer: (snickers) then risk your life and approach me

[Just as Torment had previously done, Lucifer disappears in a blink of an eye and reappears right besides Torment]

Torment: ...

[Before Torment has a chance to react, Lucifer backhands the side of Torment's head and sends him back into a mound of rubble]

Torment: (gets up from the ruble) oh yeah, this is going to be interesting...

Chapter 104

Torment against The King

[Lucifer and Torment lock their eyes on each other... both fighters ready to attack at a moments notice. Lucifer tilts his head to the side and a stream of fire shoots through the air but Torment stares at the stream and combust it...]

Lucifer: The Eye of Fire...
Torment: (winks)

[Torment takes off into the sky, his body surrounded by flames. Lucifer leans forward and arches his back, with a bit of effort he grunts and forces a pair of leather wings to protrude from his back. With one flap he takes into the sky along with Torment who is ready and waiting]

Torment: You know, it's a wonder how you even fly with those things

[Torment rushes The King head on and the two lock fists]

Lucifer: If you live more than 5 minutes then I'll really be surprised

[The two fighters battle it out in the air, both dashing in and out of the others attack range. For a time it seems Lucifer has the upper hand, but Torment manages to ram into The King's back sending him into the side of a building that was still managing to hold itself up]

Torment: Hmm, the remnants of the Azurath...

[Lucifer rights himself and before he's able to make another move, Torment dashes in and grabs him by the wrist, whirls him around and sends him into an area covered with the blue orbs the Azurath left behind. The King gets up slowly, visually in some sort of distress]

Lucifer: Useless...
Torment: Guess they're still good for something after all

[Lucifer quickly dashes into Torment and throws out a punch but Torment counters with a punch of his own. The two fists collide and a shockwave is released but the two combatants stand their ground. Torment is in visible pain but Lucifer shows no sign of backing down. Without hesitation Torment backs down from his punch and grabs Lucifer's fist with his free hand and using The King's own forward momentum, throws him over his shoulder and right into the pavement. Torment backs off a good distance]

Lucifer: How amusing, you fight like a child resorting to such tactics
Torment: You know, only Testament at his full power was any match for your raw strength, I however never really cared for strength, but I sure as hell make up for it in attacks!

[In a blink of an eye Torment unleashes his Plasma Storm. It catches The King off guard and consumes him. Moments later as the blinding light dies down, Torment seizes Lucifer's throat with his left hand and with his right hand, releases a flamethrower right in Lucifer's Face. But the flamethrower has no effect because Lucifer immediately grabs Torment by the neck and head butts him, knocking him down to the ground]

Lucifer: This is the great Fire Lord? Where's your mouth now?
Torment: In your face!

[Torment looks at Lucifer's face and ignites it into a blaze with the Eye of Fire. But the blaze dies down and is apparently absorbed into Lucifer's own Eye of Fire]

Torment: Well that sure as hell sucks

[Torment leaps back and stands his ground, fires begin to ignite around him and in no time he is enveloped with flames]

Torment: Time to take the heat up
Lucifer: Hahahaaa, bring it

[The flames that surround Torment burn vibrantly and intensely, he rushes The King punching him in the face. As the momentum knocks Lucifer off his balance Torment grabs him by the ankle and slams him down repeatedly into the pavement over and over again before swinging him around and releasing him. The King is sent soaring back but with one quick flap of his wings he rights himself only to have Torment land right on his back digging him in to the ground]

Torment: I'm tired of these damn things

[Torment attempts to literally tear the wings off Lucifer's back, but to no avail. Lucifer releases a pulse of fire from his body and knocks Torment back]

Lucifer: How the mighty have fallen, you were running your mouth not too long ago, and now look at you, thinking you alone have what it takes to defeat me. You, a peasant born of my own flames, a worm below the shadow of my power, you who thought himself a god!

[Lucifer's voice echoed through the battlefield...]

Torment: No, technically that was Testament, he proclaimed himself God King, I'm just Fire Lord

[Lucifer dashes towards Torment, but Torment unleashes a whirlwind of fire into the sky]

Torment: BURN THE WORLD TO ASH FENIX!

[From the maelstrom of fire within the sky Torment's spirit calling is released. Fenix glows a bright crimson red and has a much darker and hellish look to it than before]

Torment: Your right, I can't do it on my own!

[Fenix attacks from the sky and Torment from the ground... Lucifer manages to dodge Torment's attack but falls into the talons of Fenix who takes him high into the night sky before turning around and dragging him through the air and towards the ground. Like a meteor plunging to earth, Fenix brings its talons forward and releases its grip on Lucifer smashing him into the ground. From the crater Fenix stands up without a scratch and takes into the sky. Lucifer slowly stands up before being attacked by Torment]

Torment: STRIKE FIST!

[Torment's attack meets the face of The King and sends him flying back, but before he gets the chance to right himself, Fenix catches him once again in its talons and stomps him into the ground. Before Lucifer gets a chance to recover he is caught in the beak of Fenix and is tossed into the air]

Torment: DRAGON FIRE FLAMETHROWER!

[The white hot flames catch Lucifer and envelop him... Lucifer falls to the ground like a stone...]

Torment: Hmph, Stand up
Lucifer: (slowly stands up) I'm impressed, but not amused, you're going to have to do a lot better
Torment: I guessed as much, time to bring some old friends back...

Chapter 105

Return of the Generals

[Torment disintegrates into a fury of embers and reappears next to Testament and Halo]

Torment: Pathetic, stand up proud God King
Testament: This is just a shell of an old power...
Torment: Not for long

[In one quick strike, Torment plants his palm into Testament's chest and unleashes a pulse of white light right into him...]

Torment: Now your turn

[Torment does the same with Halo. Both Halo and Testament fall to the ground convulsing...]

Lucifer: I know what you're trying to do, but you can't create life little one...
Torment: Who said I'm creating life? I'm just... releasing them

Torment: I need to keep Lucifer away, it's gonna take a while for the demon blood in them to fully take over.

Lucifer: Think you can protect your friends long enough?
Torment: Time to find out

[Fenix and Torment lunge forward and begin their assault on The King. Testament and Halo both toss and turn on the ground as if in pain...]

Torment: As long as I can keep Lucifer away from those two for a long enough time then they will revive in full demon form and then, down comes The King.

[Torment attacks Lucifer relentlessly trying to keep him at bay and away from Testament and Halo. Lucifer tries equally as hard to reach the two before the transformation is complete, but Fenix and Torment valiantly keep him at bay]

Lucifer: To think, you'd be able to hold your ground as...

[Before Lucifer could finish Torment and Fenix both release a stream of fire at The King. The two sustain it for as long as they can... when the flames die down Lucifer is found with his wings wrapped around him]

Torment: You know, I never liked listening to you speak, it's always the same blah blah blah

[Lucifer opens his wings with such force that a rush of air is released forcing Torment and Fenix to brace themselves. Lucifer dashes off towards Torment but right before The King reaches him, a blast of fire engulfs him from the side. Torment immediately smashes Lucifer in the face with his Strike Fist knocking The King off balance enough for Fenix to rush in and take him into the sky. Fenix closes its wings and starts to free fall... once again before it reaches the ground, Fenix brings his talons forward with the intention of plunging Lucifer deep into the ground...]

Lucifer: Really think that will happen again?

[Right before they crash into the ground, Lucifer releases a shockwave of blinding heat. Torment steps back to Testament and Halo creating a fire shield that protected them from the shockwave. When the light subsided, Fenix was nowhere to be found, only Lucifer was left standing. The King shoots forward like a bullet and grabs Torment by the throat lifting him off the ground]

Lucifer: Game over...
Torment: (smirks) think again...

[Torment points to the ground where his two comrades are. Testament's body suddenly liquefies into a pool of water, Halo's body immediately follows by disintegrating into thousands of tiny lightning bolts]

Torment: Too late.

[The pool of water reshapes itself into Testament who slowly rises back up, a massive lightning bolt from the sky strike the ground and Halo reappears as a glowing silhouette... still in Lucifer's grasp...]

Torment: God King, Storm Master

Chapter 106

The last stand (Part 1)

Lucifer: A minor inconvenience

[Lucifer tightens his grip around Torment's neck but suddenly Torment disintegrates into sparks of embers and is blown away by the wind, he reappears in a burst of flames next to Testament and Halo]

Torment: Lucifer, meet God King and Storm Master, let's have some fun shall we?
Testament: This power, it is... Familiar
Halo: What did you do to me, it's like my insides are burning...
Torment: Eh, don't worry you'll get use to it in a bit
Testament: Lucifer
Halo: The devil...
Lucifer: You speak as if we are on equal grounds

[Lucifer lets loose a stream of fire at Halo, but the stream literally passes right through him]

Lucifer: I see
Testament: You, you must be stopped
Lucifer: Tell me, God King, why do you fight with this traitor, don't you remember your rightful place, don't you remember who your allegiance is to?
Testament: No, the old God King is no more, what stands before you is a tool of your destruction

Torment: YEAH! That's the way to say it

Lucifer: So be it...

[Halo still seems in awe of his transformation...]

Torment: Come on!

[In an instant both Testament and Torment dash off and begin their attack on Lucifer. Halo clenches his fist and spark of electricity arc around it]

Halo: *This is... this is too much Edge... what the hell did you do to me?!*

[Halo takes one step forward and literally splits into 3 clones, they dash off towards Lucifer]

Torment: *Heh, looks like Halo is finally getting a grip on his raw power. This has to end tonight, and not just with Lucifer, it has to end for good. No more wars, no more fighting, this is the last stand, my last stand.*

[Torment unleashes a Strike Fist right into Lucifer's face, but he counters with a flame thrower. The King is suddenly taken over by torrent of water that engulfs him. The water instantly vaporizes covering the entire battlefield in steam...]

Halo: Get outta the way!

[Both Torment and Testament leap up from the steam which Halo immediately electrifies. Lucifer is completely taken over by the surge, and is temporarily paralyzed. The three Halos circle around The King, attacking him by dashing in and out with punches]

Halo: SHOCK FIST!

[The three Halos all suddenly rush forward and strike The King at the same time... the attack electrifies the entire battlefield, expelling the steam and sending bolts of lightning through the air]

Torment: Isn't that Edge's move?

Testament: He has proven himself to be a fighter, his power is increasing with each battle

Torment: Let's hope he can keep himself under control... come on, let's do this!

[Torment and Testament land as Lucifer regains his composure from Halo's attack]

Lucifer: Impressive speed, what was it? Storm Master? Tell me, how does it feel... the raw power of a demon, does it intoxicate you?

Halo: ...it's a lot to deal with...

Torment: (sternly) quiet Halo, don't let his words fuck with your mind

Testament: If you let yourself fall now then you will be consumed

Halo: Let's hurry up and end this

Lucifer: Pfft... If only you had such hope

[Lucifer raises his right hand and snaps his fingers]

Torment: Oh for the sake of fuck

Testament: This... This is...

Halo: ...the hell is going on???

[The ground shakes violently literally tossing all the debris up into the air over and over like a popcorn maker]

Torment: HERE IT COMES!

[The shaking gets more violent until the ground explodes... a raging flow of lava comes pouring out from the fissure and begins to take a humanoid form]

Halo: What the fuck...

Lucifer: ENGULF THE WHOLE OF EXISTENCE IN HELL TERROS!

[The humanoid form begins to grow horns and hooves... the lava swirls

and curls itself into its final shape... that of a giant minotaur. The three Generals back away from Terros...]

Torment: Now it's our turn, RISE FENIX! BURN THE WORLD TO ASH!
Testament: LEVIATHAN! DROWN ALL OF CREATION IN ITS SORROW!
Halo: DYNAMO... BROOKLYN!
Torment: That's the dumbest...
Halo: (with flustered sarcasm) ...well sorry, I don't have anything fancy to say like you people

[Embers start to coalesce behind Torment into a ball of flames, it cracks and Fenix soars out into the sky and releases a shockwave of fire before landing back down behind its summoner. The ground shakes and water starts to bleed through the asphalt before cracking it. Leviathan takes form as streams of water pour out from the cracks. Finally, the sky fills with clouds and lightning races through them before tearing a hole and breaking out, the bolt of lightning lands with a thunderous roar and ends with Dynamo standing behind Halo]

Torment: The storm is here, no more waiting
Testament: Now the battle begins
Halo: BROOKLYN!

[Terros lets out a snort of fire and literally charges at the three like a bull. Leviathan lunges forward and smashes into Terros head on breaking himself apart into streams of water that wrap themselves around the minotaur]

Halo: DYNAMO!

[Dynamo moves forward in a blink of an eye and swipes its claws at Terros smashing him down to the ground. Lucifer opens his wings and lunges forward at Torment who does the same, both with their fist ready to attack. The fists meet and a massive energy wave forces the two back. Halo once again splits himself into three clones, one of them catches Torment and the other two dashes forward to Lucifer and grabs his legs. Using

circular motion, the clones speed up faster than Lucifer was flying back, bending The King's legs underneath himself causing him to bend forward smashing his face into the ground. Halo continues to drag Lucifer a good distance before coming to a stop. Out of nowhere Terros manages to whip his tail catching one of Halo's clones off guard, all three Halos show pain and suddenly disappear into just one]

Torment: Shit, what the hell just happened?
Testament: Hurting one of them hurts them all it seems...
Torment: HALO! What happened!?

[Halo gets off the floor and in a flash appears by his comrades side]

Halo: Ugh, that hurt...
Torment: What happened back there?
Halo: It's not what it seems, they aren't separate clones, I'm just moving so fast that I'm literally in 3 places at once
Torment: Interesting...

[Without warning Torment pushes everyone aside to block a jet of fire, Testament instinctively sends a swirl of water that curls around the jet of fire back to Lucifer, but Lucifer breaks the stream. Terros starts to break loose from Leviathans grip by heating its body up. Before anyone can act, Terros finally breaks free and instantly smashes Dynamo to the side. In one breath the minotaur releases a stream of fire from its mouth at Leviathan, but from the sky, Fenix comes swooping down to protect Leviathan by releasing its own flamethrower. The two beasts continue their assault of fire but Terros clearly has the upper hand. The minotaur's flames were more violent and burned hotter than Fenix's. But from the back, Leviathan opens its mouth and releases a spray of ice shards that pierces the body of Terros causing him extreme pain. Steam comes billowing out of Terros's wound...]

Torment: This is getting us nowhere, it's just back and forth attacks, we need to up the ante or this will last all night
Halo: Yeah, but what do you plan?
Torment: We need to ALL attack Terros first and bring him down, then we focus on Lucifer

Testament: Agreed

[Testament transmutes into liquid and joins with Leviathan once again taking on its serpentine dragon form]

Halo: Wow, didn't know he could do that...
Torment: LET'S GO!

[Everyone begins their assault on Terros releasing their most powerful attacks, Lucifer stands by Terros's side attacking and deflecting anything that comes their way. Terros leaps into the air and comes down with his hooves at Torment and Halo, but Halo moves away in a flash. Torment stands his ground only moving to the side just enough for Terros's hooves to miss. Once the minotaur stomps down driving its foot into the ground, Torment leaps into the air and unleashes a Strike Fist right into Terros's crotch. The attack catches the behemoth off guard and knocks him to the ground. Lucifer immediately dashes at Torment catching him by the arm and throwing him into the asphalt below. Testament takes the chance to lunge at Terros coiling his body around the beast. Two more heads sprout from the base of the first and they bite deeply into Terros's arms releasing steam as Testament sinks his fangs deeper. From deep within Leviathan Testament's voice can be heard]

Testament: Take care of Lucifer, I shall deal with this one!
Halo: Got it!

[Fenix snaps at Lucifer with its beak but is unable to catch him, Dynamo though catches The King easily and swipes at him sending him into Fenix's talons. Lucifer tries to break free but Fenix just clenches down even harder]

Torment: TO THE SKY FENIX!

[Without question Fenix takes to the sky]

Torment: When the time is right, you and Dynamo attack with all your strength!
Halo: Got it!

[*Torment takes into the air with Fenix... the two fiery demons cross in and out of each others path in a corkscrew pattern. They ascend well into the night sky and at their peak the two look like a shining silhouette in the glow of the crimson moon*]

Torment: *This is it Fenix, thanks for everything...*

[*In one fiery explosion that shook the ground and blinded the sky in a flash of light, Fenix and Torment release all the power they had left... from below Halo sees this as his sign and without hesitation jumps onto Dynamo's back. The two leap into the sky as a massive bolt of lightning that rips through the air and hits the supernova that Fenix and Torment created adding to the already massive explosion*]

Testament: Now you will meet the same fate

[*Testament begins to engulf Terros in a giant cocoon of water, but it begins to boil without hesitation. A Blinding blue light is suddenly released from Testament's core and the simmering cocoon suddenly freezes solid... Halo falls to the ground with a loud thud...*]

Halo: (in pain) is it over yet? Where is everyone...?

[*The frozen cocoon suddenly glows and shatters into a cloud of freezing dust, Terros is left as a giant lump of coal in the shape of a minotaur*]

Halo: EDGE! WHERE ARE YOU!? TESTAMENT!

[*A small figure is seen as a silhouette in front of the crimson moon...*]

Halo: No way...

[*With wings opened the figure starts a slow descent...*]

Lucifer: You insignificant eye sores thought that was enough to destroy me? ME?! WHAT AUDACITY!

[A large boulder is suddenly hurled at Lucifer, but he does nothing but explode it with his Eye of Fire]

Testament: I was once a God King, I ruled all the oceans and seas, I shall show you what that means
Lucifer: By all means abomination!

[Lucifer suddenly disappears and reappears in front of Testament, who with complete instinct as if expecting The King's actions delivers a perfectly timed punch that sends Lucifer down into the ground. The impact roared through the battlefield... far away by the small band of fighters...]

Hacker: Damn they never end!
Napalm: Got to keep this up, can't let guard down!
Hacker: APOLLO! RAISE THE SHIELD! EVERYONE ELSE FALL BACK!

[Without question Apollo crushes one last demon in a shield before erecting another that surrounds the small band of users, any stragglers left behind were immediately pulled to safety by Hacker through his gates]

Apollo: What are we gonna...
Raven: I got a plan, and it's an awesome plan!
Hacker: Say it already!
Raven: We just plug up the hole the demons are coming out from
Hacker: That's... not a bad idea
Apollo: Why do I get the feeling that's gotta be my job

Chapter 107

The last stand (Part 2)

Lucifer: God King, what a joke, I shall rip that title from you!

[Lucifer battles it out with Testament one on one. The King's speed out matches Testament's, but the God King is physically stronger. Each punch and kick that hits echoes through the night]

Testament: You may be faster, but you are predictable, and nowhere near my strength!

[Testament lands a single punch that strikes Lucifer in the face, his armor like skin cracks... far away the band of users plan their attack]

Raven: Ok so Hacker, you gate us all there, and Apollo you come last. When we all exit we attack like crazy
Apollo: What am I supposed to do just plug the damn thing up?
Hacker: Create a dome over it and stay inside, I'll get everyone who can't fight anymore to safety
Napalm: Leave me outside, I got to fight!
Apollo: You got it

[Hacker creates a gate and all the fighters step through]

Apollo: That Napalm is just plain weird...

Hacker: When I arrived I saw a battlefield of dead demons thrown all about

and still more were crawling and flying out, where's the rest of the group...
Edge, Halo, Testament.

[The fighters all step through and are instantly attacked...]

Raven: OK HERE WE GO!
Napalm: LET'S DO IT!
Dak: Oh no...
Hacker: FOR THE FUTURE!
Apollo: HOLY SHIT!

[A river of demons instantly converge on the group but Apollo raises a
shield and begins to run, literally plowing his way through. Everyone gets
behind him and backs him up, any demons that make it around the plow
are taken care of by the fighters. In no time they make it to the very edge
of the Hell Gate]

Dak: It's like, way too hot!

[Dak moves back way from the edge]

Raven: Crap, this is true
Apollo: And you want me to sit on top of that with a shield?! What are
you crazy?!
Raven: Dang, I really didn't think of that
Hacker: This is no time to argue, what's the back up plan? We can't stay
here forever
Raven: Let me think... thinking... ok got it!

[Raven plants his hands into the ground and the entire edge of the Hell
Gate lights up with electric arcs]

Hacker: What are you doing?
Raven: I'm gonna remake the edge and close it
Apollo: You're crazy
Raven: (straining) there's no other way to do it!
Apollo: Damn you're just as crazy as Edge is
Dak: I'll like, try and keep them off your back ok!?

[Apollo sees that Raven is struggling so he creates a shield to block the intense heat from Raven]

Raven: Thanks man I appreciate that
Apollo: Let's just get this damn thing closed so we can get outta here

[From far away Lucifer notices something about the Hell Gate]

Lucifer: Hmm what do we have here, more annoyances

[Lucifer takes to the sky but Halo quickly steps forward and disappears in a flash]

Halo: No way you're gettin outta here!

[Halo splits into 3 clones and they all attack Lucifer with blinding speed]

Halo: Testament! NOW!

[The clones suddenly disappear and move out the way before a jet of water crashes into Lucifer and freezes instantly]

Halo: That's not gonna hold him
Testament: Where is Torment?
Halo: I dunno, he disappeared after that attack, you don't think...
Testament: That attack was indeed a powerful attack, perhaps he did not survive it, unless...
Halo: Whatcha mean?
Testament: LOOK OUT!

[Testament pushes Halo out of the way, but takes on the full strength of the Eye of Fire. Without any hint of pain Testament explodes]

Halo: HOLY SHIT!

[Halo dashes away instantly]

Lucifer: God King... What a pathetic joke... now you're the last one Storm Master, you out match me in speed, but utterly fail in strength...
Halo: ...
Lucifer: KNEEL!
Halo: BROOKLYN!

[Raven makes slow progress in closing the Hell Gate...]

Apollo: Are you ok?
Raven: Yeah man, I'm just exhausted, using my power like this takes a lot of energy
Hacker: Apollo can you seal the rest of it off?
Apollo: I can but I'll be open to attack, someone needs to watch my back
Raven: (panting) you got it!
Napalm: I'll protect you!
Dak: We're all in this together!
Apollo: Ok, in that case...

[Apollo erects a giant shield that plugs the Hell Gate up]

Apollo: This will hold, nuttin will get past it if I have anything to say about it!
Hacker: Good, here come the rest of them!

[The fighters, Hacker, Raven, Napalm, Dak, Apollo and many more all stand their ground, never backing down, never giving up... Somewhere in the darkness Torment is speeding along... he looks forward and sends a stream of fire out that tears a hole in the tunnel of darkness, he flies out and lands in front of the Angel Sanctuary, the gates were bound by chains and locks]

Torment: (chuckles) we're you expecting me?

[Torment unleashes a wave of fire that instantly melts the locks like butter, he walks up to the gates and pushes them with enough force to break them down. An army of angels all stand before him]

Torment: Damn, you guys are really trying to make this hard for me aren't you?

[The army of angels part as Michael steps through]

Michael: Be gone from this holy place demon, your presence will not be tolerated!

[From behind Michael, Gabriel leaps into the air with his trumpet which transmutes into a spear. He stabs at the demon but Torment dodges all the attacks with ease. A river of angels followed behind Gabriel, all relentlessly attacking the demon]

Torment: Man, I do not have the time for this!

[Torment ignites his hands and grabs Gabriel's spear and throws him to the side, Torment immediately unleashes a concentrated Plasma Storm attack that wipes out the angels that were following behind Gabriel... All of the soldiers that were incinerated released small drops of sparkling light that all went in one direction...]

Michael: They are with him now
Torment: (panting) you mean he ate them
Michael: You can not keep up can you, this holy place drains you of your power quickly doesn't it
Torment: Oh shut up, you're still bitter about Uriel aren't you?
Michael: HOW DARE YOU!

[Michael lunges forward with his sword, Torment just barely dodges it]

Torment: *Damn if I keep this up I really won't make it till the end, one more time, lend me your strength one more time.*

[Torment leaps a far distance back and lands on his hands and feet like a sprinter preparing to take off, but he doesn't take off... Flames start to erupt from Torment, a pair of boney wings emerges followed by the rest of Fenix's body... but the spirit that Torment called forth was emaciated and weakened...]

Torment: *Take everything I can give you, and perform this last task for me, and you can rest alright?*

[Gabriel rights himself and rushes at Torment who does nothing but side step and trips him. The angel tumbles to Michael's side. The two Generals and remaining angels stand defiant and strong before the fiery demon]

Torment: You ready Fenix?
Michael: That emaciated beast of yours will do no damage to us
Gabriel: Accept your fate demon, you will pay for Uriel!
Torment: The flame of a candle flickers most violently before its end, you're no candle, but Fenix is probably the biggest candle you will ever see

[Fenix begins to draw out flames from Torment's body and seemingly revitalizes itself, but doing so severely weakens Torment, his skin begins to peel and lose its color... in its last assault, Fenix takes into the air and loops over itself before dashing off into Michael, Gabriel and the rest of the angel army, catching them all in a fiery bomb, the explosion rocks the Angel Sanctuary... Michael and Gabriel fall to their knees but still with life, the rest of the army were effortlessly wiped out]

Michael: Your holiness, I understand and humbly give myself to you...
Gabriel: Your wishes are my desire...

[The two angels close their eyes and crumble away into dust, they each release a drop of light so bright that it momentarily blinds Torment, when he opens them Akuma stands before him, the fiery demon drops to his knees]

Torment: You're the last to come, will you be Jehovah's "trump card"
Akuma: I won't stop you, I saw everything. If this ends the war, if this ends the fighting...
Torment: You'll be free, but will you be able to live with yourself...?

[Akuma walks forward and picks up Michael's sword, Excalibur, he then proceeds to open his wings and in two strokes severs them]

Torment: (in a severely weakened voice) there's no going back now
Akuma: Ditto

[Akuma walks past Torment, but before he leaves he turns around and looks back at the weakening demon]

Akuma: (chuckles) now I'm a traitor too, think my story will be anything like yours?
Torment: (chuckles back) heh, unlikely
Akuma: (smiles) good
Torment: What now?
Akuma: I got something I need to take care of, maybe I'll see you around?
Torment: Heh, doubtful
Akuma: Say hi to Edge for me then, I got to go now...
Torment: Yeah, time to go

[Torment pulls himself up with what strength he has left. Akuma leaves the sanctuary with Excalibur and vanishes into the black tunnel. Torment makes his way to the final gate that separates him and Jehovah and with one last effort destroys the gates that stood between him and his goal]

Torment: I hope your happy Edge, this... is... for you...

[Before Torment stood a child no more than ten years of age draped in a white toga with lengths of fabric that stretch on in all directions along the floor and mid air]

Torment: Jehovah.
Jehovah: Torment, you have no powers left here, you have exhausted everything to reach me, what did you hope to accomplish?

[The child's voice was that of an adult's, booming and assertive, but his lips never moved]

Torment: No, not what I plan to do or hope to do, I leave that up to the future, that's Edge's job, I'm done here. I betrayed Lucifer, and now I betray you, and with that my part of the plan is settled, all this fighting ends here, now...

[Torment's body begins to crack and dissipate into dust leaving a familiar body behind underneath the disintegrating shell... Edge's body... The child holds out his hand causing an ethereal hand to reach for Torment to stop Edge from taking consciousness but as the hand approaches a wave of blue fire engulfs it causing the child to scream out in pain, this cry causes Edge to open his eyes...]

Jehovah: Before the great creation, you made a deal with me, will you not honor that deal?

Edge: No. I made no such deal with you, Torment did, hell, I dunno what the fuck the deal was, so fuck the deal and fuck all this shit, I'm here for one thing and one thing only

Jehovah: To destroy me, you will be destroying the hopes of every person in the world, you will be destroying all that is good

Edge: Good? Are you fucking insane?! Do you know how much shit your name alone has caused!? The grief it's caused, and for what!? Wars fought in your name, countless unneeded deaths in your name, all so you can remain in power. You know, if you were really such a kind and loving god you'd show yourself to everyone to let them know you exist and that everyone is right, but you decide otherwise, now everyone blames everyone else for being different, everyone hunts everyone else for being unlike them, all you cause is pain and suffering, your no different than your brother

[Edge stands up and ignites his Azure Flame to full burn, it consumes the area in an instant... Jehovah stands motionless with a sad look in his face]

Edge: A god who's as powerful as you say you are doesn't need our worship, your just conceited, and a parasite feeding off of us, but that all ends right now

Jehovah: You will not do it, your human consciousness won't allow you to take away the hopes of everyone, if you destroy me, the world will fall into despair, darkness will consume everything, and all hope within humanity's hearts will disappear, there will be suffering, there will be pain, war, anguish

Edge: Yeah well guess what, you got plenty of people out there who don't believe in you regardless and they do just fine, you know why? Cuz they have faith in their own strength, their own power

[With each attack of Edge's words a wave of blue fire is released hitting the child forcing him back, causing him extreme agony...]

Edge: You have no idea what I'm capable of! What I'm willing to do in order to free myself and everyone else from your god damn hypocrisy, when I'm done here, the world will be left with a deep scar, but that scar will heal, and everyone will be able to walk on their own

Jehovah: EDGE!

Edge: JEHOVAH!

[Edge rushes at Jehovah but misses, the child leaps back and his toga takes life, reaching out to grab and bind Edge. It manages to grab a hold of Edge's legs and causes him to trip onto the floor, another stretch of fabric rushes at Edge and stretches outward sharpening itself into a blade that aims for Edge's heart. The fabric that binds his legs begins to creep up and bind his hands as well, holding him up into a crucified position]

Jehovah: I am sorry child, I deeply wish you could see the true way, the just and right way...

[The bladed fabric lunges forward, but Edge cries out, the blade reaches his heart but does not pierce through... a sharp cry is heard... similar to Fenix's but much deeper]

Edge: I WON'T FUCKING GIVE UP! CERULEOUS! BREAK FREE!

[The blade that presses against Edge's chest shatters and a torrent of blue flames gushes forward and takes the shape of a fiery blue crane, the child dodges and leaps back to avoid the lunging pecks of Ceruleous]

Edge: I WILL END THIS RIGHT HERE RIGHT NOW!

Chapter 108

Curtain call and the final betrayal...

Lucifer: Poor lonely warrior, all your comrades are dead and gone, will you continue to stand against me? Alone?
Halo: Edge would never back down!
Lucifer: Edge, Torment, Testament, your pathetic band of warriors trying to seal the Hell Gate, did you really think you'd have any chance of stopping the inevitable? All things die...

[At the Hell Gate Apollo notices something strange is happening...]

Apollo: Hey, sumtin is wrong, really wrong... I think we should...

[The shield that Apollo erected to plug up the Hell Gate suddenly glows as bright as the sun and shatters, the band of warriors are thrown back and suffer severe burns and injuries...]

Hacker: SHIT EVERYONE GET THE FUCK OUTTA HERE!

[Hacker manages to stumble up and create a gate that gets them far away from the battlefield, many manage to get through, but many more didn't even survive the initial blast wave]

Hacker: SHIT! What the fuck was that?!
Apollo: (in severe pain) I... dunno... sumtin... forced its way out...
Raven: (panting) is there a doctor...?

[Napalm lays Dak on the ground with burns covering his entire body]

Napalm: I think I'm ok, I'll go get help, Hacker where's the girl that healed me?

Hacker: Let's go to her, help me with everyone

[Hacker gates them all to the healer girl who was kept safe with the other children who were too young to fight... back at the Hell Gate, a hand reaches out pulling the rest of the body up. Covered in blood that begins to burn away into a pair of black jeans, the fiery figure leaps into the air towards Lucifer]

Halo: DYNAMO, SHATTER THE SKIES!

[The sky lights up with gigantic bolts of lightning that thunder down surrounding Lucifer]

Lucifer: Really? That's all you have?

[The pillars of lightning all shatter like glass, each of the millions of shards becoming a life sized tiger version of Dynamo. They all instinctively attack Lucifer without hesitation. Each one that manages to bite The King explodes violently... Halo drops to his knees instantly... Dynamo's barrage attack continues as their numbers dwindle down, Lucifer makes every attempt to evade the kamikaze attack but to no avail. The King manages to destroy some with the Eye of Fire, and others with flame throwers, but it was utterly useless... the assault continues until every tiger is gone]

Halo: (exhausted) if that didn't do shit, then fuck it, I give up...

[The dust begins to settle and Lucifer still stands, but with severe injuries. One of his wings is torn off, the other droops downward, broken... his armor like skin shattered in multiple places, numerous bite marks that bleed fire]

Lucifer: (in pain) HOW DARE YOU!

[From the sky above, the fiery figure that took off at the Hell Gate comes

crashing down at Lucifer with its flame lit fist, pummeling The King into the ground]

Halo: (in shock) Edge!?... Torment?

[The figure lifts Lucifer up by the neck...]

Lucifer: What the FUCK do you think you're doing!?

[It's Phenix...]

Phenix: Where's your pride now ASSHOLE? Your might, your respect, your power... all gone
Halo: Phenix?!

[The crimson moon begins to lose its bloody hue... orange and yellow slowly begin to bleed into the black sky as the sun breaks the horizon]

Phenix: That Edge is really something, dumb as a rock and never learns from his mistakes, with this asshole up here, no one was there to guard the prisons of hell, and by escaping I've become a full fledge demon...
Lucifer: YOU INSECT!

[Lucifer struggles a bit and manages to get loose]

Lucifer: I WILL DESTROY YOU JUST LIKE I DID THE TRAITOR!
Phenix: ALL THE SHIT I SUFFERED IS NOW MINE TO GIVE RIGHT BACK TO YOU!

[With one step Phenix dashes forward and combats the weakened King in hand to hand battle to the death. Lucifer is severely weakened from Halo's attack allowing Phenix to gain the upper hand. Halo tries to get up but is so drained he's barely able to sit up right]

Halo: (struggling) damn it! That attack took everything outta me, I can't even move anymore

[Lucifer's strength is clearly beginning to fade while Phenix stays strong]

Phenix: Damn, if you don't put up a fight then how am I supposed to enjoy myself!

[Lucifer growls loudly and it echoes throughout the battlefield. Suddenly the charcoal like crust that covers Terros begins to glow and cracks. As if shaking off a layer of dirt Terros comes back to life angrier and burning more ferociously than before]

Phenix: Oh shit, well if it isn't that stupid spirit calling of yours

[Terros charges forward like a bull true to its nature but Phenix doesn't even blink. Embers begin to drift off of Phenix and right as Terros's horns are about to plunge into Phenix, a massive fist smashes into Terros's head and knocks the minotaur to the side. The fist belonged to a headless humanoid body covered in flames, Phenix's spirit calling]

Halo: That's disgusting, that's your calling?
Phenix: The truth is ugly ain't it, but it's the truth, now destroy that fucking slab of meat!

[Without hesitation the headless spirit calling lunges at the minotaur wrapping its arms and legs around the bull releasing a gargling cry and explodes... the shockwave sends everything and everyone soaring back... when the dust settles down Lucifer is again found in the grasp of Phenix...]

Phenix: After I'm done with you, I will hunt Edge down, and show him the fear of death

[Phenix begins to crush Lucifer's neck, his armor like skin begins to crack and shatter...]

Lucifer: This will not be the end, mark my word, you have just made the greatest mistake of your creation...

[...*Ceruleous lunges and pecks at Jehovah with its beak, but the lengths of fabric all work in unison to fend off both Ceruleous and Edge's attacks. Jehovah only moves enough to dodge incoming projectiles and any melee attacks that get through... Edge immediately backs away and charges his Azurath...*]

Jehovah: I will not let you...

[*Two lengths of fabric extend and lunge at Edge, from their ends a blinding bright light is released and they take on the form of Michael and Gabriel. The two Generals are wrapped up in the length of fabric, clearly being controlled by Jehovah from afar*]

Edge: That's disgusting, using them as puppets!

[*With sword and spear raised high the two puppets attack, but Edge unleashes his Azurath. It rips through the puppets shattering them like glass, Jehovah suddenly shows signs of pain, but he tries to hide it*]

Edge: Like I said this all ends right here right now!
Jehovah: This will not be the end, you will be making the greatest mistake of your existence...

[*Edge and Ceruleous stand side by side, the two charge up a single Azurath that draws energy straight out of Jehovah weakening him, the young child begins to retreat but is unable to get very far... the Azurath is unleashed smashing into the child. Jehovah's skin turns black as the attack burns away the life force that sustained him... back on earth Phenix tightens his grip and Lucifer shatters like glass, a white light is released straight into the sky... Jehovah drops to the ground like a piece of burnt meat, a black light is released straight upward and continues in that direction until it can no longer be seen. The ambient white of the angel sanctuary suddenly begins to darken, the walls start to crumble and before Edge can do anything he is thrown into utter darkness...*]

Halo: You... did it, you beat him
Phenix: Only evil can beat evil, simple as that, now where the fuck is Edge...

Halo: I dunno, and even if I did...

[Phenix grabs Halo by the throat and lifts him up as he did Lucifer]

Phenix: You can't even stand, what the fuck can you do right now, if I killed you it would be a waste of time, or maybe... it would cause Edge some grief? What you say? Wanna die?
Halo: I already died, twice...
Phenix: Third times a charm
Halo: Brooklyn...

[A jet of water erupts from the ground piercing Phenix's chest at the heart, the stream suddenly stops and turns into a humanoid figure that grabs a hold of Halo and pushes Phenix back]

Phenix: Hmph, that won't do shit to me...

[Phenix suddenly breaks into embers of flames and begins to blow away in the wind]

Phenix: Looks like someone's calling me, next time I see you, you will all DIE, count on it...

[Edge is plummeting through the darkness...]

In that one moment where I thought my actions were correct, and nuttin else in the world could be more right, I saw all the goodness, all the happiness that could ever be... all this I saw as Jehovah lay motionless. I didn't feel bad, I didn't feel sorry, cuz I know that nuttin was lost, it's still there, we'll just have to find it again, that's all... in the end, after all that's happened, after all the long battles and hard fought victories I finally felt content, I felt that I did enough. I wonder though, did I do it for myself? Was this all a personal goal, my own agenda? Hacker said I couldn't save the world with fire, but I guess he was wrong, or maybe I was wrong... in any case, what's done is done, I have no regrets. I don't feel ashamed of my flame, my life, and especially my decisions. I only wonder though, will this stop all the fighting between everyone? Probably not, at least people will have one less thing to fight about. Now everyone is equal, when we die the same thing will happen to everyone, no heaven, no hell, but what comes next I dunno, we'll have to wait and see I guess, but either way, I feel so much better now...

[Everything glowed bright white and then suddenly a dawning sky...]

I think I'm back, it's over... I think I'm free... I'm free. I felt the cold air rush over me, but at the same time the warm sun... I fell, I just fell.

Epilogue:

Lucifer and Jehovah were no more, but unknown to everyone was the consequence of their destruction. Edge continued to fall, but not through earth's skies as he had thought, and in all truth he wasn't really falling to begin with at all. What of everyone else? From Edge's perspective they were all alright, because to him where he was at the moment, everything was alright, but the truth was farther than he could ever imagine. Phenix took Lucifer's death into himself, and so his powers and strength. In doing so he had inadvertently awoken the destruction of all existence... but that was not where his reign of destruction starts. Now Edge, upon his defeat of Jehovah, managed to grab the attention of a long slumbering entity. His decision to destroy Jehovah showed he was willing to defy everything and anything in order to get the job done.

Phenix left the battlefield leaving Halo and Testament behind in a blaze but his words echoed loudly...

Phenix: ...next time I see you, you will all DIE, count on it...

As the sun rose from the horizon the great tree that Mei had left behind soaked up the sun's warm nourishing light and came to life. The wind rushed past its leaves and was purified, from the base of the trunk the baron land began to grow flora at an unstoppable rate. The great tree's roots shot through the ground reaching all the major bodies of water purifying it all. The great tree's purpose was to clean the world and give humans another chance to get it right this time. This was Mei's gift, my sister had given the world and its inhabitants a second chance to make the right choices, hopefully they don't mess it up.

But like I said, there were consequences to everyone's actions. You can accept this as the end of Edge's tale if you want, because to some, this is truly the ending, but for others, this was just the introduction...

About the Author

Being an avid fan of science fiction, fantasy and anime, I would always see the world as a giant adventure. There's always been a story I wanted to tell, something that defines my character, my beliefs... I wrote this story for the primary purpose of getting it out there, but hidden in its world is also a message to those out there that feel they are different or don't fit in, that they are not alone. The greatest strength that one can muster up comes from themselves first and foremost... find the strength in yourself to help yourself, and you can help everyone else around you. If everyone in the world looked inside themselves for strength then what a world that would be... I live in NYC, like they say, if you can make it here, you can make it anywhere right? Right???